Sometimes the cause of civilization is best served by a hard stare into the soul of its opposite.

The Botany of Desire - Michael Pollan

First Edition

ISBN 978-0-9793958-1-9
Text copyright ©Rebecca Guevara

This is a Panoply Publishing product
Printed and bound in the United States

PUBLISHER'S NOTE
This is fiction. Names, characters, places and incidents either are the products of the author's imagination or are used fictitiously, and any resemblance to actual persons, living or dead, events, or locales is entirely coincidental.

Dedicated to the understandings and misunderstandings
Of love that are said and unsaid.
And
To Sam's and my family.

Acknowledgements

Many people helped with their information, wisdom, advice, time, questions, doubts and suggestions. Thank you to Curt Astin, Ken Atkin, Jennifer Blomquist-Willis, Donna Gaydon, Lori Giovannoni Roper, Sarajane M. Guevara, David and Marilee Ibarra, Lee and Ernestina Martinez, Cynthia Maw, Gloria Spiking, Andrew and Joyce Valdez, Susan Vogel, Karen Wilson.

Also published by
Rebecca Guevara

The Trading of Ken

JUNIPER PRESS

*Write Your Book – A Writer's Guide to
Combining Creativity with Project Planning*

PANOPLY PUBLISHING

Glossary and Discussion Questions For

My Family, Mi Familia

Located in back of book

My Family, Mi Familia

A Young Anglo Woman's Journey into a Mexican-American Family

A NOVEL BY

Rebecca Guevara

Panoply Publishing
Salt Lake City, UT USA

1

*I wish I could choose who to love;
and who to love me.*

- Kelly McCullough

An angel gently held her fingers under my chin, lifted it and made me watch Maury walk through the door of Wanlass Optical. There wasn't a reason to look up, except to watch him enter my life. My mouth fell open to catch store dust and flu germs. The frumpy customer I was helping was preening over silly looking glasses named Rigoletto that made him look like a cross-eyed otter.

Peripheral vision kept Maury and his two friends in sight as they walked the cases looking at sunglasses. "Excuse me, please." I leaned toward Mr. Rigoletto, "I'll be right back." He was studying himself in the mirror and fiddling with time I needed to trip a stranger into my life.

"I'll be right with you—let me know if you need anything," I brushed by Maury making wide arm movements. I felt like the guys wearing orange jackets docking airliners signaling the two other sales people he was mine as I returned to Mr. Rigoletto. I hoped he would drop the glasses, walk out and leave me free. Sometimes a standing sales person pressures a slow customer, so I stood above him with my arms folded. He wasn't hurried. "I need to try a few more," he finally said.

"Sure. Take all the time you want. I'll be back in a few minutes." Again I walked toward Maury. "Can I help you?"

"Just checking sunglasses."

"This is our best selection," I pointed where he was looking, "but there are some others over here." He nodded to what he already knew. "These would look good on you," Conversation wasn't flowing. Clumsily, I handed him a big European pair named Gladiator that would swallow his thin long face. He knew it and looked away without touching them. His two friends looked at each other and I knew my intention was clear as glass. I picked up the more sedate Stalwart frames and handed them to him.

"Well, if you need anything, I'll be over here," and I pointed to Mr. Rigoletto who was waving at me. I finished the sale pleasantly enough, but when I looked, the choice of customers was an obvious return to Maury or walking up to a mother with two children under five. I decided to loiter at the cash register and pretend busy.

"Could you open this case for us?" the older friend had walked up behind me. Sure I could.

"Abby Baker," I introduced myself. Maury motioned toward his friend who he said was Jerry, and the boy was his fourteen-year-old brother, Oil Boy. Later I learned Jerry was Americanized from Geraldo. He was meatier, stood taller and straighter and had a square strong face. His short thick dark hair glistened with golden strands. Jerry was the most handsome of the three, with his walk of a rolling down the stairs slink and Elvis smile. Oil Boy, was cute, about my height at 5'4", and his eyes laughed as he looked at me with the strangest color of yellow brown eyes I've ever seen.

But it was Maury I watched as he tried on six of the most expensive sunglasses. His thin face was a triangle, the wide part holding in brains that seemed to look directly through laser straight aware eyes. The guy needed sunglasses to protect what could be called challenging when all he was doing was seeing more than you wanted. His nose had a bump and widened at the bottom. His thin goatee circling a practically sized, not full mouth was perhaps for the first time last week thick enough to be manly. Not a hair showed under his black skull cap and he needed to adjust each pair of sunglasses carefully to get them straight on his ears.

Oil Boy and Jerry continued trying on glasses while Maury paid cash for Stalwart. "Haven't we met before?" I was floor sludge. I'd stooped to worm eye level using my mother, LoBeth's, meet-the-man trick. He

2

grinned like I was a first grader who said something cute. "No, but if you'd like to see a movie here tonight at the mall when you get off, I'll buy tickets."

"I'll buy popcorn."

"I'm Maury Arias," he finished, and turned away when I told him the time I'd be off. Mauricio was his full first name, but he didn't say that until the third time I saw him two weeks later. It could have been Merlin and it wouldn't have been any more magical to me. But it was his sister, Renan, who would give me lessons in love. Her startling weave of undisguised open friendship and breath-deep sensuality were a dark chocolate milkshake, whipping cream and maraschino cherry. As inviting as it was frightening with a rich hurting satisfaction. But, that's getting ahead of the story.

Now as I look back it feels like I'm making up an unreal memory. It couldn't have started so simply. It's difficult to re-feel the beliefs I had then. I was ready to fall off cliffs for love and I expected the return of goodness when it was given away. Now scenes gather in my dreams and I wake, breathing in emotions I don't understand and can't control.

As I walked out of the store that night looking for Maury, I put on frames named Bahía. It's marketed to girls who look like they have beds with striped satin duvets and pillows in complimentary plaid and floral. They had a cat eye shape and were blood red with black tiger stripes. Real cool. I was hoping to look through Bahía as though I was one of them. LoBeth taught me costumes work.

Maury wasn't impressed. He was a few yards down the mall watching people come in the opposite direction. When I walked up to him Bahía seemed to startle more than entice. I wanted flirty Bohemian Mystery Aura, but it landed on him with a thudding Girl Needs Attention.

The movie ticket taker put an arm in front of Maury, "Whoa, there brother, got a ticket?" I saw Maury was Mexican, but it hadn't connected that was any different than admitting being Presbyterian. I should have realized that was odd here in Utah, too. Maury shifted his weight, didn't look at me and showed the tickets.

I sat in the theatre staring straight ahead, interested in the movie but wondering about the guy next to me. During a change of scenes from bedroom dark to morning cereal bright, lights flashed in the theatre and I side glanced Maury. He was slim, straight and silently strong. His shoulders

3

were lank, loose hungry bones without meat even through the tailored leather sportcoat.

We went to Denny's after the movie. In 1985, coffee shops only existed in Utah as twenty-four hour breakfast restaurants. I was sure the light was making me look like Godzilla's green-scaled mother. "You didn't wear your hat tonight. I like your hair." It was forest bark in a hundred shades.

He nodded and looked at the edge of my left eye. "That's quite a pair of glasses."

"They're called Bahía. I think it's Spanish for bay." I took them off and handed them to him to inspect. Call it ingrained customer service.

"No, thanks," he didn't touch them.

"They're supposed to be for rich spoiled girls with sex appeal," my voice dropped sure Bahía hadn't the right effect, but my explanation was rewarded with a belly laugh, which I later learned was a freedom he didn't like to share with strangers.

"So that's why you bought them?" He spilled sunlight as he grinned and sat straighter.

I held them, studying to discover why I ever thought they were rich and sexy. "No, I didn't buy them. They're clear plastic. My manager, Alicia Christensen, lets me take a pair when I ask to discover if they really hit the customer they're supposed to. I entertained her once by pretending to be a nerd in a chemistry experiment gone bad behind some glasses named Erudite. After I wear a pair for a day I tell her how they make me feel and sometimes it helps make a sale to a person who needs that." I'd talked for a long time and he hadn't said a word. His quiet made me shift on the seat. "But I think I'll tell her Bahía misses its mark. Perhaps its more for a girl like this," and I put them back on my nose, moved my left shoulder under my chin in a vamp attempt, batted my eyes big, crossed them ever so slightly and said, "Mr. Arias, so good to meet you. I'm sooo tired of this receptionist job. Phones are driving me crazy. I'm trying to look perfectly sophisticated and brave in these over-designed soul shades. Wouldn't you like to take me home and love me for the rest of your life? I can cook."

The laugh was gone and his eyes were a sad dry teardrop. LoBeth's voice rang in my head, "Develop a little artifice, girl, you're far too needy for a good man to want you."

Predictably, he didn't give me a kiss, phone number or any idea where he lived when he left me in the Fashion Place Mall parking lot. He took me to my white Toyota with twenty-eight months to go before it was paid off and waited for it to start before walking back to his Chevrolet something. "Oh, well," I thought watching him drive away, "one more down before I meet someone." I didn't expect much. Just a someone. Maury had been too good.

"You're late," LoBeth was sitting in the dark living room, listening to Jim Croce sing *They can change their life but they can't change me,* and drinking scotch. Once more I regretted still living with my mother at age twenty-one, and my excuses in arranged order were: I didn't make enough money to support myself, but when my friend Kelly McCullough finished beauty school and we could split the rent, I'd move. I was afraid LoBeth would sink to personally chosen weirdness if I wasn't around to keep her a little bit straight. Mothers who try to stay as she says, 'hip,' are a special burden.

LoBeth needs explaining. To the point, I prepare people to meet her, or perhaps I think if I excuse her ahead of time I'll be less involved instead of a self-serving bitch daughter. She doesn't fit. Never did fit. Never will. And doesn't really want to because its her badge of honor. By fit, I mean she doesn't fit in Salt Lake City and if you talk to anyone who lives here and say, 'fit' they will know what you mean. It's an, are you Mormon or not issue. Except Salt Lake City fits LoBeth like Cinderella's slipper. There are two reasons. One, underneath she believes she was forced by God to do penance by being born to her parents in Utah. It gives a proud mantle of doom she hadn't a choice but to suffer among hypocrites. The other is she is a direct descendant of pioneers who trudged their way into Utah history by living in a wagon for six months. If you didn't come over the Rockies in the winter of 1847 with Brigham Young, the next best thing was to be a descendant of the goofballs who followed. So, LoBeth, and I (one generation weaker and more importantly, invaded by a distracting gene pool from another state) have locally recognized heritage. Heritage LoBeth chooses to alternately deify and de-sanctify with me as an accomplice.

She was born in 1940, and I think Grandpa and Grandma Baker must have looked at the baby LoBeth and known trouble had arrived. They gave her the blessing of a bastardized Utah name so they could say, 'Well, we tried, didn't we?' LoBeth was named after Great Grandpa Lowell on her father's side and Great Grandma Elizabeth on her mother's as a tribute to family history. She was the third child of five, which gave her good cover to be a problem while progeny at either end better comforted parental expectations. Glen was seven years older which she complains felt like a generation when he and his friends ignored her. He just kept growing up ahead of her, finishing a business and CPA degree from the University of Utah and moving to Minnesota with a wife who was terrified she would die here. He visited Utah so seldom, his son Leland was five before Grandma and Grandpa Baker saw him.

Marjorie joined the LDS church when she was fifteen and fell in love with an LDS man. They live quietly and faithfully with their five children less than an hour's drive away in Orem. When they visit Salt Lake during church conferences or to study in the genealogical center they seldom call and we never visit Orem. I tell LoBeth to be thankful for Marjorie since she fulfilled Grandma Baker's hopes of womanhood and she suffered less with one daughterly success under her belt when LoBeth fell so far short.

Lee and Owen were the brothers two and five years younger. Lee fled to Phoenix, Arizona where he works in an office. He's on his second wife and third child. At Christmas he sends us a postcard of a saguaro cactus with a Santa Claus hat on it and says he may visit the next summer. Owen had a slow start to adulthood and never made it through the gate according to LoBeth. He tripped into the local Hippie scene where he had no business being. The pot, alcohol and other drugs he played with messed up his sense of purity and worthiness and after seven years of too much fun, he never had another fun day in his life. After drying out, crying and praying, he took a boring paper pushing office job in a Salt Lake bank, never married, was baptized LDS, always goes to church and stays away from us.

They were all successes for Grandma. One was a CPA in Minnesota, one a good woman, one a pioneer to Arizona and one a returned sheep to genealogical history. Even as a non-LDS she could have a conversation with neighbors by leaving LoBeth out and being careful what she said.

A week after LoBeth graduated from high school in 1958, she left for New York on the train. She said she wanted a chance for satin skirts, champagne breakfasts, and men in tuxedos. The movies of the 40's and 50's made it very clear New York had kept all the sophistication when it sent Joseph Smith's saints to Utah. In 1964 she returned to Salt Lake with superior secretarial skills, a rebellious and therefore glamorous smoking habit, and a swelling belly of me.

Her parents were happy to see her, unhappy to see me, but they generally adjusted to LoBeth's 'new situation.' Grandma and Grandpa Baker re-opened the girls' basement bedroom. The brave rebel who had shared a bedroom with her 'holier than thou sister,' soon shared one with a squalling, diapered me. It was a lonely time for LoBeth as she re-adjusted to Salt Lake, put away dreams of New York culture and slept with a poopy baby. For two years she worked part-time clerical and waitress work to buy food and give Grandpa sixty dollars a month for rent.

Then Hippies came into existence. The rumble of the Viet Nam anti-war movement was an annoying dandelion in Salt Lake's manicured yard according to LoBeth but it did exist. The tiny number of long-haired, moccasin-wearing love children who listened to Janis Joplin, Jimi Hendrix and The Fifth Dimension stood out of the general population like Marilyn Monroe stood on a stage singing Happy Birthday, Mr. President. Alone and friendless, LoBeth looked for the Hippies and found them in cubbyhole bookstores, University of Utah off campus groups, and apartments in the seedy old neighborhood of the Avenues.

Nothing permanently bad happened to her at the brownie eating, bong smoking, speed swallowing parties, and she did make forever friends. I tortured her by referring to them as the Open Heart Anguishers because they took such joy in confronting God with their anguished questions without a church as referee. They eventually evolved into New Agers. It wasn't the same group Owen found.

We lived with Grandma and Grandpa Baker until it was time for me to start kindergarten. LoBeth plucked me out of her childhood neighborhood, reasoning it was not good for me to run into the ghosts and progeny of the jerks she had gone to school with. We started living in a series of apartments until Grandpa died of a heart attack when I was twelve. Three years earlier Grandma died of a stroke. Broken, tattered, weak and multiply fractured hearts run in the Baker family. After all was said and done, each child of Harold Bean and Jessamine Owen Baker received thirty-five hundred dollars.

LoBeth bought a house and her luck held because the next year she got the job she kept. She was hired as a secretary in State Family

Resources where she witnessed domestic violence cases collide with the law on her desk in black ink on white paper. Family privacy rights and cultural customs boxed with spousal safety and dignity in round after round. In 1980 the title secretary was replaced with Administrative Assistant, which didn't include a raise, but she received business cards to give people who needed to call the office and men she wanted to meet. The job was perfect for complaining endlessly about the plight of women and children and occasionally she made a difference with timely correct notes and well-written correspondence.

In truth, if I had to stand before God, and I suppose we do some day, I would say she was a good mother. She tried to explain things, kissed me, kept me protected from cold, gave me food, sent me to school and said I should….. Well, here is where she forked from Utah's road. There wasn't a call to find a good man and breed an adoring family. Which, except for her and her leftover freaky friends, who wore the 60's like purple hearts, was all that lived in the white frame houses up and down the block. No. She told me: Live life with feeling and truthfulness to your heart. God will understand. I hoped God would understand. But what feeling? Whose truth? By age eight I knew there was LoBeth's truth and everyone else's in my school.

I had four mothers. The first was Missy Mommy. "I don't want any daughter of mine playing with that jack rabbit," LoBeth declared, straightening her shoulders, wriggling her nose and it was understood. Local boys of all and any sort were under this label, which in the end left me very little to choose from to please her. The second was Golden Bitch. "Mormons are peacekeeper missiles to those of us who want to live in peace," were her words. Ruby Reverie seldom visited, but if you gave her a hug, a teenager might get ten dollars to go to the movie. "Your baby hair searched for sun like grassy sprouts on a wheat field in early spring," she said remembering me at four months. I took that to mean I had thin flapping old man baby hair. The last mother was Drunk. It happened and happened often. Scotch was a first choice, but she could as easily do it on gin, vodka or rum. She said beer interrupted her body's water flow, which she needed to keep pure to remove all toxins. Alcohol was not considered a toxin unless it created a headache the next day. Friday and Monday were the most common drinking nights. The first to celebrate the end of the week, the second to celebrate that she made it through the first of the week. Now I understand that selfless routine of send kid to school, work all day, come home, fix dinner, complain of all co-workers, sleep, do it again Monday through Friday interspersed with Drunk. As a child, I didn't.

We had an understood co-existence. She was interruptable at all times except when she talked on the phone with friends or men were present. The only time I seriously avoided her was when she drank, but that was easy because she didn't like getting up from the couch. It was during these evenings she was both lucid and stupid as she imagined she was preparing me for the world. "Men love bodies first, brains last, and humor only if you have money." "Or is it deception they love," she murmured to herself, followed by "at least in practice to protect themselves. I'm not sure." It should be easy to understand why I introduce LoBeth to friends in small doses.

After the movie with Maury and his send-off good-bye, I sent LoBeth a jab. "Instead of Croce, shouldn't you be listening to Elvis or Buddy Holly? That's more your time," I kept walking to the kitchen for a drink of water, but decided to answer. "I met with a friend for a movie after work."

She was on the couch, her straight dark hair barely laced with silver draped her shoulders like a well-washed blanket. Luckily I didn't get her full chipmunk cheeks but I would have liked her clear blue eyes that sat in her face like ready bullets. "Male or female?"

"Male." Pride and inability to lie to LoBeth resulted in truth even when it wasn't to my advantage.

"A jack rabbit?"

"I really don't know, LoBeth. Just a guy I'll probably never see again."

"Some friend." My mother. The original dispenser of tough love. That's what I returned. She watched as I turned away.

"Love you, honey," she said. She better. I love her.

Five days ticked through dateless before Maury called at Wanlass. We became movie and coffee shop partners. Every seven to ten days he'd call, we'd meet at the movie theatre, or a couple of times just for coffee. After a movie we'd sit across from each other in a booth with two coffees and a shared grilled cheese and fries.

"I never liked school," he looked at the fries with a cross of shame and disgust.

"No, neither did I, but you do like thinking. That class sounds hard." He was taking a logic class at Utah Technical College. If I had decided to go to school that's where I would have gone, too. It was a good state owned 'move 'em in, move 'em out,' two year school for barbers, auto mechanics or carpenters. They were there to teach people to earn a living, not to try and convince each other they were smart.

"Some of it's hard but the one on BASIC programming is fun. You have to outthink the machine."

"Are you sure computers are going to be a good thing to graduate in?" All computer training was still listed under Data Processing with secretarial classes. It seemed geared more to LoBeth than a guy starting a career. It seemed a little feminine.

"I'm sure they're coming. The schools are just starting to teach what will be an explosion. I'm in on the ground floor."

"Dentists never go out of style."

"They start with two years of literature and biology and I don't like touching people's faces."

He wasn't touching my face either and I knew if we didn't get a better connection soon nothing would work. It seemed all he wanted was to be friends who met in an optical store and I wasn't bright enough to turn it into anything more. Finally, he called on a Friday afternoon with a different idea.

"You going to Slicker's tonight?" It was a dance club in an industrial part of town where people could sneak in and out of Utah's idea of disapproved behavior. I wasn't planning on it. It was Friday night which worked for a lot of people, but was another work night for me.

"Jerry and I are going to be there with a few others. If you're there, I'll see you." Not my mother's idea of a proper date request from the 50's but good enough to start a little friction in the 80's. I called Kelly, my remaining friend from high school. She was busy with beauty school and dating Dave, but she was my best bet.

"Ya, I'll go and I'm calling Gen. I know you're not crazy about her, but she attracts guys." Gen, or Genevieve Newbold, as she would sometimes roll in fake French followed by a last name with the thud of a stale English biscuit, was going to beauty school with Kelly, but she thought it was queen preparation academy. Her attitude was stretched way beyond being the underpaid female who does hair to believing she should be the overtipped love goddess who accepted accolades.

"How's Dave?"

"He saw his old girlfriend last week."

"Oh."

"Oh, well, I'll see you at 9:30."

Through the sounds of Michael Jackson and Tina Turner, cigarette smoke so thick I pretended it was London fog and two hundred bodies posing for allure, Maury and I managed to find each other. We danced like cotton candy; sticky, happy to be there, and sweetly insubstantial.

Between dances he explained his love of jazz. "My Uncle Virgil learned to like it when he was in the Marines. He lived with us for a while when he got out and he would play his music and I'd listen with him." Later, I introduced him to Kelly and Gen. Kelly was friendly, Gen the usual ice queen. From across the room Jerry gave me a cheery salute and the three other guys with him looked my way. Straight-lined mouths, glaring eyes and shiny black hair made them a little scary looking compared to my neighborhood boys of teakwood hair and honey freckles. Two of them were being held so close by females they may have become fathers that night. One female was the only blonde at the table and her hair shone like a single headlight on a freeway.

"Who are the guys with Jerry?" I asked.

"Old neighborhood friends. I don't see them often now, but we go way back."

I wanted to end up with Maury that night, but when the dance club dumped us at closing time into the glare of streetlights, he said the next best thing.

How about if I pick you up tomorrow night? Jerry's having a party." At last. A nibble.

"If my mother's there tomorrow, remember, she's only a show."

The next night LoBeth purposely kept the front porch dark until Maury rang the bell. She beat me to the door and flipped on the light to put him under scrutiny. "Sit down, daughter. He's mine."

"Welcome, young man. Please come in." A tentative foot entered, followed by the gangly guy I was crazy over. "Please, LoBeth," I thought, "don't kill this for me."

"I'm LoBeth Baker. And you would be?"

"Maury Arias." They shook hands.

11

"Maury." She said his name like it was a period at the end of a sentence. "Seems to me, Abby said you had a more formal name. Only if the police need it, you understand."

Maury glanced at me. "Mauricio Antonio Arias, second son of Juan Bastidas and Chepita Arciniga de Arias."

"Thank you. I'll write it down. Did you grow up in Salt Lake?"

"Yes, ma'am. Rose Park. Went to West High School. Presently a student at Utah Technical College in Data Processing and part-time delivery and stock boy at Pace Office Supply."

"Abby also is from Salt Lake. So you understand how uneducated and unworldly that makes her?" At least he had the presence of mind to just stare at LoBeth without agreement.

She looked him up and down. "However, perhaps it does the same for you. Therefore, I entrust my daughter to you for this evening, but bring her back in the same pristine condition you take her."

"See you later, LoBeth. Don't wait up," I grabbed his hand and headed out.

"Nice to meet you, Ms. Baker," he sort of said as I pulled him. Maury waited until we were in his five year old Chevrolet Impala, it was started, backed out the driveway and halfway down the block before he pulled over and laughed until tears glistened his eyes. He laughed so hard, he pushed the seat back so his body could move freely with releasing guffaw sounds. I knew LoBeth's act, but I had not seen a victim laugh.

"Okay, so I'm not pristine, what's so funny?" LoBeth had unpredictable effects.

"Who would believe it?" he wiped his eyes and straightened himself, "Who would believe? I've never had a Mexican girl's family ask me those old questions. Maybe because I already knew them and they knew my parents, but the formal old ways are dead to this country. Who would believe I had to go to a white girl's house to stand up for my honor?"

"Honor?"

"Well, that's how the old way looks at it. I'm surprised a cousin isn't here. If you had a brother he'd be with us right now."

"Don't bet on it. LoBeth isn't as protective as she sounds. She was just showing you she knows how to hold a brick." I needed to save money faster to get away from LoBeth. To keep him talking and change the subject I asked about Jerry. "Tell me about Jerry. What does he do?"

He cleared his throat and started the car. "A few years ago he went back to San Jose, California to live with cousins while he went to school to be an electrician." He was still snickering and trying to lose his smile as we drove down the street.

"Why didn't he just go to school here?"

"Free rent in California and school's cheaper, too, but he also wanted a foreign diploma."

"Foreign?"

"Yes, he said it would be more impressive to get a job in Utah with a certificate from California."

"So he's an electrician?"

"Si, senorita. Be careful with me or I'll send Jerry to take your house lights out."

I'd already decided to go slower than I did the first night with Maury. I suspected an emotional depth that maybe he didn't fully know he had. To be allowed to sink into his kindness, reasonableness and reliability, required caution.

Jerry gave spontaneous parties at the apartment he shared with his friend, Brian Goodman. Jerry and Brian each made two well-placed calls early in the day and the invitee list would grow through the jungle. Over the next month I learned Jerry often had a semi-date who I'd end up talking to for longer than I wanted while Maury caught up with the guys he knew from his neighborhood. The dark guys from Slicker's wandered through looking at the crowd as though they were choosing meat for breakfast.

Jerry was the only friend Maury still saw with any regularity from his teen years. When his parents, Juan and Chepita, bought their house on Nocturne Street Jerry's was the only other Mexican family and they became friends. It was Jerry's mother who taught Chepita to be careful wearing red because gringos thought it was for putas, and it was important to have parties in the backyard instead of the front. There was a curious need for street-side privacy in this northern country. Jerry's two older brothers were married when their parents died in a car accident, and though Jerry spent his last year of high school living with his brother Bellesimo and his wife Collette, he also became an accepted son to Juan and Chepita.

I liked Jerry. For as good-looking as he was, he was friendly and natural.

Everyone was welcome at his parties, especially if they brought more beer than they could drink themselves and he was a genial host. There was little conflict or dangerous over-drinking. I attributed it to his happy open face outfitted with a square jaw and solid chest and shoulders that said, "Welcome to my home, enjoy your time here, relax where you are liked but I'll help you get the hell out if you don't behave." He never worried about who was popular or not, good-looking or not, known or not. As I stood talking to Mandy or Lisa, Maria or Elena for Jerry, and holding a third beer at midnight, it began feeling like an overcrowded train station for the well-groomed. People walked by in paths through groves of people to the kitchen, bathroom and front door. They were tall, short, red-haired, blonde, stark black-haired and my brown cat fur. Mixed and matched with skin and eye color, the room was a Ripley's Believe it or Not—This is Salt Lake City postcard. Three men LoBeth's age were there and pre-school children ran among legs until they slept in a parent's arm. Twice I saw a baby who didn't look three months. The richness and variety of color, age and education was an exotic syrupy after dinner liqueur Utah didn't realize was maturing. Like a train conductor, Jerry moved about his apartment, quietly assuring the peace and being gracious to his temporary visitors.

The apartment was the expected cheap third hand furniture two guys might collect except for two pieces. Mandy showed me a seven foot French tapestry sofa hidden by a blue bed blanket protecting it where six people sat. Then she showed me the thin bone, delicately flower rimmed china arranged in a cabinet like a woman would do for something she loved. Mandy said when Jerry's parents died the household goods were divided among the three brothers.

I liked the way Jerry said good-bye to me. When Maury and I were ready to go he jumped to my side, threw his big arm around my head, pushing it down to his chest so I couldn't see or breathe, and he'd knuckle the top saying, "Si, Maury, listen, there's something in there. Could be brains. Could be a ripe sandia," and then he'd give my hair a big smoochy brother kiss. His hold was as solid as falling into a life size full bag of flour. A girl met secure surrounding earth force in his arms. When he let me go it felt like being released by gravity to Maury's realm of God's musical angels. Maury's hold was a kiss that made me shiver in cashmere, a softness that made me want more, more, more.

By this time I'd shown Maury the neighborhood park with two tennis courts and a children's play area within a mile of LoBeth's house. It had a hidden driveway behind lilac bushes to a maintenance shack. We would park and lock together, secure and buttoned against the cold, like a single warm winter coat. I'd watched LoBeth begin several fits of passion that looked like temporary lobotomies with several of her men, so I appreciated Maury's gentler, tender ways.

When Maury wanted to go for a movie, to a party or for something to eat I was always ready, but he still enjoyed spending time in the boy group on a Saturday night so I kept up with Kelly and Gen. On a summer night Maury, Jerry and a few others had been in the club and Maury and I danced twice, but the guy I talked to the most was Craig Spencer. We recognized each other because we both worked at the mall. He bought me a drink and when I walked over to thank him he motioned to sit down. Maybe Maury would see and consider me more valuable with competition. Craig sold shoes at Florsheim and went to the University of Utah. Required classes were filling his time and he hadn't any aim. After Maury he felt like standing by a cousin. Same skin, hair, eyes as me, but he was a better looking guy than I was a girl. Another girl walked up to us with the light of liquor in her eyes and asked him to dance. Maybe she thought I was his sister.

I went back to Kelly and Gen. At 2:00 a.m. the club kicked us out to find our way home. High school may have been history for three years but it still felt like a summer vacation night as we left the dance club. June nights in Salt Lake can feel like an oven warming rolls. Even standing on asphalt and casually kicking pebbles and aluminum tab lids that were still legal, summer nights have a resonating sexual fullness that LoBeth said frighten some people to sleep and pull others to stay outside to follow wicked ways. Then she laughed with secrets. I looked up from comforting tab lid kicking before getting to Gen's car. Streetlight behind Maury made him a visage of arms sweeping to eternity with his head nod defining horizons.

"You're making a dust storm, Abby. You'll ruin your shoes." We looked at each other. "How about meeting me at Liberty Park tomorrow? I'll buy lunch." He suggested north of the paddle pond, where it would be easy to find each other in the city's main park.

Gen and Kelly were waiting in the car, equally busy watching us and other people walk by as they fell out of the bar, yelling and saluting God, country and sex. "Well, okay. What time?"

"How about 2:00. Gives you time to sleep in."

I pulled Enlighten out of my purse and put the heavy set library glasses on my nose. "Be careful what you say, young man." He tousled my hair.

"You like that guy too much," said Gen. I was climbing in the backseat of the car.

"What do you mean?"

"He makes mincemeat of you."

"Aren't you supposed to like someone too much? Maybe get someone to keep for life?"

"Getting someone isn't the answer," she swept beauty school coiffed hair off her shoulder. "Getting somewhere is the answer. He won't get you there. He's a bus stop."

"Stop it, Gen. He's not so bad," Kelly waved her arm over the car seat. "This is fun, right? Not real life yet." Her one too many drink eyes looked at me. That's what my friends thought of Maury, an exotic way stop like a trip to Tijuana where you wouldn't want to live.

The summer night hadn't put LoBeth to sleep. She was in the dark, holding a drink, listening to Eric Clapton and remembering New York.

"Isn't Bobby Darin more your time?"

"It's still my time," she was silent before saying, "Don't let that boy sucker you," I didn't answer. It's best to leave Drunk alone. Missy Mommy waved good-night when I said where I was going the next day without mentioning Maury.

Sunday was full-on summer when grass smells sweet and dandelions sprout like miniature chrysanthemums. Leaves were still shiny, stretching young limbs and reaching a new distance. The smells of the chicken, fries and soda lunch mixed with the paddle pond water, wet earth and the cries of seagulls. I felt wakening, a realizing of life just looking at this person, Mauricio Antonio Arias as we sat on the blanket he brought. Lunch was Maury's offering as he put me through an interview to discover if I liked him, could like his family or would freak out at all the Mexican-ness. He was so skillful I didn't realize it was a grill until later. His quiet talk and slow moves were protection for his family, but the grace was for me, since he understood the game and I did not.

It was impossible to fully explain his family, but his musical voice chose words and phrases to make each person a full note. The household included his parents, two brothers and a sister, Renan.

Pedro was the oldest brother at twenty-eight and the only one born in Mexico. The name Pedro was used on all tax forms, but publicly he chose the name Paul which was more properly from Pablo, but it was his private joke and smokescreen to keep white men a controllable distance. Maury described him as slim, ever quiet and secretive in a crowd or at the family dinner table. When their mother saw an old silent film on tv she began calling him Rudolfo Valentino's godchild. Pedro was sailing his life away as a cook, or short order chef. Meats were his preferred specialty but whatever needed doing in a restaurant was what he did. Whether it was Mexican, hamburgers, pizza, Americanized Chinese or Greek there was always money for his parents. A paycheck was never cashed that was not shared. Even when he disappeared anywhere from a month to a year and a half, he would have someone, usually the woman he was living with, bring by an envelope with cash.

His father, Juan, was the next person he described. "He works so hard his little butt is tight as a drum and pushes him down the street because its got too much muscle and Catholic guilt to stay still." The 4:00 a.m. alarm would go off by the bed on a table covered with hand crocheted lace and Juan's beefy calloused hand reached over to kill the noise announcing the day ahead of the sun. His mother, Chepita, rose to go to the kitchen, walking across clean linoleum floors to lead everyone into the day. When the warm balls of tortilla dough were covered and resting she would heat the black thick grill, releasing the lard and flour smells of a thousand mornings. Then she would go to Juan to say the sun was calling his name for the pleasure of working his back. Slowly and heavily, to waken his old muscles, he pushed back the sheets and walked like the older man he would be in ten years to pick up crusty clothes from the back of the closet. On his way out the door he took three tortillas filled with meat and beans he began eating as breakfast between gulps of a pineapple juice from Mexico. In his lunch bucket was a can of Coke, a Twinkie, banana, chips and two bologna sandwiches on white bread. Juan had worked for the same construction company for five years which sent him from job to job but always doing the same. Heave ho. Heave ho.

Pedro followed his father out the door to a twenty-four hour restaurant where he ate free. He took a warm tortilla with melted butter and leaned for a kiss and to hear his mother's words, "!Cuídese mi hijo. Vuélve vivo!" Maury told me what that meant and I asked why she would say that. He only shrugged and continued looking ahead.

Chepita made six dozen tortillas while only one child and a husband were out the door. "Everyday she makes that many tortillas?" I was incredulous.

"No, every other day. She takes them to two houses before 8:00. Two dozen are given to Tia Manuela, my father's sister. She's a widow with her daughter, Carrie, who's eighteen and my Abuelita Felipa lives with her. Then she gives a dozen to a woman who lives around the corner with two little ones. She's too busy and has to be at work. Mamá makes the tortillas and watches the boys after school. That only leaves three dozen for us and as you've heard, they walk out of the door with every person leaving."

Renan, his older sister, was next in the kitchen and the first to offer her mother conversation. When Maury enters the kitchen they are talking about Tia Manuela's new haircolor. Definitely too red for her already pink skin. Maury refuses his mother's offer to pack lunch, but leaves with a tortilla dripping in butter. Blue dawn is spiking the valley in sunshine through mountain canyons as he drives to Utah Technical College. Renan usually leaves within five minutes after Maury for her job at a healthcare company where she enters data into a computer. It was a dead-end job for middle America. A job of prestige and security to others. Everyday the people in her office talked about how long it would be before computers replaced them. It was Renan who encouraged Maury to study computers. She said it was best to survive with the most powerful and she could see the fear in white people, so the computer must be powerful.

Only Oil Boy remained. His mother had to wake him. At fourteen his body soaked sleep like a sponge and didn't easily give it up.

"Why is he called Oil Boy?" until then I was afraid it was nosy to ask but now it felt uncaring not to inquire.

"He was a quiet bebé but he was a mover. Where we lived was tiny, but he'd disappear. Put him down and off he wandered. He wouldn't answer when you called. Tomas! Tomas! Mom's voice was more frantic each time. On the third Tomas! We were all trained to jump and start looking with her. We found him swishing toilet water, in the backyard eating dirt, or throwing Dad's socks and underwear out of a drawer. But one day we found him in the cupboard under the kitchen sink. He was drinking cooking oil like it was root beer. So the name stuck. He's been called Oil Boy ever since." He turned with a half smile on his face. "That's mi familia, Abby."

"That's a lot of adults in one house. Everyone's over eighteen but Oil Boy."

"Si."

"How does that work? Doesn't Pedro want his own place?"

"Why? He'd have to clean and pay for it. If he wants to be alone, he goes off."

Neither of us spoke for several minutes while I gathered greasy paper, napkins and leftover food bits to throw away. When I sat down he began again.

"We moved to Salt Lake when I was eleven. We lived in a basement apartment at Bishop Erickson's almost a year before my parents bought the house where we are now. Jerry lived down the street when we moved here and since his parents died he's spent a lot more time with us. Sometimes his brothers and their families come, too."

My thinking had stopped on Bishop Erickson. "Who is Bishop Erickson?"

"I'm LDS, Mormon, Abby, and he's the bishop of the Mexican ward. Cisneros Ward."

I was doomed and blindsided. There was no escaping. It had been my unresearched opinion that even in Utah, a pinprick in the world, where the Catholic Church did not hold historical dominion, it would still claim all Mexicans as its rightful children.

"I'm not active anymore. I haven't gone for three years, but I like Bishop Erickson. Mamá has a lot of friends there."

"I didn't know the Mexicans had their own ward."

"Yes. I think it's supposed to make us feel special."

"Oh." I was without wind. We began walking through the park's Tracy Aviary when he said, "I forgot to mention the aunt and uncles. There's Rafael and Bernice, Leon and Marta, Nicholas and Ruth and Uncle Virgil. Remember? He's the one I learned about jazz from. He's my mother's brother and he's widowed. Tia Teresa died three years ago so he's raising Armando and Maria Elena alone." They might have all been a grocery list for a month's worth of food for all I could remember.

I passed the oral exam because the next week Maury took me to his house. We stopped to pick up his schoolbooks before he dropped me off at Wanlass while my car was serviced.

"Come in and meet my Mom. She'll be the only one here." I wanted to stay in the car but it seemed rude to avoid meeting a mother. Even I would have been offended if someone hadn't wanted to meet LoBeth. Introducing a mother is like making an invisible well kept secret part of you suddenly transparent and baby-like.

The front yard of the 1950s wood house built for returning WWII veterans was straggly. It looked like somebody mowed the lawn when ordered but trimming and well-kept, weeded flower and shrub beds was asking too much. Grass sprigs eighteen inches high entwined in chain link fence on the sides and three evergreens six feet high dizzily leaned toward the front porch. I expected the inside to reflect the same casual approach to necessary housekeeping.

LoBeth and I agreed only last week during a drive to the grocery store that house front neatness, originality, sloppiness or neglect must logically reflect the insides of the house and therefore give hints to the people within. We imagined ours did.

Our straight row arrangement of spring-blooming forsythia, lilac and snowball bordered each side as natural barriers against neighbors and though they were boring for the rest of the summer they stayed green and we didn't have any desire to do the work to replace them. Any eye appeal of LoBeth's 1930's green aluminum sided house that looked like a frugal cookie jar was in front. She had dug a five foot circle on either side of the cement walkway, which held roses, delphiniums, geraniums, alyssum, nasturtiums and a canna lily on each side. LoBeth summarized as we walked into the grocery store, "Our house shows we like privacy from neighbors and we are uncommonly full of need for bursting flower beauty."

"As long as it's well-ordered, weeded and seen as decent from the street?"

Above the mailbox by the front door it read Arias Arciniga. Simmering beans and flour tortillas is what I smelled when we walked in Maury's front door. An overwarm space heated by cooking and vented only by a fan is what I felt. Reflecting shiny wood floors, stiff doilies on tables, knick-knacks fighting for space, a red crocheted blanket on the sofa and a vivid painting of Mexican landscape over it all jumped for attention. On the long wall in the back, opening to the kitchen was a print of a bleeding Jesus with thorns. Below was a small table with a dozen small candles in round glass holders. Beside the Jesus was a photograph of the Salt Lake LDS Temple and a popular photograph of Brigham Young I had first seen when I visited an LDS Church as a child. I didn't absorb everything in that room. It was so busy, clean and precisely arranged I didn't want to sit and leave LoBeth dust. From the kitchen popped a short dark haired woman with long hair pinned like a pastry twist.

"Mom, this is Abby." Apparently I'd been mentioned. "Abby, my mother, Chepita Arciniga." We eyed each other, but it was me with the veiled eyes and sudden tongue tie. She was open and welcoming. Not 'daughter I finally found you,' welcoming, but rather 'oh, another new friend of my Maury's.'

"Hello, hola, welcome to our casa. Would you like something to eat?"

"Haven't got time, Mamá, I'm only picking up my books," and he disappeared.

Chepita surveyed me and seemed pleased enough. "Here, come sit down. Do you go to school with Maury? I don't understand why he takes a class in the summer. It is so hot." She stepped into the germ free clean red room. I barely had time to explain we had met at the optical store when Maury returned and made our good-bye easy and quick.

Back in the car he turned to page 143 and asked me to read the sample test questions so he could practice. I had never been with anyone who introduced a mother and as soon as it was possible, not say something like, "Is she crazy or what?" "Didn't I tell you?" or "Next year I'll be out of this place." Since his brief affectionate family review during the picnic, Maury assumed his mother was likable and his house acceptable.

As we exchanged small family stories, we were alternately envious and horrified by what the other lived around and how we had grown with our families. Foreign life wasn't just China; it was a fifteen minute drive away. Maury was working class Rose Park neighborhood first generation Mexican family meeting me; a dissipated Murray area Scandinavian heritage family of ex-Mormons who had moved 'up' to Sugarhouse, a stuffier working class neighborhood.

We tried to understand the psychological mess the other had to overcome. That was my view. Maury simply found my life different and a little sad and lonely which I sank into like a hot tub. No one had ever acknowledged my Utah life and split family without cover of

Rebecca Guevara

Mormondon might be a tiny bit lonely. He didn't think that was sufficient reason to be a psychological mess. Why would anyone be messed up from my childhood unless they were weak? Growing up with a smoking, drinking single mother who had boyfriends in the same neighborhood as prim LDS families was a trivial reason to mess up your own life. He envied the sanctuary of my bedroom.

He shared a bedroom with his brothers. Pedro had the bed on the opposite wall, Oil Boy had the top bunk and Maury was in the bottom. Renan had a space between her parents and the boys, created with three feet from the parents' and three feet from the brothers' bedroom by Leon, a carpenter cousin. The single door walked her through her brothers' bedroom. Two fold out couches were in the living room, facing the tv that were used for visiting relatives. The high season was April to October when construction was more active in Salt Lake and friends and relatives came from Mexico, California and Idaho to stop by for a few nights before finding their own place or driving to where the fruit was ripe. A few families preferred the boys' room so they were shooed to the two foldout couches. Pedro got one and Maury and Oil Boy shared the other.

Maury saw LoBeth's house was the same size as his on the ground level, but with an unfinished basement used for the luxury of storage and lived in by only two people it was an estate. If Maury dropped a shoe while sitting on his bunk bed the noise was covered by music playing, his brothers teasing, his sister humming and his mother stirring food. Juan seldom made noise. If I dropped a shoe, the thump would disturb LoBeth's reading in the quiet living room and she would ask what I was doing. At LoBeth's there wasn't a synchronized wait to the bathroom. We each had our own closet. Sheets were bought for specific beds, not traded like sleeping bags.

"But where are your people, Abby? You said you were born here." Distress crossed his face and I was charmed.

"They're around. We just don't see each other often. Everyone's busy," I listed their names and how they made a living but bypassed family drama, disinterest and loathing. We were in his car behind the lilac bushes almost ready to go home after a party at Jerry's. Crickets were beating their legs off, ruining the peace of darkness.

"And your father? I've seen your belly button so I know you have one," he wanted to hear the story I'd skipped. The quick version of

22

LoBeth's lost years in New York was all he needed. I told her hackneyed story of attending a wedding at St. Patrick's after she discovered her pregnancy and being overwhelmed to responsibility of motherhood that whooshed her back to Salt Lake. My head was resting on his chest when I finished the short story and I heard the thump of his heart. When he could tell I wasn't going to say more he gave me a two arm squeeze, "Abby Baker, my little immaculate conception." That one I'd never been called. I didn't understand his casual mixing of LDS and Catholic thinking.

"Well, Abby Sabby," he had taken to calling me this and I didn't know why. "How about coming over for Sunday dinner tomorrow and meeting the tribe?"

When I arrived the next afternoon, cars and trucks lined the driveway and several houses down the street. As I parked my Toyota down the block, Maury walked toward me. He'd been waiting and watching.

"Now, don't let the number of people surprise you, Abby. Most are relatives except Renan's boyfriend, Bishop Erickson, and you know Jerry. You don't have to remember all their names. Just be your cool self." We walked into a nine hundred foot house that felt like a full box of cookie people ready to be crushed at any second, leaving arms, legs and cookie heads everywhere. In reality everyone had the necessary grace but me so I held Maury's hand tight.

"This is my brother Pedro," he stopped in front of a man sitting on a folding chair watching tv who got up to shake my hand. In all of Maury's descriptions of his family he had not prepared me for the intensity, the feel of summer rain on bare skin without privacy. Pedro looked at me with eyes that in the first instant knew something about me I didn't. He smiled, said hello and kept his secret about me to himself. I felt looked at like a sister and a woman and felt soul naked both ways.

To the side of him was his father, Juan, who also rose. The solid rough ridged hand took mine like butterfly wings and turned my palm down as he half bowed. The look was imposing strength from an Indian face trained to tell only what he allowed.

Beside him was Oil Boy who waved from his chair and again I noticed the laughing yellow brown eyes.

Maury's guiding hand was my grounding. Everyone was friendly and they all introduced themselves and each other but it was trying to memorize the phone directory. Toddlers were Tiffany, Isaac, Maria Elena,

Roberta, Morrison and two year old Blooper, who was a surprise baby. Children included Armando, Frankie (Francisco), Jeremy, Red (Amber) and Sharon. Adults were Yasmina and Ernesto. I think they were together, but Ernesto could have been married to Willie (Wilhelmina), but not Collette because I remembered she was married to Bellesimo, Jerry's brother nicknamed Barry. Jorge was with either Willie or Yasmina. I recognized the name Tia Manuela from Maury's family description and I met her daughter, Carrie. Carrie and her boyfriend, Marcus, looked like brother and sister with wide shoulders, narrow hips and the same body shiver when they laughed. His grandmother, Abuelita Felipa, sat in a chair like a nucleus with the universe spiraling about. Her sprouting thin hair was the baby hair LoBeth described as mine but the deepness in her eyes had a loneliness I'd never felt.

As we went through the kitchen he stopped by a tall pale man with receding blonde hair and dark eyebrows shaped for a Maybelline ad.

"I'd like you to meet Abby, Bishop Erickson." I recognized his name and family placement. We nodded heads in the style of those days when a man and woman were more likely to nod a polite hello than shake hands, as if all touch were sexual or dirty.

"Lovely to look at, Maury." Ignored and complimented at the same time.

"Time to meet Renan," Maury led me out the back door, beyond the smoking barbeque of chicken. Several men with silver belt buckles were circling it. The small backyard was filled with tables bright with table-cloths. Two people sat alone at the back one.

"Renan, this is Abby."

"Hi, Abby," she held out her hand and I took it. Early rising sunlight, rosy and warming, looked at me. She turned to the man beside her, "this is Brad. Brad Evans." His hand was warm and large as an oversized oven mitten.

I was busy trying to remember dozens of faces and names, but the feel of their space on the picnic bench under the shade of the grandfather age maple faded everyone to background. It was dense passion and emotion that wanted to be apart from everyone. Instinctively I stepped back; not believing I was welcome and not sure I was safe. Maury didn't notice and stepped closer. Maybe it was the smell and feel of LoBeth and her lovers when I knew I needed to leave. Maybe kids like Maury who live with real parents didn't know the feeling, but it was large, deep and whirling. Re-aligning an entrance of safety, I moved behind Maury to follow his lead and stand close. I was dizzy and over stimulated; afraid and baffled.

Inner framework of belief patterns, neat and tidy boxes of well-ordered thinking faced unknown choices that could destroy or give birth. But those words did not come. I did not know what I was looking at. I only knew I had left the structure of my life and willingly entered one I didn't understand.

2

The Estados Unidos is a land of plenty,
but it is not a land of everything.
We want our children to have the grace, love
and respect of México.

- Chepita Arciniga and Juan Bastidas Arias

Love fell from a cloud in Renan's earth brown eyes and her clear brown skin was relaxed, at peace. The smile was restful, accepting, sexual. Dark, straight hair fell evenly from a middle part past her shoulders. Leaning to her left side a lazy end curl of hair teased her breast's beginning curve from a light blue blouse. Brad had a man's swagger strengthened by pushing work, women and even traffic his way. He had good shoulders, proportionate face a little wider at the eyes and small close ears. His hair was more styled than Renan's in groomed careless-ness. Renan's eyes may have been fallen clouds meeting earth but Brad's were lasers and he didn't like being interrupted.

Renan moved on the bench, "Here, sit here. There's plenty of room." She indicated her other side so she stayed close to Brad. "We'll watch all the crazy relatives from here." The mist evaporated from her eyes as she laughed and at the men around the barbeque. "Think the chickens are being timed for cooking or how long a beer takes?" Brad took in a breath, ran a hand through his hair and shifted his six foot frame moving like rocks in a burlap bag. When Renan moved closer to him he gently placed the hair on her left side to her back and looked at her with something I had never seen before. There wasn't a word in my experience.

LoBeth's imagined words ran through my head. "I doubt she plays chess," but I knew if Maury's sister touched a love wound, it would heal.

26

My Family, Mi Familia

My nodding uneasy smile was hidden by Maury's conversation and then I noticed Renan's easy talk hid Brad's watchful quiet. I compared Renan in my small experience to find a comfortable place to put her. She was graceful, but so was Gen in a runway fashion hip thrust. Renan's was a quiet confident ballet, moving from her heart center, not hips. The invitation in her eyes was melting candles, old family silver, the feel of yellow satin on perfumed skin while Kelly's was spring's apple blossom love without doubt and wrapped in flannel to always keep you safe. Renan's may not be safe. She looked to be slim due to age because from head to toe the only bone popping up like my knuckles, cheeks and ribs if I cared to look, were her ankles. "One baby and she'll split the sails," Golden Bitch had said of some forgotten female she was jealous of that we had seen in the mall. It was Renan's face that truly held attention. The nose was straight, the lips full without being cotton balls, the eyebrows a little high, long and straight and the eyes almond shape and brown. Her face was mechanically symmetrical, made light as spirit with a searing life energy that surveyed with appreciation, honor and a love both sexual and motherly.

Maury was called to help his father arrange chairs, leaving me as the third person at an awkward party for two. When I saw Jerry peek out the back door I smiled and gave him a small wave.

"Hi, Jerry," Renan said and Brad nodded hello as he rubbed his hands. The party with Renan was clearly interrupted so he exhaled and took a long swallow of beer. "Do you know Jerry, Abby?"

Yes, we both indicated and she continued, "But do you know the real Jerry? Where he comes from?" Jerry shifted in the bench, slightly embarrassed, but let Renan continue. "My family is simple country people from Jalisco, Mexico. Never anything great or educated, but Jerry is more norteamericano than George Washington."

I looked at Jerry who was not denying it but seemed to be playing along with Renan. She spent several minutes explaining while Brad looked with boredom at the silver buckled chefs and sucked his beer. The Sandoval family had heritage reaching back to Mexico and then Spanish California.

Generations ago Jerry's family were original settlers in San Francisco. "In the late 1700's his ancestors left Sonora with who was it...de Anza?" she looked at Jerry.

"Juan Bautista de Anza."

"Yes, and they founded San Francisco."

"It was called Yerba Buena then." He went on to say a few years later his family went to help settle San Jose. They built haciendas and lived by European manners chiseled from the grace and history of the Catholic Church. By 1846 California fell to the upstart and voracious U.S. government during a time of Mexico's military weakness when fighting both the French and Spanish. The Sandovals and thousands of others practiced diplomatic and survivalist tactics for the next two years expecting an equitable bargain could be made. In preliminary drafts and cocktail party promises Mexicans were assured. The private land and businesses they held for generations, would be retained in the Guadalupe Hidalgo Treaty of 1848 that ceded northwest Mexico to the U.S. Unfortunately, the U.S. Congress omitted that paragraph from the treaty in its final form and the war torn, over extended mother country could not protect them. 'Hay, pobre de México. Tan lejos de Dios y tan cercas a los Estados Unidos,' was Mexico's lament.

Jerry's family was stripped of land and business connections but remained in San Jose until his grandfather, Ernesto, believed a fortune could be re-made in Salt Lake City. He reasoned his ancestors had prospered by moving from Mexico to the open land of San Francisco and then moving to San Jose. Perhaps the young Salt Lake City would hold his fortune. In the 1920's when opportunity seemed possible everywhere, he brought his wife with her thin bone china and heavy furniture that was in Jerry's apartment, to Utah.

"He's shown me his mother's silver hand mirror, Abby. It's beautiful," Renan said she had never seen anything like it. After a year, of continuing struggle Ernesto was grateful to find steady work at Kennecott Copper. Neither he nor his wife, Luisa, ever adjusted to the rugged isolation of Utah's high mountain desert. Utah never felt like home and Jerry's father followed his parents' wishes and sent his wife, Maria, to family in San Jose for the birth of each child. "They need to be born in their homeland," Ernesto taught.

During a Sunday dinner served on thin flower rimmed china, Ernesto announced he was sending two sons back to California for college but Jerry's dad, Alberto, a boy of twelve, stayed here to remain a comfort to his parents.

"Your family history is grander than mine," I said at the end.

"It's grander than anyone's here," smiled Renan. "Let's eat." She led us in the house to be last in line for food. "Now these are tamales and they're steamed in corn husks. Just take them off," a blonde girl of three grabbed Renan's leg while she delicately demonstrated how to retrieve the treat inside and throw the husks in a garbage can under the table. A big night out with LoBeth through my childhood was never any more authentic than Greek shishkabob, ham fried rice or stiff dry corn tortilla tacos.

"Si, and when you have enough husks, you make baby shoes," an uncle offered his help from across the table. Further down the table of beans, rice, salsa and tortillas was potato salad, jello salad and pickled hot carrots. As we passed the barbeque to the tables, chicken was put on our plate.

The blonde child twisted her head and shoulders between Brad and Renan before sitting to eat the six beans, tablespoon of rice and fistful of jello. She was a pretty child with wavy, light brown sparkling hair and eyes that were intensely interested in what the other children were doing.

"This is Crystal, Brad's daughter," Renan said. Brad was trying to interest her in a piece of tortilla with three beans on it. Renan wiped her face when she wiggled off the chair to rejoin the children I recognized by the color of their hair.

"Welcome to our family. We are noisy." The friendly statement was Chepita leading Red and Sharon as they held a plate of square cut sheet cake. Isaac trailed in a white shirt, tie and dark slacks handing out paper napkins as seriously as blessings.

"Thank you," I took a piece of offered cake and hoped I wouldn't explode.

Pedro's observant hello, Renan's suffocating sensuality, Brad's decisive disregard and Jerry's history was a boil stirred down by Maury's easy walk, light hand hold, gentle brush of my side. As I listened to Maury talk to the children, aunts, uncles, cousins, mother, sister, brothers and whoever walked by, I watched large family ease for the first time. There was comfort and acceptance that didn't sit at Grandma and Grandpa Baker's Sunday dinner of scalloped potatoes and roast beef so many years ago.

When the sun moved far enough to the west that tree shadows

reached to the house, Juan brought out a Mexican mariachi hat. It was bright blue with gold stitching. He threw it on patio cement and bowed to everyone. "Heoyy, heoyy," came from the crowd in male and female voices and then music blared from the house. Whoever wanted danced in a large circle around the hat in steps that looked both practiced and a feeling of the moment. The silver belted men, children of all sizes, women in skirts and tight fitting jeans circled the hat as an altar to their hearts. They laughed toward the sky and to each other as they entered and stepped out of the circle.

Jerry sat beside me, aware I was a new spectator. "Surprising isn't it?" The spell was broken and I looked at him. "What do you mean?"

"When you grew up being able to hear your mother's slippers walk in the kitchen this is a surprise."

"Yes, I guess it is."

"Enjoy the party, Abby. They never last forever." I looked at him, so square shouldered, solid and strong, but with a woman's face skin. Eyebrows were straight and honest. He watched Renan with her arm around Crystal.

"And a good one is hard to start." It was a fitting reply to LoBeth.

Light flooded his face as he turned, "You are a wise little sister."

I would come to respect Jerry. His mind was always vacuumed, cleaned, polished and rid of wastefulness, meanness and laziness. He was a force of self as simply real as a handful of dirt in your hand as you plant roses.

The rhythm underpinning Maury's childhood household was his mother's constantly lyrical Mexican music blaring from scratched records on the old stereo. The love songs were passionate, lamenting and proud of strong emotion ripping hearts, sending longing across a thousand mile desert through Utah and Arizona to Mexico. Celebration music of proud heritage, rousing trumpets and longing guitars inclusively drew everyone to smile, participate and live happily under God's Tuesday morning hand of responsibility when Saturday was far away. It was the last melody I didn't hear; an undercurrent of private laments kept with razor blades in each heart. The songs of loss and remembering what can never be found again. They were resonating notes from the dirt of a country left behind; the tearing of children from a parent's soul. Juan, Chepita, Pedro, Renan, Maury and Oil Boy all held separate straining sad notes.

Music was Maury's restoring hiding place. He was always a pleasant, soft-spoken person and I would become too aware of my every so often too big laugh or careless temper when I was with him. Stupid drivers, slow sales clerks, rude waitresses never bothered him like they tormented LoBeth and by her example, me. Maury took his frustrations, sadness, angers, questions to music that played up and down, over and out of him, removing the crust of anger or hurt until he was his soft self again. He listened to popular music with me and shared the understanding and vitality of its youth, but he took his soul to jazz. Ray Charles I'd heard of, but John Coltrane and Dexter Gordon were new. With or without me he could lean back in his car seat, listen to the soulful notes of life playing in midnight magic from the car cassette and settle his mind with tomorrow.

"How was the Sunday dinner?" LoBeth was sitting on the couch reading when I came home.

"Good. Lots of food. More people." I tried to walk toward the spit-size hall that every room in the house wagon-wheeled off to my room.

"How did they make you feel? Who were they?"

"A little claustrophobic there were so many of them and the house isn't any bigger than this. They were just a bunch of aunts, uncles, cousins, friends, his parents and brothers." I wanted to get away from her questions. I felt unfaithful to our non-existent family and what they had never given and I hadn't been able to ask for and LoBeth had treated as unimportant. Now I had seen what I hadn't been able to ask for. "Oh, I did meet his sister. Renan. She's really pretty. Two years older than Maury. We're going to a movie with her and her boyfriend next weekend."

"Old for a Mexican family to not be married."

"Old for a Utah family," why did she have to jump to that? "She's only twenty-four or five. Didn't you say to wait to thirty?"

"What is good to do and what people do are two different things. I had you when I was twenty-four. I should have waited until I was thirty." It's always comforting to hear your arrival would have been better postponed or cancelled.

The week after I graduated from high school LoBeth had an appointment for me with her gynecologist. She didn't go with me but she did inform the doctor and me that the purpose of the appointment was to discuss birth control options and give me a prescription for birth control pills. I think she imagined something with Thurman Wade. Thurman and

I had been friends the last year of school and went to a few movies and parties together, but he was going out of state to school the next fall and I wasn't going to any school, no way, no how. Half the time we were together he'd try to talk me into going to school, saying he thought I was smart enough, but I wasn't interested. School took the joy out of learning. School was a stunter. It was time to try exciting, grown-up living. Besides, LoBeth wanted me to go to school. I needed to rebel. When I got the sales job at the optical store, I thought I'd started a career. The other half of the time Thurman and I spent together we played around with sex, but nothing requiring birth control.

The two times I could have used the pill were when I was seventeen with Shane Cooper. He was a shadowy no-good great-looking guy who may have had the girls in the junior class alphabetized to properly lay in good order. I'm glad my last name was Baker, but it was me who ended it. I was scared to end up like LoBeth and have to say, I should have waited until I was twenty-four. Since I'd had the prescription, maybe I'd taken it half the time and usually without reason. I wasn't on it when I met Maury and didn't start. That was too plotting for a self-styled good girl like me whose lack of virginal purity should at least not look slutty by LDS standards goddam. I told him it was his responsibility and he handled it well. Turning over birth control to his condoms allowed me to keep a sense of female decorum that I had loose but not lost morals.

When Maury, Renan and Brad picked me up on Friday for the movie, Maury and I sat in the back seat. It was a black two year old Camaro and the shape reminded me of spacecraft for evil aliens hiding on dark side streets for victims. The three of them talked and I didn't say much. As easily as lighting a match these three people caused the air in the car to be heavier, sexier, more intense than I was accustomed to and I wasn't comfortable. The first time I was aware of the feeling I was fourteen and I walked into its reaching vapor when three of LoBeth's old New York friends stopped to visit on their way to California. The air was germinating and sensual. I was packing a pillow and pajamas to spend the night at Kelly's and I made sure I came home late the next day. I didn't fit with LoBeth's friends and I didn't know if I fit here.

Renan shone in the carlight as a Mexican Madonna in surreal fire. Her hair was up with pins but what wasn't fastened fell along her neck and forehead glittering like a halo. Her voice had a lilt that made sentences flute notes. Maybe if I said too much someone would notice I was a bitchy cocker spaniel and put me out at the bus stop. Brad was harder to see because he was watching traffic but when he glanced at Renan his sculpted profile had a mixed American business earnestness and vapid manikin perfect pose.

"What work do you do, Brad?" it seemed a normal question.

"I sell." A twitch of his head said he wanted it dropped, but Renan turned in her seat and cheerfully added he sold ATVs and motorcycles. She clearly thought it was great work and the carlight, streetlight and her light radiated a larger halo. Automatically, I recoiled into the seat, self-conscious and confused. Baffled as to why I felt dismissed by Brad and still trying to adjust to the full air, I returned attention to Maury. "Got any glasses tonight?" he asked when I looked at him.

"No, I didn't want your sister to think I was weird."

"Oh, it's okay. I've already told her that, Abby Sabby." I rolled my eyes and he pulled me into his arm.

The week before Kelly had agreed Maury was cute in a quiet, magnetic artist way. Dragging out my words for effect, I said his searing eyes and lanky spare bones made him hungry and sensitive. His brown eyes were deep pools of thought and his hair was thick and warm and strong. Very alluring to me. Gen impatiently sighed and reminded us cute only worked well with dogs and babies and artists weren't paid at all. I countered he was going to school for computer programming and data processing. Nothing artistic in computers. LoBeth's office had installed them last month and she was taking a special class, which got Gen and Kelly on a new subject.

Gen's objections to Maury made me think about what did attract me. There was a lurking gentleness behind a teasing smile, an easy manner, and when we walked into the movie his long arm around me felt like a summer shawl. Standout handsome or doctor potential would have looked misplaced by me anyway. Gen and I never confused prey.

After the movie, a shared pizza and two pitchers of beer, I was dropped off at the doorstep wondering if Maury thought I was a conven-ient cooperative date or a love interest. Maybe he hadn't noticed the embracing wrap of warm air that tickled desire in Brad's car but it made me start taking birth control pills. Sex had never felt magnetic or crazy urgent. With Shane and Thurman it had been discovering chocolate and enjoying more than friendship. Even with Maury, the attraction was pleasure that was more fun than washing dishes to keep his kindness. Our sex had been satisfying and gentle which is all I had ever expected. If I'd been one to drive men to physical madness and no control, I would have known it by then. While other females got male lust, I hoped to look interesting when someone needed a little long term loyalty and an occasional laugh. But when I began taking the pill that night I consciously joined the ranks of deliberate planner and participant.

The next Friday night Brad had to work and Renan came with us to Jerry's party.

"Brad doesn't usually work Friday night does he?" I asked as Maury drove.

"No, and he didn't want to tonight but sometimes it's the best sales night."

"Really?"

"You know, Abby," Maury broke in, "a man's got to be ready for a hot Saturday night date."

"We're going dancing tomorrow after he shows me how well he does with a handgun at the shooting range." Renan stated.

"He has guns?"

My question made Renan smile and Maury snicker. "He is a gun. Straight and ready to fire at Renan."

"Stop it, Maury. He's a marksman. He has ribbons and trophies to prove it. Brad has a few guns but mainly his dad has a collection. When Brad was a kid they would hunt together. He wants Maury to go with him."

Maury's shoulders shook in mock disgust, "Not for me."

A strawberry blonde who looked like vamp meets cosmetic counter sale had her arm wrapped in Jerry's when we walked in. When he saw Renan he patted her on the shoulder and sent her to get something.

"Renan, I didn't know you were coming tonight."

"Brad had to work so I invited myself with these two."

"Come with me to the kitchen. I've got real beer there, not this Utah pee water." Renan followed while Maury and I stayed behind to get our legal 3.2% pee water out of a cooler in the corner. We talked with Brian, his girlfriend Shaya, two cousins I'd seen at Maury's and a woman who lived down the hall and had to go back to check on her sleeping baby. An hour passed before I got up to go to the bathroom, knowing I'd have to wait by the door for a turn.

As I stood third in line I saw Jerry and Renan sitting on his bed talking. Their heads were bent toward one another. The other people in the room were laughing and talking in two different groups. The strawberry blonde whirled past me in military stride to stand in front of Jerry. I couldn't hear what she said but her face meant, "Why the hell aren't you paying any attention to me?" Jerry stood, his head leaning for pleasant compromise but she took a good look at Renan, turned and whirled past me again, before leaving with two friends who were not happy to go.

When I got back to Maury, Brad had arrived and they were talking. Without understanding the instinct I went back to the bedroom and told Renan Brad was in the living room. A crease crossed Jerry's forehead until Renan hugged him, kissed his cheek and said, "I love you, Jerry."

"Another woman gone! Another life lost! Three more children devastated and torn to shreds for the rest of their lives," LoBeth lifted one arm high while the other poured scotch. It was 9:30 p.m. the following Thursday, and I had walked in the door from work. Maury hadn't called since we'd been at Jerry's party. I could have called but now that I was on birth control, I wanted him to play a part.

"A bad day at the office, huh?"

"A bad day." Drunk sometimes had sad tales about work and life. She didn't see first hand the thrown chairs, broken dishes, blood or bodies, but she had imagined the broken, vacant and ravaged eyes of adults and children who witnessed the death of their family as the paperwork passed her desk.

"The man killed his wife with a hunting rifle. In their kitchen. At least the children were in another room, but the oldest one saw. An eleven year old boy. He was the one who went to see what happened when his father left the house and it was quiet for an hour." I opened a can of soup, heated it in the microwave and sat down with that, crackers and a glass of milk while LoBeth told the most recent tragedy.

"Senseless," she finished with the n left in the glass of scotch.

"Power and control. Like you've said." I repeated her mantra to keep conversation general and uncrazed by Drunk.

"There's got to be something more. All men like power and control but they don't all kill."

"What makes you think all men like power and control? There must be a few exceptions." Maury for one.

She eyed me, "Live life, Missy." Golden Bitch had a tone in her voice that could pierce Drunk. "But it didn't make him too happy. They found him dead two blocks away. Shot himself in the head with a smaller gun."

The picture on the 10:00 o'clock news of the dead couple showed two normal people sitting at a picnic table. He had round cheeks and springy hair that held its own away from his head. The wife looked a little tired but she was working on a smile and she didn't look any more tired than any other mother who wandered into Wanlass. All of it, the whole icky ideal family of mother, father and kids under one roof was not my life. We continued talking about the tragedy and the horrible burden the children and two sides of a family would carry forever. There was a communal nod at the end that flourished a near self-indulgent wave of pity and prayer to them.

On Sunday I caved. LoBeth had taught me friends could be called anytime but lovers needed intrigue. Gen and Kelly said, "Just call him for goddsakes. If you want to see him, let him know."

"Hola," it was Pedro sounding comfortable away from Anglo restaurant people. Mariachi music and at least a dozen people were in the background. LoBeth and I would have to invite her whole office to our house for sounds like that.

"Hi, Pedro, this is Abby. Is Maury there?"

"Si, Abby," he held the phone away, "Maury. Phone." It was clunked down on the table. Sound casual, sound casual I repeated.

"Hello." He was relaxed and friendly.

"Hi, Maury. Abby."

"Hi, Abby. How things going?" I could have been his bank teller calling.

"Oh, fine. Just called to say hi. Hadn't heard from you."

"Had a few tests this week. Been intense. How about if I call you tomorrow?"

"Okay," I was disappointed even with a promised call. He could have sounded more excited or pleased.

"Hey, Renan wants to talk to you. Here she is."

"Hey, Abby, how things going?" were those words a family secret code? Now I could sound bitchy so I needed to be careful.

"Fine. Just a Sunday."

"Yes. I need some sunglasses and Bro here tells me you have some great ones. When will you be in and I'll come by?"

"I'm there Tuesday through Saturday 10:00 to 6:00, sometimes 1:00 to 9:00. We do have some great glasses. A new shipment is coming this week. If you wait until Thursday they should all be out to see." The words were paste.

"Great. I'll see you Thursday or Friday. Probably during my lunch hour." She worked three miles from the mall.

In the days before cell phones, LoBeth remembered to tell me two days later Maury had called the next day. She said, he said, he'd call again.

Renan and Brad came Saturday about 2:00 p.m. That's the busiest time so I rushed over while I was helping another customer and showed where to look for the best sunglasses. Another man with an observant steady look of belonging where he stood was on the other side of Renan. When Alicia noticed them a minute later she presented a huge Wanlass welcome smile and walked to Brad.

"Can I help you?" her voice rang across the store. It was a far different tone from the one for cranky old people with their own spectacle ideas. When he said they were waiting for me she slinked back ever so slightly but to her credit, relieved me of my last cash register moments with the customer and let me go help them.

Brad had mentioned his friend Travis Patrick. He wasn't quite as tall as Brad but he had the broadness and sense of space. Thinning brown hair was compensated with a carefully trimmed goatee. After introductions, Brad pointed to a jeweler's plastic bag Travis was holding.

"Travis wanted Renan's help choosing a birthday present for his wife."

"I wanted her to like it; not just say she liked it," he smiled.

"They've got the cutest kids, Janna and Jason," Renan added.

"Don't forget the third kid, a black lab named Jag," Travis grinned larger with Brad's words. He was a happy family man.

"See anything you like?" Brad returned us to business.

"Here's the face," Renan waved her hand in front of her face like a princess wand, "what do you think?" She held Artemis in her fingers like they were already home.

"The glasses you have in your hand are good ones for you. But here's another couple to try. You have a rounder face, a little broader at the eyes so something with a little height and depth gives length to your face. You wouldn't want cat eyes." I brought out Beach Party, the least expensive, Calliope from the same line as Artemis, and Extravagant. They all looked good and Brad, Travis and I nodded at each pair. It was only a matter of preference and these glasses appeared well-named.

"I think I'll go look in that full-length mirror. Be right back," she took all four and walked away.

"How things been, Brad?" I thought I might as well be pleasant and I was smothering jealousy of this female who moved like Snow White and had a handsome devoted guy slobbering behind her and a married man who took her advice. Travis folded his arms and watched me.

"Great. I've got Renan. Isn't she beautiful?" Brad was a crossword puzzle. When I had a word figured out for him like 'foreboding', as he looked across a Sunday dinner table when I met him or 'evasive' when he was asked about his work, up would pop 'cheerful' when he introduced his friend, or 'glisten' when he looked at Renan.

"Yes," we all watched her across the store.

"Maury likes you," my ears perked and I looked at him. "He thinks you're okay. But he's been with Erica for a long time." I stared at him; aware Travis was leaning to watch me.

"I didn't think you knew about her." He looked closer, "Renan didn't think it was right to string you along. She likes you so she got after Maury. He and Erica have been off and on for almost two years but six months ago she made more excuses and it's been on and off again since. Who knows how it will turn out." Renan was walking back. Travis moved back, aware of Renan behind him.

"If that hunk ever becomes available, let me know," Alicia watched Brad walk out the door. I also watched them go, thinking it was out of my life. At least I'd get the commission for Artemis.

A few days later while LoBeth and I watched 60 Minutes and ate Hamburger Helper the fork suddenly felt too heavy to lift. My simple boring white life of comfortable routine was not resuming. Something in me was changed by Maury and his haunting family. I told LoBeth it was over with Maury. My admission of mourning was met with a smile, "You're building a resume, Abby. You're looking for the best man, not the first man."

What sympathy I could get was from Kelly while she cut my hair.

"I'm sorry, Abby. Now you know how crappy guys can be."

"I already knew that."

"Yes, I guess you did." Sometimes you have to hold tight, aim right and stab hard to get milk from coconuts or sympathy from humans.

Two weeks later Gen and Kelly talked me into going to Slickers. I hadn't been with them for over a month and wasn't excited then, but LoBeth almost kicked me out the door when they stopped by to see if I would come. "Meat and croissants have to be displayed before they are bought, honey. Go." Missy Mommy sent me cruising.

I danced a little with two guys and then Gen and Kelly, but standing by a table with first a beer and then water was my evening. Gen was making progress with a hulk of a guy that made her five foot nine short and Kelly was talking to me and a group of people she knew at the next table. When the music ended Gen came back alone, a little dewy after dancing. "Maury's on the other side. With that looker Jerry and a few others. Maybe a girl."

I spent the next half hour trying to see through dancers to the other side and finally spotted him. He was uncurled and loose, a pose I associated with comfort and a third beer. The female sitting by him was Velcro on him from shoulder to elbow. Long blonde hair puffed out in extraordinary 1985 curls, high cheeks, slender neck. When they danced I stood a little behind Kelly and tried to talk to her group. When he held her for a slow dance, I knew he and Erica were together.

"Abby, listen to me. Whether he's the best or the worst of them, they're all replaceable with fifty watt light bulbs," Kelly watched me. If I needed a second opinion I knew LoBeth would agree.

Almost a month of not seeing Maury and then seeing him with another female was an ache. Watching them dance made me see that possible future evaporate. His musical, gangly, gentle, a little foreign self standing by my side as we walked into a future wouldn't be. Instead, there was now another desert of aloneness to walk over while hoping there would be an end where someone would want me.

For silly reasons I believed when a person graduated from high school life finally arranged itself in a neat little children's hundred piece puzzle. The footwork of living through school, childhood, dependence, parental observation and indifference would be rewarded with true love, stability and good income. By age twenty-one reality was sinking in, but hope lingered. When I met Maury, and the angel made me watch him walk in the door, I foolishly let childhood dreams have one more try.

I knew I was not premium first quality fruit, so to say. Boys didn't hand-pick me as the first one off the tree for looks, family money, or a popular local favorite, a 'good' girl of high moral character. I needed someone a little off the mark himself in standards to be okay with average. So, it didn't occur to me to fight for Maury's affection. I could see Erica was blonde, pretty, slim and smart enough to get the man. I wasn't conceding. I was admitting I didn't have an arsenal for a first round. When I walked out of Slicker's that night the desert of aloneness was the Gobi and all of Nevada combined.

Large Guy came with Gen to the car. "We're dropping the two of you off. Anyplace you want?"

"Home," I said. "Home," Kelly said. There wasn't any talk in the car while Gen drove. Large Guy put a cramp on it by staring at Gen like she was a double burger. The air started having that charged electrical energy like around Renan and Brad and I sunk deeper in midnight Saturday gloom.

3

Life is what you make it.
It's as hard or easy as you believe it to be.
Success and failure are chosen.

- Mauricio Antonio Arias

On the drive home twenty-one felt old. Routine returned to pre-Maury: work, time spent with Kelly, Gen and My Lady LoBeth. Looking for a Maury replacement didn't make the list. Casual dating just to be busy or for the sex without a first and last name and at least one meaningful conversation never interested me. If a guy fell out of the sky, fine, but I was not a born hunter. It was growing up with LoBeth that ruined me. Through the years she dated enough for both of us though she never brought anyone home for a single night. If she had one night stands they were away from me. I only got to see the dates and the six who lived with us anywhere from a week to a year and a half.

Two of the men LoBeth brought home I wanted to stay. The other four were never missed. One of them came on to me when I was ten, though I didn't know what it was. After he gave me a big hug and quick soft kiss on the mouth he said I could have that every day if I didn't tell LoBeth because it was special for me. He didn't know how proud I was that LoBeth's boyfriend liked me, too and at that age not to tell LoBeth was not to tell myself. He was out the door that night and I was rooted to the couch for the next hour and told what and how men could and couldn't touch. Well, that's good, but to explain how dumb I was, I knew LoBeth was telling me something important so I came to the conclusion men weren't to like me. Only LoBeth was likable and kissable. From that moment I was more a spectator, sure of my lack of allure. Four of the six ordered me around when LoBeth was gone. "Get a beer." "Make the bed." "Fix a sandwich." She was more lenient with that behavior.

Looking back I realize they were nice enough men and if it hadn't been for me maybe LoBeth would have stayed with one. Boyfriends of a daughter's mother hold keys to two hearts and their twisting turn is felt as much in the sex life of the daughter as the mother.

I hoped Gen and Large Guy had a meaningful conversation about the band that night because time was running out before they'd be alone and my suffocating moral standards were not being accommodated. Yet, Gen wasn't what I called easy. Of the three of us she was the pickiest about who she thought was good-looking or Gen-worthy. Watching her sidelong glance him at the red light, I felt cheated that uncontrollable sex heat didn't run through me like hot water to a shower.

"Nice to meet you," I stuck my hand out to Large Guy before sliding out the door in front of LoBeth's. "Now, what did you say your name was?"

Flustered away from his hungry stare, he looked at me while Gen twitched her shoulder at me like a pushy little sister, "Rick Hanes." It could have been Hanes, Haun, James or Kanes, but I now had that much information for police if needed. LoBeth tutoring has a way of seeping into the skin.

I would like to say it was a broken heart I felt when I walked through the darkness of LoBeth's house to my room, but from the distance of these years a lot of it was self-pity. Her gentle sleep breathing was background to pad to my bedroom, change to nightwear, walk to the bathroom and remove dancehall dirt from my face, brush my teeth and go to the kitchen for a glass of water. I took the glass to my bedroom, went to the pre-World War II closet that measured four feet wide, three feet deep and reached inside the rarely used suitcase in the bottom corner. Deep in a zippered pocket was gin. Through the moonlight that touched it on the bedside table it looked as clear as my purpose. Get drunk. My insides needed comfort. Needed surcease. Needed not to feel for a few hours. I mixed the water and gin with my finger and drank gulps, tasting bitter stinging baby green tree limbs.

When I drink like that it is to quell. I need the drink to blunt knife sharp edges and slow flowing melting fluid glass that is my insides. Gin needs to cool the liquid poised to boil, poised to kill with surging feeling I don't want to feel. Glass that was cold and sharp, jutting and cracked during the workday as I waited on customers at Wanlass, tried to be happy with Kelly and Gen, saw Maury and Erica, and watched Large Guy, gave way to a heat of tears, anguish, mourning that melted to a moving thick hot glass that needed gin to thin pain; lower temperature. Gin to soothe edges and help return sharpness so I could manage tomorrow. I stopped taking birth control.

Tuesday I asked Alicia if I could start testing the new Emotions line from a popular manufacturer. She said yes and I began working through Internal Spin to Discovery to Peaceful.

1986 started with the Challenger exploding in Florida and dating Craig Spencer. He reminded me of Thurman. He talked about school and wanted sex. Craig was a good person but he didn't seem to want me anymore than Maury. We were both spending time. I never did meet his family but he said it was the usual assortment of crazies and hidden skeletons.

"They're pretty good people, though. At least they all talk to each other on major holidays." I had just finished telling him about my family on the way home from a movie.

"Is love important to you, Craig?"

"Yes," an automatically reasonable response from a guy hoping to end the night with sex.

"What does love mean to you?" he hated the store glasses, so I was not behind a façade. Maybe if I'd slapped on more makeup I would have been more protected.

"Love," the question made him sit up and rub his chin. "I guess staying with someone through thick and thin. Caring if they are happy." I let the conversation drift to silence. Happy. The boy who thought happy went with love. He was too much for me.

Late on a Friday afternoon Alicia sent me for take out food at the food court. Balancing our Greek souvlakis on my way back, I saw Travis sitting at a table. My impulse was to turn another way, but he had already seen me. "Abby."

"Hi, Travis," a woman and two kids were at the table.

"Meet my family," A wide arm sweep to introduce Mistie, Janna and Jason, with nods all around was finished with a disclaimer to his wife.

"Abby dated Maury, Renan's brother." Then he turned to me, "How you been?"

"Fine. Taking dinner back for the crew right now."

"Still at Wanlass?"

My small routine life was a paperweight and all I could do was nod. "Say hello to Brad."

"I will."

On my way back to Wanlass I saw a poster in a shop. A dark skinned angel with black hair was flying over power lines. She held a message she was delivering and its white scroll, her white dress, clouds and moon surreally blended into reading patterns and shapes of feeling. There was a message I didn't understand in it, a warning and foreboding I felt through a memory dreamed but yet to be lived. It turned out to be a print by Mexican painter, Tamayo. The next day I bought it during my lunch hour, had it framed and hung it in my room.

Six months later I left the store at 6:10 p.m. Thirty feet down the mall, seated on a bench facing stores was Maury. A skull cap was keeping his beautiful hair a secret. I stopped. Magnets in front of strong forces don't think, they just fall on target.

"You didn't call back," he said. At first I didn't know what he was talking about and then I remembered LoBeth's late message. "No," I answered. The mall wasn't busy and anyone listening could hear our words and the silence.

"Hey, Abby Sabby, how about a movie and something to eat tomorrow night?"

"Okay," was a whisper.

"Good," and he got up perky and quick as a wind-up toy. "Pick you up at 8:00. Still living with LoBeth?" I nodded, afraid anything I'd say would be in tears. On the way home Robert Palmer sang 'might as well face it, you're addicted to love,' on the radio. I didn't know what love felt like, but I did feel addicted to Maury.

LoBeth insisted on answering the door that night though I was ready and waiting with her in the living room. "He said he was coming," I told her staring off to middle distance afraid it was a delusion I had suffered in the mall's walkway.

"Well, if it isn't Phantom Man," LoBeth greeted Maury with a half bow at the door. She had a way with men.

"LoBeth, mi Corazón, me embriaga con su bondad," Unassailed and unrepentant, Maury stepped inside.

"I have no idea what you said, lovely young man, but once inside this threshold you enter LoBeth land."

"I'm ready, Maury, let's go."

"I didn't know you spoke Spanish," I said in the car.

"I don't. But a little can flip up when I want to be heard but not understood. My parents speak it."

"What did you say to her?"

"LoBeth, my heart, I am drunk with your kindness." The night proceeded with tentative polite conversation. He held my hand as we bumped past knees to a place he wanted to sit. Self-righteously, I didn't offer to pay for the shared popcorn. On the drive to a Chinese restaurant we talked about the movie, Color of Money. After ham fried rice and barbequed beef it was twelve ten a.m. and the promised events were completed. Closing prayer was all we needed to live through the night.

"I've missed you, Abby," we were parked outside LoBeth's.

When I had seen LoBeth at this point with a man or two, she would raise her eyebrows in sexual indictment and come-on. She expected apology and abject retreat. All I could do was bite my lip and keep from yelling, "Well, then, why didn't you come around?" I felt my breath. "Why didn't you call?" I asked quietly. I was wimp city queen thinking of Erica.

"Come here," I moved toward the console between us in his car. His fingers were dance steps on my shoulder blades, backbone, ribs and as he held me I only wanted to sink and sink and sink lower to where his fingers would always be mine and inside all of me, to love that's all I wanted, to be touched.

"What happened to Erica?"

His surprised back stiffening said he didn't suspect I knew. "She wanted a Frigidaire." My blank look prompted more, "Inside joke. You know. No coffee with her cream."

Why did these phrases make me feel like I was settling? Was choosing a human being ever settling?

"She's gone." Notice I was too afraid to ask him if he was settling.

Brad, Renan, Maury, and I and sometimes Travis and Mistie began hanging out together. I didn't give it a pretend future. Hearing Maury's voice on the phone, sitting beside him, having his company, his daily good cheer, his arms around me was enough. I felt in love but I didn't expect or ask anything of him. I let the pleasant illusion stay mine. I didn't want his real opinion or feeling to dissolve it.

Being with Renan was still unsettling. I had to dump high school stereotypes and remember school yard cruelties and judgments wouldn't make a difference in who sat with me at lunch. Renan would have been part of school's social underworld. Her every move would have been watched by the cheerleaders and class officers and I'm quite sure Shane Cooper would have come up with the alphabet approach just for Renan Marolita Arias. She would have been a danger to girls who expected hand holding to secure a lifetime allegiance.

Brad seemed a suitable and dangerous dark outcast. The first look he had given me was dismissive. He didn't need to look beyond my nose to know I was afraid and inconsequential. I didn't need to look beyond his eyes and shoulders to know darkness and strength that could evaporate my presence.

That was the orange skin of their appearance. Brad could stand with an arm touching Renan in a movie line or in a Jazz basketball half-time crowd, and ice cream and beer crowds separated. They could walk into a restaurant and the blonde pretty hostess skipped three couples who walked in first to ask Brad how many were in his party. He didn't hit six feet, his belly wasn't a washboard and months later when LoBeth met him she rated him 7.25 on her handsome scale. According to her, he didn't have DNA; he had body exudence. On a snowy night when I was fourteen LoBeth and Open Heart Anguishers, Susan and Judy, explained their secret phrase.

"It's been called aura, charisma, personal space, electromagnetism and a bunch of other things," scotch was starting to get to Susan's clear thinking.

"But the point is," LoBeth broke in, "body exudence is power, strength, health, sex. Real attraction power." All three nodded toward me as though they were imparting sacred knowledge.

Her next lesson ended with, "Don't be a target. Sensitive is only practical during sex."

"Yes," LoBeth explained Brad in her man rating system. "He's a well-made girl scout cookie. You like him because he's consistent to the recipe."

"What does that mean?" I slurped over my Saturday morning breakfast cereal.

"He's got the market cornered—fairly tall, blondish, strong, owns it and like most girl scout cookies when you bite he's soft in the middle."

Brad and Renan both had something that alternately drew people toward them and sent them away. They were compelling and dangerous. From my inside distance I learned a surprising secret of their outsidedness. Being outside and not caring to be part of the group gives freedom to love and hold without boundary. A slow peeling under the orange skin revealed their insides as sweet fruit, tender and in need of each other's care.

When Renan looked at him like he owned the earth he went for the next glass of what she wanted, when she stood he went for the coat. When she sat he handed her a napkin or sat beside her like a sentinel. I watched her go for a kiss late one night as Maury and I got out of the car. She leaned over on him with her arms wrapped as though he were a birthday present she wanted to give her life to hold.

On a rainy Friday night when Travis and Mistie joined us, I began to call Brad Sir Brad. We were headed out of Sizzler, one of the first chains to believe in Utah, where we had eaten a day's worth of food in one sitting. Brad opened Renan's thin coat for her arms to slip through, but as they walked out the door into the rain, he held his coat over her to give headcover and space. Like a carriage, he spirited her away in safety while he stepped briskly alongside, soon wet and soppy as a puppy. Maury and I ran behind, each wearing our own coats. Travis and Mistie ran to their car under an umbrella Mistie made him keep in the car.

"Brad, you are wonderful," I said as three wet bodies slid in the car. "From now on I will call you Sir Brad." They laughed and I didn't always call him that when others were around, but between Brad and me, I did.

"Thank you, Sir Brad, and I want you to know I say that with the utmost respect," This time I was standing behind him in the Arias family Sunday buffet line. Brad handed me a fork and napkin as though I was following him like Crystal.

"Well, keep it quiet. And my mother wouldn't agree."

"Maybe she doesn't know you very well." I meant it as a casual return of the conversation. It was what two contemporaries say about parents or what parents say about grown children, but the sudden darkness in his eyes was startling. I tried to make-up. "I mean, I don't think my mother knows me very well. You've met LoBeth."

"Yes, and Maury told me about her," he shrugged. "I don't understand mothers, Abby," we were almost at the end of the food. Fog echoed his voice.

"No one does, Brad, no one." I followed him out for hamburgers off the grill. Crystal was with her mother today. Maybe that was a reason he was off. We found Renan sitting at the table talking to Tia Manuela about sewing. Tia Manuela's red hair was dull and broken in the sun that tried to brighten it. But her true spirit was counterbalanced with the red and green threads woven through her tight dress and dancing along her large bosom. Sitting with this family I knew puberty cheated me. They had to think I was a medical example of girl imitating woman. I looked around for Maury.

"Tia Manuela and I are going to work on Carrie's wedding dress Tuesday night. Would you like to come, Abby?" Renan's question broke my surveying concentration. Sewing was not my favorite thing to do, but I did want to see what Maury's female family was like and I might learn patience if not skill.

"As long as all I have to do is sew pearls in a tight space in random order." They laughed and agreed. I saw Maury was on his way over with a plate of food.

"Does that mean we won't meet after Crystal?" Brad's voice bordered accusatory.

"You said you were working late before going to Crystal's." The terms of Brad's custody with Crystal were two weekends a month from Friday 5:00 p.m. to Sunday, 8:00 p.m. and one weeknight every week there was a visit to read a bedtime story and kiss her goodnight. Brad didn't answer, so there must have been an understood misunderstanding.

"I see you found the food," Maury teased as he put his plate on the table. I had also found him. I was back on birth control.

LoBeth was impressed I was going to spend an evening sewing as long as it did not become a feminine interest. Her parting words as I walked out the door were, "Keep it a practical skill for survival and then keep it to yourself."

Learning to sew was in the same category as learning to type. "Never learn to type, Abby, they'll make you do it." This was feminist logic in pre-computer days that was her odd mother blessing to keep me from dreary office jobs. She observed not one male boss ever typed so she once again was maneuvering me to higher education. Since I asserted my right to independent thinking by avoiding college altogether, I was left to retail.

The invitation to sew with Maury's family was offered after I told Renan about my embroidery experience. Eight is the age of religious consent for the LDS and as soon as I turned that age I was invited by three classmates to attend weekly children's meetings called Primary. LoBeth was reluctant to let me go to the after school event but I begged and then threatened to go anyway since she was at work and wouldn't be able to stop it. My classmates were very pleased and polite as they introduced me to the girl's primary class and I was welcomed. The first project was embroidering a tea towel in a geometric stretch across the bottom.

LoBeth picked it up from the knob attached to the side of the cabinet by the back door when I was seventeen and refused to apply for college. She screamed and threw it to the floor, "Learn a little brain work, Abby, since you have no skills with your hands."

Cross-stitching Bless this House and Family was the second project. LDS beliefs were discussed during sewing sessions which was fine because I didn't need to be talkative and friendly the whole time. But when I realized I was expected to memorize and recite the Articles of Faith I stopped going. One of them had to do with not smoking or drinking hot drinks such as coffee and it seemed God was asking for a choice between him and LoBeth. Maybe if I'd been asked when I was a teenager I would have made another choice but learning embroidery forewarned me God's church didn't need my skills or like my mother. My three new friends fell away. I felt like the unnecessary toy put back on the shelf or the sister kept from dinner because my room was messy, or the ugly child.

When I arrived at Tia Manuela's small brick house I knew Maury was sitting on his bunkbed studying, Brad was being a father, Pedro was working a dinner shift, Juan was watching tv with a soda can in one hand and a bowl of unshelled peanuts by the other. Oil Boy was by his side. Tia Manuela's husband had passed away and Carrie's groom, Marcus, was working on his car in his parents' driveway. All men were accounted for. The thought stopped me from ringing the doorbell. It was the first time in my life men could be accounted for. In a blinding flash I understood Kelly's confidence, Gen's brattiness, LoBeth's assumption of daughterly privileges, and all the other girls I went to school with who pitied me or thought me not good enough. They had society's cachet of men. The seductive warm glow of knowing where the male pieces of life were placed shocked me. I didn't deserve this. I didn't know what to do with it. I didn't want it to mean that much to me. But I wanted it.

The door opened without ringing. "I thought I heard you, Abby. Come in." Renan opened the screen. "We saved the largest pearls and easiest sewing for you. The bathroom is through the hall." All seamstresses washed hands before touching taffeta. On my way I passed a round table filled like a gift store with photos, trinkets, a small tray with jewelry, candles and ribbons of red, yellow, blue and green weaving through everything. A polished silver frame with an old black and white photo of two babies in white long dresses seemed to be the center from which everything began. To the side of it was a larger color photo in another silver frame of a man leaning on a car with his arms folded. He was relaxed and smiling. Above was a cheap print of a bleeding Jesus, his eyes forgiving me of sins my guilt only suggested.

On my way back through the short hall I heard Carrie. Her voice was a sullen whisper gaining volume. "Gringo hands on a bride's dress are bad luck."

"That's a lie from fear, Carrie," Renan answered, her voice almost hidden by Tia Manuela's noisy rise and re-settling of scissors, taffeta and pins hiding words.

I wasn't sure what to do. I stood hidden for a few seconds before walking carefully into an awkward silence.

"Hola, Abby, come sit by me. I want to hear how handsome my son is." Chepita broke the silence and patted the chair beside her. The first time she asked me how handsome Maury was the vacant afraid look on my face made everyone laugh. "Maybe she thinks you're a toad," Oil Boy said.

"Oh, no," I rushed in to answer, not realizing I didn't need to say anything. The truth was I was afraid they would see my prudish pioneer desire for their gangly loose-limbed son and brother. They did with a simple oh, no.

I settled by Chepita and sat without moving. "I think he's so handsome that if I had to choose between him and a frosted brownie, I would need time to think." Soft giggles let me know I had caught on. Chepita picked up a fake pearl and handed it to me.

"We saved the largest for you." Maybe I hadn't heard anything. Chepita, Tia Manuela, Carrie, Renan and Yasmina, who I learned was a friend of Chepita's from church, were around the living room on chairs and the couch.

Carrie had modified and elaborated her dream dress from a Butterick pattern used for three brides. Tia Manuela and Renan were the engineers and all of us were dream makers. The conversation was a soothing bath of female privacy. Sounds trilled like birds in morning song. Daily life was accepted and reviewed in words I had never experienced.

"Juan is home with his peanuts," Chepita's voice was resigned, yet not bitter.

"Oh, Mamá, what's a little mess of peanut shells? I'll clean it up," Renan knew Juan was home being messy in Chepita's perfect living room.

"Mas vale vivo con cacahuates que muerto con rosas," said Tia Manuela.

"I wish papa was going to be at my wedding," whispered the bride.

"Well, I'm sure he will be watching over you," offered his widow. "I know he watches over me when I open his drawer of jockeys and socks. I want to throw them away, but he yells at me." Everyone laughed but me.

"He doesn't want the drawer cleared for another man," Renan said.

Tia Manuela moved her shoulders flirtatiously, "As though another man would want me at this age. Carrie's age is when men want you."

"So go get one. Waiting in line for a man to give you what you need doesn't even work at the hardware store," Yasmina offered.

"That is a picture of my Cliff, Abby," she waved toward the framed picture of the man leaning on the car.

"Is that Nolan still bothering you, Renan?" Carrie didn't lift her head to ask.

"He's a frog. He watches with big eyes but no threat," she could see my unasked question. "He's my boss, Abby."

"Just remember, mi hija," Chepita stated, "that old saying has some truth. El servicio a Dios es mas grande que el pecado."

This time Renan interpreted for me. "The conquistadors were

supposed to have said it before raping us after they had killed our men. It means the service to God is greater than the sin."

"Oh."

"And since we are a sin, a man like Nolan looks at us imagining something he never gets with his wife. But he's still a frog."

I sat sewing pearls and small white flowers for three evenings but the wedding dress took more sessions than that. My status was guest, not required family. In the last three weeks before the ceremony Renan and Manuela set up their sewing machines in Manuela's living room to fit four pink bridesmaid's dresses with emerald green trim on the bodice and hem. The wildly different bodies the pattern was adjusted to fit were a friend, a niece and two cousins. Luckily, I was not involved in any more than attending a shower, being present with Maury at the wedding and I offered to help at the reception.

Normally Tia Manuela, Carrie and Marcus' family attended Our Lady of Guadalupe Church on Third North, but they requested the stately Cathedral of the Madelaine on South Temple for the wedding. It was the first Catholic ceremony I had ever seen and I was impressed to reverent silence. The towering church reaching to God, the prism of light filtering through Bible stories in the stained glass windows, the touching human smallness of the bride and groom before the priest in religious vestments with braid, the quiet listening of over a hundred people. All of it was soul stirring. I thought of LoBeth over twenty years ago sitting under God's direct scrutiny. She must have felt shamed and alone to have me growing deep within while sitting in a church where rules are clear and female sexuality is monitored.

I offered to help serve food at the party afterward which was held in a rented building at the State Fairgrounds used for home arts. Pedro was in charge, and he soon had the assembled know-nothings like me arranged and working efficiently within amateur ability. Renan was also helping since Brad was spending the weekend fishing and camping with his dad. Maury claimed to be helping with gift storage and assuring garbage did not overflow, but whenever he walked by to wave hello, he was enjoying himself watching girls with Oil Boy and his male cousins Frankie, Armando and Jeremy while Blooper and Isaac circled eights around them.

At the end of the evening Pedro and I were boxing leftover food and

Renan was on the other side of the kitchen stacking dishes. Jerry walked to her, drew her to him and closed his arms around her. I stared for a second, but shook myself and returned to putting shredded lettuce in a plastic bag. Renan's head shook no against Jerry but she did not move away for several seconds. As Jerry walked out of the room I saw Pedro watching me. He leaned down and whispered, "Love has many faces, Abby."

When Maury drove me home at midnight I smelled of corn and shredded beef flavored with bay leaf. He was humming. "Maury, why are you LDS and not Catholic?"

"Oh, it's a long story," he stopped humming.

"The rest of your family is Catholic isn't it?"

"The cousins, aunts and uncles, yes. Not all practicing, but they claim it."

"But your family, Juan's family, is LDS?" I wanted to be sure.

"Mostly Mom. The rest of us yes. Dad, no. Renan and Mom are the only ones who go to church."

"When did that happen?" I couldn't imagine Chepita doing anything without Juan, let alone take a different staircase to God.

"Oh, years ago, Abby. I'll tell you about it sometime," he smelled my corn hair. "You seem tired tonight."

He was right but I didn't like him telling me. Still, I opened the door of his car and went in LoBeth's house.

The next morning sun warmed the kitchen, brightening the yellow walls and painted cupboards. LoBeth and I sat apart in the built-in breakfast nook so popular before WWII. She was drinking coffee and the only noise was me slurping cereal.

"How did it go last night?"

"The wedding was beautiful. I've never seen a Catholic ceremony."

Her eyes unfocused, "Yes, you know my story of being in St. Patrick's. It was near overwhelming with all the grandeur when all you've ever seen is pioneer austerity." Smoke from her cigarette twirled through sunlight beside her face. "When you're not accustomed to it a good church ceremony can reduce a person to jello. As you know, that was the week I first knew you were on the way."

I looked at her, not expecting anymore. She had always been quiet about her time in New York and my untimely appearance. "I felt so comforted by the silence of three hundred people listening to the chanting of a man in the greatness of that church. It was in Latin and it seemed a private conversation with God. We were all so small, so insignificant. Even the bride and groom. I knew it was time to be a mother, to be the best mother I knew how." Ruby Reverie didn't appear often, so I stopped slurping cereal to quietly acknowledge her confession that God and I had a place in her life. Enough of that, she must have thought, because she straightened quickly and her eyes focused on me, "So, what I really want to know is how serious is this with Maury? Helping at a family wedding is big."

"I don't know. We like each other, but it's just floating along."

"Marrying a Mexican would be a weight on your life, Abby. You need to think about that." These words were surprising from LoBeth. Die-hard hippies who still wore long straight hair were duty bound to preach people were equal and there should not be discrimination in society.

"You've always said everyone is equal."

"They are in God's eyes, but that doesn't make it equal or easy in everyday life. And marriage usually brings children so you need to think of that."

"Children?" why I sounded so dumb I don't know.

"Yes, children," Golden Bitch mimicked me and bobbed her head back and forth. "I don't want my grandchildren to live with unnecessary disadvantages," she looked straight at me, "like I made you live with."

Maury was not an unnecessary disadvantage. I bristled ever so slightly, but we ended the conversation as pleasantly as possible. It was time to move on and once more I pleaded Kelly to share an apartment, but graduation was three months off and she didn't want to jeopardize her situation.

I hated myself for starting to notice. I hadn't noticed before. Only two members of Maury's family were over 5'10". Pedro hit it and a cousin, Jeremy, who claimed a little Irish blood on his mother's side. Skin displayed this continent's history and hair color was midnight black, bark brown, tawny golden, rampant red, grandma white, beach blonde and my favorite was Maury's Deep Forest Thunderstorm. I wasn't a geneticist, but I could see it was a real crap shoot to tell how children would filter out. Not everyone told me how they made a living, but what I did know had a score of five unskilled to three skilled (members of trades and unions) to one cushy office job (bank employee of some kind who wore a tie), not counting Renan's office job with superior benefits. Maury and two cousins were in schools beyond high school. If I only counted

Maury's and Tia Manuela's family, five out of nine were born in the U.S. and they were the youngest. If I counted the extended cousins, uncles and aunts, which may have brought the number to fifty, the proportion would have been the same. Five were Latter Day Saints and everyone else was Catholic.

Good science required the same assessment of my family. They hadn't been seen in over five years, but I analyzed what I could from gossip and memory. Adult height ranged from my 5'4" to Glen's 6'2". Hair color was dull blonde to LoBeth's chestnut with silver strands. No red and no black. Skin color was white, beige and cream. Education ranged from high school drop-out who was being pressured into night school (Lee's daughter), to Glen's CPA degree. The average was high school, and maybe a little beyond to look like we tried. My three month, one evening a week, customer service class sponsored by Wanlass that was about selling more needed to count for something. Everyone was born in the U.S. and three had visited Mexico. Glen's family went to his wife's Lutheran church. Marjorie's family was all baptized LDS and so was Owen. LoBeth's and Lee's family had remained, as they say on forms, without affiliation, but Lee's rebellious teenager was threatening to be a vegan and picket expensive steakhouses in Scottsdale. That sounded righteously religious to me.

The families were a draw with Maury's winning the family together-ness title with fifty living in Utah, a few scattered in California, Arizona and Mexico and they all spoke to each other vs. our ten who lived in Utah, seven in Minnesota, five in Arizona and we seldom spoke with any of them. Mine won the snobbery title with white self-satisfaction, pioneer heritage and a self-proclaimed need to have a chip on my shoulder to mentally survive Utah society. The Arias family won the title of actually being pioneers with gratitude that they were able to live comfortably in this great country.

LoBeth's question about where it was all going forced me to think. I was twenty-two now, aimless except for showing up at Wanlass on time, still living with my mother, and dating a guy who seemed interested but not breaking down the door to be with me. It wasn't a dream set-up. Maury didn't pretend I was more important than school. Between Monday and Thursday when he had classes, studied and worked the delivery job, we saw each other once. He would call with, "How about tonight?" and I agreed to a bacon and tomato sandwich that I paid for at a cheap restaurant and the long interrupted ride home that was always very pleasant. Weekends we spent more time together.

I don't think Jerry meant to break my flow with Maury and our weekends but he did. We were at a party at his apartment on Friday when he said, "Come on, Maury, your absence has been a presence. Be with the men tomorrow." He was asked, so he went. My gravitational pull of Maury's affection lost to duty and outside interest whenever the two met. He wasn't trying to be Prince Charming. It's just that his natural self filled my requirements. The short conscious list was: kindness, reliability, affection, like me well enough, and assumed future job security. When Maury went with Jerry I stayed home and watched tv alone while LoBeth was out with Open Heart Anguishers.

Not long after LoBeth went camping with a few of her friends and I invited Maury, Renan, Brad, Travis and Mistie to the house on Saturday. Surprisingly, it was more comfortable than Chepita's superbly kept room. LoBeth and I had lower standards and the furniture was worn, so it was fine for a pizza box and beer cans.

When it was my turn to go to the kitchen for beer my head was deep in the fridge when Brad walked in the room. "I've got to ask you something, Abby."

"Yes?" I shifted, and quickly handed him a beer, aware he was looking at the wrong end of me.

He popped the tab and opened the door under the sink to throw it away. Good self-cleaning man training, I thought, and was as quickly angered I was using LoBeth's standards. Brad's overhanging forehead shadowed his eyes and tried to keep a pleading look from reaching me.

"I want Renan to marry me. Do you think she will?" Why he imagined I would know the inner curls of a beauty's heart I don't know.

"Well," I gained slowly, "I don't know what Renan thinks about marriage, but she's crazy about you. She wouldn't be with you if she wasn't."

He smiled, indicating my answer was acceptable. "Do you think she'll say yes?" The hope in his eyes was as clear, still and innocent as the air in the Salt Lake Valley on an April morning after a rattling, shaking midnight windstorm. "I hope so, Sir Brad. The two of you are beautiful together." At that moment, I hoped it more for Brad than Renan.

"Travis thinks it's a slam dunk," he sounded like he was saying supporting ad copy for a sale.

It baffled me why Brad had started asking me questions like this. Over the last month he had cornered me several times and I wondered if he was asking my opinion because I was handy or could be counted on to give the answer he wanted. Last week Maury had gone to get us drinks at the Sunday family dinner and Renan was still inside getting her plate. He zoomed over to my side and without preamble whispered, "Abby, my sister, Sandy, thinks Renan looks too Mexican. What do you think?"

"Too Mexican? She is Mexican." I thought. The chicken leg in my hand stayed held high. "What do you think?"

"I need her." I'd never heard men needed women and admitted it in strained voices that sounded ill from the effort.

"Why do you think your sister thinks she's too Mexican?" We were whispering under rounded shoulders among fifty Mexicans.

"Renan's too darkly beautiful. Maybe sexy. Different than Sandy's used to."

"Maybe Sandy doesn't know her." Knowing Renan would underscore beautiful and sexy, but the words seemed to soothe him. I had never met Sandy but I wondered if she could ever feel like I did with Maury as light new fallen snow resting on rich brown earth. It had been since Never that a handsome guy like Brad asked my opinion on anything except which glasses warranty to buy, so I was a little lifted he talked to me beyond hello and good-bye. He changed the subject as we stood in LoBeth's kitchen. "This is a nice little house, Abby. It's hard for a mother to bring up children alone."

Brad surprised me with words that sounded like he was a fish who knew about air. A short description of his life was he was brought up Mormon with a sister, stay at home mom, and white shirt working dad in a four bedroom, two and a half bath house with a formal dining room on a little cul de sac in the high tax district of the city. My understanding was that problems didn't exist in his neighborhood. It seemed the only banana peel he'd ever stepped on was his ex-wife, Karla.

"Hey Travis," Brad said when we walked back with six beers, "Abby said you have to clean the kitchen to earn your keep."

"Abby, baby, I didn't even earn Mistie. Why would I care about a kitchen?"

"Just earn your paycheck, baby," Mistie giggled, "Mistie needs new shoes."

When Brad was around Travis his softness shaped into corners. He had an edge, losing the voice he used with me.

Maury began flipping through LoBeth's music collection. "I'll play my song for you, Abby." Soon Ernest Tubb and the Texas Troubadors were singing, *I know my baby loves me in her own peculiar way.* At least I had some place in his heart. Sir Brad played Juke Box Hero by Foreigner and gave us a karaoke version straight from the heart. As I watched aching beery Saturday night emotion sing *That one guitar felt good in his hands,* through middle class LDS lips, I wondered if I really understood why either he or I were with these two clearly grounded good people of another culture. Perhaps Renan and Maury should run like hell.

Gotta keep on rockin, Brad mimicked, as he later led Renan, Travis and Mistie out the door, leaving Maury to me.

Chapter Four

4

*Sometimes I wish white people
would stay away from us.*

- Carolina (Carrie) Rodriguez Garcia

Brad and Renan scheduled their wedding for the last Saturday in March 1987. This time I helped six evenings with the sewing of the wedding dress. My job was attaching hand-swirled pink roses in two alternating rows along the bottom and then beading a pre-marked lazy path between them which felt like a mile and a half. Tia Manuela carefully marked where each rose was to be placed and tenderly noted with a sweet smile that it was always lovely when the back of sewing looked as neat and beautiful as the front. On the third evening when it was time to leave Renan suggested she and I go for a beer. I replied sure and we ended up at a pool and beer place on North Temple on the way to the airport. It wasn't far from Tia Manuela's or Renan's and Maury's. Before we sat down I realized the difference of walking in a bar with Renan. Men looked. Eyes sometimes followed Gen and Kelly with curious assessment but these were smokier, sweatier.

"There's a lot to do for a wedding," Renan looked a little tired, in a sleepy Aztec princess way.

"I bet," I swallowed beer.

"Thanks for helping with the dress. You really don't need to."

"I know. But I enjoy it and I like being around your family."

She nodded, aware of that. "How are you and Maury doing?"

"Fine. Fine." If I really had anything to say, it would have been to Kelly, not the target's sister. "How did you and Brad meet?"

A smile dripping desire crossed her face. I felt warm just watching her think about the man she loved. "I was with a man named Everado at a beer party up the canyon. Brad walked up beside me while I was listening to Everado's friends brag about how much they could drink. The first thing I noticed was a wave of heat on my shoulder from behind. I turned and he was looking down at me like I was a potato bug he wasn't sure whether to flip or gently open. He nodded, not quite looking in my eyes. 'Hi, I'm Renan,' I offered, nice and neutral since I was with Everado. 'Brad, Brad Evans,' he answered."

Everado saw them talking and walked over to show off. She said his chest puffed out like a fighting cock. 'I've seen you at Jerry's. Renan's with me.' Brad's eyes recognized Jerry. Connection was made and though he avoided Renan the rest of that night, she saw him watching and wasn't surprised when he called three days later.

"What do your parents think of Brad?" May as well get the whole story.

"He's what Mom wanted me to find. Her only disappointment is Crystal."

"Crystal?"

"Just because that means he's slightly used and Crystal needs to be cared for. Otherwise, here's the list," and she put her beer down to start holding fingers up for a count. "From a good family, has a good job, is reliable, good-looking enough to be proud of and make beautiful children, but not so good-looking that women chase him."

"That's close to LoBeth's list. Plus, will do favors for mother-in-law."

"Man in blue plaid sends his regards," two beers were placed in front of us. Renan and I nodded at a guy sitting at the bar.

"Walking into a bar with you is a lot different than walking in with my friend Kelly."

"Abby, that's because you have a look I will never have. Maury's lucky. You look like you love only one man."

"You love only Brad."

"I love Brad and he's the one I want, but I don't love only Brad." People talking at another table filled the background while I thought of

Jerry. Renan's voice became irritated, "Does your Mom also have not Mexican on the list? Because that's what is preferred by mine."

"Really? Your Mom said that? Why?" I avoided LoBeth's opinion.

"She never really said, don't marry a Mexican, it just came to be understood a better life could be gotten without one."

I looked down, unsure what to say. "She just wanted me to have an easier, more secure life than she did."

"But she's got a good husband and three good sons." Maybe I shouldn't have said anything, but it was my impulse to defend men who were simply and apparently pleased to be present. I wasn't including Mr. Blue Plaid who was making me uneasy when he looked at Renan.

Renan shrugged, took a drink, and looked at me. "She does now, but when we were younger we lived in Pine Creek. Dad worked at a sugar beet factory. It wasn't much, but we were okay," she named a town with less than a thousand people in northern Utah. "He went to Mexico to pick up Abuelita Felipa when his father died and stayed for months. Rafael and Bernice and Leon and Marta and Virgil followed not long after. He met Aunt Teresa here, but what I was saying is with him gone it turned all of us into fruit pickers. Mostly apples and cherries. We tried never to do sugar beets but we did a few times. It was hard. Mamá spoke English well enough by then, but we didn't know many people. The other fruit pickers were there just for the season. We were the only Mexicans who lived there all year." We paused looking at each other, "It's been a long time now." Blankness of purposeful evasion fell across her.

"He brought Grandma Felipa back then?"

"Yes. And Tia Manuela and Carrie. We didn't expect them, but Tia Manuela begged to come. Her husband beat her and Carrie's older brother, Hector Jesus, had died of a fever." Empathy for Tia Manuela was what I imagined caused Renan's sudden frailness. She was melting caramel.

"The husband who died beat her?"

"No," she sat up, latching on a new subject, "she left her first husband in Mexico with her baby's bones and came here. She met Cliff Rodriguez a year later. He was born here in New Mexico. He didn't have any children of his own and he adored Carrie. He adopted her and tutored her until she became a citizen but Tia Manuela has never given up Mexico. Let's go." She started sliding out the booth.

Seeing there wasn't more time to meet Renan, Mr. Blue Plaid came over.

"Thanks for the beer," Renan said straight as looking at a traffic light.
"Got time for another?" He stared at Renan.

"No, I don't, but I'll remember your kindness," and she led me out.

In the car, I told her the truth, "That sort of beer buying doesn't happen to me."

Looking ahead she shrugged her shoulder, "He's like a million other white guys. He wants to know if I'm Natalie Wood or Rita Moreno from West Side Story. Virgin or whore. Either way they want to use it."

"Does your mother know that?"

"She thinks there's men's lives and women's lives. Mamá doesn't know ways here."

On the last Saturday night before the wedding, Maury, Renan and Brad waited for me in the mall center court where they could watch children play on a plastic playground. When I got off work we were going to see Superman IV. They were sitting on a bench facing me with Renan in the middle, but all three were watching the children scoot about up and down slides and walkways. Sculpted they would have been interesting bookends. Two could be teak or maple; one quartz or marble. This was the first time I was far enough away to see them as an observer in public. I saw why people occasionally lifted a head for a second look or nudged a partner before we passed. In 1987, we were on a cusp of no longer looking exotic with two brown people and two white people casually together, their futures entwined as emotionally as electrical wires.

"Thanks for waiting for me."

"God, Abby, did you expect we'd go sit in the movie and let you hunt us out?" Maury's greeting. What I saw as an imposition of other's time for my convenience which needed appreciation he saw as the natural law of people who were together.

"Maury, it was just a thanks," Renan understood female politeness. Brad laughed understanding what I'd meant. A wait was worth a thanks.

Maury took my hand and kissed my cheek, "Thank me for the big stuff. Don't waste it on this."

When we walked to the cars after the movie Maury and Renan walked ahead and Brad fell back to talk to me. "I got a visit this after-noon," he leaned toward me and his voice was softer.

"Yes?"

"Juan, Pedro, Maury, Oil Boy and Jerry were waiting for me after work. The boys."

I looked at him. "Why?"

"Juan did most of the talking. Pedro, a little. He said Renan was his daughter and he expected she would be taken care of in marriage. That meant food, a house, all children would have my name."

"Wow," I'd never heard of such a thing.

"That's what I thought. The last thing Juan said was, don't ever hurt her."

I paused, thinking before saying more, "Is she a princess or a traded horse?"

His laugh was good enough that Maury and Renan glanced back. "She's going to be my queen. I can live with that. Forever." We stopped at Brad's car to plan where to meet for pizza and then Maury and I walked to my car which he drove.

Brad and Renan settled on marrying at Cisneros Ward which had a Mexican flare of surrounding high adobe wall. It may as well have been a log cabin in Manhattan for as well as it blended in the Salt Lake City architectural landscape. Every other LDS building in the city was stone or brick. I reasoned the Mexican Cisneros Ward was either a gesture of comfort for new converts or an unconscious veneer of herding all Mexicans to a controllable area.

My duty was the guestbook and I was surrounded with nieces Danielle, Morrison, Maria Clara and Tiffany who hopped about in girl frenetics, grasping at gifts.

"Well, I'm here." I thanked LoBeth for her court's favor as she looped the arm of a current amour, Johann. I saw the tight waves on his forehead as a sign of prissiness, but LoBeth thought it Continental. Her ethnic dress with butterflies fell from her body, but her fuller than my chest was advertised.

"Give my regards to Broadway," I said as they walked away. She turned, giving me a queenly nod to commoners before swaying away and saying goodbye with loosely held hair ribbons of bright yellow bouncing behind.

The last to come were Maury's old neighborhood friends. The lead man nodded my way and I held the pen toward him. Each signed in turn down five lines: Chucky Martin, Little Benny, Dust Valadez, David and Veronica Ocampo, Hermie and Irene Gonzalez.

I slipped in after them to sit on a folding chair by LoBeth and Johann. Maury was busy settling Abuelita Felipa. Bishop Dennis Erickson stood in front of a spray of pink roses at the front of the room waiting to begin the ceremony. Until best man Travis and then Brad stood before him beaming light, it was impossible to tell if the pink roses were for a wedding or a funeral. The dark business suit he wore would work for both. He was a slim man in his fifties with blonde thinning hair. Peace or perhaps calmness surrounded him. Bishop Dennis Erickson was a man who knew where he was standing and why.

I grew up in the neighborhoods of LDS boys and men. They seemed a rock garden of kindness, self-righteousness, deliberate patience and a desperate need to financially succeed. As a child I feared them. They were male strength, voices and size I didn't understand. As I grew beyond eighteen and dated Shane Cooper, Thurman Wade and Craig Spencer, they had the feel and look of teacher blackboards that, like me, once knew secrets, important words and phrases written on their souls, but all was erased, cleansed away, and now they were as needy as me. My Sir Brad kept his place in front of Bishop Erickson and stood motionless for the civil ceremony.

The beautiful Renan and Sir Brad had an LDS civil ceremony that was by custom, abundantly austere. I called it a wedding and Maury never corrected me, but by LDS standards it was a disappointment it was not a proper wedding held in the Salt Lake Temple. It was understood but left unstated they were not religiously approved for a temple marriage. As an outsider uncomfortable with asking for details I'd been told through the years in local gossip it was usually because the bride and groom were not virgins.

When I was seventeen LoBeth tried to explain civil ceremony. "It is a Mormon step above illegal fucking, but a step below blessed by church fathers because it isn't in the Temple."

"Jeesh," I'd said, keeping decorum, "how can you be so tough on them when their very pioneer blood is yours?"

"That's why I'm so tough on them. I know what underbellies hurt me the most."

"All right. I wasn't born to a married mom. You never even asked to be blessed by them."

"This hasn't got to do with me. Or you." She mashed her cigarette in an ashtray. "Haven't you ever wondered why we're not LDS?"

In all naïve truthfulness, I hadn't. Whatever happened was a long time ago and at seventeen I thought the only embarrassing family secret was my birth. Besides, things not thought about maybe weren't important. "No."

"Your Grandma Jessie's grandmother, Anna, was a young widow with a son in Denmark. She worked on her parents' farm but two older brothers would inherit everything. There weren't any marriage prospects so she was attracted to the Mormon missionaries, as much for the gospel as the promise of more men like them in Utah. So she and her son came to Utah. She left Denmark where she was a burden to her brothers and their wives and ended up being the third wife of Brother Clark. She was not happy with the male arrangement but she liked the female companionship and there was no where else to go from this godforsaken desert."

So? my eyes said without words.

"So desire for adventure and stupidity are a heart to brain link with the females in this family and your great great-grandma is the first screw-up we have on record."

"She didn't think she was a screw-up. It worked out."

"Ask me about your Grandpa Harold Bean Baker sometime," she finished before turning up Journey and leaning back on the couch to look out the window through the dark.

"Besides," I finished, "I haven't done anything adventurous or stupid."

"Give yourself time." I forgot to ask why we weren't LDS.

Now, as I waited beside LoBeth at Renan and Brad's wedding, I looked at Brad's family. On the groom's side, people were loosely scattered with their smaller nuclear family. They used about half the provided folding chairs. In the front were Brad's parents I recognized from when they signed in. His father was tall, impeccable, cleaned with razor blades and starch. He looked to be an office man who understood rank. Beside him his wife held a handkerchief to her eye and though her head was bent, her shoulders were as self-disciplined and sure of how seasons change and hearts love as her husband's. Her close-cropped hair was loose and wavy, the sandy soft color of white pepper. They could have been sitting as the parents of the groom in any city in the country and you would know their children and Saturday morning lawn mowing always came first. Brad's childhood family was security, parental direction and first steps on a well-worn path of agreed goodness. Envy for their belief of rightness and pity for the same belief fought in my heart. Sandy sat by her mother. The flowered dress and demure turn of her young lovely head made me as full of disgust at people's presumptions as jealous of their security that God only claimed them.

Bishop Erickson smiled and motioned for quiet when he saw the assembled wedding party in the back. Rustling clothes and scraping heels of two dozen children under age ten was all to be heard.

The neighborhood church had not dressed for the wedding. Its family living room feel was carpet worn and working man plain. The Sunday school meeting room had gun metal folding chairs and worn cream color drapes in back of the roses. Renan and Brad stood in bridal splendor, flanked on each side with pink dressed and black tuxedoed attendants. LoBeth leaned and whispered, "Beauty outlives," as she had many times in my childhood.

Her example was dead bodies on a battlefield. "Where is the beauty?" she asked. "There is none," I answered, "It's all ugly." Golden Bitch gave me her I am smarter than you, look and slid into Ruby Reverie, "Beauty is in the moon ending the soldier's last painful day, in the soft cushion of grasses under his bloody deserted body cradled by earth." Another time she talked of sick old people dying in a rest home smelling of urine and bleach. After my shudder she said, "Beauty is in the wisp of dry, white hair protecting the grandmother's old skull that could recite a lifetime if you would only ask. Beauty is in the kindness she left in other's lives. Beauty is in death's gentle steady tapping on old knuckles calling us home. It is relentless, steady and loving for all of us."

Connection with death in war and slowly decaying old age with the marriage of Brad and Renan was a tenuous poetic imagination of beauty wasted in human cruelties. As I watched the two people standing as close to God as their church allowed, I thought they were the deserted beauties who had already forgiven.

"When you are ready, Bradley Conrad Evans and Renan Marolita Arias," Dennis Erickson entoned, "you will be blessed by the fathers before you," or something like that. I stopped taking notes after high school. Bishop Erickson wished them well, reminded them of the need to live within church doctrine, practice forgiveness, have joy with each other, and strive to be worthy and seal their love for time and all eternity in the Church's monument to God, the Temple. It could have been cross-stitched and hung in a kitchen until the last thought.

"I have observed," and Bishop Erickson stood straighter before the wreath of pink roses Brad's family had sent, "men love women beyond what they should. Women love men for what men give. You must meet in the middle before God."

Go to hell and die, is what LoBeth's eyes flared when she looked at me. Johann squirmed. It was later, during the reception, I heard what others thought.

"Ella entra al matrimonio. My hija, al fin, es bendecida," said Chepita time and again. She goes into marriage. My daughter is at last blessed.

One less worry, was in the shrug of Pedro's shoulders.

"Mi hija al fin sera cuidada," Juan repeated. She was taken care of and he sounded full of regard and admiration for woman.

Dear Renan, sister of my soul, please rest in happiness, Maury felt not hearing the words in the beat of his heart. I saw it in his eyes and the thrust of his chin.

Oil Boy wanted to follow her. She was sweet reassurances and dearness and he was afraid she was leaving him for a man he didn't trust with her care.

My prejudiced thought was it was re-assuring to the hurts I had received as a child that the LDS Church inserted a commercial in a marriage ceremony belittling the bride's and groom's morality that they hadn't married in the Temple. The bride received a wounding jab on the biggest night of her life that she was a conniving female, incapable of loving her man while she was overly adored by the groom. Cruel pleasure to take at Renan's and Brad's expense.

Everyone moved to the church gymnasium for the reception. The first through the line were the five late friends and their wives. "I didn't know they were friends of Renan, Maury," I said.

He was puzzled. "I said I knew them from early years. They're mi familia."

"Oh." As I watched them at a table two of the men turned away and drank from a flask.

"But Oil Boy's been seeing them lately." When I walked by them later the women glared and the men all nodded recognition toward me and watched me walk.

For the first hour the reception line stood under the basketball net flanked by foul lines. The tired wooden floor also held an iron coat rack and gun grey metal folding chairs around white tableclothed tables. There was a box of basketballs in the corner.

Brad was euphoric. One arm wrapped Renan at every possible moment and the other arm held Crystal whenever she wanted. "Abby, come here, I want you to meet my mother." Several people were standing together while Brad's father was in a male group with Juan and Maury.

"Mother, this is Abby Baker. She's Maury's girlfriend."

She looked at me for value beyond knowing Maury. "Oh, you're the one who works in the optical store."

"Yes, nice to meet you."

"She helped sew my dress," Renan tried to make me important.

"I'm sure that was a lot of work." Her voice was measured.

"It was, but I enjoyed it. Do you sew?" I was grasping.

"No, I don't." She looked at no one. "I gave that up when Marlon became department head. There were other things to do."

"Isn't Renan's dress beautiful?" Brad said it like he was sweeping up crumbs and hurt feelings with a dustpan, a sensation I had around LoBeth at times. "She couldn't have bought anything so beautiful." She turned to leave.

"Nice to meet you..." I said.

"Bonnie. Bonnie Evans, Brad forgot to mention it."

"Bonnie."

"Renan, I need to leave now," a male voice accustomed to giving direction interrupted. I turned with Renan to look. Brad still held Crystal and was pulled away by Sandy and Bonnie.

"Thank you, Mr. Nolan, for coming." I recognized the name as Renan's boss.

His eyes were glassy looking at Renan. The woman next to him was stiff but virtuously, precisely pretty, a western beauty pageant winner. Certainly prettier than me.

"See you after the honeymoon next week. This is my wife Rosemary."

"Yes, nice to meet you," Renan extended her arm and then the new Renan Evans was interrupted another way.

I sat with LoBeth and Johann. "Who is that man talking with Renan?" LoBeth asked.

"Jerry. A friend of the family."

"He certainly likes the bride doesn't he, Johann?"

"Brides are meant to be liked," Johann diplomatically observed.

"They've been friends since early teens." With Brad's back to them, Jerry pulled Renan in his arms and squeezed her like bread dough that needed hard and gentle at the same time. Then he turned away to leave Renan's wedding.

"Yes, he likes the bride very much," LoBeth finished with a drink of red punch held to her lips. Mr. Nolan's eyes also followed Renan and Jerry as he led Rosemary out.

It seemed everyone watched Renan and Jerry except Brad because not ten minutes later Travis stopped me as I walked toward Maury. Mistie and the kids were seated at a table eating cake.

"Renan's a beautiful bride."

"Yes."

"She has a lot of friends."

I hadn't noticed any except family and a few women from work and church so I didn't answer.

"Jerry is a friend," Travis' statement was not a question.

"Jerry's a family friend to everyone. He and Maury are like brothers."

Calculators seemed to be adding, subtracting and multiplying in his head. He forgot he was talking to me, turned and walked to his family.

"Pedro, can I ask a question?" I approached him near evening's end when mariachi music was ending and kitchen duties had slowed enough that he would pay attention to me. Leftover cake was being picked up and heaved in plastic bags. Corn tortilla bits and lettuce shreds were being swept from the floor. Pedro was in the kitchen's doorway to the parking lot smoking a cigarette. Chepita's choices of love music was in the background, slowing conversation and telling people it was time to go home. His dark direct look always put me under a spotlight that understood sexual female intent in his airspace. He looked at me like a yellow light before red. Brother's woman. "I have a question," I sensed gentle laughing at female wiles.

"What do you think is the difference between love accepted by the church and love not of the church?"

His eyes measured me, "Why you ask me of love, La Flaquita?" Little skinny girl he sometimes called me.

I needed to jump back to safe ground. "I, I only want to know if it matters if a person is a church member. If it makes a difference."

I could tell the question filled his brain. Pedro wasn't one to be concerned with inconsequential details or silly and unnecessary philosophy without final and verifiable answers. He was a product person, a producer. He directed prep cooks who made radish flowers and waitresses who flirted for their customers. Behind their obvious actions, he was in charge of grand production, the full plate, the total meal; the sexual encounter, desired end result. He understood women's bodies and customers' meals. What was ordered he produced. Pedro seemed like the person to know the overlapping similarities between nourishing body needs and a love question.

He straightened against the wall, thought through a slow arm lift, cigarette inhale, holding of breath and exhale before looking at me. "I think there is no difference in love. It is the same. It is love. Si, love."

"Pedro, thank you." I took that as a sign his family could accept my lack of religious training, greater lack of desire for it and might believe I was okay for Maury.

After Brad and Renan's wedding our circle of date friends changed. Twice we went with Kelly and a guy she was with, but chemistry between the guys was non-existent the first time and rising to confrontation the second. All Kelly and I could figure was it was upsetting to both of them that the females were the nucleus of planning power which they both tolerated out of a percentage of lust on the first date but on the second they each felt duty bound to skirmish for first male position. Either that or Kelly's guy was bored stiff hearing about going to school for computer programming and Maury thought a man vainly self-absorbed and shallow who lifted weights for shirt protruding abs with the single ambition of being headwaiter. I wondered about that, too, but knew Kelly was in her 'fun' period and still mourning Dave who she'd been with over two years. So Kelly and I held our men apart to prevent a schoolyard scuffle.

We also decided to hold off getting an apartment. She needed to get a student loan down and I wasn't home enough to be too bothered by LoBeth.

Once we double dated with Gen and someone she met at a frat party she'd crashed the week before. He was in Urban Planning and was intrigued when Gen said she was good friends with a Mexican who lived on the wrong side of town who could give him insight into the poor people living over there. Gen didn't realize that while his snobberies were elite his pocketbook was still a student's and she chose a place to eat that was too expensive for us all. Maury and I split the cost of dinner but half could have bought two at Sizzler. He looked out the windshield on the drive from the restaurant. "You've got fancy friends, Abby, and at least right now, I can't keep up with her." He didn't mention the student interrogator he'd exaggerated to about growing up on the Westside.

"What were you talking about, 'the Brothers wouldn't let me be part of the heist'?"

He smiled at a secret joke. "They wouldn't Abby. They didn't call it a heist either but I thought college boy would understand it better."

"Are you serious? What are you talking about?"

"It's true Abby. They knew I wasn't one of them. So they let me go."

"Go?"

"You know them. Hermie, Little Benny and the rest. They're my neighborhood. That night they told me to stay home and I did. They opened an eighteen wheeler along Seventeenth South past Redwood Road after the driver thought he'd put it away for the night. It was full of microwaves and they sold them at discount," again he smiled as though it was a high school prank everyone experienced. "They never got caught. Made a lot of money. That's when I signed up for school. They wouldn't let me in so I had to go somewhere." Sarcasm didn't suit him.

"Was Jerry part of it?"

"He was that night, but two of them got caught doing some dealing and he decided it was time to get out, too. Little Benny's brother, Dominico, is still in jail. They've all been in at one time or another." Maybe he hadn't exaggerated. "Hey, we're lined up to be at a party next Saturday. A girl in my programming class is having it."

"Oh. Okay." I wasn't sure about new friends but he didn't need the old ones.

As I walked in the dark that night to my bedroom LoBeth's voice was a disembodied ghost. "Woman found dead in a parking lot from gunshot wound to the face."

71

"Sorry LoBeth."

"Husband drunk with blood spots on his clothes. Six children motherless."

Wednesday Maury called while he was doing homework in the school library and I was putting dishes in the dishwasher. "I'll pick you up at 8:00 for the party."

"Great. Jeans or dress?"

"Didn't ask them what I should wear. Hey, you ready to buy a poor student dinner ahead of time?"

"Sure. I'm in the mood for a pastrami burger. I'll wear jeans and bring a dress."

On Friday LoBeth greeted Maury. "Maury, it's your responsibility to introduce Abby to the valedictorian. I want her to realize how stupid that person is next to her. Then maybe I'll get her to school. You're with me in this aren't you?"

"Yes, Ms LoBeth, but only if it's a girl and what does valedictorian mean?"

She shoved him on the shoulder, "Don't play stupid with me. Or too greedy to share the spotlight with my Abby." That's as good a Missy Mom as I got.

The party was at an apartment in the south end of the valley where families grew like crabgrass and 'still singles' latched onto apartments hoping vapors of domesticity would gag them into security and fertility. Five people were lolling about the apartment and I was insecure enough to put on glasses called Starlight before going in. The straight top and deep blue frame had a whimsical s curve on the side. They felt omniscient and brave.

"Hi, Maury," a girl with long straight brown hair, loping shoulders and biscuit round cheeks greeted him.

"Hi, Wendy, this is Abby," he motioned toward me. We settled in with Wendy, her girlfriends Sue and Stacy and the boys, one name I never caught and the other was Tom. When we walked in the door everyone stopped talking. I couldn't tell if it was to be polite to new people or we had interrupted something. Conversation syncopated and five people were either bored with each other or suddenly interested in new people because we seemed to change the course of the evening. For the next hour we talked to one stranger and then another. A couple named Laura and Dale came, their pale skin and freckles looking more like brother and sister than an engaged pair. I thought they were sweet dolls, to be kept on shelves where they would not face life. Starlight gave me grace to spread. Talk and drinks were in a dance with chips and dip, beer, ice and water or Coke. When the fluorescent kitchen light becomes cruel to people who have been drinking I've learned it's time to go so I stepped to Maury's side.

"Maury," the male voice was a little into beer, "I hear you're in computers." Tom asked the sort of question.

Maury turned and looked at him, "Yes, second year."

"Repair?"

"No," Maury straightened and I should have taken the hint, "Programming. Wendy and I are in the same class."

"Any bigger sights?" Computers hadn't yet convinced everyone they were a good future.

"Right now just the diploma."

Dale moved into view with Laura behind him. I heard the hum of the refrigerator. "Nothing else, amigo?"

My knuckles closed around my water glass.

"Just life and getting ahead. Like everyone else," Maury's voice was the only one where moments before over half a dozen moved about the air.

"Abby." A declarative use of my name, "you from around here?"

"Tom, let's go sit on the patio. You've had enough," Wendy stepped beside him to take his hand, but he shook her off like water from a dog.

"Yes, I was born here."

"Then you know," his words sank to dungeon level and held in barred isolation until years later when I was ready to hear the judgment on skin not white. Maury took my hand, motioned me to put the glass down, thanked Wendy for inviting us, handed me my purse and led me out the door.

"I'm walking you to the doorstep tonight and giving you a sweet goodnight kiss. Please tell your mother the valedictorian was not at the party or I would have introduced you." When he kissed me goodnight I wanted to hug him and I wasn't sure why which is I'm sure why he didn't take me to the lilac bushes.

When I walked in the door the house was darkly quiet and I moved through shadow to my room when the phone rang. "Hello," I said, afraid it was Wendy following like karma.

"Sunshicloud?" the deep nasal voice was not one I recognized but the name was. LoBeth's hippy days were still re-visited by Open Heart Anguishers who never left those years. LoBeth said friends would sit around smoking pot and making up cute nicknames for each other when the real names their selfish, boring, middle-class parents gave them sucked. The wine drunk pot head version of Sunshine Cloud did hit a mark in LoBeth but I hated it anyway. I screamed letting the evening out, "Sunshicloud, you in?" I went to bed.

LoBeth gave up drugs long ago but she kept the friends and loves to remember the story of how they met. A stoned wacko from San Francisco came through Salt Lake sure he was on his way to the Garden of Eden in Idaho. For a year he lived on the largesse of those who thought potato chips and clam dip were gourmet and preached everyone needs to love everyone while providing personal demonstrations to any interested party. His listeners formed the World Love Light Center to formalize their friendship and sound important. Rent was paid for a garage without heat six blocks from the LDS Temple in the industrial section by the railroad tracks. Open meetings were held to announce belief in love and nicknames were given to show affection. I suggested this was to protect everyone from responsibility so real identities could not be traced, but LoBeth said it was to bond as a family. After the charming wacko was gone for a year without sending new teachings, the group let the garage go and invited people to Saturday parties in an Avenues apartment. The World Love Light Center left a legacy of several dozen friends who became lawyers, pharmacists, housewives, teachers, administrative assistants, auto mechanics, mail carriers and dead drug addicts.

Open Heart Anguishers was my name for them and when they heard it they took it good naturedly, even teasing themselves. Only LoBeth didn't think it was funny so I tortured her saying they were old hippies who realized worshipping John Lennon and hating Yoko could be a religion like loving Christ and hating Mary Magdelene. They had only turned to personal redemption of their own standards to avoid the well laid out historically tested religions of their Catholic, LDS, Baptist and Presbyterian parents. Golden Bitch mumbled and then clearly called me a godless heathen. "You're paving a boutique damnation to your own very special hell, Abby."

Noon the next day I called Maury. "He's in the shower, La Flaquita. I'll tell him to call," answered Pedro. At 5:30 he called and I dragged the overlog phone cord into my room, closed the door and paced.

"What was that all about?"

"What, Abby?"

"Those people. How they questioned you?" I couldn't say their names.

"That's just how some people are."

"No it's not. I've never seen that." He didn't answer for enough time that my words fell into a void.

"Now you know what some college friends are like."

"No," I sat on the bed and explained LoBeth was in mourning over Johann's move to Denver so for comfort she was making grilled cheese sandwiches and a made from scratch chicken noodle soup. "Want to come over and complain about men with LoBeth?" I knew he'd already had a full Sunday dinner, so if he said yes, it wasn't to fill that underweight body.

"Tell LoBeth I'll do the dishes if she'll do my homework. But no man attack. I've had enough."

Our friendly, easy going romance felt as comfortable as a worn tee shirt to wear while strolling through the zoo holding hands or sharing popcorn in a movie. Reliable love, friendship, comfortable sex and peace with each other's presence were ours from the beginning. For me it was a long awaited arrival of someone who liked me. I thought Maury saw me as a safe harbor to be trusted with the sincerity and gentleness he could not hide and left him vulnerable to anyone who saw it.

Gen thought we had drifted into Consolation Gulch. "You're just too comfortable to find better." She was disgusted with how I had a kind, reliable, quiet friend. But I didn't believe the series of pampered angry boy/men she attracted gave her what Maury gave me.

A year later when Maury graduated from Utah Technical College and I paid off my Toyota, we decided to marry. Our words of love were what expert tea brewers suggest. Heat the water until just before the boiling point, then pour over tea and gently steep for full flavor before pouring and straining.

"What do you think of our relationship, Maury?" I asked one night when we were sitting alone in LoBeth's backyard. We had returned from a movie and he'd been reluctant to leave though I didn't think it had anything to do with being attracted to me. I thought he wasn't tired. We'd been sitting on lawn chairs for ten minutes without a word between us while we watched the spring sky turn to summer. My question made him sit up and look directly at me.

"I like it very much. I'm happy with it, Abby."

"Good. So am I." The stars above my head felt like mine and I almost lifted a finger to touch them.

"Abby."

I turned to look at him.

"Abby, let's get married."

LoBeth's method of brewing tea is to boil the hell out of it, twirl the teabag and then squeeze the last bit of strength out before throwing it away. I was plenty happy with before the boiling point.

Maury left the date choice to me. After five minutes I decided on Thursday, August 18, 1988. Eights are a wonderful do-si-do of infinity and circling partners I hoped would bind him to me.

The wedding was the only party I had ever given. I worked to take off the uncivilized edges of life with LoBeth to Maury's family, and make myself acceptable to their Catholic Mormon background, but there was only so much I could mask.

Chepita peeked behind the mask at my wedding shower that was graciously given by Kelly and Gen in Kelly's parents' house. My gentle mother-in-law to be who had family and friends stretching a two thousand mile radius looked with shocked fear from her side of the living room where she huddled between Tia Manuela, Grandma Felipa, Carrie with her new baby, Sofia, Renan, Yasmina, Bernice, Marta, Collette and Willie with collected children. On my side, were LoBeth, Gen, Kelly and two Open Heart Anguishers, Judy and Susan, who had been surrogate aunts.

The next week when I was with Maury so he could change his shirt before we went dancing, she hugged me, "Mi probrecita. You need us. You need a family."

Then there was the thorny issue of who would marry us. I respected Judy, who seriously took up another touchy feely church where she became a legal leader and could marry people. But perhaps because I knew the seeds of the local movement, it was too experimental. The do it as you feel it ways didn't tie Maury tightly enough to me. On the other hand, a justice of the peace was too strictly legal and didn't call to humankind's greater spirit.

"Call the Congregational or Unitarian Church," suggested Kelly. "They'll marry anyone." So I opened the phone book and due to scheduling ended up with a man from the Congregational Church. He let me choose between his costume of official black robes or a suit. LoBeth convinced me to choose the robe so there could be 'some drama at this garden party.'

We didn't have the money for a religiously neutral reception center so it was in our small backyard. The Open Heart Anguishers, rallied by LoBeth, generously came through as cooks and servers. Juan, Pedro, Oil Boy, Brad and Jerry quietly provided all chair and table setup and silly ribbons from the street to the backyard.

A week before the wedding I bought my dress at Penneys for $159. It felt like wearing Niagra Spray Starch but it fit well enough. LoBeth made me try it on and when I walked in the living room she actually got a scrunchy almost cry face. She had me sit on the couch while she got an old photo album. For twenty minutes I patiently sat, trying not to move in a dress I didn't want to wrinkle because I didn't know how to iron it. We were re-looking at photos I had seen before, but she stopped at the old black and white of her parents on their wedding day. Her skinny finger touched it. "It's lonely when two people truly care for one another." Ruby Reverie sniffled, stood, and threw the scrapbook in my lap. "Don't let that stiff as hell bride's dress give you any illusions."

Renan was matron of honor and Kelly my bridesmaid. Except for Kelly's talent with orange blossoms in my hair, they both looked better than me, but I was the one who got Maury so it was okay.

5

Anglos think they settled virgin land. They did not.
They took my motherland, but as in King Solomon's
story, the real mother gave up to save
the life of the child.

- Geraldo (Jerry) Sandoval

The morning of my wedding I looked at the Tamayo print and believed the brown angel brought me Maury. Later I wondered if she was bringing a warning on the paper in her hand. But I know that is wrong. Brown angels never warn anglos. Perhaps the message was for Maury or Renan. A month after we married, the angel opened the paper and held it for me to read. Her smile was soft and loving. I struggled to make out the words. Fear rose as I fell into hieroglyphics and I fought to pull my head out of the symbols holding me by my neck as I gasped air until waking.

The skeleton of my life was now in place. Brad and I had made decisions and brought ourselves in marriage to a circle of people we thought we knew. We thought we knew ourselves.

Our apartment on Fifth East was less than a block from the I-80 freeway, which Maury and I hadn't noticed when we decided on it. Groans of trucks speeding to get out of the city woke us at night and the steady drum roll of commuter traffic was the morning alarm clock. The night of the Grateful Dead concert left our ears deaf to freeway noise and we never heard it again unless we tried. We lived in a 1960s brick fourplex with an outside door and carport. It had the personality of vanilla pudding which was a fitting backdrop to figure out what marriage meant. It was fairly clean and a blank canvas of living room, kitchen with eating nook large enough for a card table, bathroom and two bedrooms.

At Christmas LoBeth went to Guatemala to build a latrine in a village with a few Open Heart Anguishers and a university professor. Before she left I stopped on my way home from work for tea and to hear about her trying week at work. A girl two years younger than me was beaten and stabbed by a boyfriend and a woman in her forties who had filed for divorce, was shot by her husband as she crouched hiding behind a couch. Through a bitter laugh she told of a man who was shot by his very drunk wife when all he had done was walk through the kitchen door.

"Don't tell me you're feeling sympathy for the husband." Maybe because I missed her from everyday life I returned to a childhood habit that I self-righteously refused to do at age thirteen. 'I'm not your slave any longer,' I had said, leaving her to suffer her tired back pain. Now, I offered to rub it as she lay on the floor of her living room.

"Not sympathy. Just despair."

"So the bastard deserved it but it still may not be right?"

"I don't know if he deserved it or not. What I don't understand is how what's supposed to be love can end up that way."

"All you need is love, da, da, da, da, da" I mimicked a Beatles song she played when I was six until I ran to a neighbor's house. Let the left over love children suffocate in their silly pretensions.

"The Beatles didn't have anything to do with this either. Are you looking forward to Christmas?"

"Without you? Not at all."

"You are my baby," Missy Mommy said with eyes closed. "I'll miss you Christmas morning. But we'll both be off to new adventures and we'll tell each other all about it when I come back."

It's been years since that first married Christmas with Maury's family but what I remember feels like lessons in a Mexican soap opera drama. Christmas afternoon Maury's family with Juan's mother, Tia Manuela, Carrie, Marcus and their new baby, Sofia, were at the kitchen table. Two cardtables twisted like a tail into the living room. On my right was Maury and on my left was Renan whose pregnant belly reached to the table. We were eating turkey and all the usual trimmings smelling of Puritans and east coast history, with the addition of tamales and chilies when the doorbell rang.

Oil Boy opened the front door and we saw David Ocampo. Voices welcomed him with holas but he stood grimly. "I came for dinner. Puta waits in the car, Pedro."

Juan silently stood, facing him from the head of the table. "I don't know any putas."

David bowed, flourishing in arm, straightened and said, "Then you haven't met my woman." He looked at Chepita, "Good to see you again, Mamá. I miss your tortillas." He turned to Pedro who was jamming an oversize piece of turkey in a grocery store roll.

"Pedro, Pedro, no!" begged Chepita as she raised herself from the chair. Juan sat down, shook his head and lowered it to not see his wife.

"Eh, Mama, it is just for a time. I'll be back." When the door closed Oil Boy sat down between Marcus and Crystal and asked for potatoes. Brad looked at me from behind Renan but we both looked back at our plates before anyone saw us.

Pedro was gone. Entirely gone for six months. Maury knew where he lived but spoke to him only twice to verify he was alive. No one else asked where he could be found. It was known he held his job at the greasy twenty-four hour restaurant. Chepita and Juan continued receiving his twice monthly envelope of cash by US mail or a personal visit by Little Benny who always had time for food. He did his duty to family and himself. There was nothing else to ask of him. Since he was sixteen he had disappeared from two weeks to almost a year and a half.

After dinner the phone rang and Oil Boy moved for the phone with the grace of a leopard. He was seventeen with complete incoming call control. His hair was a curly bird's nest, inviting touch, his eyes an evasive darting look of teens and his posture was Hollywood cool.

"Hello," he whispered as lemon meringue and pumpkin pie was being put out.

"Yes, meet you at the parking lot," he turned toward the wall, "I'll have it, Hermie, I'll have it."

"See you later, Oil Boy," I whispered as he left an hour later with nothing evident in hand. He looked at me.

"Juan, por favor, su madre needs your help," Chepita whispered. The meal had ended and Abuelita Felipa who was near toothless and deaf, was alone at the end of the table. He shrugged but stood and went to the papier-mâché woman who stared onto the empty plate and struggled with a last sip of water. Maury also rose and stood nearby if needed. More patiently than I would have bet, Juan waited for his mother to finish putting down her napkin before he moved the chair away. As she made her slow way to the couch, I smelled rotting wood and hair oil.

Renan, Chepita, Tia Manuela, Carrie, and I went to the kitchen to do dishes and Sofia rested in her father's arms watching football with the boys and Grandma Felipa. Through dishwashing Tia Manuela and Chepita murmured about Pedro's women. Carrie, Renan and I talked about decorating Christmas trees. As the last pans were wiped Renan stood in the middle of the room. "I've got a special present for Abby, everyone! I want you all to see."

We turned. She was a wrapped present with Christmas ribbons in her hair falling to her shoulders and wearing the oversize dark green velvet dress she had made to hold the lines of shoulder, growing breasts and belly. Then I saw the small gift with gold paper and red curled ribbon. Smiling, she held her arm straight out with the gift. All of us looked at the small wrapped box. "Well, thank you," I slowly took it, feeling self-conscious. "Whatever it is, you didn't need to."

"I know. But it's important."

Inside was a compact mirror. A deep pink rose pattern with swirling leaves and thorns was painted on bright black enamel. It was good quality with a snappy clasp ready for years of daily use. I looked in the mirror. Same face as last time.

"There. That's what you're supposed to do. Look in the mirror and see yourself because from now on, you're surrounded by brown and if you don't look occasionally you'll forget who you are." The other four brown faces around us laughed good-naturedly. I was the only one unsure of a right reaction. "But don't wear any of the store glasses when you look."

"That's right. Especially that Helena you were wearing Halloween. Ugly," Carrie drew out the last word and again they all laughed. I was confused. Why did I need to look in a mirror? Vanity? To see how poorly I stacked up? Mirrors were for beautiful people and to check for tooth spinach.

"Did you give one to Brad, too?" asked Carrie.

"Are you kidding? Brad surrounds himself with mirrors. No needs to remind him how handsome he is or who he is. All I have to do is agree." There was appreciative laughter accepting male preening. Chepita put water on to boil and the women sat at the kitchen table.

"This is a lovely basket of fruit, Chepita." Winter fruits were piled high in a reed basket between us.

"Si, I'll move it for now," she said. Renan jumped up to move it to the counter for her mother. "Bishop Erickson brought it by from the church. He brings us something every holiday. It is so thoughtful." I remembered the black suited missionaries LoBeth snarled at through the years as they stood on the front porch. She should have been polite enough for fruit receiver list.

"I'm starting a new sewing project for the baby's room." We all looked to Renan. "It's a painting only in sewing. Because I don't paint. But what it is," her elbows were now on the table and she began moving her hands in ways we were supposed to understand, "is scraps that remind me of people or events and I sew them together, kind of like a quilt. Only not a quilt. It will hang by the baby's crib for it to see."

Silently, we all considered something to say. Carrie was first. "So you might use a scrap from my wedding dress to mean me?"

"Yes, yes, that's exactly it. I want the baby to be creative and surrounded by the people of its life." Renan hadn't wanted ultrasound so the baby's sex was unknown. We patted her belly and made our guesses, calling the baby it; without an English word that gave life without sex.

"And a blessed bebé it is, Renan. What you are doing is making a retablo. A Mexican altar in fabric," Tia Manuela sounded excited and her Catholic heart appreciated symbolism presented to God.

Chepita shook her head, smiling, "Manuela, es una colcha."

"Una colcha con corazón e historia desde el principio." Spanish could erupt into any conversation and when it did I waited for the next English. I was the only one in the room who didn't understand and I came to know Chepita and Tia Manuela's use of English was politeness to me and acquiescence to their daughters' urgings to adapt. "Oh, Renan, that is a wonderful idea for a wee one to start its way," her aunt finished.

Renan preceded the days of how-to books encouraging working for a passion with disregard for Puritan and pioneer pain. She was a gentle footfall that opened the door of thought and made me consider love as art. "Yes, I do want love and beauty to lead the way. I shall call it a retablo because I want my child to be blessed with knowledge of love, where it comes from and how to walk in this world toward work that is its talent and love. There is better work than what I have."

Chepita was the only person at the table not envious of Renan's job. It was secure, she could wear nice clothes, it paid well and it had superior health care, vacation and retirement benefits. That it was boring or repetitive didn't matter to Tia Manuela who worked in a near sweat shop sewing sport clothes, or Carrie who worked in a warehouse or me, who would have to be dying before health benefits kicked in.

"I know you're all jealous but believe me, it's a job at the bottom around there." We all understood that, too.

"How's Brad's new job?" Chepita asked.

"Good. He's enjoying it," her brow creased. It had been a month since Brad left selling motorcycles and ATVs. Now it was new cars. It was for the same company, but in a different location and with a larger sales commission.

Chepita changed the subject. "Geraldo was here last week. I made extra tortillas and called to see if he wanted them. Poor boy. He doesn't get enough good cooking."

"How's he doing?" Renan asked.

"Fine. He makes his dead parents proud. He even came in and had lunch with me. He was hungry to the bone. I wish Oil Boy would eat like that. Or Maury."

"Last week he applied for a good government position. Such a good young man. He wants to be an electrical inspector for the county."

"I hope he gets it then," Renan said without looking up.

"I will pray for him and his parents," Tia Manuela gave the sign of the cross.

"Will you and Brad pick me up for Church Sunday?" asked Chepita. Renan explained to me she and Brad went to church, often enough to keep her mother happy and not too often to make Brad unhappy. "Actually," she added, "he is more peaceful there than me. He would go more easily if he had never been ordered to go."

LoBeth's Christmas Guatemala report was that everyone who couldn't afford a plumber should build their own latrines and next year she was looking into Hawaii.

All the adults I would come to love more deeply in my life had gathered.

Rose Graciela Madrugada Evans was born at 4:02 a.m. on January 8, 1989. Brad stumbled through the name when he called at 4:30, but it became family lore that he chose Rose and Renan decided on Grace in the Small Dark Hours Before Dawn.

Renan later told me as she breast fed her daughter, "Where there is grace in the nightmare hours there will be renewal."

"Do you have nightmares, Renan?"

She nodded and turned away.

Monday was my usual day off and it was often lonely since Maury was in school so I was happy to help, watch and wait on Renan for a few hours. I parked on the street of the old neighborhood that separated the University of Utah from downtown Salt Lake. It was their compromise between the east and west sides of the city. Brad didn't want to live west of Fifth East, sure that was dangerously near the wrong side of town. Renan didn't want to be too far from Chepita. The hundred year old two story Victorian had been carved into two downstairs apartments and their upstairs one. January's cold clear air followed into the dark hallway of suspended cooking and dust smells. Renan and Brad's apartment was a warm island at the top of the stairs.

For three hours I washed dishes, vacuumed, mopped the kitchen floor, took garbage to the dumpster, changed baby sheets and made sandwiches for lunch. When it was over I sat in an oversize stuffed chair across from Renan. Watching Renan breastfeed gave me the sensation of seeing a Rembrandt painting move. The diffused day light slanted behind heavy brocade drapes over starched white sheers. Originally, the apartment had cheap drapes I would have kept but Renan replaced them with a remnant she found. Brad begged her not to paint the walls any darker than taffy chocolate but she teased his middle class devotion to white walls and painted them a water blue, that when the sun hit sent out red lights to meet it. The plush burgundy sofa and dark wood tables were being paid for monthly. A brass bowl was full of oranges and jonathan apples. A vase on the tv spilled purple silk flowers.

"Do you prefer Rose or Graciela or Madrugada? That could be Maddie."

"Rose. It will be easier for her. But she will come to know all of it."

"How do you like being a Mom?"

"It's wonderful Abby."

"I think I'm pregnant."

Her excitement was genuine and she was as thrilled for me as for

Rose and Maury. "She'll have a first cousin and they can play with Sofia. When is it due?"

"I don't know. I haven't been to the doctor, but not till the end of summer. So please keep quiet. Why haven't you opened this present yet?" There was a large box against the wall with a smaller one attached on top.

"I will now. Here. Take Rose," and she handed me the squishy blanket with protruding hair. "It's from Jerry. He brought it this morning on his way to work. He got the job mamá was talking about. He's an official electrical inspector for the county." The four-legged rocker had six tunes to soothe baby and could rock for twenty minutes.

"Aren't you going to open the smaller present?" Rose was warming my arms. I didn't know babies gave out heat. I thought they only needed it.

"I think I know what it is." She opened it while I waited. "Yes, it's *Beautiful*." The Estee Lauder fragrance was not the smallest bottle.

"That's nice of him."

"He's given me that since it came out three years ago. It does smell good." On cue my replacement knocked on the door. "That must be Bonnie. Here. Will you put this in the bathroom?" She handed me the *Beautiful* and took Rose.

The fabric retablo hanging over Rose's crib caught my eye as I walked past the nursery. It was an apartment size room and it would be hard to fall down and not hit a wall. Renan had it as bright as Easter Sunday morning with the small tablecloth-sized retablo bordered on four sides with gathered scraps of Carrie's wedding dress taffeta. Standing like a well-tended orange lawn was a vertical tuft of yarn Chepita donated. On either side in random circles was emerald silk from Tia Manuela, worn white cotton shirt pieces from Pedro, black nylon of Maury's discarded backpack, plaid flannel from Oil Boy, pink grosgrain ribbon that had been in my bridal bouquet, a lace handkerchief Sandy gave from her hope chest, a cut up donated hotpad from Bonnie and parts of a shredded golf towel from Mr. Evans. Swirling through spaces and uniting the circles were weaved stripes of ivory satin pillow cases Renan said were what she and Brad slept on their first married night.

"Hello, Bonnie," I said when I returned. Mrs. Evans may have been the best name, but I had already said it.

"Hello, Abby. Nice to see you." Polite sounded unbending. She had arrived so I left to return to my vanilla walled apartment with the

85

marshmallow shades, sage colored used sofa and scratched coffee table with schoolbooks thrown about.

Maury was scheduled to graduate that spring. Instead of easing up like everyone did in high school, he chained himself to a stricter routine of school, study, and his delivery job. I saw him in the morning before he left and felt him in the dark before we went to sleep.

"What's this?" he was truly alarmed in February when he sat up in bed in the dark and the blankets fell from his shoulder.

"What?"

"You. Your breasts are larger. What's this?"

"Well, Maury," I scooted up to rest my back on the headboard. "Well, Maury, I think I'm pregnant."

"Pregnant?"

What should have been a wonderful nearness of you moment felt like I had given Maury another schoolbook to read. He turned on the bedside lamp and looked at me. "I didn't expect it now. The pills?"

"I, I, I." His look could have bored a closed door. The distance and anger surprised me. It was an emotion I'd never seen in him.

"You forgot the pills."

"I don't know."

"Yes, you do," he turned away. "I don't want life out of control, Abby." He got out of bed and went to his schoolbooks.

I didn't tell LoBeth the depth of my guilt or confusion, but her piercing eyes that always saw unfairness to females, looked at my unsure, avoiding brown ones.

"What did Maury say?"

"He was surprised."

"And then?"

"He was surprised. That's all."

"Imagine that. Surprised at results. Isn't he the young man I remember hearing was taking a class in logic for computer studies? People aren't surprised when they get a cold from shaking a germ covered hand. Even if they are taking vitamin C. They're not surprised when they fail a test if they haven't studied enough and I know Maury studies often. Why are they surprised when a woman is pregnant from sex?" Golden Bitch was oddly comforting.

"By the way, I'm thrilled to be a grandmother. Do it again soon," and we hugged.

Three days passed before Maury's anger fell to fear. Timidly, I approached. "We can manage, Maury."

"Yes, Abby, but that's not the point." It was a week before the fear at least went into hiding.

In May when Maury graduated, my belly had the gentle slope of a sand dune. It was the inbetween stage of looking in need of a diet instead of pregnant. Renan gave me a blouse she had worn, but though my chest was bursting by my standards, it was still The Lesser Sand Dunes in that blouse. But I wore it. I would have looked better in Maury's black graduation dress except I couldn't duplicate the shining smile he wore from the moment he woke until he fell gently back to the pillows after midnight.

Chepita cleaned and directed cooking for a week. She slow-cooked beef for burritos, made bowls of salsa, and argued the finer points of chicken molé with chilis, chocolate and almonds with Tia Manuela and Grandma Felipa. The day before I stood at Chepita's sink hand sifting beans to remove dirt, ruined beans and rock remnants.

"I remember doing what you are doing when my brother, Rafael married Bernice, Abby. They had the happiest wedding I have ever seen."

"How old were you, Chepita?"

"Oh, let's see, I believe I was nine."

When I was nine the smell of a Baker family meal was beef and potatoes floating in the dry air from an oven. The circling steamy bean, tamale and fresh tomato smells of Maury's childhood wrote different stories.

Guests brought homemade tortillas, salad, soda, beer, paper plates and so much family love I choked tears as he was man-handled by a hundred well-wishers. I was sitting at the back table under the tree where I first met Brad and Renan with a photographer's long view of the house. It needed paint but dots of color were moving with life. Streamers in red and green ran down the butcher paper covered tables. The men broiling chicken flashed silver belt buckles below turquoise, red and yellow shirts. People of all ages were running to and from the center magnet of Maury in a black skirt.

I waved at Brad as he came to sit in the shade. He held a beer dripping with ice water. We watched the scene. "Bet you're glad it's all over."

"Yes," my head bobbed as I worked on steadying my voice.

"Are you crying?" He looked to verify.

I cocked my shoulder, avoiding voice.

"Women and tears. Renan can look at Rose and tears run down her cheeks like a drippy faucet."

"Sorry. They just come." We were quiet for a few minutes while he drank beer and I wiped my eyes. "I'm happy for him. He's worked so long. I'm just glad it's over."

"Yes, I hated school."

"So did I. Glad to get out of there."

"Think it will pay off?"

"I hope so. We could use it. I still don't really get what he's supposed to go out and do. Work with computers. Seems like they change all the time. And will they be around in the long run?" I felt like the only person in the state who wasn't impressed with WordPerfect, the Utah based company that was growing better than weeds in LoBeth's flower garden. LoBeth called computers one more secretarial supply.

"That's why I like the car world. You know people are going to buy and there's money to be made."

"You do well, Brad. I know you do. Renan said you're looking for a house." Crystal ran up to her dad and he opened his right arm wide to balance her as she sank into him. "Hi, Crystal," I finished.

"Hi, Abby. Dad can I go with Oil Boy and Frankie and Jeremy to the store? Tiffany and Roberta are going. Chepita needs ice cream and with the ice out of the freezer there's room now."

"Okay. Here's money to help." He handed her a five dollar bill.

"Good of you, Sir, Brad," he smiled gratefully.

"We're looking or Renan is. I don't care what she gets as long as she's happy and it's not too close to either parents."

"I can understand that. I think if it were possible Maury would spend the week here with Chepita's cooking and Juan's tv peanuts and weekends with me."

"Not with that little one you've got coming. He's excited about that." Oh, good, I thought, verification from an outside source. Quietly we watched Renan, Carrie, Jerry and Pedro talking at another table.

"I like that retablo Renan did for Rose's room."

"She's talented. Now she's making one for Sofia. Scraps of stuff are all over the living room. We need a house." LoBeth was walking down the side path of the house so I excused myself to accompany her. I was still her lady in waiting.

Maury had his first job in July with a company named frinTz starting under the rosy aura of Wordperfect's parent company, Novell. Novell started in 1979 and its Cinderella rags to riches story was shaping as legend, creating a hardy undergrowth of companies, like Utah lawn mushrooms, hoping to imitate or live off them. Everything seemed to be falling into place and even a baby wouldn't be a financial freefall.

In the early computer days companies were having as much trouble naming themselves as I was having naming a baby. While they made up words like Novell and frinTz to prove they weren't daddy's LeRoy and Sons, I faced a pride and prejudice I didn't know I had. The name Arias was rhythmic and connected me to a man I loved, but having a child was a problem. Enrique, Rudolfo, Esteban, Selena, Carlotta, or Maria or any other Mexican name would have flowed more easily than Henry, Rudolf, Steven, Sally, Charlotte or Mary with Arias to keep a smooth melodic flow. But that meant I had to loosen my grip on the importance of my genetic input that I didn't know, respect or feel loved by, but I was still walking around in its skin. It felt like I was serving tea and crumpets on the same plate as enchiladas.

I talked to LoBeth. "Naming a baby Mary instead of Maria just feels like mixing ketchup and ice cream."

She wasn't any help. "You're a funny old fashion matron, Abby. You keep me looking young."

Maury's family had a two month running conversation about naming the baby that I didn't hear about until Brad said something as we all said good-bye on a Sunday. He gave me a big beery hug and patted my belly saying, "Name that kid anything, Abby. Herbert Hoover's a good name if you like it," and he leaned whispering, "It doesn't have to be Emilio." No one beyond Maury and Renan heard him but they looked at each other and their eyes darted away.

"Why would he say it doesn't have to be Emilio?" I asked in the car.

"Oh, Abby." His voice wilted and I looked at him surprised while he repeated himself. "Oh, Abby, all of it was so long ago and I don't like thinking about it." The whole drive home he repeated it was so long ago and didn't matter and we didn't have to name a son Emilio. Finally, I faced him across our kitchen table with his choice of beer, water, tea or vodka. He chose vodka.

"You know we lived in Pine Creek," he looked at me with a plea, took a breath, and a second vodka shot. "Well, Abby, Pedro is really the second son of my parents. Emilio was the first." He paused. "Oh, hell, I don't want to spend time talking about this. The story is: Two boys were born in Mexico. Emilio and Pedro. They all went to California where Renan and I were born and then they came to Utah because California was getting too mean and Oil Boy was born. We went to school in Pine Creek and sometimes traveled to Idaho to pick sugar beets but Utah was home after Dad got a job at the sugar beet plant. One day Emilio got in a fight with local boys and he was stabbed and he died. That's all."

He didn't look at me as he recited his soaped and towel dried version and I didn't press him. What he said was awful enough and contained all the story I made him suffer. At the end he whispered, "I don't want my son to be named Emilio."

"Then it won't be."

A man came into Wanlass the next week looking for replacement glasses. He was a large full man who took up space and pushed his chest ahead. Quietly he tried on six pair. When I tried to make small talk he peered at me with distaste so I shut up.

"I'll take these."

I took the black frames, put them on the counter and wrote the pick-up day.

"Arias," he read it from the copy I gave him.

"Yes."

"You don't look Mexican," he eyed my swelling belly.

"No. My husband is."

His stiffening was so sudden I froze. He growled low and close to my face, "What's the matter with you?" He turned and left. A fearful breeze from dark nights when I was the last one awake at LoBeth's ran its rough hand across my cheek.

Jonathan Arias was born September 14, 1989, as a brown and chubby muscled earth guardian, first disguised as a delicious 8 lb 2 oz basket of cinnamon donuts.

My Family, Mi Familia

Being a mother did not come to me as easily as a baby shower invitation. Jonathan was the first baby ever put in my care. After leaving the hospital, Maury drove his tired unsteady wife and newborn son home. Within the hour a steady stream of people bearing presents and broad smiles made it their purpose to hold or stare at Jonathan or ask how I felt. Over the next four days Maury looked as though he was in a commercial, saying cooing sounds to the baby and patting my head like I was a collie that had done well. A spontaneous event that had started with a black see through babydoll lace thing that jumpstarted that wonderful hungry look in Maury's eyes, ended in a yellow and white flannel nightgown with stupid virginal ribbons and a frightened look of kindly respect from a new papa. I noted to God He was very crafty and had a wicked sense of humor.

On the morning of the fifth day of Jonathan's life the house was clear of LoBeth, Kelly, Maury's family and Maury himself when he closed the door at 7:32 a.m. I lay in the middle of our bed, covered to chin in the flannel nightgown, sheets, a blanket and a green cotton bedspread. Rain spattered gently outside the window on the accumulated rocks by the rain gutter. Perhaps grey daylight was already associated with people and activity because Jonathan began to cry as though he was the last abandoned earthling left to carry on. I got up and went to the kitchen to warm a bottle before getting him. His little fists were curled like a fighter's when I got there. Deserted and forlorn, his lost wail asked God why he had been thrown to me. He was cheated and afraid. The cry transcended the need for food but food was my only answer. I picked up the human being weighing less than LoBeth's dictionary, and we went to the bed where he was conceived.

A low vibration stirred my now empty uterus and recognition of black power rose from inside to a realization in seconds. A consciousness was opened like watermelon with an ax and I believed I heard and felt everything in that small apartment. The hum of the refrigerator, lint moving through the air, light peeking through drapes, a car driving down the street, Jonathan's sucking sounds. I looked at him. This baby was mine. Its life was mine to shape. It and he were still interchangeable. This little pile of flesh was helpless against me. Unearned power over helplessness was mine to use as I wished. As I desired for my benefit. In the next moment I realized I had never, never in my life felt in power and authority. I was the child, daughter, student, employee and wife. Now I owned a baby. I could use it, hurt it, pinch it, withhold food, not clean it, love it, nurture it, never let it be without and it would have no choice but to think all was as it should be.

Jonathan's and my tears mingled with the rain as I realized how easy it would be to hurt one tiny person so I could know the lust of power and give back to the world the cruelties and painful neglects given me. I imagined when LoBeth returned to her childhood bed with me. I had ended her dreams of New York. I was in a marriage bed of comfort but still wondered, as she must have wondered, what I had done to myself. Being a loving mother with cookies and milk, kisses on cheeks, bedtime stories and clean clothes was a consciously chosen path on a rainy morning while wearing a flannel nightgown.

Maury was also path choosing. He was learning about the corporate working world, being a daddy of a crying gassy baby and husband of an alternately weepy and claws bared mean female who only wanted to hold her baby and sleep. It is not surprising he accepted Brad's invitation for a deer hunting weekend in October. Brad had asked him for several years, but this was the first time Maury needed a restful time away.

The hunting party was Brad, his dad Marlon, Travis, Maury and Oil Boy. Brad, Travis and Marlon took care of everything but orange vests and hats.

"I look ridiculous." Maury was standing in front of a bedroom mirror with the vest and hat on. His precise dress code of conservative pressed matching clothes that were never frayed or not tucked in was offended.

"Are you a decoy? Where are you going that you need that stuff? Don't make me a widow or I'll kill you."

"I'll stand behind Brad and enjoy the damn great outdoors." He turned and looked at his butt in the mirror.

"Liberty Park is not a protected wilderness, Maury." I was bitchy and he was a sulky boy king.

Friday at noon he left the office early and headed to the Uinta Mountains to set up camp before deer hunting season began at dawn. The report I received from the lips of a man who Sunday night walked in the door and claimed to be our husband and father was disjointed. He looked like a pampered prize winning thoroughbred in shock after a lost weekend with wild horse cousins. My handsome racehorse had been dragged through the mud, left unwashed and unshaven with dirt in his hair and the surprising boyhood feel of grit on his hands. His eyes had a clarity and sharpness of new understanding.

"Brad got a buck. Big antlers. He and his dad had us sitting on rock in bushes before the sun came up. Travis was hidden at an angle behind rocks and trees. It was still grey black sky and nightmare time. We sat and sat and sat. I was so cold my nose ran. Brad saw the buck at the same time as Marlon. I never would have seen it across an open field and into another forest. Then he whispered. It was spooky. In God. For food. And he lifted his rifle, pulled the lever, followed that deer and waited. He seemed to be talking to it. Somehow communicating. When he did finally shoot the sound of the gun exploded. The deer cried! Then the gunshot ricocheted down the canyon until I heard it over and over."

Words fell out of him like a six year old repeating every scene of a movie in perfect order. His eyes blazed excitement and horror. "Before the ricochet Marlon, Brad and Travis were up and walking to the deer. Halfway across the field Marlon lifted his rifle to show Oil Boy and me where the deer was limping out but it was Travis who aimed and fired. It went down. Good shot, boys, Marlon said and then I learned why we didn't walk too far from camp. That thing was huge and it took all of us to carry it back. Oil Boy and I just watched as they cleaned the guts out. Mom took me to a Mexican market as a kid where meat hung like that. It's disgusting. I like meat under plastic."

Maury wasn't a convert but he did listen with a closer ear when Brad talked about guns and hunting. "I've used a few of Brad's hold steady and listen techniques at the office. They work." Three times over the next week he told me how impressed he was watching Brad wait, anticipate, aim, wait, kill. "His eyes were focused with the gun as though it were a third eye, Abby." He also appreciated the feel of a gun in his hands. He said it was the best handshake he'd ever felt from a friend who gave everything. Maybe the Uintas is where Brad went to sales school.

"You never did tell me what Oil Boy thought."

"He told me Little Benny's a better shot. He gave me this," he pulled out an ounce of marijuana.

"Oh."

"Think I'll go visit Jerry with this Saturday."

Successful hunting had a prize. Renan insisted we take the twenty pounds of meat wrapped by a butcher. Our apartment freezer wasn't big enough for all of it so we passed some on to LoBeth who nostalgically made a stew like she had at a cousin's as a child. I made a pot roast and later meatballs, but we were slow to get through it.

Overall, life was quietly lived as Maury and I slipped into a comfortable routine of necessity to fulfill responsibility. I continued working at Wanlass but with Alicia and Maury's encouragement I applied to be a manager and was accepted into the training program. Work took on a purpose I'd never meant to give it. Being manager didn't look like fun. It's just that being under a manager, even a good one, for the rest of my life seemed like less fun and the cost of daycare while trying to save for a house gave money a new value. It would also mean one more week of vacation and a retirement option. I began to try to care about work.

Tuesday through Friday Jon rotated between Lil Kidz and Chepita or Tia Manuela when she was sporadically laid off because there wasn't enough work. Crystal, Rose and Sofia might also be there when their mothers' schedules or regular daycare hours didn't work. Oil Boy was sometimes directed by Juan to drive everyone home so the house would be quieter sooner than waiting for parents.

On a Thursday I came home to Maury and Oil Boy arguing in the living room. I heard their voices before opening the door and when they saw me they shut up. I heard Crystal, Rose, Sofia and Jon in Jon's room throwing toys out of the toy box.

Oil Boy lifted an open beer from the coffee table and headed out, "Bye, Abby."

"Bye, Tomas." When he turned sixteen he announced he was no longer Oil Boy though that's how I thought of him. I asked Maury what it was about.

"When I got here the kids were playing Yahtzee in the car and Irene Gonzalez and Oil Boy were in the front yard yelling at each other."

"Why?"

"Hermie's in jail and she wanted bail money. She found Tomas here with the kids. I told him never to bring her or any of them around again. Now he's mad at me. I had to give her a hundred dollars to get rid of her."

"A hundred dollars?"

"It won't happen again," and he walked out of the room.

Maury loved his job with frinTz and he was never late or missed time, but on the third Friday in April when Jon was seven months old, there was not a paycheck for time put in or apology. "Hey, you all knew this was a dream," the owner said as he dismissed the last of the staff and drove off in his Mercedes.

frinTz taught him he'd always be a student. Night classes and seminars became his hobby as the changes in technology moved from walking speed to time travel whizzing. From the beginning he knew computers would be mentally challenging, but he was too caught up in it before he understood how fast and unpredictable the pace would stay. I conceded computers were a real career.

He was quickly hired by another start-up company in May, but Jon wasn't a year when that company cut the staff by sixty-five percent saying, "The banks just don't understand this new technology game so to follow our dream we must build a brain trust." The brain trust was only university graduates.

For the next week, in the dry heat of August, Maury spent his days listening to John Coltrane, Journey and Santana. I came home after Wanlass to a dark curtained apartment with saxophone soul notes spilling over teddy bears, a toy red truck and building blocks. He showered every day but his slicked back air dried hair and stubby chin made him look like a scrawny, weather beaten, but still jazzy cactus. Jon crawled over and around him all day, happy and content to be with a compliant nearby parent who introduced potato chips and indulged every desire but diaper changes.

"Tomas, Chucky and David came by today." We were sitting at the kitchen table eating macaroni and cheese and hot dogs with Jon.

"Uh-huh."

"They had some grass."

I didn't say anything.

"Relaxed my mind. I was Coltrane." He had glazed eyes. "He's dealing bigger now. Moved up the pyramid scheme. I told him to get out."

Jon squirmed so I got him out of the high chair and put him on my lap to pick at my plate. I wondered when Maury graduated, why Oil Boy didn't follow Maury's education example. But years of school and sacrifice that led to being fired two times in five months wouldn't seem successful measured against the cash flow and hours of marijuana.

"I thought you told him not to bring any of your old friends here."

"I'll remind him," he paused. "Abby, I'm applying to the University

95

of Utah. They're the people who kept their jobs. My program was good. Taught me as much. I was showing a few of those graduates how to get around DOS but they have the dog paper and that's how bean pushers and brain thieves decide."

Some of the credits from the trade school were accepted and he calculated it would be over in two years and he would have a college degree in Computer Science. Pace Office Supply took him back part-time, but it felt like we were back to where we started. In guilty moments I felt nostalgia for being twenty, boyfriendless and without dirty laundry. The flip thought was I never, for a second, wanted to be without Maury and Jon, but tears fell on top of Jon's head as we watched Sesame Street reruns while Maury studied in the bedroom.

My most selfish cry was when we took out a student loan for enough money to be a house down payment. We were sinking in debt, I felt more like Maury's housekeeper and cook than lover, and I was tired of wearing the same black shoes every day of my life. At 9:00 p.m. I still hadn't put Jon in bed. I needed his close movement and approval. While I held him with his last bottle of the day in the blinking lights of tv, I drank gin and water and felt my stiff glass heart, lungs, belly, hips start to melt and warm to sliding syrup down every cell through my legs and out my feet. The college boy voice of Jay Leno and audience laughter were playing when the phone rang.

"Papá." There was silence. "Si, Papá, but only poco tiempo." When he hung up he turned to me. "Hang on, Abby. Oil Boy is being kicked out of the house and dad wants him to live here."

"What?"

"He'll sleep on the couch. He's on his way."

Oil Boy's steps on the stairs were slow and Maury opened the door before he was at the top. "Hola, little brother. In trouble?" His voice was the accented English of a new speaker.

Oil Boy struggled. He looked tired and half drunk as he fell in the door.

"I want a beer."

"If you tell me why in the hell you're here, Oil Boy."

"Don't call me Oil Boy."

"Then be a Tomas."

Maury and I headed to bed.

In the morning after he showered Maury stood over his brother on the couch. "Get up, burro. The sun shines. Remember Mom saying that? You live here you're up and dressed before I leave in the morning."

"¡Que te chíngues! I'm hanging out today."

"Suit yourself. Place has a bathroom but no morning tortillas."

Maury came back to the bedroom to say good-bye but before he could say anything I said, "No morning tortillas?"

"It's just an expression."

Tomas got dressed but when Jon and I were ready to leave he was asleep on the couch. "Bye Tomas." Jon crawled over and held the couch as he patted his back. Tomas waved an arm but didn't move.

Both Renan and Chepita called me that day and said thanks, don't worry, it will be temporary. When I got home Maury was studying and there was no sign of Oil Boy.

"What's happening, Maury?"

"Family emergency. It won't be long. I'll be as strict as Dad."

The only thing he made Oil Boy do was be dressed when he left for school. That was a compromise for Oil Boy because it was his middle of the night. He got up about noon and more than once had his friends over for breakfast. He began leaving a dirty frying pan on the stove and his friends left a late night bar odor in the air.

On a Sunday while Maury studied, I escaped with Jon and visited LoBeth. "Hand me my grandson and tell me your woes. The tea is over there to pour."

Who do I get to boss around, I thought, on my way to the tea. Not even Jon was listening when I said no. "Nothing you don't already know. Since Maury's return to school, a house won't be any too soon. And with Tomas around food is costing more."

"You're in school, too."

My two hour weekly management classes on Saturday mornings before my regular shift only felt burdensome. "It's just learning Wanlass propaganda on a national scale."

"Which you can take anywhere in the future. And when Maury graduates, it could be your turn for college."

"I want a house."

"You've got time. Houses need care, apartments don't. Enjoy that. Don't give him that. He needs healthy food." I'd leaned to give Jonathan a cookie from the plate she'd set on the table. She held him while she foraged the cupboards and produced a wheat cracker.

"Oh, sure, that's a lot better. Let's compare the sugar content with the salt."

"And then let's have a little respect for Grandma. At least it's got wheat instead of bleached flour. And if you like, I'll introduce him to sprouts. I have some in the fridge."

"That will kill his lifetime interest in green things."

"All right, enough of the avoidance. Tell me all the flaws of Young Married Love Skids into Motherhood, Housekeeping and Brother-in-law."

So I named each one with a supporting sentence. Money worries. Everything expensive. Boring job. Too much homework. Extra housework and cooking. Self-pity's daughter sat beside me as a friend and was the only one to feel sorry for me. LoBeth laughed at my complaints. Perhaps it was the slow discovery that getting my dream of a husband and child was not as easy as carrying a purse around as a new springtime accessory. As a sister to three brothers, not even Oil Boy's stay surprised her. "Now you know, Abby, how wonderful a large family can be."

The contrast was Renan's life. "Look at this plaid," she said of a material we were passing in K-Mart, "it's so precise and well-ordered." It was fall and I had trailed her for something to do with Jonathan so Maury could have a quiet apartment and Oil Boy could sleep.

She was looking for material to make Chepita a dress like the women wore in Jalisco. There wasn't a store that sold them and recently Chepita wistfully admitted she missed the simple clean femininity of her girlhood dress. U.S. fashion was garish, uncomfortable or dull and all of it was without history and connection between grandmother, mother and daughter. We were also looking for satin or taffeta remnants that could be used as an artist's canvas for a retablo for Chepita.

"What do you mean?" Jonathan had orange fish cracker crumbs on his chin and I lifted his coat sleeve to wipe them away. He began licking his coat sleeve. Rose was holding a single fish cracker like a pearl.

"Plaids look so military. So carefully put together. You have to match them up, yellow to yellow and red to red, or they are a mess and they take extra material."

I shrugged in boredom. Plaid was something I would never bother wearing. A single plaid square could be as big as my face. What was her point?

"Plaid gets attention because it's so strong with lines this way and that way," she crossed her arms, not knowing the word perpendicular, "and complicated because they are designed so many different ways."

Her life was a well-ordered plaid. She was settled with a handsome guy who was crazy over her and wanted to spend every second away from the car lot in her exuding, feminine presence. She had a clean job sitting at a desk where she didn't have to deal with the public. She and Brad had bought a twenty-year old house with four bedrooms, two bathrooms, a family room, a sliding glass door to a backyard full of roses and a double car garage. Brad was not shy describing sales commissions of one week that were more than we made in a month. She hadn't even split the sails after Rose's birth. If anything, she evolved from beautiful to lush while hen waddle walked beside her pushing Jon.

"Did you know Brad called Maury this morning to see if he wanted to play pool while we shopped?" she asked. She had one hand on Rose's stroller and one was fingering white poplin.

"No, I didn't."

"What was strange about that, Abby, is I knew he had to work. He didn't know I could hear him talking from the kitchen."

"Maybe he forgot."

"I heard Hermie and the boys have been visiting your place."

"Irene, too. It's not when I'm home. Maury gave her that hundred dollars for bail months ago but nothing since."

"You can't leave anyone in jail. I'll tell Tomas not to bring them, though. She must have hit every house in the neighborhood to get enough hundreds."

"Thanks," he'd listen to Renan.

"Come over Friday with Jon. Brad will be gone and we'll have pizza," she said when she dropped us off on her way home.

6

*I told Abby when she turned eighteen,
'Hell, Abby, stupid women run in this family.
Of course you wouldn't know anything about men.'*

- LoBeth Baker

"I'm taking Jon to Renan's Friday night so you and Tomas can have the place," were my sexy words to Maury before falling asleep on Wednesday. "Crystal might be there, too," I added as I packed Jon's gear on Friday for a three hour visit. "It will be a real female family visit."

"Maybe if LoBeth was there."

"My mother?"

"I miss not going with you and Jon tonight. To a movie on Saturday nights. A beer with Jerry. My mother's tortillas. Sleeping."

"Talk like that anymore and I might feel sorry for you."

"It's worth it, Abby. Someday it will be worth it. I promise." I kissed him a quick good-bye.

"Be careful what you smoke with Tomas."

Crystal's white star girl hair had deepened to sun yellow and her brown eyes were beginning to widen from baby fat face to leaner muscles and lines of a girl. At nine she was a child but the dawning of a grown face was shaping. Custody was very split between the parents but Renan and Brad often had her extra weekends to accommodate Karla's dating. I never met Crystal's mother but she once showed me a picture she carried in a purse when she visited her father. Her hair was full and long like Renan's but a lighter Anglo girl shade of brown. The eye into the camera

100

was straight and purposefully seductive. It was a synthetic, cheaper mirror of what Renan had naturally flowing through her eyes and lips. What Renan owned, Karla had in degrees.

After she took the kids to the tv room with pizza and drinks I told Renan what Maury said he missed and what he wanted to do. "Where would you want to go?" We were using fingers to eat pizza and smearing the oil and tomato sauce on beer cans when we drank.

"I miss dancing. But I got to dance last night. A few of the women from work went to a place on Thirty-ninth South for one of their birthdays. Guess what! Jerry was there and I danced and talked with him." She closed her eyes, "I miss being in dresses that feel like underwear, wearing shoes with sparkles and feeling my bare shoulder on Brad's shirt during the last dance."

"That beats Maury's list."

"It's the same thing really. We miss something that went away to make room for something we need to do now." She paused for a drink, "What do you miss, Abby?"

"This is what I wanted. A guy. A family. What I want is a house and to see Maury in it. I don't miss much. Well, I do miss seeing Kelly and how easy things were. Life seems a lot more complicated now." She was quiet so I continued. "I wasn't leaving anything behind I wanted. I just want life to go well. Along a simple, little path of happy husband, healthy children, clean house."

Renan closed her eyes and saw in her mind what she must have pictured many times, "I want to feel love, know how it breathes. I want to be surrounded with color, music, people I love need to be close. I want to understand something about life I haven't even put into words and feel it beat in my heart."

Crystal came into the room from downstairs with Rose and Jon. "I need to call Mom now. Can I use this phone?"

"Yes, Crystal. Let's go downstairs, Abby." I didn't know how to respond to Renan's wants so I waited for her to talk. "Brad always gave me that, but marriage and children put a hair clip on it. But I don't blame him. When he's not working he almost follows me around like a puppy. Last week he was waiting for me in the parking lot at work when I came out." I knew they drove separate cars.

"Why?"

"He said he missed me. Nolan was with me and it was awkward. He got out of the car and just stood there when he saw us coming. His arms were crossed." She reached for pink quartz beads to restring from a necklace that was Chepita's. The three strands would be placed by the cut up felt of a hat Juan wore in California as a young man when he was so sexy, Chepita declared the bees by the oleanders would faint in his presence.

"Was he mad?"

"Yes, but I don't know why."

Crystal's whiny girl voice yelled a few unintelligible sentences starting with Mother! "Sometimes she does that," Renan said, "just ignore it." When Crystal came down she sat by Renan; her face a wilted sunflower. Renan opened her arm and pulled her head to rest on her shoulder before kissing the top of Crystal's head.

"Why does she have to be that way?" Crystal sounded like I did at that age and I talked about LoBeth.

"I'm sorry, honey. I'm sure she didn't mean it."

"Yes, she did. Yes, she did. Her and her boyfriends. When one's around she won't even talk to me."

We watched tv a while longer until I hoped Maury wouldn't mind if we came home. While she wrapped pizza for Maury and Oil Boy, Renan said she was a little ticked at Carrie. Carrie had told her mother a secret and Tia Manuela told Chepita who had called that afternoon and been both angry and worried.

"Brad and I had decided to get married when Jerry came by the house on a night when he knew I was alone. Brad was with Crystal. Mom and Dad and Oil Boy were visiting Grandma Felipa and Tia Manuela, Pedro was at work and Maury was with you. I was ironing a good shirt for papà when Jerry brought a wedding present.

"He's given me something every so often since he was in high school. That night he gave me his mother's silver hand mirror. You've seen it on my dresser. I refused it, he insisted and I told him when he gets married his bride will get it. He was friendly and casual at first, keeping me company and drinking a Coke I poured him. When he got up I thought he was leaving but he came over to the ironing board and slid his hands along my breasts as he wrapped himself around me and buried his face in my neck. 'Renan,' he whispered, 'be careful of Brad. Gringos are too often puffed corn. They've lost grit. He doesn't understand much. When you need me, call.' We kissed once very long before he looked at me for permission. He saw desire, but I moved him away and he left." She shrugged, "it is a long time ago. Carrie shouldn't have talked. I'm glad I didn't tell her about when he came to this house just after we moved in. At a Sunday dinner I told Jerry we hired an electrician to install two lights on the back patio. The next time Brad was at work Jerry showed up and did them before the electrician came. I do like seeing Jerry. I do love him."

We heard Brad drive in the driveway.

"Hi, honey," Renan turned and fully hugged Brad when he walked in.

"Hi, Abby, what's up?"

"I was kicked out of the house tonight for homework."

"Too bad. Want to stay and watch wrestling?"

"Thanks, no."

"Hi, Dad," Crystal ran up the stairs holding Rose who opened her arms for Renan.

Brad's eyes followed his wife as she warmed his pizza. It was a household of brave bright colors and textured materials that moved around Renan like planets around the sun. My stoic pioneer women ancestors with a do it on your own and never complain attitude while wearing a practical black dress felt like a bitter lonely heritage. Except for Renan's good-bye, Jon and I slipped out unnoticed.

The next Sunday Tomas was still with us. He, Maury and Jon were on the floor stacking blocks and I sat on the couch watching. Jon loved the attention. His delight encouraged Maury and Tomas to stack the blocks ever more oddly until his squeals became so free they were interspersed with hiccoughs.

Maybe this is family, I thought. This is what it means to help one another. This is only a new experience in a large family, large familia. Tomas, has always been a pretend little brother. Now, maybe, he was becoming a real one. This must be what it feels like.

"Abby, when's lunch?" Oil Boy said.

The spell was broken. Maury looked at me worried with his eyes pleading, "Abby, we all need a snack. I'll help you make sandwiches."

After Oil Boy left for his night work I stood in front of Maury. "I love your family."

He nodded.

"But I'm not making anymore sandwiches like that. And does he know how to hold a vacuum?"

"It's only a short time."

"A short time is getting longer."

"He needs help."

"Then give it to him." The glare I got started melting my glass insides.

"You've never had family. This is what it is."

"I have family. They just never take advantage of each other."

"You've never had family. They're all over hell." Jon began to cry. "Jon's crying."

Screw you, I thought, and turned to Jon.

When I woke up Tuesday morning Tomas wasn't on the couch. "Didn't he come home?"

"He went home," Maury didn't look at me. "I told Dad the stay was over and he agreed to let him come back."

Pedro started bringing a dozen tortillas every Wednesday for Maury. Tomas told Chepita about our apartment's tortilla barrenness. She assigned Pedro to bring them to us. Usually he quickly handed them to me on his way to the grill and salad bar restaurant where he now worked, but on a late fall morning he came earlier than usual.

"Here's the tortillas, la flaquita Abby." His dark eyes looked at me through volcano light to a little sister.

"Garcias."

"Gracias, I tell, you Abby," his voice was kind and deep. We'd teased each other with this before. Maury thought my joke was stupid. "Can I come in to see my nephew?"

I jumped out of the way. "Uh, sure. Come on in." After he picked up the willing Jon from the floor he sat on a chair. "Would you like a drink? Coffee? Coke?"

"No, nada," he played with Jon, not looking at me. "But perhaps water." I had the sense he didn't really want the water either but he needed the time it would take me to get it. He didn't like ice in his drinks, so I ran the water for a few seconds to get it a little colder. Eyeglasses named Composed were on the counter where I had left them before going to bed the night before. I put them on.

"What do you think of these, Pedro?"

"You have ojos muy bonitos, Abby. Very pretty eyes. You don't need them."

"But what do you think about the glasses?" I couldn't answer such an answer.

"They are for a woman who is dull and afraid."

"That's what I thought, too." I took them off and put them on the coffee table before sitting on the couch across from Pedro. We listened to Jon babble to Pedro. I was always surprised by the looks of attention and softness Juan, Pedro, Maury, Oil Boy, and Marcus had when they held babies.

"Abby, you are friends with Brad."

Unintentionally I crossed my arms. "Yes." I answered slowly.

Sensing my reaction without looking directly at me he said, "You know Brad perhaps in a different way than the rest of us."

"What do you mean?"

"I have been watching. He has changed." His words were a slow walk. "He has been a good man for Renan. He makes good money, very good money, but I watch and some things I don't understand. All his nails are not in the floorboards." He was quiet for long seconds. "Renan feels much but she doesn't always see what she should. She is an apasionado mujer, a passionate woman, and such beauty attracts much it should not." His early years with California fruit pickers and parents struggling to learn basic English lingered in his use of Spanish as though it was a favorite boyhood toy. "Pine Creek is much of her heartbreak." This was twice the words I had ever heard Pedro say at one time.

"It must have been hard on all of you to lose a brother and son."

Pedro regarded me as an innocent child. "It was more than that for Renan." We looked at each other. "Someday ask Maury about it. When he is not busy with school." Pedro kissed Jon's cheek and put him on the floor before standing, "Brad is a good man. He cares much for Renan. But, Abby, watch for me."

He turned when he was three steps out of the door, "Perhaps it would be best to ask Tia Manuela about Pine Creek."

Kelly or LoBeth would have called Tia Manuela that afternoon but I had lived under the sentence of silence about my father and I thought it kept life simpler.

Vicente Fernandez sang in the background during the annual tamale

105

making for Christmas holidays. Jon was the only male in the kitchen and he, Sofia and Rose were following each other through legs and under the table in patterns that appeared to be designed to aim for whatever woman held out the best treat or softest arms. I wondered if I evaporated if Jon would notice.

My task did not require years of tamale experience. Once Chepita showed me how to shred pork, I was trusted to follow direction. It was a Saturday and I was only off from Wanlass because I begged a vacation day to fulfill this family holiday tradition. It was a new sensation to have anything more repeatable and traditional than helping LoBeth cut sugar cookies beyond her bedtime on a work night.

"Damn these cookies. Next year I'm buying something at the bakery," she declared when the dough was too warm to cut well. Next week Jon and I were invited over for the sugar cookie fest. It would not be the same female party for his childhood memories but it would involve grandma devotion and sugar. Tightly knotted feelings about families and traditions were what I was thinking about to a background of English and Spanish when Renan made the announcement she was pregnant and there would be a July baby.

"Oh, Renan that is wonderful! Lo que mas quiero es tener muchos nietos!" The excitement defaulted Chepita to her native language, "You must listen, Abby. This is your call, too!"

"And, Carrie, do not close those ears under that thick hair. Sofia needs a brother and sister." Tia Manuela chorused. Sitting at the table drinking tea, Grandma Felipa smiled with few teeth but a lot of cheer. Arias grandmas always asked for more children yet their voices were never high school teachers before a test expecting to expand the kingdom. Instead they were earth mothers inquiring about new saplings. I shook my head.

"I would scare Maury away if we had a baby now. School takes much."

"Si, and when school is finished there will be money for a dozen." Tia Manuela consoled Chepita and me.

I turned to Renan who was dressed in church indigo and glowing like a candle. I wanted Pedro's words to fade like a dream. Sir Brad was important because he was Renan's husband and Maury's relative, but he was also my hand in the dark. It was Brad, more than Maury, who helped me to breathe in the heavy air. Since marrying Maury I realized I was in a family I didn't understand at all. There were so many I would never know all the cousins, aunts, uncles and godparents that circulated through the house on Sundays and the states of Utah, California and the country of Mexico. Their history, customs and closeness made me feel both loved by a real, breathing, blood family and a funny trinket from the outside world Maury had brought home to amuse them. He was my entrance ticket, but Jon who was now in a near sensual kiss game with Grandma Chepita, had given me a center seat.

"I've put the extra tamales in the bag for you," Chepita said as Jon and I left. I had asked for six to give Kelly. She had never had authentic tamales and I missed seeing her. They would be my Christmas present.

"Sorry, Kelly only gets five and you better hide them in the fridge or be ready to lose them," Maury greeted me when I told him what was in the bag. From the fridge I handed him salsa.

"It's Saturday night. I don't have to work. Got any ideas?"

"I'll call Jerry. Maybe he can come over."

"That's not what I meant." He was already walking toward the phone.

"Oh, Abby, I almost forgot you." He turned and smiled. I didn't answer.

"Okay. Come on. What would you like to do?"

"I don't know. What is there to do? We don't have a sitter. Or money. I don't know why I said anything."

He went to the couch and motioned me to slide into his arms. Jon pushed trucks and made vroom sounds while Maury kissed my neck and nuzzled the back of my neck. "We got married didn't we?"

"Yes. And I am glad we did."

"So am I," Jon was crying 'up, up' and climbing Maury's legs to be included in the affection so he lifted his son and held the two of us.

It was a rare time I was both without Jon and not at Wanlass, but on Sunday I went to Kelly and Gen's apartment and Maury took Jon to see Jerry. As I walked from the car to their apartment I had the rushing fear and loss feeling when a purse is suddenly missing in public. I was alone and empty of who I was; Maury and Jon.

"Haven't seen you for a while," Gen said. "Kelly's in the shower."

"I haven't been out much. How have you been?" Their apartment was about as decorated as Maury's and mine, but it was newer and had a view over growing young trees that looked out to a six lane highway that crossed the valley east to west.

"Been fine. How do you like this haircolor?" She turned so her locks fell like a stream down her back.

"Nice. It's a little lighter than I remember. But it works well on you. You like it?"

"Yes, I think it picked up the light in the bar last night and looked brighter."

I hoped Kelly wouldn't take long. "I met three studs last night but only one of them might work out." She stuck her chest out at me.

"I was with a stud, too. A proven one considering we've got Jon."

"Oh, you're funny, Abby. Stud is just good-looking." When Kelly appeared in a robe with towel-dried hair Gen left to get dressed for a party she'd heard about.

"Am I keeping you from the party?"

"No. If it's good she'll call. Otherwise Sunday is my day to catch up around here. And just sleep."

It was past 1:00 p.m. but she hadn't eaten so I scrambled three eggs and she had tamales with eggs and toast. "These are good. They look hard to make." I repeated the process which let her quietly eat while I rambled. Her shoulders slumped to the food. Perhaps it was last night's party. A tiny line fell like a hairline crack in glass from her eye. When not chewing, her lips were quiet, keeping unsaid words. I saw the same line and hold of my lips when I looked at the bathroom mirror. Married with child and unmarried with hope looked straight at each other.

"Jerry and I have become friends." The announcement stopped me.

"Friends?"

"Yes, friends. It started just because we'd see each other at the bar and since we knew each other we started talking. Sometimes about you and Maury."

"Oh?"

"Nothing much. Just how are you doing. About Jon, too, of course. He said he doesn't see Maury very often."

"That's true. He's off seeing him this afternoon."

"That's good. We'll get a laugh over that." The glow in her eyes, told me it was slightly more than friends. "Did you know he bought a little building? It's got some kind of repair business in it. He bought it as an investment."

"No. I didn't know."

"He's a good-looking man," Kelly's voice was soft.

"Yes, he is."

I couldn't stand the suspense, "So have you slept with him?"

"Like I said. We're friends. I'll let you know." I decided bringing up Renan would only be gossip that could backfire. A touchy-feely moment before marriage, perfume, installed patio lights and dancing after work didn't prove anything. Jerry needed someone and I wanted Kelly happy.

The next week before Jon and I left for LoBeth's Christmas cookie baking event Maury was working on a paper about indigenous people of the Southwestern U.S. for an anthropology class. "Did you know I'm considered indigenous? Whereas you and all pale skins are trespassers?"

"Yes, thank you. But weren't the Native Americans here first?"

"We were all Native Americans until the Spanish found us."

LoBeth greeted Jon and me at the door with, "Welcome to my home for a festival dedicated to a simple act of pure love."

"It's a sweet idea," she was making fun of the current LDS soundbite to its flock along the lines of doing a random act of kindness.

"Yes, if it didn't seem directed to control women's lives. Coming from the women makes it sound like a cross-stitch pattern. Couldn't they flatly tell men to do it, too? They're simple enough." She reached in the refrigerator for cold cookie dough ready to roll. She gave Jon, who stood on a chair, a piece of yellow playdoh but he started mixing it in the real dough. She gave him a chunk and he mixed the two together and made cookies with us.

"Why did we start making sugar cookies at Christmas? Why not fruit-cake or tamales?"

"Heritage my dear. You have Danish heritage."

"Sugar cookie heritage. That's substantial. At least you don't ask me to put burning candles in my hair."

"Well, sorrrry," Golden Bitch moved her rear end to synchronize with the rolling pin. "Your ancestors practiced beauty, delicacy and sweetness to survive the harshness of forbidding winters. What more can you ask of them?"

"Not to be killers of indigenous defenseless people who were generous of land and spirit."

"What and change world history? Not be daring adventurers? Forsake our own natures for a little world peace?" Her voice fell to regret, "As I've said, what should be done and what is done, are usually two different things."

"I remember you telling me a few years ago to ask about Grandpa Harold Bean Baker. So what about him?"

"He's a man," she cocked her head like a flirt and put her cigarette down on the counter across the kitchen, away from Jon. "Are you sure you want to hear about him before Christmas?"

"Did he do something lewd with an elf? Why would Christmas make a difference?"

"You have no sense of drama, darling daughter. I'm sure Maury would appreciate it if you developed one."

Secretly, I agreed but I focused on not letting my head nod a hundredth percent. "So what about your father? My grandfather?"

"What do you remember about him?" she was lifting cookies from waxed paper to cookie sheet. Jon put a finger through one for a perfect round hole. LoBeth took his hand and licked his finger of dough. Grandmas could be very kissy touchy with my boy.

"He would read to me, Dr. Seuss, stuff from a fairy tale book. When you went out at night he took me for ice cream. Grandpa was a nice man."

"Yes. He was a nice dad, too. He was sincerely sad when grandma died. It seemed like he turned into a rotting live thing ready to die the last few years. Though the man had failed. He had a mission from the day Grandma Jessie agreed to marry him until the day she died." I held Jon's hand to steady it as he threw red and green sparkles on the cookies. "Something ugly happens to the human spirit when it needs to prove hour after hour, day after day, year after year that it is acceptable. Grandpa was a handsome man. His eyes gleamed. His forehead was wide. His smile strong. Well, you've seen that photo, too, and I hope you keep it well for Jonathan to remember his pale side."

We silently worked. Even Jon tottered quietly on his chair. "I doubt he'd been a very good Episcopalian until Grandma Jessie couldn't be Mormon anymore. Suddenly he had to prove himself and the worth of all European religious history to keep his young bride happy when she was thrown from her family and told never to return." LoBeth took a long breath of cigarette.

"He had a terrible responsibility. Picture this." She put four fingers covered in sprinkles in a framed square. "Young virginal flower protected by four polygamous mothers, a father and a dozen older brothers comes from a prosperous respected family that own a furniture store and acres of peach orchards. They spent winters in a large three story Victorian house in the city and summers at the peach orchard in a house with a wrap around porch. That house still stands in Holladay. Did you know that?"

She named Brad's childhood neighborhood, a fifteen minute drive from the downtown Salt Lake Temple. "No."

"Well, neither did I until I was ten years older than you are now. Mother didn't like to talk about it. To continue the story. In the Gentile area of Salt Lake, on Third South, around Main and State Streets, there was a mercantile store with a reputation for carrying decadent laces and ribbons that were too bright and frivolous for the serious LDS good woman. But Grandma Jessie is another example of the pitfalls of desire and adventure. She didn't leave Denmark for Utah, but she thought she could sneak away from her comfortable secure home of prestige and entitlement and make one little visit to a store that sold pretty lace and ribbons.

"Wouldn't you know it? That fateful afternoon your grandpa was working the counter and lace and ribbons turned to puppy love. She didn't realize what was at stake for her, she only knew he was a charming and attentive young man who was more Germanic than Scandinavian so he would have been exotic.

"Observe how that runs in the family. Dane attracted to men of the cloth from the cowboy West, Scandinavian LDS attracted to Germanic Episcopalian, inbred Utahn attracted to New York poet, pale Anglo attracted to handsome Mexican." She shook her head. "We're not altogether smart but at least we go for the exotic. Perhaps, and I say this truthfully, Abby, perhaps if people had allowed this to play out the two would have parted ways before it went too far, but their flirty friendship was discovered and when they each stood accused by their own kind, they defended each other to the death of marriage."

"You don't think they loved each other?"

"I believe and it is only my imagination, that by the time they exchanged vows in the Episcopal church they both had to believe it was love. And as the five of us were born so did we."

"So how did Grandpa need to prove himself?"

"Do I have to spell everything out for you, Abby? She was disowned. Her parents and at least half her brothers and sisters never talked to her again. She was given up because she married outside the LDS faith. Your Grandma Jessie suffered deeply. But to answer what Grandpa needed to prove. He was a man with a conscience and he knew any love for him had taken her from her family and shown her very plainly that her family hated him, and respected their religion more than they cared for her. Grandma Jessie lived with an A on her chest like Hester in The Scarlet Letter but it was E for Episcopalian. No man can be worth that for long. A woman without her foot in the emotional ground of where she came from is always lost."

"Or a man."

"Or a man. And she cried a lot. She never truly stopped crying."

"The Mormons wouldn't do that now."

"Probably. But consequences don't disappear in other people's lives just because we change our mind after we've done something."

"So what put you in St. Patrick's for a wedding a thousand miles away from Utah when you expected me? Why didn't you stick to Mormons and Episcopalians?" The timing seemed right to get more of the story.

"Trying to breathe air. I only wanted to get out of here. Catholics had carved the earth from Rome to South Africa and through South America so they seemed historical beyond anything Salt Lake offered. New York was life and heartbeat. It called to my youth," and she snapped her fingers a few times with sugar flying off. "Besides, I was only a guest at that wedding. Only an observer."

"So tell me more about my father."

She sat on the breakfast bench beside Jon and looked at me. "I thought you'd never ask, Abby." I didn't say anything but I also sat down and faced her. Melting cookie dough, playdoh and sprinkles were spiking Jon's hair and running down his donut cheeks. "Why are you asking now?"

"It just seems like a Hallmark moment."

"That's not it. Why haven't you ever wanted to know more?"

"I don't know. Why haven't you ever told me about him?"

"Because I was afraid. Because I didn't know what to say. I was

112

responsible. You were born without half your history and it was because of me."

"Well, I was afraid, too. Afraid to ask about someone that important who didn't want to know about me. It seemed safer not to ask."

"I met him in a coffee house in a basement of an apartment building on 115th Street. A group from my office stopped in after more than one drink in a bar two blocks away. We were on our way home when we saw a flashing sign pointing down the stairs that said live poetry and coffee, and we wanted to laugh more. Anyone could walk on stage and say any stupid thing for applause. It was our way of saying, your parents are stupid but I understand you. Before we sat down I saw him up on stage. He was so goddamn handsome in that turtleneck and his lanky brown hair, just like yours. It swayed like a hip calling my name. He was standing under lights that looked like police were questioning him when I first heard him saying some inane thing about a train whistle sounding like a mother's screaming voice. All of us from the office where I worked thought it was brilliant that night." Jon was rubbing goo on LoBeth's sleeve but she didn't seem to care.

"When he finished he asked everyone to yell out where they came from so he could pick the strangest one. Utah won over Nova Scotia and Oregon. "When the house light turned on me he said, "Utah wins a drink with poet. Virgins must be rectified."

"I'm glad Jonathan doesn't understand all this."

"It's his heritage too. This child holds all world blood in him somewhere." She picked up the tray and put it in the oven

"Want to know more?"

"Yes, let's pull the baby tooth."

"Good, Abby. It is a baby tooth to not face your parents." She picked up the teapot, added water and put it on the stove to heat before sitting down. After she lit a cigarette, she sat away from Jon. "If we talk of this much longer I will need a scotch."

"I know where to find it."

"I started going to the coffeehouse, of course. Even wrote a few lines myself, but never showed them to anyone and finally ripped them up. I still have the lines your father wrote for me. 'Lilacs spill fragrant life fading in death before the purity of stamens calling to sex, calling to breath, screaming to exist.'" She was silent; her eyes closed.

"That was to you?"

"He named it, Ode to LoBeth." I silently agreed it was an odd to LoBeth.

"So glamorous and wonderful. He was the fantasy I hadn't had until he existed for me." Again we were quiet except for Jon and the whistle of teawater which LoBeth got up to prepare. Lipton. LoBeth poured scotch in hers and I silently vowed not to pass lilac history to the next generation. I'd rather he drink Lipton and scotch.

"We went on for six months, Abby. It was not a one night deal. But in the end I was pregnant and we looked at each other and discovered two frightened people. The veneer of New York fell away. I was from Utah and he was from Indianapolis. We had made a baby and didn't know what to do. He didn't go to the St. Patrick's wedding. It was for my boss and he wasn't invited. I was alone to think of you." She poured more scotch in the tea. The oven timer went off and I checked cookies. One more minute.

"To make a horrible story short, I decided in St. Patrick's to give him freedom to make a choice. His reaction would determine the future. I believed we could marry but I didn't know what he thought." My hands needed to be busy so I picked up Jon who was unhappily squirming from dried sugar on his cheeks, a dirty diaper, thirst and a need for better food. I kissed and snuggled him tightly, gave him milk and banana and hoped mother love would erase the words from his ears of the story being told, but I needed to listen.

"The next day I called him and said I loved him and would do what he wanted for us, but one hundred dollars could change things. I never said abortion. I just gave him a choice of the two of us or one hundred dollars." For the first time I realized it hadn't been only me the man hadn't wanted. It was also my mother.

"By noon the next day his friend brought the money in an envelope while I worked at my reception desk. I used it to come home. Caught a late night bus and landed in Salt Lake three days later at the Greyhound Bus Station on the southwest corner of Second South and West Temple at 8:03 a.m. I waited until 9:00 to call home."

Jerry was at the apartment when I got home. My return seemed to irritate him and he left. Maury immediately began talking.

"Jerry's ticked at Brad."

114

"Why?" I was listless. My family could be kicked out of religions, banished from families and take money to leave town while expecting illegitimate children and his family would trump it.

"He thinks Brad's closing in on Renan. When he took them a Christmas wreath he told Jerry not to give her presents again."

"Oh." He took the sleeping Jon from my arms and put him to bed and I offered cookies he turned down. Maury went to bed, perhaps expecting I would follow. Instead I went to the kitchen, poured room temperature wine we had opened two weeks ago with a spaghetti dinner and watched the stars fall across the sky.

The first week of January I still hadn't told Maury LoBeth's story. My conception felt like a brick on my heart and belly. I'd always suspected something close to what she told me but innocence kept it away. Besides, it was a boring typical white story.

————

The next Sunday was Rose's second birthday and everyone was expected. Brad's family of three and Bishop Erickson and his wife were also invited, making over forty people. Sunday dinners were beginning to rotate to Renan's and Tia Manuela's to give Chepita a break. It would be another six months before I heard the reason was because Juan was getting tired of his house being overtaken and he wanted some peace. He was agreeing with God to get older which thrilled Chepita because he had not had a conversation with God since the move to Salt Lake eighteen years ago.

I walked in holding my assignment of salad, not a bestseller. Through the wood railing of the split level brick rambler I saw half a dozen children walking around and touching the birthday piñata of Kermit the Frog made by Willie and Jorge. Maury told me on the way to the party that Willie and Jorge were Salt Lake renowned for their traditional piñatas shaped as a star to lead the three Kings to the manger. Only in recent years had they become dissolute enough to do Kermit.

Bonnie Evans walked in behind me carrying a pan of chicken. Beside her were Brad's father, Marlon, and his sister, Sandy. They looked like the three spirits of Disdain, Curiosity and Conceit. Sir Brad walked to his mother, quickly kissed her on the cheek and took the chicken before leading us through the crowd. Crystal ran to Bonnie's side.

Pedro was in a chair with his head bent, playing a game with Tiffany and Maria Elena. We had not talked again of watching Brad and until I saw Pedro I had forgotten. At the dinner table, Bonnie was on my right and Jon on my left. "Great chicken, Bonnie."

"Yes, Mom always makes great chicken," Sandy was on Bonnie's other side. She wore a dark smooth knit that looked like an expensive book jacket for a Bible.

"Thank you." Bonnie's cooking had been acknowledged before.

"Quite a crowd isn't it?" Maybe it was just the number of people that seemed to keep Bonnie's eyes wide and watching.

Her eyes followed Tomas to the kitchen. "Isn't he the one who was called Oil Boy?"

"Yes."

"How in the world did that ever start?" I told her what I'd been told and at the end she shook her head. "Children." She seemed to empathize with all parents.

"Yes. You had good ones. I like Brad."

She turned and for the first time, looked at me. "Yes, Bradley still is a child."

I was startled to silence and stopped chewing while she continued. "It's way beyond time to leave that dead-end job, go back to school and finish his degree. He's got Crystal to consider."

"Going back to school is hard."

"Yes, it is. And not going is harder. Marlon wouldn't have finished without me and Renan should want that for Bradley." Both of us turned to Renan who was at the next table with Brad, Rose, her parents, Tomas and Pedro. Her eyes were luminous and soft as she looked at those she loved.

"Well, he seems to be doing great as it is. This is a nice house and even the new baby will have its own room."

"It's a beginning house. A starter. Rose will need to start school in a better neighborhood."

"How is Crystal's school?"

"Crystal goes to school by me. Brad and I take turns taking her and picking her up when Crystal's mother is too drunk or strung out."

"Doesn't she also work?" Renan said she wasn't as bad as her reputation.

"She does nails. Is that work?"

I stopped talking and so did Bonnie. As I took dishes to the kitchen I passed Marlon sitting and smiling, at ease with a group of guys, including Maury as they watched football on tv. Carrie cut my walk off and stood in front of the men, "You'll need to make some space. Everybody move. The piñata's coming."

"But it's not half-time," one of them dared.

"It's half-time for the party," she answered and Pedro turned off the tv when Brad brought Kermit the Frog dangling on the rope from the stiff stick he held. Furniture was moved to the side, lamps were put on the floor and Blooper was gently blindfolded. His cowlick stood at attention and his white shirt hung out one side. Fair weather birthdays held out doors gave children more space but also increased the torment adults could make them suffer as the piñata was danced around their stick, close enough to feel and never easy to hit. Jorge held Kermit through a full round of all the children before letting steady battering take a leg, arm, nose and finally a good swat from ten year old Armando. Candy and party favors spilled out to the diving children who were accustomed to rough play Grandma Jessie would have mistaken for family violence.

Jon was in the fray, wildly laughing and grabbing candy from the floor and other children's hands. When Pedro asked who was going to share with him all the girls and Blooper went to him. He compared and inventoried candy with them like it was Halloween booty until everyone else had straightened furniture and lamps and turned tv back on.

"How's su madre, Abby?" When I returned to the kitchen, my mother-in-law's question was soft. She seldom required my attention and her gentleness was so different from LoBeth's mighty presence that I often overlooked her. I was gathering forks and napkins for the birthday cake table.

"She's fine. She gets after me if I don't take good care of Maury or Jon." Chepita smiled at my lie.

"Si, that is women's work."

On my way through, again carrying napkins and plastic forks, the tv was on a news report. The January 15, 1991 date for Iraq to be out of Kuwait was a week away. Again tv was turned off. Rose was ready for presents.

She was a budding princess sitting on her mother's lap while every-one sang the Mexican birthday song, Las Mañanitas, with the music of

Vicente Fernandez. Dark flowing hair and lips like opened petals were the gifts of her mother. Hazel eyes and a carved face of angles and strength were gifts of her father. Small, dainty and with the brightness of being where she knew she was loved, she moved quickly and darting, flirting and as unselfconscious as a butterfly in a field of dripping nectar. Clapping and laughing with her, all the adults and children watched Rose's second birthday as she discovered the unexpected joy of a present in every wrapped box.

Bishop Erickson and his wife, Anita, were to my side. "Isn't she a beautiful child?" He leaned in my direction.

"Yes." It was the only answer. I wondered what it would be like to always be seen as beautiful. She was a child born on the same day as Elvis Presley and David Bowie. Rose Graciela Madrugada Evans would hold her own.

"I never had a birthday party like the children in your family," I said to Maury on the way home.

"Pretend Jon's birthdays are for you, too." His first birthday had been like that, with thirty-five people stuffed in our two bedroom apartment. Half a dozen trucks, three ball games and four toddler outfits made our apartment feel like a store.

"No, that's okay. I don't need it myself. It's just so big. The kids must miss them when they stop."

"They stop after the eighth birthday and everyone understands that."

"Still, they must miss the attention."

"Their own smaller families can do something."

"But you don't do anything for adults."

"I've learned from you it doesn't have to be that way. Thanks for the birthday cake." I had sung Happy Birthday a cappella with Maury holding his ears and pretending it hurt, but I could tell he felt very special.

The Tamayo print with its angel holding an urgent message was ignored when we lived in the apartment. Still in its frame, it faced the wall in our bedroom closet with shoes propping it up. Arias households all appeared to be simply and naturally living normal lives. Juan's held the familiar routines of men being cared for by a content woman. Renan's family circulated in fire and life, held by passionate love. Maury's small household was building its pattern of quiet love and easy deep friendship. We had talked about another baby. Maury hadn't any concept of the only child, but he didn't want one while he was in school.

The other side of me was LoBeth who seemed at peace if not joyous, but she did not complain. For the first time in years she visited Lee in Phoenix during a three day holiday and enjoyed it. Another time she had lunch with Marjorie and surprisingly reported they laughed over chocolate desserts. Kelly wanted Jerry but he was as elusive with her as anyone until May when she called to say they were officially dating.

"So have you slept with him?"

"We didn't do much sleeping Abby. That would interrupt things."

Daniel Juan Evans was born thirty months after his sister on July 15, 1991. Curls, the color of strong coffee with flashing Mexican sunshine through it, cradled his alert bright face. The smooth saddle brown of his skin followed his mother's history. From the first day he followed movement and seemed to sense the world as a surrounding symphony.

Brad was ecstatic. "Two beautiful girls and now a boy. Everything is wonderful." He had his best sales month in history and bought Renan a mother's necklace with the birthstones of a small diamond to represent Crystal above a garnet and ruby of equal size. She wore it at Daniel's blessing.

The ceremony was at Cisneros Ward during regular Sunday church services. Maury and I wore scratchy dressy clothes Jon's first visit to a church. Catholic Tia Manuela sat beside Chepita who was by Renan and Daniel. Rose sat between her parents. By Brad was Bonnie, Crystal, Marlon and Sandy. I waved at Yasmina, Ernesto and Carrie with her family.

Little Daniel cuddled with his mother while his father stood tall. Brother Erickson welcomed Daniel Juan Evans to God and the LDS church, where he joined his parents, sisters and grandparents. Juan's absence was expected, but I wondered why Pedro and Tomas had not come.

When it was over we stood in the foyer waiting for everyone before heading to a buffet restaurant. Chepita walked directly to Maury, her brows knit. "Mauricio, mi hijo, I need to tell you bad news. Dust's Mamá called last night. He died from a gun shot. A drug deal. Poor, poor Florina. Tomas wasn't home yet. We didn't sleep."

"Was Tomas with him?"

"No, no, Mother Mary, Church Fathers, no. He came in at 6:00. Torn clothes, drunk. He left poor Dust and Chucky moments before. Chucky's in jail."

Maury's eyes opened and he swayed but he said nothing.

At the buffet Maury ate little and Jon filled his plate with orange jello and chicken. Juan joined us to sit in a chair Chepita had saved. As soon as we got home we changed clothes and put Jon down for a nap. We sat in the living room. "Want to talk about Dust?"

"No."

"Why didn't your dad come to the blessing?"

He looked for the tv remote. "Dad's mad at God for a few things. He may be talking to him about age, but he won't give God the satisfaction of prayers or a church visit."

"Talk about conversations with God. Did I ever tell you LoBeth's story of church, poetry and one hundred dollars?" I told him the story as LoBeth told me, finishing with her return on a Greyhound bus.

He got out of his chair, walked to me on the couch and kissed me on the forehead. "Jon and I thank LoBeth." He turned on tv and I started a load of laundry.

Monday at 3:40 a.m. I thought the phone ring was my dream, but before the second ring I was in the kitchen where we kept the only phone. Great sobbing filled the apartment, shaking Maury out of bed. Before I finished saying, "Chepita," he took the phone from me. "Mamá?" His head began to go up and down as he paced while I heard Chepita's voice a mixture of crying, English and Spanish.

"I'll take care of it, Mamá, I'll take care of it," he said louder the second time and when she didn't quiet after the third time he hung up. Maury vibrated a readying stillness. "Tomas has been arrested and she wants me to go get him."

"Oh."

"She thinks it was drugs, but I'm going to find out. Get Jerry on the phone."

Again, all I said was, "Jerry," and Maury had the phone. Later I learned Juan was making his brothers see it. Pedro was with a woman and that left Jerry to help Maury.

7

I'll get through.

- Tomas 'Oil Boy' Arciniga Arias

LoBeth seldom called Wanlass, but when I became assistant manager in the spring of 1992, she decided I should have more liberties so I was paged to take her calls. Her liberty, my daughter duty.

"My retablo is ready. You need to stop by Brad's work and pick it up."

"I'll try and do it during lunch."

"Good. I can't wait. When you get it let me know and I'll come by," and she hung up to answer a call on the other line. During my break I called Brad and asked if I could come. He said yes and why don't we go for something to eat, too. My strawberry yogurt and ham sandwich would keep until tomorrow.

When I drove in the car lot to meet him he was talking with a thin male customer who was lovingly gazing at a dark red car with a shape suggesting speed and sex. The heavy, wet April spring snow of the night before had melted to fading white clumps of reflecting light holding the car in heaven's light. He waved, but returned to his customer, his pose suggesting he had all the time in the world to also lovingly gaze at the car. I went inside where it was warm and fingered brochures, wondering if there would be time to eat a hot meal or if I would be returning to yogurt and cold ham.

"Got him! He's bringing his wife tonight and I've already given him a deal he seems okay with on his old car." I hadn't heard him come up behind me. He was carrying a plastic bag with the retablo. I'd heard about it but not seen it. It looked to be the size of a baby blanket. "I'll put this in your car and we'll go in mine." I followed Brad and a whiff of alcohol passed my nose.

Without asking my preference, which was fine but still noted, we went to Wendy's. He paid for my lunch and we settled at a window by the sidewalk.

"I've already closed one sale today and he'll make two."

"I wish I could get as excited about eyeglasses."

"Think of it this way, Abby," and he put out his hand like a teacher calling a kid to class. "I don't sell cars. I sell speed, freedom, a man's sport coat to the world, sex. You sell beauty, better sight, personality. I know you know you sell personality."

"Yes, but it's usually nerdy personality."

"No it's not. Have you seen Renan take off her sunglasses? God, it's like she let the strap fall on a summer dress."

"Brad, I can't keep up with you and Renan. It's sex, sex, sex. Haven't you two been married long enough?"

Pride laughed. "You and Maury need to get school out of the way. When does he finish?" His kind eyes were puffy and tired.

"December, this year."

"Why don't you come this Friday for dinner? Leave Jon and pick him up Sunday."

"Renan might want to know about this." White girl politeness I knew.

"She'll be happy about it. She loves Jon and another kid keeps Rose and Daniel busy. But tell you what. We'll pretend we didn't have this conversation at all and she can call and invite you."

"I'll wait to hear. Now tell me about Crystal."

A crease fell from his eye and I was sorry I'd mentioned her. "Ten years old with an attitude. Ever since I objected to her being baptized Mormon she's been on my case. Every Saturday night she calls and asks if I'm going to church with her the next day."

Everyone had heard about the screaming fights between Crystal and Brad over her becoming LDS two years earlier. Brad started with persuasion that it was an adult decision to choose a religion and she should wait until she was old enough to vote. Crystal's response was in the meantime she might die and go to hell all because of him.

"You were raised LDS, Brad, why don't you want Crystal to be?"

"In our house religion was a freakin military. Mom was the general who made me go every week until I was too big to push out the door. Dad stayed a corporal. He drove us there, quietly sat and drove us home. Crystal is being raised LDS. She can make it official when she's older. And I've seen what it's done to Renan's family to be Catholic and LDS. But I'm okay with church now. We go sometimes, pay some tithing, starve ourselves on fast Sunday every month and sometimes we send the kids with Chepita or my Mom and have a Sunday service of our own."

"Maybe that's why Sunday school was invented." Since I couldn't keep up I could at least wish them well.

"I envy you, Abby. A nothing," he continued like I hadn't said anything. "What could be greater? Since God's supposed to like everyone, he has to take you anyway, doesn't he?"

I felt like a special nothing. "Maybe. Unless you believe I'm cast to hell as a non church member. I thought your church taught you guys are the only saved ones."

"They do, but the sales numbers don't add up. Doesn't make sense."

Now was as good as any time to ask a question I'd kept in isolation, hoping the answer wouldn't hurt. "Brad, years ago, why did you tell me about Erica?"

His tired handsome face softened from talk of religion to love. "You were being deceived, Abby. You needed to know the situation so you could decide with full knowledge whether to share or not." He leaned back in the chair, comfortable with his reasoning. "If you were dating other guys or stringing Maury along it might have been different, but we all knew you weren't. It wasn't fair." His eyes flashed and he looked harder. "Karla fucked every dick in town before I swore I wouldn't watch anybody else be that kind of sucker again."

"Every dick?" I rolled my eyes, trying to tease him.

"Not Maury's. She didn't know him. By the way, how was Brian's wedding last week?"

"Good. Shayla's parents bought everyone dinner."

"Now if we could get Jerry married."

Believing it was polite I asked Brad how his mother was as we said good-bye in the car lot.

"Part-time bitch; full-time mom, and still mine." A fair description of LoBeth, too, but I hoped I sounded more affectionate. It was curious. On the way back to Wanlass I wondered why it seemed ninety-eight percent of every Anglo person I'd ever met had a similar mother sentiment and at least ninety-nine percent of every brown person I'd met never did.

Later that day LoBeth ran into Wanlass for the retablo. What Renan had spontaneously sewn to inspire and comfort Rose became a time consuming hobby. Her artistic wall hangings combining Catholic shrines and Mormon craft were becoming very popular personal histories. LoBeth was her first paying customer.

"Isn't it beautiful? I could just weep," I hadn't seen Missy Mommy for a while, but she stood before me, her long hair touched with white falling like an knurled tree trunk. "Look Abby, remember this dress I so loved when I could fit into it years ago?" She touched blue polyester. "And Mother's embroidered kitchen curtains I've stored for years? And the dress you wore to your junior high graduation? There's Jon's baby blanket when he visited me. And worn out dishtowels that were the first thing I bought when we moved into the house? They were the only little pretty thing I could afford. And here's the old blue ribbons the Open Heart Anguishers used for bookmarks so many years ago."

Considering it was all junk, Renan had pieced together a beautiful thing of some sort that was artful. Eclectic was a new word I'd learned when a new line of glasses arrived. It was eclectic. "It does look good. What are you going to do with it?"

"Hang it in my bedroom where I can see it before I close my eyes and as soon as I open them in the morning."

"Good lord, LoBeth, you are weeping."

"Here is my universe. The people of my life."

"Except for your father, sister, brothers and Maury."

"Mother's kitchen curtains represent all my family. She is the matriarch and well, Maury….I decided to leave him alone since he's yours." We paused, looking at the retablo. "Abby, what's happening to Oil Boy? How is he doing?"

"He joined the Army. Juan told him he had to work full-time, leave the house or join the Army. That's what he chose."

"He was lucky he didn't get jail time."

"Yes," He was lucky he'd only been charged with possession of the half ounce of marijuana he'd been found with at the drinking party held in Dust's memory. The law had been one sentence. Juan was another. He insisted Tomas stay away from the old neighborhood friends, which killed his social life. Tomas Arias, now twenty-two, was leaving in a month for nine weeks of basic training. The time had come for Chepita's baby to move in the world.

Everyone was surprised how excited and prepared he was getting as the time came closer. It was seeing the quiet kid in class, who never tried to do anything, become the brightest student who only needed the right inspiration. He began a diet that drove Chepita crazy with calorie counting and fat content. Chepita and I were drying dishes when Tomas walked by, "That was great Mom, but you've got to cut down on the lard in the beans, it's not good for you or Dad."

She didn't say anything until he was out the door and on his way to meet Jerry at the health club. They were going to grow abs together and compare heartbeats. "Food is to be enjoyed as God's blessing, not turned into pennies to count for the mortgage." She put her hands on her full hips and watched him walk through the backyard to the driveway. "Whose food does he think put the handsome in those eyes, Little Debby?"

Renan called that night saying Brad had a great idea for the weekend. Sometimes her voice irritated me. It was so genuine, full-measured and sultry that my Utah girl niceness was hardening taffy next to warm dark chocolate. I hung up the phone feeling like a two year old who disliked an indulgent older sister because her goodness laid bare my flaws. What's more, pioneer stoicism and western big sky independence felt challenged by south of the border free-flowing good will, generosity and sisterhood.

Maury's reaction to the invitation was a wrinkled brow and five seconds of silence while he considered his disrupted schedule.

"We'll keep Saturday normal, Maury. I need to work until 6:00. All we'll do is go to a movie and out for a cheap dinner. How's that?" Relieved I wasn't pretending a honeymoon, he agreed. While I secretly shopped for a nightgown I hoped would please Maury and not make Jon curious when he saw it, I promised myself not to make a big deal out of the weekend.

Sex was a playing card that needed strategy in dealing before marriage, but now it was a card I was unwilling to trade. It was enjoyable on a date but so were the movies and conversation over coffee or beer, and I was in

125

control of if, when and who. A slowly moving axis was changing how sex felt in my bones. It was beginning to ooze through muscles and breathe out skin. It was beginning to own me.

On Friday, before Jon was out of his coat he ran to Renan for a full four-arm nuzzling hello. Rose greeted all of us and Daniel squealed. Travis and Mistie waved from the downstairs family room. Sir Brad brought Maury and me beers.

"That's the first pair of glasses I've liked on you, Abby. What are they called?" Brad asked. No one in this family minced words. It might be nice once in a while.

"Martini." They were a slim frame with a slight uplift and sparkles along the arms.

"They do have a more glamorous look." Renan liked them.

"She wore them just to get me tonight." Maury was getting into the spirit.

"If she wanted, she could have you every night," Brad said. "Come see the guns Dad gave me."

Travis was the first one up, "He gave you guns? Really? I didn't think he'd ever part with them."

All adults followed Brad to their bedroom where he opened the closet door and reached to a far corner along a top shelf. "He gave it to me last week so I've still got to get a safe but Rose doesn't know I have it." When he lifted the handgun down he held it with both hands on the handle like he was holding a baby chick, lifted his arms straight and looked forward to aim out the window. "It's not loaded. I don't have any bullets." He placed it on the deep green bedspread and it was ready to be photographed.

"It's a Colt 22 Woodsman, made about forty years ago. This is the first gun my Dad let me use. I think I'll take up target shooting again."

"I'll go with you. Remember when we'd go up Butterfield Canyon and shoot? I thought your dad was Wyatt Earp." Travis' voice bounced.

"Brad's dad has quite a gun collection." Renan's voice was flat.

"Here, Maury, hold it."

Maury took it like he was figuring out how to hold a girl to dance for the first time. "It's heavy, but not as heavy as your hunting rifle." He twisted it around in his hand for a minute before giving it to me. I took it with both hands, held it without knowing what to do and handed it back to Brad.

"This Colt is a friend who sits through a night with you. Rock real." he turned to put it back in hiding. "Reminds me of being a kid having this around. Dad would take Travis and me target shooting out west where homes are now. We got more than one Stop sign, but we did most of our practice at the gun club on Wasatch Boulevard. It was close to home."

"Did Sandy go?" I was curious.

"No. Mom wouldn't let her. Said she wasn't raising Annie Oakley." He turned abruptly back to the closet and reached to the shelf again.

"I think Sandy would have turned into Clyde's Bonnie if she'd had a chance." Mistie hit Travis on the arm for his comment.

"Maybe that's why Mom wouldn't let her," Brad's voice was serious. "Here, Maury, a little history." A long skinny rifle with hammered nicks and scratches that looked thrown and hit like LoBeth's bakeware from the 60's, was put on the bed. "This Winchester 1866 was probably owned by an Indian or it could have been used to kick Maximilian's French butt out of Mexico. Juarez bought them. This rifle changed history."

"Brad's Dad has a real collection." Renan repeated, standing by the door.

"Sure does. He still has my old Winchester 22 for deer hunting, some 1873's, even an old 1885 single shot and Henry first repeater that are worth something. Some Brownings. Now there's a Utah gun. And some handguns. A few others, too." He stopped talking when the air around him felt heavy with everyone else's silence. "But, that's all history now. I don't buy guns. Still like to go hunting with my dad, but no one likes the meat around here." We nodded. We ate some of the meat he had given us, but they weren't our favorite meals and the last two pounds of hamburger were thrown out.

Between the clack of Jon and Rose's forks and pounds of sippy cups, to the tune of Daniel's coos from the carryall, and Janna and Jason's occasional calls from the family room, dinner conversation jolted. We talked about Madonna's Sex Book that was coming out, if Excel was going to make it in the computer world, or something else would take its place, Travis' work of predicting inventory and sales to keep cash flow high for the lumber company where he worked, and Juan's new hobby of spending hours water coloring and pencil drawing with the grandkids, nieces and nephews. There was a sentence about the starvation and growing human rights crises growing in Somalia.

Brad, Maury and Travis took the kids to the tv room when it was time for clean-up. Mistie and I looked busy but mostly watched Renan move about her kitchen. Mistie explained a school car pool arrangement like it had the value of stock certificates. Her job was the children and the biggest one of all, she said, was Travis. We laughed but I didn't get the joke. I never felt like I was taking care of a man-child. I looked at Renan and a question moved to consciousness. Why did Maury run from connections of his boyhood? Where had his childhood gone? Why didn't he ever recall a memory like Brad did with his father and hunting or I did with LoBeth and the Open Heart Anguishers?

There was also a moment spent envying Renan's dishwasher. I envied the way her hair dripped in curls from the careless ponytail she wore. I envied LoBeth's excitement of Renan's artistic ability on her retablos.

"So how is life treating you, Abby?" she interrupted my thoughts as she bent into the dishwasher.

"Okay," I cleared my throat. "I'm an assistant manager for Wanlass another six months and then I'll be ready for my own store. How's your work?"

"Same as usual. Another computer change taking place and we have to relearn a new system but it's supposed to be better. Nolan promised me a promotion next year, but it won't go far. He's moved others up and out faster and I know my work's as good."

"Maybe he just wants you close," It was a joke that applied to other men but work was supposed to be fair and equitable.

"He does and he's said so, but I told him I need my career to move. Want a beer?" She looked at us.

"But he can't do that. Wanlass managers couldn't get away with saying that." She handed me the can and I poured it in a glass.

"Men. Sometimes I think they believe they can say anything when just women are around."

"I agree," Mistie said.

"So would LoBeth."

Renan brightened. "How did she like the retablo?"

"She loved it. You're a star daughter," jealousy was behind the words so I veered away. At least I was that conscious. "You really are talented Renan." A slight compliment might redeem me.

"I'm making one for Yasmina now. She brought me a sack full of stuff yesterday. It will be a fun puzzle." Her eyes unfocused, "If I had my dream I would open a fabric store. Beautiful materials would be piled to the ceiling and I would show people how to make their own."

"Maybe you should do that. Leave Nolan and start a company," suggested Mistie.

Renan moved toward whispering, "I want to. I want to, but I can't yet. I've been saving whatever I can squeeze in a box upstairs and someday I will.

"Good Renan. We'll both be store managers."

"Or maybe," and she shone like a small sun, "you can manage it and I'll buy and sell fabric and show people how to love it."

We laughed in the joy of her enthusiasm. She touched our arms and made us look at her, "Don't tell anyone I'm saving the money. It's a secret."

Before going home I went to the bathroom. The guest bathroom was midnight blue, peach and stark surprising red hot pink. Textured peach wallpaper was the background for joyous pink towels, soap, lotion container and rug. She had made the midnight blue velvet shower curtain and window dressing. As I dried my hands I saw the two bottles of *Beautiful* on the toilet back. One was open; one was not. Brad was her husband. Where did Jerry, Nolan and men like Blue-plaid guy fit in a woman's life who was beautiful and loved in a way I didn't understand?

Jon's eyes questioned when Maury and I said goodnight as he was in Renan's arms, but we heard only one short wail. The comfort of his aunt, her family and house were soothingly familiar and Renan knew how to keep male attention.

Saturday I woke to a house without baby breaths. I hadn't realized Jon's breathing was a refrigerator hum I heard while sleeping. As I lay there, listening to Maury's gentle breaths I also remembered I was in the cheap new nightgown that was slightly scratchy and I wanted to fix Maury breakfast in bed, and lastly I remembered it had been since Tuesday that I had taken birth control pills. Startled, I jumped from bed, moving Maury.

"Why so fast?" he asked from half sleep.

"I'll be back," and I went to check the pills. Four days still there. I took one, went to the bathroom, threw water on my face, brushed my hair and teeth, and went back to bed. I should be okay but a woman at work who had been married only three months said she missed five days and wham! Cumulative fell like tinker toys.

"What was that all about, Abby Sabby?" He pulled me closer.

"Oh, nothing. I just woke up fast."

Maury surprised both of us by suggesting a restaurant that night we'd never been in and didn't to cater to children. I felt a little naked. I'd left my identity in Renan's arms. Motherhood was consuming and without its little head that needed brushing and its little cotton ball butt that needed cleaning hanging on my hip, I felt undressed. I will use that as an excuse, along with the wine at dinner. I chatted like a familiar loving girlfriend with a thousand interesting things to say who was an easy yes at the end of the night. We had a great weekend.

On the way to pick up Jon on Sunday Maury said he had talked to Jerry last week. "He's seeing more of Kelly now."

"Oh?" A week ago when I talked with Kelly she was coy as she cut my hair.

Maury continued, "Jerry called when you were in the shower this morning and said she was moving in today."

"She's moved in his place?" That I did not know. It was only a month since Brian's wedding.

"He asked if you still made chili and they'd come over next weekend," he winked, "I didn't tell him LoBeth made chili and you carried it in mason jars."

"I could try."

"I'll call Jerry and tell them to come over Friday."

When I called to verify the news Gen was irritated, "Whose going to pay half the rent?"

Kelly called me at Wanlass the next day, "You won't believe it, Abby."

"I might."

"Jerry and I are living together." Her voice sounded like a cassette tape gaining speed. I wanted to feel excited for her but I only felt dread.

The minute I looked at Kelly and Jerry when they walked in the living room, I saw Kelly radiated gooey love happiness and Jerry was his gracious friendly self. His job with a title and the need for clean clothes had strengthened the air around him to a confident denseness. His shirt was pressed. His hair was Kelly's perfect cut. As soon as beers were poured all around I went to the kitchen and Kelly and Jon followed.

"We'll watch and help where we can," she beamed like a six year old and picked up Jon to be warm in her light. Jon was moving in on two and a half years and was heavy enough that Kelly moved to a chair and cuddled him in her lap. That boy of mine was a sure magnet for female affection and he never backed away from any of us.

"Okay, so what's going on with you two?"

"We started seeing each other every day. Last week we were together from Friday night until Sunday afternoon and he suggested I just stay. So it's going pretty good."

"Is it serious or just fun?"

"Both, both, both. I'm crazy over him, but that's where it is. Nothing more yet."

"I've never seen Jerry settle with one girl. If he's seeing you that much it says something."

Confusion and sadness mixed above the chili as Kelly talked about the Friday date that turned into housing arrangements. Dinner at an Italian restaurant with real tablecloths turned into a weekend of late nights and washing breakfast dishes. When she went on about his hair being so dark it reminded her of caramel and chocolate, and he was affectionate and sexy and romantic and strong and vulnerable I had to interrupt to say dinner was ready. It was before I was about to burst into tears and the glass shards inside were going to melt and burn suspicious edges.

"Isn't she cute as candy?" Jerry motioned to Kelly as we sat down, his eyes a liquid river of beer and sincerity.

"Candy?" Jon inquired.

"After dinner, Jon. Everyone, here's the ladle. Just take what you want." Maury had assured me the chili was as good as LoBeth's and I made him eat a cupful before they came to prove it. He nodded the whole time and made mmmm sounds. I watched now as he filled his bowl to know he wasn't lying. He caught me watching, smiled and showed his full bowl before picking up his fork. Inside glass had melted enough to let my heart throb for Maury. Dear Maury, ever so sweet and dearly teasing. Never trying to use me for something I was not. I loved Maury more than I could say. More than I was willing to feel.

"Yes, she is Jerry, but if Kelly's candy, I'd better say Abby Sabby is something good. Let's see, how about beer or tamales or Wheaties?"

I knew he was being conversational, teasing Jerry and even declaring I was worth saying a kind word about, but his comparisons were fine lace to burlap. Worse, I knew both Kelly and I were dimmer lights to another. I smiled and pressed in best LoBeth fashion to stop the flow of glass and bring order to my insides.

"If I'm beer and Kelly's candy, what's LoBeth and Renan?"

"Your mother is steel, a fine sword meant only for an Aztec warrior," Jerry hadn't taken a moment.

"Or a hard-wired Microsoft computer, stronger and smarter than any of the competition," Maury and Jerry laughed in a private joke. "And, Renan, well, my sister is a shrine, a retablo just like she makes."

"That's a good description," I wanted more information so I held the talking door open and noticed Kelly who was more interested in feeding Jon a bean.

"Renan is an orchid. Delicate and in a jungle." Kelly nodded in agreement.

Maury hadn't heard the details of Dust Valadez's funeral now several months in the past so he asked Jerry about it.

"His mother threw herself on the coffin."

Maury closed his eyes for a second and then talked, "She was a nice lady. I used to go to Dust's house after school. She always had pozole on the stove."

"Hermie and Irene had a huge fight at the dinner after. They were both drunk when I left. I hear they're separated."

They changed the subject. I didn't understand but I was no longer surprised by the newspaper headline stories in Maury's past. Years ago when LoBeth got a speeding ticket, it seemed a major law was broken.

When they left, I pretended interest in finishing up the kitchen mess and Maury was happy enough to fall to slumber without me. I dumped the last half of my beer down the sink and made ice water before sitting on the living room couch in the dark.

I was afraid. It had only been a week since four days were missed on the pill, but I had a feeling as sure as knowing when I needed to pee. My body was re-arranging itself to accommodate new life. Maury might be impressed with the technology of computers but I was a captive to a computer of semen and egg command that made babies. He might not be so impressed with me.

When I told him he wilted down to sit on the couch. "I better not go for a doctorate if this is what you do every time I graduate," he was watching me like a banana he'd just peeled to see where the bruises were. Thelonious Monk was playing in the background. Spring sun hit my face through the curtains so I moved to the shadow of the living room. A book on algorithms and data structures was on the floor where he had placed it after my announcement.

"I didn't do it alone." I felt guilty and didn't look him in the eye. We were in the living room after Jon was asleep.

"I married you because you were different. Not from where I came."

"You're confusing skin color with just being female."

He patted the seat next to him. I sat down and we stared straight ahead. He sighed, "We'll be fine, I know."

On a late May day when standing too close to a heavy hanging lilac bush could fill your lungs like a vacuum bag, Tomas left for basic training. Bishop Erickson, Jerry, Tomas' two girlfriends and twenty relatives walked down Terminal C to say good-bye at gate thirty-four. He was hugged by the women, shook hands with the men and giggled over by the children. Chepita stood like a five foot water statue with tears on her cheeks as time closed in. When the waiting area was quiet because most of the passengers were seated on the plane, Bishop Erickson gave a prayer. Pedro, Maury, and finally, Juan stood their turn to tightly hug their little brother and youngest son. Juggling a duffle bag tucked with tortillas, Tomas stooped to kiss his mother before walking quickly away.

Everyone silently stepped to the window and waited ten minutes to watch the plane holding three hundred people back away. Children began to talk and ask for cookies and grapes tucked in pockets and purses, but not one of the adults talked as we started to return through the terminal.

Jon was in Juan's arms and Maury walked with his mother and Bishop Erickson. Pedro and Jerry came beside me. "Brad had a good sales month I hear," Pedro looked straight and then glanced at Brad, about fifteen feet back.

"Uh, yes," and then I realized he was waiting. "I think Brad is okay." He fell back to take Jon from Juan's arms. Jerry still walked beside me. He whispered before we parted to different cars. "How can something so good for Tomas, feel so bad for us?"

I told Maury what Jerry said when we were driving home. He blinked his eyes that looked heavy, "We don't like to see family go."

"But Maury, it's only basic training."

"It doesn't feel good. Parts get taken away."

A tone of experience shadowed his words and I wanted to ask more but his near tears kept me from pressing a very tender spot. I treated the tears like floodwater to be kept away so Maury and I wouldn't be engulfed. Maybe I should have treated it like drenching spring showers breaking open hard seeds after winter to bring flowers.

Summer slipped into a pleasant routine allowing me to not think about where I was headed. Life was tasks and duties filling requirements. Take care of Maury, Jon, the apartment, go to work, don't think too much about the swelling belly. Maury appeared happy another baby was on the way. Jon needed more people than his mother had as a child, he said in perfectly reasonable tones I was supposed to understand as he outlined my flawed childhood. And I did. I wanted another baby for me as much as for Jon. I wanted a fuller table at dinner time. I wanted to know what family felt like. My only disappointment was the baby would come home to a crowded apartment, not a house with an attached garage, rose garden and wallpaper like Renan's two children.

"A house is on your horizon, Abby," LoBeth said when I visited on my way home from work. We were having a cup of herbal tea. "If Maury won't buy one, you will always have this one."

"LoBeth, this is your house and you will live in it forever."

"Yes, until I'm finished watching life's parade, and isn't it getting more interesting?"

"What do you mean?"

"Look at little Utah. This backwater can lead the country in surprising ways. We may be in the top three states for suicides, and wife killings, but how many states have a female lieutenant governor, attorney general and mayor of the capital city all at the same time?"

"So now women are equal opportunity political failures."

"Olene, Jan and DeeDee won't fail me. And neither will you. Have a girl this time."

"Hear that kid?" I patted my belly. "Penis to pussy or no Grandma LoBeth for you."

LoBeth stepped back. "I hope you don't talk like that in public, Abby." She paused staring at me, "Besides, if you'd gone to college you'd know it's pussy to penis."

I was surprised to silence. I had shocked LoBeth. What was I turning into? I was crabbier lately but I thought it was only being tired and feeling ugly and stupid. The day before I bought a larger size pair of pants than I had worn when I was pregnant with Jon and I was putting a pair I'd outgrown in a drawer, when I saw the mirror Renan had given me that first Christmas.

I lifted it like I was holding my second born for the first time. Sitting on the floor, I heard the tv in the other room where Maury was reading and Jon was scribbling in a coloring book. Maybe this was a magical mirror I held. Bathroom mirrors were business, used to make sure hair didn't stand out and eyebrows were plucked. Car mirrors were for driving and to make sure nothing was dripping from a nose. Mirrors in building lobbies were to be walked by very quickly. Perhaps this mirror held a bit of Renan's feminine beauty, assurance and easy charm that could be mine in the smallest way since she had given it to me. Before opening it I used my fingers to brush my hair, tilted my head and closed my eyes as I squeezed the latch.

I looked at the same eyes, nose, lips and hair as in the bathroom and car mirrors but I had to hold it away to see my whole face. In the darkened room, it looked slim, soft, not objectionable or alluring. Just the same simple and unmemorable face I'd always had. For the first time I truly consciously regretted my female normalness of modesty and attempted goodness I had strived to achieve like a good grade in school.

I confided in Kelly. She called to see if there was anything she and Jerry could bring when they came to visit Friday. I would be working late, so I suggested a pizza. I'd have a salad. Maury was in the bedroom studying and Jon was asleep while we talked. I lowered my voice and turned my head in guilt. "Kelly, have you ever felt beautiful?"

"Beautiful?"

Of course she had. Every female in the world had but me. "I mean, I know you are, but what does feeling beautiful mean?"

"Beautiful." She paused and seemed to consider so I gave her time. "My dad always said I was beautiful."

"Anyone else?"

She seemed not to hear me. "But he doesn't count." Yes, he does, I only thought.

"I felt beautiful on my twenty-first birthday when I went out with Dave. Remember him? He made me feel very special and I'll always remember that."

"Is that all?"

"Well, my life hasn't exactly been a beauty contest runway. When did you feel beautiful?"

"I haven't really. I've felt like I looked okay. Or that I was presentable enough to leave the house, but that's all."

"You were beautiful at your wedding. Really beautiful."

"Thanks." And we were silent for a few seconds.

"What's brought this on? Why are you asking?"

"Oh, I guess being pregnant makes me feel like an elephant," I inhaled for strength, "and being around Renan has made me think about it more."

"I know Jerry thinks she's beautiful. He's told me so."

"Everyone thinks she is. Does he tell you you're beautiful?"

"You know what he's said? He says my eyes are great. He'll put his hand on my cheek like he wants to touch something deep inside me. And he likes my boobs. He's said that."

Maybe I was nosy. I wasn't sure what I wanted to hear so I stopped talking but Kelly quietly continued. "I never thought I was beautiful, either. I wanted to be. I was okay and I liked it when my dad said I was beautiful even if I never believed him. But, you know, what's funny, Abby? When I'm with Jerry and he's smiling and happy to be with me and I can tell he is, well, I feel kind of beautiful."

It was a long time before I fell asleep that night as I lay in the dark staring at the ceiling while Maury softly slept. I wanted Maury. I wanted Jon and this new baby. My life was in good order even if it had been a long time since Maury had stared at my chest in awe. Beautiful never had been my self-description. Synonyms for that word had been vanity and self-absorption to keep it unwanted.

I needed the soulful gangly loose limbed man with the gentle sense of humor and quiet smile to tell me words that even on our nights of greatest passion I had never asked him to say and they had never tumbled from his heart in hope I would need them. The next Saturday I slow cooked a pot roast to be ready when I came home, stopped for fresh bakery rolls and bought olives for a salad. After Jon was put to bed at 8:00 I changed to a dress, combed my hair and added lipstick. When everything was ready, I lit the candles on the small kitchen table and called him from the living room where he was reading. When he saw the lit candles, cloth napkins we'd used twice since the wedding and me in a dress, he stopped like a cat suddenly circled by dogs.

"What's up, Abby?"

"Nothing."

He slid into his chair, unsure if he was in trouble or the center of a celebration. "Then what's this all about?"

"I want to have a nice dinner with you." LoBeth taught me liquor, meat and potatoes are male soul soothers. If you have questions or worries, use them as the intro. "I'm happy, Maury." He looked at me pleased, as though I'd told him he'd passed an English exam. "I love you, Maury and I'm very happy."

"I love you, too, Abby."

I put my fork down and looked at him. "Do you think I, I look okay?"

He was startled. A slow smile crossed his face and lightened shadows. "Of course I do Abby. I think you are very pretty. To me, you are always the prettiest."

We did have a nice dinner. It was very congenial between two people who genuinely like each other. It was how I'd imagined married life when I was twelve with security, peace, simplicity of feeling, loyalty.

I sent him from the kitchen after we finished, trying to make him feel special and unthreatened. He was asleep when I walked back to the living room. At first I wanted to shake him awake but I decided to attribute it to my improved cooking and success in making him comfortable. I watched his resting face, with his mouth slightly open and his loose arms that fell away from a book. Here was the life friend I'd always wanted. A man to encircle me with gentle love and security. I'd never asked for anything more. I didn't know what life could offer or whether all options of love were open to everybody or just a few with stronger passions or needs or understanding.

I looked at this man peaceful enough with me to sleep without guard. We watched and tended each other's days but I wondered if we tended each other's darkest needs. If he said the words that would piece me together, that would melt the glass shards once and for all, I wouldn't recognize them because I didn't know what they were. If I said the words he needed would it open his childhood?

It was over a month since I had seen Renan, when Chepita and Juan had the Labor Day picnic. Seven years had passed since I first attended an Arias family gathering. Life's merry-go-round had circled with the children behind us. We were always and only a movement ahead and they seemed to be waiting for us to step aside. With only LoBeth to watch my childhood, I hadn't realized how time moved people through bodies.

Tomas had changed from young teen to young man and now was finished with basic training. He was at Ft. Benning to train as an electrician. He'd watched Jerry's career and thought that would be a good life. Jon, Rose, Carrie's Sofia and her new baby brother, Marcus II, with the toddling Daniel, were among the youngest as they chased each other. Crystal, Tiffany, Morrison, Maria Elena, Roberta, Isaac and Blooper awkwardly stood about as children and teens. The merry-go-round had started with one set of faces and circled around with time well-marked on all of us.

Pedro had invited a woman, Irene Gonzalez, which was rare for the darkly private oldest brother who never truly left his parents. Her thin blonde hair was the color and texture of a Sears white lingerie half-slip and she had a look of half demon possession and half still in need of basic reading, writing and arithmetic skills. She was also ten years younger than Pedro, which made her three years younger than me. Brad, Maury, Renan and I were sitting at a table watching Pedro and Irene say hello to Chepita. Chepita's shoulders dropped when she recognized Irene. Maury and Brad laughed.

"Stop that, both of you," admonished Renan.

"Where's Hermie? I thought they were still married."

"No, divorcing," Renan said.

"She won't last long, mi mamá," said Maury quietly.

"How do you know?" I asked.

"She's just hungry for brown meat and Pedro doesn't mind being sampled."

"How do you know?" I repeated and Renan looked away.

"First, the only reason she's got Gonzalez for a last name is she married Hermie. She's been kicked out of the country," he turned to wink at me, "and she misses the flavor. So she's making an illegal run across the border."

"Mauricio!" Renan seemed to be protecting me.

"We'd all miss the flavor, wouldn't we, Abby?" Brad sunk into Renan's hair.

With a little borrowed LoBeth drama I slowly turned to Maury,

"Perhaps." No one said anything so I continued, "but why would he bring her here? He's had plenty of others without bringing them home."

"Blonde gringas are always a prize Abby Sabby. See how I must love you? Maybe you'll go blonde for me one day." He laughed again. "Look at her shape. She needs the food."

"Yes, it looks like mine before Jon."

"I knew you'd get some texture with a baby. After this second one, you should be Marilyn Monroe." I shot him a look. "Hey, I love you any way you are. Brown hair and all." He held his palms up and I let the conversation die with that and Brad's small laugh.

After chile verde, rice, beans, corn on the cob, barbequed chicken, salad, tortillas, jello and cake, Maury and Brad left to talk with other people. Carrie came to sit at the table under the tree with Renan and me where we were eating frosting off our cake for a direct sugar high right along with the kids.

"Hi, Carrie, how have you been?" Carrie and I were friendly when we saw each other, and never missed each other when we didn't.

"I'm going to have another baby, too, Abby. It's time for you to have a blonde one isn't it? Mine's not due until the end of March. Our babies will be close." Carrie's cross currents confused me. Starting with Rose we talked about how many babies were within a four year ring of time. When the children were named we were quiet, licking our fingers of frosting or drinking tea through noisy ice cubes.

"I wish I could quit my job. If we weren't so in debt I would." Renan was more resigned than I had ever heard her.

"In debt?" Carrie looked up.

"Oh, Abby, Carrie, please don't tell anyone," her eyes were a plea and her voice lowered. "I've got to tell someone. Please don't say anything to Maury or Marcus. Between the house payment, the payment for Brad's new SUV, childcare and the credit card and the bedroom furniture we shouldn't have bought, it's really tight. We can barely handle it and last month Brad had a terrible month and we lived on the credit card."

"Oh. That's too bad. Maury and I struggle, too. At Christmas we only paid some on all our utility bills. It took till May to catch up."

Her shoulders fell, "But you and Maury know you're working toward a better tomorrow. He'll graduate, get a great job and you'll get everything. I never needed as much as we have." She moved closer and her whispering was the clutching feel of fingers gripping a cliff as she looked from Carrie to me, "Something's pushing Brad and I don't know what. Lately he seems afraid like I've never seen him. Work's been tight but that doesn't explain it. Last week he shoved me."

I leaned back and Carrie's eyes widened as she put her drink down. Renan glanced around to make sure no one was listening. "He was so frustrated and I was just the nearest thing to shove, but it was so hard I fell back and got a bruise on my shoulder. Nothing bad, but he's never done that."

Renan sharply sat up, calling our attention to Brad heading our way. "Can I get anyone more cake? Do you need anything, Renan?" His smile was friendly and his body comfortable and relaxed.

"No, thanks, Brad, I'm fine," his wife answered. No, both Carrie and I said. He sat with his arm around Renan who looked confused and unsteady.

"I'll talk to you later, Renan. It's time to round up two Marcuses and Sofia for home. Bye, Abby."

"I'm not sure I want to go home yet, but I also don't want to help with dishes."

"This is your window of time, Abby. Use it well." Brad's eyes laughed.

"I think I'll look for Maury and see what he wants to do."

"He's in the living room in front of tv."

Hearing Brad and Renan were in debt and he had shoved her was a secret about the football star and prom queen. It could be kept quiet so they could privately improve their situation or they could be publicly embarrassed by gossip and innuendo. Responsibility twisted and enlarged to include their financial problems, Brad's frustrations, Renan's safety and my promise to keep a confidence. If she didn't want Maury to know about bills and money problems, I assumed she didn't want anyone to know about the shove. My knowledge of how brothers and sisters operated among themselves was vague. What they needed to know about each other and shouldn't know was a mystery.

Pedro's request to watch Brad resurfaced and felt ominous with a sliver of merit which made me feel I was unfaithful to family and suspicious of my own brother.

Maury hadn't hit me. I had wanted to slug him when I found him asleep after the pot roast dinner. Over the last days I had pieced together what I wanted to hear from him. Could he remember something in me that he truly loved, something he found exciting and bound him to me as no other female ever could? Even if Jon hadn't been born. Even if my income wasn't helping him go to school. Even if I wasn't convenient for sex. Even if I didn't wash that night's dishes or was angry with him while I picked up his dirty clothes pile. What Renan had told Carrie and me was as deep and private as this and I would never tell anyone of this ache. Renan's ache needed to be healed by Brad and mine needed to be healed by Maury. Not festered by infection and gossip.

I had my own worries. Maury's classes had started the week before and he announced on the third day he was part of a study group that was meeting Saturday afternoons so I needed to make arrangements for Jon.

"What kind of study group?"

"English Lit."

I nodded expecting more but when he didn't say anything it felt like me avoiding LoBeth's questions. I turned and looked at him. "How many are in the group?"

He turned away and shrugged. "I don't know yet. I will after the first meeting. Three, four." The words were straight. The delivery wasn't.

I called Renan at her office on Friday. It was timed to give a follow-up call of concern to find out if she wanted to talk but since four days had passed it couldn't be called an emergency, make a bigger deal than necessary, call.

"If you have any leftover big girl clothes from Daniel I might be interested."

"I've got a few, but you may not like them. Remember the fuschia blouse and the gold pants? Bright color isn't usually your choice."

"No, but if I wear something you've worn maybe I'll know what it feels like to be beautiful and proud of it."

"You're beautiful, Abby," her laugh was tender. "It's just a matter of belief."

"Yes, I believe your face is perfect and mine looks like God was in a hurry."

"I'll have them at Mamá's tomorrow night. I'm visiting her while Brad works."

When I stopped by for the clothes, Chepita, Juan, Jerry and Renan and the kids were finishing dinner. I imagined Kelly was still standing and cutting hair. Renan picked up a magazine about small business from the table. "Look at this Abby. Jerry found it for me. I've never heard of a demographic before." The headline was 'What's Your Demographic?' with six bulleted points below. Wanlass had customers when I started there but now they were a demographic.

"We've been told at Wanlass ours is high school education, twenty-five thousand to sixty thousand household income, believes tv news and has bad sight. Are you getting ready to start a store?"

"Not yet, but I'm trying to learn so I'll be ready. Nolan is impossible."

"What's he doing?"

"He follows me out of the office every night. Pretends it's just coincidence. For years he's suggested we go for a drink so we can discuss my career future. Things must be cool at home." Juan walked out of the room, Chepita shook her head and Jerry listened.

Brad's shove fell into history and I was glad the door closed. He was my friend. He'd sit beside me at family dinners and his friendly car sales self was a comfortable brother friend I'd never had. Pedro and Tomas always gave a polite hello and accepted me at family gatherings, but they kept family small talk and private jokes for Maury. Brad was my outsider friend who understood I felt accepted in this large overwhelming family that always gave me a welcome but like him, I saw the friendliness and acceptance in their eyes held a secret they would always keep and allegiances above me.

At 5:30 on the third Saturday in October, Maury called at work. "I'm going to be late. The study group is going for something to eat. Don't fix dinner for me."

I started to protest but stopped. It was just a study group. I could hear a web of interrupting voices in the background.

On December 4, President Bush agreed to send U.S. combat troops with the U.N. to Somalia. Twenty-five thousand troops were ordered to Somalia and the first marines landed on the beach on December 9. No one talked about how close Tomas might be.

Perhaps it was the emotion of the holiday season or worry over Tomas but Chepita called a few days later and asked me to stop by. My parka wouldn't cover my belly, my shoes felt tight, my hair was limp and my lips were winter chapped as I stood at the door. When she saw me her face got LoBeth's mother worry look that made me think I must look like an orphan cat with no hope of learning from mistakes. She looked like a welcome to Mexico travel brochure featuring a family hotel. Her hair was up and smooth, her eyes large and caring. The dress Renan had made softly held her.

"Would you like tea, Abby? I was about to make it." One look at me and mothers ran for teapots. "I see you're wearing Renan's blouse. Color is good for you."

"Sure. Tea sounds good." I felt out of place in Renan's blouse.

Three old photographs were on the kitchen table. "I want you to have these photos of Maury. I want to make sure your bebés have pictures of their father as a boy."

"Thank you, Chepita." I picked them up. The first was Maury, about age eight, standing in Sunday best with Emilio, Pedro and Renan. In the second, the year old Maury was standing on wobbly new lamb legs looking as directly and casually attentive as he did this morning before he left the house. Reflective lines of Jon were in his face. The third was a school class picture and Chepita leaned over to point Maury out, third from the left in the second row of Miss Hathaway's class.

"I haven't been very good at keeping a scrapbook but these might get me going."

"The photos are more important than the scrapbook. It's important you have them." She poured the water in a teapot and the oversize dress collar draped her arm and fell in even soft folds. "I gave Renan some last week. Oh, I had beautiful children, didn't I?" Her heart sounded near exploding.

"Yes, you did, Chepita. I think Maury is very soulful looking."

"Si, Abby. Not everyone understands that about him. I knew you did." I smiled, pleased I was observed positively.

"And I think Maury saw your beauty, too." Now I squirmed. She took a sip, watching, "Ah, Abby, don't be afraid of your beauty. It is a woman's gift to herself and to man."

"I've never thought I was beautiful," hoping to shift the focus I added, "Renan is beautiful."

"Yes, she is, and it is important for her to make it cut through dark. It is almost her mission, my poor hija. Yours is a very different kind."

Curious, I looked at her. "Yours joins light from different places, uniting new peoples and friends. You should use it more. It would make the world happier."

The kindest description of my coping with being an outsider I'd ever heard. I changed the subject. "Tell me about when you came to Utah, Chepita. I've only heard Maury's version."

She settled in her chair and her eyes lit. "So long ago. When I had a figure like Renan's. I had never been outside of Jalisco until Juan insisted we move to California. It was to be temporary. Two years he said. No more. So we could have money for a house. I was eighteen and a wife and mother but my whole life was spent within a few miles of my little mountain village outside of Puerto Vallarta.

"Mi mamá wanted me to stay like other wives but Juan insisted. 'I married you to have you with me,' he said. Juan was from Puerto Vallarta and I thought him very worldly, so I believed he could lead me anywhere. We came as braceros.

"I was afraid to leave my beautiful home. Oh, the colors Abby! They are all so much more alive and singing in the sun in Mexico than anywhere in this country."

She looked in rhapsody. "Renan has them in her soul. I cried so hard when I was pregnant with her because I missed my mamá and I would be having a child without her help. Renan brought the colors of Jalisco to tell me I would never be without my country's colors and my mamá's prayers."

"That's beautiful, Chepita."

"But I am sad."

"Why?"

"It was with Renan I stopped using my family name. It should be Renan Arciniga Arias. To leave your family, Abby, is to leave your soul. The man of marriage is but dessert, a sticky flan. But we were here." She drank a sip of tea.

"But our story. My dear babies, Emilio and Pedro, and Juan and I began our bus ride north up Highway 15. When we got to Sonora it was so dry and ugly. Cactus and needles on everything. I looked to Juan for protection and saw he was as afraid as me. We had never seen a desert before.

"Puerto Vallarta smells of perfume, ocean, water, leaves. My village smelled of grass, chicken feathers and morning. Sonora smells of death and thirst. Suddenly rains began. So much water I thought the ocean was calling us home but when I looked at Juan he smiled, 'See, Chepita, it rains here, too. We're under God's arm.'

"The next morning I saw a sign. A pair of frogs as green as leaves were sleeping outside our door. Away from the rain, they were as close to each other as Juan and I had been with our boys." She laughed gently, "I thought it was to show we would be okay in the U.S. and when I opened the door and saw you tonight I remembered the frogs. But Maury was missing."

She told me about the long wait to pass the border as papers were checked. They moved with the growing season in California between Salinas and Santa Barbara along Highway 101. Everyday was work. When the boys were young they often went with Chepita, but just as often they lost her day's pay when she stayed with them. Her head bowed, she made the sign of the cross when she told me as soon as Emilio and Pedro were old enough they sometimes went with their father. "It was not good work for boys." The family tried to live in the closest town for schooling, because many farms were too far away when they lived in the camps on the farm. Weeks would pass before Emilio and Pedro could return to school. When Renan was three Chepita got work in local stores where she could take Renan and have better hours.

About 1965 Cesár Chavez started the unions and Juan supported him when he could. A first strike was called when the Filipinos asked Chavez for support for their strike. Juan went to the meeting. She leaned forward, "Can you believe, six thousand of us showed up. Juan thought things would change then. Finally, it would be easier."

"My dear Juan believed in Chavez and the cause, but our children were growing and he could feel the weight of years. Two years became eleven. Our families back home needed the money we sent. Perhaps other parts of this country were a better place to live. We came to Utah because it was away from cities. We ended up in Pine Creek." Her shoulders hunched and her voice crushed in on the last words.

What worries I had felt small and mean fisted after hearing Chepita. The blouse's bright color under the parka felt stolen. I hadn't earned the earthy strength of suffering, I didn't understand the pull to beauty and love that despair and pain forces. After picking up the boys at Chepita's, I pulled the ugly brown pants off and put on the gold pants. I'd worn

Renan's fuschia blouse with brown pants and the gold pants with a black shirt but I hadn't worn them together. When I looked in the mirror I cringed slightly but thought, oh well, let's just see what it feels like.

The boys were asleep when Maury returned from his study group. I stood and looked at him. Stopped, he looked at me in his sister's clothes. "You're not Renan."

"It's 10:30. Where have you been?"

He walked past me to the bedroom and I followed. "Where have you been?"

He turned and held my arms flat against my sides with a full grip and stared at me unblinking. There was a glint of the fierceness when he heard I was pregnant with Jon. "The group went late, Abby. We got talking about other things. Nothing to do with you." He let me go and sat on the bed to take his shoes off.

I didn't wear Renan's clothes again. They were soaked in her story. They bled deeper questions and were sewn to hold a woman who didn't question emotion's truths. The emotion not leaving circled Maury's story about the study group.

Kelly called the next day. "What's with this family?"

"Why?"

"Jerry came home last night laughing and when I asked him why he said, anglos are so soft."

"What about?"

"That's what I asked him. He said he and David Ocampo went to Renan's office and waited for Nolan to come out. When he did, they walked up to him and said if he ever bothered Renan again he'd be sorry."

"Oh."

"He thought it was funny. He said Nolan went white and said of course he wouldn't. I asked him why he did that and he said he'd do the same for me. It was easy. What is with this family?"

"I don't know, Kelly. Sometimes, I don't know."

The next Wednesday a woman in Maury's study group called. "Will you tell him Corinne called and the study group's cancelled?"

When I told him he looked at me and his jaw dropped slightly.

"How many were in your group, Maury?"

"Doesn't matter, does it? It's been cancelled."

My Family, Mi Familia

Alexander Arias was born December 12, 1992, weighed less than Jon at 6 lbs. 14 ounces and was twenty-one inches long. He was my boy smelling of crushed geraniums, musky and sweet with sunshine eyes and raspberry bright cheeks. Cornsilk fuzz didn't hide the skull ridges that looked like the landscape of Widowmaker Hill rimming the south end of Salt Lake Valley. His pale milk skin over baby soft muscle was a ripple of cottonballs gathered under white mink. The crooked gassy smile he gave Christmas Eve that parted his thin lips like country roads on a map, would be the smile all of us would know as only his. Alex was nonperfectly perfect from the beginning.

"This one will keep us from applying for minority status," Maury's grin kept his statement clearly in the realm of smart ass. He was holding Alex in a swaddled blanket and they were on the couch with Jon beside them. Jon lifted a finger to his brother's forehead, pressing and twirling like he was leaving a fingerprint in water colors.

"Gentle, gentle, Jon. He's not ready for someone as strong as you yet. But he will be one day," Maury said. Tears rushed from my eyes before I could hold them and I felt my face so contorted I put it to my lap so Maury and Jon wouldn't see.

"Oh, Jon, we've got her crying. This is where men are stumped, son. What's the matter Abby?"

"I'm just crying. I'm just grateful. Grateful you're all here in front of me and I can see this and it's real and I just feel like crying." My words were muffled through nightgown and robe. Jon came to pat me on the shoulder so I lifted him to my lap and cried in his neck. He started to whimper while repeating, "Mommy don't cry," so I lifted my arm and held him as a newborn as Maury held Alex. Our two boys were each being held by a parent and I hoped they always would be.

"Don't cry, Abby. This is a happy time." I blubbered to a stop.

In January 1993 Maury graduated from the University of Utah, I returned to Wanlass and Tomas was sent to the supporting army sidelines outside Somalia.

8

*Sex is only and all for love. That is why people
are afraid of it and treat it like shit.*

- Pedro Arias

I no longer try to feel empathy for strangers. I am not sure of the
virtue or value of abandoning one's own joys and responsibilities to feel
the weight of a stranger's tragedy. Perhaps someday I will resume the
childhood habit I once found mature and cute, believing myself awash in
Joan of Arc feelings. I felt wonderful feeling another's pain.

When I was living with LoBeth her announcements of murders by
husbands, wives and lovers forced me to think about the children and how
they had lost parents. We talked about them while I drank tea and LoBeth
drank scotch, shaking our heads and feeling a communal loss mixed with
relief that a horrifying human event had bypassed our lives.

Before the Vietnam war ended when I was eleven, I watched news
reports night after night showing fighting and dead U.S. soldiers and
Vietnamese. The curliness or straightness of their hair rimmed my thinking for days and their faces would loom ahead of me as I walked home
from school or as I took a first bite of dinner before LoBeth talked about
something else.

Famous killer Gary Gilmore was executed at the Utah State Prison
when I was twelve, beginning a new wave of capital punishment across
the country. LoBeth and I talked about the sadness his and his victim's

families lived through and for perhaps an hour I felt a whiff of claustrophobic vapor mixed with the cloying sweetness of my superiority that I had a human heart capable of feeling another's hurt and pain.

Now I acknowledge the news of the destruction of lives, close my eyes to send care to them instead of bring their sadness to me, and I try not to think of the tragedies bounding through the air hoping to latch heavily on open hearts. Instead I recognize when life has a pleasant rhythm and problems that can be handled. I will myself to be grateful. Perhaps it is only a new way of believing I understand more when I understand less.

The years 1993 and 1994 should have been treated with gratitude for a pleasant rhythm. Maury got a job with a company named Virid, which he had to tell me meant green, and in the imagination of his boss, money and sound waves. The owner told all new employees of his vision one night after a fight with his wife about the tao of sound waves and particles. I interpreted it as he needed to prove her wrong. Virid had a business plan written on dreams of the internet that, with the force of a hundred other companies being founded, would create digital sound and demolish the need for cassettes and bulky home music systems.

Maury was more practical when he outlined his job expectations: 1. discover how dreams materialize. 2. understand specifications and scheduling of the business world. 3. manage the development process. 4. understand the realities of bringing dreams to market with maximum margin and minimum cost.

I became manager of a Wanlass store located ten miles further south in the valley, and began wondering how long I could continue to sell glasses and be proud of my career at the same time. There wasn't vision like Maury's or a desire to express beauty like Renan. I was just trying to earn money. I felt very practical and carry your own weight righteous, but I also felt the walls of life inch closer. For a reason I wouldn't acknowledge, I hadn't let Maury sell many of his college books. After he graduated, I picked up *Norton's Anthology to 20th Century Literature* and then the *Essentials of Geography* to quietly read.

My boys were healthy and growing. Jon insisted his body follow as fast as his mind as he pushed, jumped, ran, probed at everything with a concentration that demanded answers now and attention sooner. He was also becoming more thoughtful and I needed to stretch mother thinking muscles. I signed him up for a second six weeks of swimming class but he clearly did not want to go. Deeply browned arms blessed with Mexican heritage were folded across paler Scandinavian boy belly as he regarded me as an enemy.

"I know how to swim." He was refusing to let me put a pajama top over his head to underline his sincerity.

"You are learning to swim, Jon, but there's more to it."

"I know how to swim."

I paused trying to out think him. I wanted him to like swimming, not do it simply because I was still bigger and meaner. "What if you are invited to a party? And they have cake and ice cream. What if you have to swim all the way across the pool to get the cake and ice cream? So far away. Wouldn't it help to have a little more practice?"

His eyes clouded in thought. "That's possible." He agreed to swimming lessons and a pajama top with blue and green cowboy hats.

Alex saw his first and second birthdays during those years. While Jon went to people and expected to be included because he now existed in their circle, Alex sent light from his own circle and drew people to him. More than once his daycare keepers mentioned his calmness and when the expected madness of a dozen children under five was about to erupt, they looked for Alex and used him as a hub to subdue chaos. He had a favorite yellow blanket he used as a marker for private audience. Maury reported that often when he opened the door to pick him up, Alex would be in a far corner, sitting on the blanket with one other child. They would be quietly bent over a toy truck, doll or six piece puzzle. With their two heads over one toy they seemed to be communing in a silent baby language adults forget.

What attention I paid to the lives of others was shallow and more like watching daytime serial tv slowly pace itself. The storyline furthest away but with the most drama was Tomas. He was stationed in Mogadishu, in one of 25,000 U.S. troops sent to work with the United Nations. His letters were infrequent and either had the tone of a son who had been ordered to a desk to write his parents as a duty job, or they had a gush of a young man's raw surprise that he really did miss those people and Mamá's food.

In the first week of October 1993, the evening news report of dead American soldiers being dragged through the streets was an automatic roundup call to Chepita and Juan's living room. It didn't matter Tomas was not in the fighting services, he was in the nation's service and at risk. The children played and wandered to all parts of the house. Renan, Carrie and Manuela hovered around the sobbing Chepita, bringing tea and cookies she did not touch and occasionally wiping their own tear. Maury, Jerry and Pedro circled Juan. They were trying to break through a telephone maze to find out about Tomas. Their short sentences to each other and strained voices to strangers on the phone held the most aggression I had ever heard the three of them use to each other. Marcus was in charge of changing tv channels to find news while he held his newest son, Roberto, and I had no duty at all except to be present and worry about Tomas. Kelly sat shyly beside me watching and helping where she could. Brad was working late. He came at 11:00, as David Letterman was finishing his top ten list. Alex was asleep in my arms, Jon was playing with Rose, Daniel and Marcus II in the kitchen. Silently, Brad slipped in and sat on the couch to watch tv. Even in Chepita's softening reds reflected through television light he looked yellow green and tired.

At 11:30 Maury thought to call a television station. Tomas Arias was not on their incomplete list of the dead so we all went home, only half relieved. The first thoughtful call of Tomas' life came at 4:32 a.m., 2:32 p.m. for him. Chepita said Juan sobbed for half an hour after they hung up while she called everyone. The Battle of Mogadishu claimed eighteen lives and wounded seventy-nine. But not Tomas.

Pedro's love life was easier to watch. It became entertaining rather than a curiosity. Irene Gonzalez was somewhere in the middle of the train I watched and certainly not the most interesting. There had been Daria, a short dark-haired patent lawyer, who he left when she reportedly joyously encouraged his type of entertainment until the moment of sleep when she preferred to be surrounded by her dogs and if he could find any room he was welcome to cling to the edge of the bed and slap jealous and territorial furry tails away from his neck. There had been the tall blonde Barbara who looked exotically beauty queen Texan and I learned later had been a dancer in Las Vegas. A schoolteacher named Ms. Carr tutored him in Hemingway and Marguerite Duras and only broke up with him when her fiancé finished his residency at Johns Hopkins and came back to Utah. He gave me the book, *The Lover*, she gave him with her good-bye. "Maybe you'll read it, Abby." There were women I never met and was

151

only aware of because he wasn't present at family gatherings and Chepita shook her head when Pedro was mentioned.

Since I had met him, perhaps twenty women ago and that was only the ones I had heard about, he never complained. Even his comment about Daria preferring the night warmth of animals seemed more a punchline to a private joke than a jab at him. Pedro had never used a woman's sexuality against her or to belittle any woman. Perhaps his real name was Pedro Truly Love Women Arias. Well, Maury's better be, Mauricio Truly Love Abby Arias.

Maury had a cassette tape by Etta James singing, "I Want a Sunday Kind of Love." That's what I had. Blips seemed inconsequential to the whole. Kelly and Jerry were living a Monday through Friday kind of love. They were up and down, mostly together and round and round with their feelings and commitment to one another. Kelly pretended they were married. She kept the apartment up, nagged Jerry to take vitamins and changed the kitchen curtains. Jerry seemed content to be very well cared for and Kelly enjoyed the work. Her parents were upset she was living with Jerry without marriage, but as she said, "That will come."

The Saturday kind of love was still being played by Renan and Brad. Eight years of marriage and two children and they could still smoke a room when they looked at each other. They were the only ones I knew who went out of town and came home like contented purring cats after raising hell everyone else cleaned up. In early spring of 1994 Rose and Daniel stayed with us when their parents drove to Las Vegas. Renan had sprained her wrist from falling down the stairs at home and it was in a brace. Brad wanted to give her a vacation from using it.

There is no control of four children six and under in a two bedroom apartment so Maury and I surrendered to macaroni and cheese, corndogs and orange segments while pretending a picnic by sitting on the living room floor. Knowing Renan and LoBeth would cringe at the overwhelming orangeness of our dinner, I tried not to look at my plate. Maury and I hunkered down with the kids in front of tv amid trucks, dolls and building blocks until the next to the last one was sprawled and sleeping. Hopefully, one of us was the last one awake. That adult was then in charge of rousing the other adult and Jon and Alex were taken to their beds, Rose and I got the big bed, as it was called during those weekends, and Maury and Daniel camped in the living room.

As I fell asleep for the second time I looked at Rose's five year old face through moonlight. All little girls are lovely. Even I had a girl charm in the few photos LoBeth has of me before I was six, but it was only youth reflected in young fat skin and clear eyes. I had the charm of new cheap furniture that needs to be carefully tended if it is to remain lovely at all. Rose's face held clues of adult beauty that would mold and stretch as she was ready. Her beauty waited as a devoted lover for her to realize what had always been hers and would be ready as she grew into it. It was good Rose would learn from Renan. It was probably good I didn't have a daughter. Looking at the sleeping possibilities on Rose's beautiful young face I felt strangely lonely that I would never experience being desired, vulnerable and sacred in a way I didn't understand.

Sunday afternoon Brad and Renan returned in their bug covered dark silver SUV to claim their children. I had sloppy joes to offer but they weren't interested. Imagining the endless champagne, seafood and dessert buffets they had, I wouldn't have wanted to crash on sloppy joes either. I offered beer or soda pop. As we slurped drinks from glasses and the children slurped juice from sippy cups they told us how boring the drive home was and how bright the lights were in Nevada.

"Brad was up five hundred dollars on Twenty-one," It wasn't Twenty-one or the money that made her eyes sun rays through an April rain smelling of hyacinth and dirt.

"It was great while it lasted," Brad was alive in her light. Maury looked down at the beer can he was squeezing. "Well, we've got to go. Work starts again tomorrow," Brad stood and stretched. Renan and I went to gather kids and paraphernalia.

Lowering sun came through the boys' room as it hadn't in the living room and when I looked up from lifting a child's suitcase I saw the side of Renan's face.

"What's that?"

"What's what?" she seemed to not know what I was asking.

"Your face."

"Oh," she touched the purple and blue bruise cascading from her eye down her cheek.

"What is it? What happened?"

She put Daniel down and walked over to me, speaking in whispers she didn't want heard in our small apartment. "Don't say anything, Abby.

It's nothing really. Brad and I had a fight and it's over."

I felt my eyes opening wide in horrified recognition. "What really happened to your wrist, Renan?"

"I fell down the stairs." Her whish past me was strident.

For a week the bruises on Renan's face rose up in front of me as I drove on the freeway or looked at someone's face in the hard glare of Wanlass light as they tried on glasses. I didn't know what to do, who was in danger, what consequences could happen if I said anything to Pedro. I didn't want Renan hurt. I didn't want Brad hurt. I wanted my found family to stay intact and insoluble. But Renan's face wouldn't go away and the sound of Maury snapping a chicken bone at dinner made me jump.

I couldn't think about it. I couldn't talk about it. I couldn't think about it.

On a Saturday when I needed to work regular hours and Maury wanted to put in extra hours, Tia Manuela agreed to watch the boys. When we arrived she put Alex in Great Grandma Felipa's arms that draped him like withered dry vines. Fear crossed his face and I almost went to lift him from her lap when Jon walked over to demand attention by pulling at one of the withered vines to also be sheltered in their dying grace. The presence of his brother settled Alex but I watched for a minute.

"Alex had a little diarrhea this morning, so I've sent extra diapers, Tia Manuela."

"I'll give him rice water."

"Rice water?"

"An old recipe. You make rice with too much water and give a few spoonfuls to the baby. Stops the runs fast." It sounded harmless enough, if not very tasty.

When I got to the store I slipped Swan Lake on my nose. I seldom wore glasses outside the store anymore to assess their appeal. "But you don't need to wear glasses, Abby." Chepita equated them with bandages and neck braces and was appalled I wore them without necessity. "If you're going to be an actress get on stage," said LoBeth. "Not all of them do you justice," Renan was tactful. Juan once took a pair off my nose, put them on his, lifted his face in prissy imitation and danced a few steps of flamenco with his pinkies held high, while everyone laughed. "Somewhere there's a you behind those frames, my lady" Sir Brad's voice was eerie and sounded as directed at himself as me. I remembered Pedro's words, "You have ojos muy bonitos, Abby." "I love you, not the glasses," Maury's reasoning was my favorite. What had been a silent friend like a child's imaginary playmate, had become simple sales pitch.

When I walked into Tia Manuela's living room that evening, I heard my boys' happy voices but what I first saw was Tia Manuela's shrine. The Jesus discount store print still overlooked the busy arrangement of jewelry, half-used candles, ribbons and photos. The silver frame was tarnishing around her photo of Cliff leaning on his car. A new photo of Carrie's family smiled from a gold frame and there was a picture of Cesár Chavez. Tia Manuela honored him since his death over a year before in April 1993. Nestled in the back, was the photo I saw on my first visit of two dark babies in the white long dresses they wore years ago. They appeared barely old enough to sit on their own and not fall into the heavy drapes behind. Since she had moved the photo toward the back I felt safer asking who they were.

I hugged my boys and began gathering toys. "Manuela, who are the babies in your shrine?" As I asked, I simultaneously knew it was a dangerous question.

"Beautiful boys, aren't they?" her brow knit. Grandma Felipa was in the kitchen, her head rhythmically bobbing over a bowl of food. Curious, I looked closer at Manuela.

"I'm sorry. Is one of them your son? I shouldn't have brought it up."

Quickly she sat in a chair by the shrine and folded her hands like a shy child about to be scolded. "I'm not ashamed to talk of my son, Abby. Hector Jesus died a sad death. He burned in fever and only God knows why He took my bebé. But the other bebé is Emilio, Juan and Chepita's first born. Has Maury told you about Pine Creek?"

"Well, yes, he's told me about it,"

"Did he tell you about Emilio?"

"I know Emilio died while they lived there."

"Sit down, Abby, it is time you heard all the story. I'm going to get tortillas and beans for the boys so we can talk."

Unsure, but directed by a woman who was trusting me with a story, I took my jacket off and sat down in Manuela's smaller than LoBeth's living room with twice the furniture and doodads and none of the dust. "We're here a little longer boys, so please play quietly."

Tia Manuela directed them to Alex's yellow blanket in front of tv and gave them each a rolled tortilla with a thin paste of beans and a handful of corn chips. "Alex is all better, aren't you, Alex?"

He nodded as she sat down. "Heartbreaks cannot fly away if they are kept in dark boxes or frightened hearts," her eyes were small dark flames. "That is why I keep my life on display on this shrine. I want God to know what I care about and where I need His help. Lives held secret in a heart can never be healed because God might not know you ache. Have you ever noticed this box, Abby?" She held up a small tin box.

"I've seen it there."

"Inside is Abuelita Felipa's necklace that was given to her by our father, Emilio, the day they were married." She opened the box to show an opal pendant on a silver strand. It was not large enough to impress LoBeth. "It belonged to his mother, our grandmother, Clara Renan.

"The necklace goes back further. When the French occupied Mexico during the time of Maximilian and Carlota, a French soldier said it was his mother's, whose name was Renan, and he gave it to our great grandmother Clara." Now the French name in a Mexican family made sense.

"We were told it was a union of love though there was never a marriage. The necklace is on my shrine because I want the Virgin and God to recognize and bless a love that was scorned when their daughter was born. Perhaps the French soldier never knew he was to be a father because the family story is he was in the village for six months before he approached Clara and he left under order within weeks after their first words. The descendants of a French soldier and Mexican Indian peasant need releasing."

"Releasing from what, Manuela?"

"I don't know, mi hija," calling me her daughter was so tender and unexpected I couldn't hurry this story along.

"I only know there is a streak in the Arias family that needs special blessing so I keep my shrine and cross myself in front of it every day, hoping to chip away at unhappiness for all of us." Beseeching Catholics always baffled me so I remained quiet. "Perhaps the necklace was not the French soldier's mother's but a payment for Clara's purity. It took her life and made her an outcast. That is why I haven't given it to Carrie. I want a sign it is of love and not bribe or guilt.

"You need to know about Pine Creek because though Maury was not present, he is part of the story." Manuela motioned me to be quiet as

Abuelita Felipa slowly walked from the kitchen, through the living room and to her bedroom. Before her bedroom door closed Manuela changed the tv channel from news to cartoons and then returned to me.

"Juan had a good job in Pine Creek as a handyman in a sugar beet plant. He and Chepita lived very quietly with their children. It was lonely so far from family and the blazing wild beauty of Jalisco. The land felt barren and far from God though it grew food the white man liked. The closest church, St. Thomas Aquinas Parish, was in Logan, but Father Stoffel tended the needs of all northern Utah and a poor brown family, alone and quiet who asked nothing, fell unnoticed into the earth like the rotting leaves of fall.

"When our papá died our mamá had our priest, Father Omar Gustavious, send a letter telling Juan of the death. Juan decided to go get our mother because an old woman alone needs her son. For money they all picked fruit and after cherry season he had enough, so he asked his manager at the sugar beet plant if he could have a week off. He was fired. Before he left he made the children promise to pick tomatoes and peaches and give the money to their mother. Emilio, Pedro, Renan and sometimes Maury joined the tired pickers through peach time. They all started getting very worried about Juan when he didn't return before apple season. Money was getting tighter and tighter."

Tia Manuela took the silver framed picture of Hector Jesus and Emilio from the table and held it to her chest. "Days get shorter quickly during apple picking time and Chepita didn't like sending them to pick. Emilio, Pedro, Renan, and Maury would always walk home together down the long dirt road through the apple trees. Quarters would clink in Emilio's pocket for the next day's food. Chepita finally begged for work in a small grocery store sweeping after the butcher and cleaning under the vegetables. Oil Boy would cling to her skirts as she worked.

"When Juan arrived home my baby, Hector Jesus, had already returned to God," she closed her eyes and made the sign of the cross. "He was blessed by the church. My husband, Hector, was a good man before but he blamed me and beat me every day. He said I was a whore mother who God saw as unfit. There was no life for me, a woman with a dead son, a daughter who did not have a loving father and a husband who was a grieving cruel man. At first Juan did not believe my life was so bad, but perhaps God and Hector Jesus watched, because he stayed longer than he had planned knowing it would be the last time he would ever see where he was born.

"One night Juan and Hector got drunk together with old friends and Juan came to our house to sleep it off because our mother does not like it when a man drinks too much. As soon as he finished eating the day's beans and squash I had traded tortillas to get, Hector began hitting me. He was so drunk he forgot Juan was there to see. Juan could not stop the strength of the drunk man turned into a raging bull, so he grabbed me when Hector fell back and I grabbed the crying Carrie. We ran to our mother's house. He still did not want to bring us but he knew he could not leave us. It was a blessing for me. I met my love man, Cliff, here and he was a sweet father to Carrie. I am not a whore mother."

Her chest gave one heave, "But it was not good for Juan's children. White children are always sick at school. One bad air flies around and they chill to sickness like flowers in fall. They need more chilis to keep them warm and their blood strong. White skin must not cover well. Sorry, Abby." I smiled and said it was okay.

"While Juan was gone the air of fall began flying around and cold sickness got to Pedro and Maury. Chepita made them stay home from school and apple picking. Renan and Emilio were told to go to the orchard from school and be home with last light.

Now I must tell the story quickly. Local white boys had been watching Renan as she blossomed from a girl. She was only thirteen, and Chepita did not realize the dark forces her daughter's presence made swirl and boil in the local boys. They saw their chance when Renan was with only one brother instead of three which had never happened before."

On the way home as Renan and Emilio walked alone in early moon-light, four boys came out of the trees and grabbed Renan. Three of them dragged her to the orchard and Emilio began fighting the last. When he knocked the boy down he ran to Renan whose screams led him to her. "Two boys jumped on Emilio while the third was tearing the frightened tender insides of our Renan."

She continued, saying the boy Emilio knocked down was following only steps behind and pulled his knife from his belt. Farm boys carried knives like city boys carried combs. As natural as it felt to have a right to the sex of an unprotected fruit picker who did not show shame as she walked in front of them, it felt natural to pull the eight inch utility blade dangling from the monster's waist. So strong were Emilio's efforts to rise and help his sister, the knife was plunged a first, second and third time before he fell.

Tia Manuela dabbed her eyes. "His last gasps for air woke Renan in the night for years. She would scream in morning's blue blackness. Perhaps it still does but she no longer talks of it. The only blessing of the day was the boys ran, leaving Renan's blood from her female place mixed with her brother's. She lay alone beside him. Alive and dead before God."

Her words began running together as days in an unremembered life. Renan lay shaking in shock, watching darkness flutter black and grey through apples and leaves. She watched the night sky open, each star a cry she could not scream. The side of her body felt her brother's.

"Chepita became worried and walked to meet the children. My poor cuñada. She heard beginning cries from Renan and discovered the scene. Chepita saw the violent death of her first born at the same moment she saw the need of her daughter. Que sea lo que Dios quiera!" I didn't know what Tia Manuela said but I felt the emotion.

"Renan could only remember the faces of one boy and one man because the boy had picked apples with them and the man lived in Pine Creek. But they denied everything and no one in Pine Creek wanted to believe it possible. Still, the dead body of a sixteen year old would not go away and something needed to be done.

"Juan's manager at the sugar beet plant who had fired him, came to Chepita with a Book of Mormon and the promise of a burial spot. Behind him stood two kindly men with lowered heads and fingers touching in front as though they were about to pray. They listened to Chepita's cries and offered God's blessings in the new country where they were alone. Seeing the poverty of their lives, they sent their women the next day with food, blankets, old pots and a few dishes.

"Chepita had only lived in her small village where rain cried in Catholic tears, and California migrant farmlands where her children fell asleep hearing drunk men and putas into the night. Here, she was alone and far away from the comforting smoke of incense and the heavy skirts of priests. She was drowning in tears of bitter desertion, grief for her first born and need to feed four children," She sighed and swallowed a tear.

"We are hermanas, Chepita and me, with deaths of first born sons. We were all relieved Renan's and Carrie's firstborns were daughters. Juan was gone longer than expected and she believed herself alone in the world. These were days before easy telephoning. How would she know where to call? Phones were for police or wealthy people only."

Tia Manuela's shoulders fell, resigned neither would help. "She was very far from the God of her parents. Perhaps the LDS held God's truth and blessing in this new land. Mexico and its perfumed full flowers, fresh food and full-skirted dancing no longer existed.

So Chepita and her children were baptized the day after her son was buried and the day before church members gave her money and help to move to Salt Lake City. They were taken to Brother Dennis Erickson, a young married man of high virtue. He spoke Spanish from his mission and he had a basement apartment where his mother-in-law had lived until her death a year before."

As Manuela helped gather the boys and pack everything in the car she finished the story. This was the struggle between brown and white my boys would need to settle as their blood history.

A month later when Juan arrived in Pine Creek with his mother, sister and niece, he was given Brother Erickson's address in Salt Lake. He would take him to his family. While Felipa, Manuela and Carrie ate cookies and sipped milk in the clean living room of Brother Erickson, Juan was told in English about the unfortunate death of his son. His cries stopped their snacking and they moved around him without knowing what he had heard. It was left to Chepita to tell him about Renan.

There was a silence of tree roots when Brother Erickson closed the door to leave Juan with his family. Chepita's words in Spanish, a tongue that was a conqueror to her Indian ancestors, told the story of Pedro and Mauricio being sick, that Emilio and Renan picked apples and were followed by devils. She told the whole story and when she finished she bowed her head.

Long seconds passed as Juan looked at Renan, the attractor and witness of his first born son's death. Now a dishonored impure woman. He stepped to his daughter, lifted his arm from his side, around to the back as a baseball pitcher and struck Renan full-fist and straight on the chin. Except for the small dark throat sound of released air, the room was at first soundless. She fell and crouched without movement.

Tia Manuela looked deeply into the picture of the babies she held. Perhaps she heard Hector Jesus cry as I could hear my boys' voices merely by thinking of them. "Chepita told me that what she thought at the moment was the dirt floors of Mexico must surely be warmer for her daughter to fall on than the cold linoleum basement floors of this country."

The fifteen year old Pedro and eleven year old Maury stood but did not move toward their father. Tomas and Carrie's cries were all to be heard.

Chepita ignored Tomas and stepped before Juan. "Pues, ella viene de tus huevos, pendejo! Estamos parados en un México muerto y abadonado, separado del corazón donde la bandera gringa vuela. Protéjela."

It was much later when Maury told me it was at this moment, feeling the dampness of winter in the basement, seeing his sister's broken spirit and his parents' torn souls, that he no longer spoke Spanish with the ease of a child. English was the survivor that killed and won.

"I came to die here and I have done so," Felipa's words in Spanish that night were the last said.

I was wordless to ease pain or attempt understanding. Before getting in the car to drive home, I gave Manuela the longest, fullest hug we had ever shared. She was an oversize cuddly teddy bear in my arms. As long as my Toyota drove her street she stayed at the curb and waved good-bye.

Sorrow was so heavy that when I arrived home words were simply too difficult to form. I gave Maury a small kiss and moved to the kitchen to fix dinner, leaving the boys to him. He didn't notice my silence until we sat over dinner.

"You're quiet tonight, Abby."

"Yes."

"What's up?"

"Tia Manuela told me the whole story of Pine Creek."

He looked at me stricken, as though I had picked up a board, hit him broadside and his head was ringing. Slowly, he looked down at his food.

"I know you told me some of it but you hadn't told me all of it."

"No."

"Why not?"

"Pine Creek, Pine Creek," Jon repeated as a children's nursery rhyme.

"Pine Creek," Alex laughed, mimicking his brother.

"We'll talk later," I said.

When the boys were in bed we sat on the couch facing each other.

161

There was nothing either of us wanted to say so after a few awkward minutes looking at each other, I held my arms up and opened them to him. More quickly than I expected he wrapped his arms around me. We rocked each other slowly, as we had our sons when they were babies and almost asleep. Tremors heaved suddenly from Maury's chest like spurts from a cold and unused engine.

He tried to stop the sobs but could not and his steamy tears slid down my neck. He held so tight I wanted to move his hands away but I could not. I breathed through my mouth to silence pain. Only minutes went by before his tears slowed. His grip eased and when he pulled away the eyes of an old man looked at me.

"It is best you know." Stupidly I nodded. He gave a half smile, got up, went to the bathroom, cooled his hot face and wiped the tears. Dazed and punchy I sat without moving. A bank vault's door slamming and twisting its lock shut created itself in my mind. I was left on one side and Maury had closed himself on the other. The sudden switch was a Jekyll and Hyde engulfing ocean of wild unsettled, unfaced emotion hidden by a façade of polite, intentional normal.

"Don't shut me out," I said when he came back and sat on the couch. Staring at the tv he turned it on with the remote. I took his hand and watched him.

"Let it fade, Abby." When he didn't look at me I got up and walked away.

As the first day of kindergarten separated my baby days from the school years, I came to mark the day of learning about Pine Creek as separating my girl adulthood from woman adulthood. I thought being twenty-one, getting married or having children made a girl a woman, but I no longer think that. I only started hearing as a woman on that day in 1994 when I was thirty. I believed Renan was forced to start living a woman's landscape at thirteen.

The next time I saw her was at the Halloween party she had for the children. Rose was a princess and Daniel was Robin Hood. Renan made both costumes which became family property to be borrowed by dozens of children through the years. Rose's dress had the detail of gossamer wings sprouting from her shoulders. Robin Hood's hat stood at attention with extra lining and RH was embroidered on his vest. Jon and Alex wore store bought costumes of Poo and Tigger.

As they straightened costumes and opened bags wide for the expected loot, Daniel fussed by me with a sack that wasn't opening. I pulled the sack sides as wide as possible and then gave it to him. His eyes brightened and opened like Jerry's. Renan had arched his eyebrows for effect, giving him the languid lines of a man. I leaned back, looking.

"Thank you, Abby," he said and I stared at the black hair with gold light and square jaw.

He disappeared into the crowd of neighborhood children and cousins. Everyone seemed invited to stop by, so there was constant coming and going of Draculas, princesses, rock stars and clowns. Parents or older siblings were marking time until they could take the young ones home and have their own party.

In the light from decorative skeletons and pumpkins Renan was a Christmas angel instead of the witch she was dressed to be. She took pictures and served cupcakes and caramel apples while Sir Brad looked tired but polite and courtly. He wiped Daniel's runny nose, took out the ever growing garbage and talked with Maury, Travis, Marlon, Marcus and Jerry. Crystal, Carrie, Mistie, Kelly and I moved about under Renan's direction. Chepita, Tia Manuela and Bonnie sat at the kitchen table with coffee or juice.

When Tia Manuela came back from a bathroom visit I stopped her in the living room. "Can I ask you one question about Pine Creek?" She side-stepped me further from the kitchen. "Why didn't Renan or anyone ever get any help in recovering?"

Quickly she pulled me further and sat me on the couch by her, facing so she could see anyone enter the room. "Abby," and she took both my hands, "Abby, you cannot wonder. We were new to this country. We saw murder was legal. Renan could not cry and endanger her father and brothers further."

There wasn't anything to say to Renan about Pine Creek. She probably thought I knew the whole story years ago and I'd been told twice history should fade and stay quiet. Instead I took greater notice of the elaborate care Renan had given this party. Orange and black streamers crossed the walls and laced the walkway from the living room to the kitchen. Skeletons were taped to the wall on the stairs to the family room and carefully placed to appear to be walking alongside and snickering at fear. Hand-carved pumpkins were throughout the house, while a dozen

163

fresh ones were stacked with a scarecrow on the front porch. Open-faced children's sandwiches with pimento smiles and olive eyes were on trays, the juice had cinnamon sticks and orange slices as did the coffee offered adults. As each child in the family left they were to be given a wrapped present with their name on it of a Golden Book about Thanksgiving. Everywhere I looked there was something shouting have fun, enjoy life, be joyous. Laugh at and survive death.

When the last neighborhood child was taken away by their parent and only family remained, Renan brought out tequila. Everyone had it except the children and Bonnie who held simmering apple juice with cloves she swirled with a cinnamon stick.

"To my family and how important it is to me," she held her glass high and was answered by Mexican hollers and "To Renan." Jerry kissed her, "To the most lovely witch here tonight." Kelly was dressed as a gypsy fortuneteller.

Half an hour later, when Renan saw I was headed for four coats she took my arm and led me downstairs to the family room. "Let me show you something before you go." She opened a closet door and bent to a cheap filing cabinet.

"See this? It's a lease for a store at Mountain Plaza by Fashion Place Mall."

"You're going to start the business? Really?"

"I hope so. Mountain Plaza will give me a lease for one year to see how it goes and they're close to the mall so it gets traffic. I've saved some money and if I can get a loan I think I can do it." She held the lease up, causing a black lace sleeve to fall away and I saw a bruise the size of a plum with two smaller ones beside it.

"How about Brad?"

Her shoulders fell like a slow leaking balloon. "Well, he's not so sure, but he's also not saying no and I'm trying to show him what it could mean for both of us." When she stopped talking I touched the bruise and looked her in the eyes.

"It's nothing, a hard hold. That's all." There was nothing on her face.

Before walking out the door that night I walked to Brad with Alex in my arms. In a one-female-gives-two-guys-a-squeeze pose, I spoke into his shoulder, "Sir Brad, are you okay?"

He laughed and then saw my seriousness. "Yes." When I backed away, feeling insecure about my words and impromptu hug, he seemed to rethink his answer, "But thanks for caring." He tousled Alex's blonde hair.

On the way home I brought the store up to Maury. "Did you know Renan is trying to start a business?"

"Is she talking about that again? I thought she gave that up."

Wednesday on my lunch break at Wanlass I went to Mario's Cucina where Pedro worked. It was after 2:00 so the lunch crowd was gone and I asked my waitress if I could see Pedro.

"Who?"

"I mean Paul. Paul Arias."

"Oh, sure," she smiled. "I'll go tell him. What's your name?"

"Abby."

When he came out his apron and hat were removed but he still had on chef's white. He slipped into the chair opposite me with curiosity in his eyes. I looked away.

"How's the food?"

"Very good, Pedro. You should make lasagna for Sunday dinner."

"Cooking is the last thing I want to do on a day off."

We stopped talking and I drank my soft drink. He asked me how Maury was and the boys. He asked me about LoBeth and gas mileage on my Toyota. I don't know if I met his eyes once. When I finished eating he took my check.

"I'll sign for it, Abby. Garcias for coming." His lips tried to smile but the ends turned down. I had never said Brad's name but he knew. He knew where to find torn pieces in a woman's heart. I cried my way back to Wanlass.

1994 was closing when LoBeth invited us for dinner on Christmas Eve. "We're having a traditional Danish dinner. It's time your boys tasted something besides tortillas," was the invitation.

Since this would be a first for me as well, I couldn't tell Maury what to expect. Being Danish had never meant anything beyond skin that didn't tan well to LoBeth. That she would bother to prepare an historical footnote of our ancestors so the boys could be aware of her heritage would at least be entertaining. I certainly wasn't adding to their education. I had none myself.

When we arrived we were unexpectedly greeted at the door by LoBeth's newest friend, Grant Hawley. It was difficult to tell what he really looked like with his full face beard but his eyes sparkled and his clothes were very well pressed.

"I thought the more the merrier, especially since we are toasting," LoBeth said as she introduced us all. She was wearing a red Christmas elf hat, floor length purple rayon dress and silver belt. For the first time I noticed a roundness in her shoulders as her head moved forward. I touched the elf hat to make amends for noticing the passage of time on my ever young and fighting mother.

"I like your hat,"

"Do you dear? I don't believe it. You've never liked hats, but I did get one for each of the boys." So LoBeth and the boys wore elf hats while Grant, Maury and I looked like the audience of parents for them.

"Tequila is wonderful," LoBeth nodded toward Maury, "I've had my share and only regretted it the next morning, but it is also time you learned the grand toasting style of the Danes." She gave the boys cranberry juice and then she opened the freezer and brought out four tall shot glasses and a bottle of Aquivat.

"Bring that tray, Abby," I was told. Small round slices of black and white bread were decorated with ham, cheese, pickles, sliced boiled egg and olives in artistic casual collage.

"Salaad! And merry Christmas," she charged us before we kicked our heads back and gulped. "This is a simple act of pure love."

"And what flavor is love?" Maury nearly wailed when his head popped back up.

"Can you tell, Abby?" Grant Hawley was laughing and pouring himself another.

"I know I've had it before but I don't recognize it.

"Caraway, my dears. Caraway. The flavor of Denmark as cilantro is for Mexico." So began our introduction into a Danish meal starting with the hearty vodka type drink with finger sandwiches that made it natural to have another. There was roasted goose, creamed potatoes, and a little touched bowl of turnips, parsnips and carrots.

After the table was cleared and leftovers were in the refrigerator, we went to the living room, leaving LoBeth to bring us cake. "It's a Danish recipe, a little dry, so I've added a layer of raspberry jam and whipped cream on the top." Six plates were on a tray. "I can't serve you because you must be allowed to pick your own and be the lucky one to find the one almond in the cake. If it is yours, you will have good luck in the new year."

"If it is one of the boys, we'll never know," I said.

"I know which piece it is in and it is not the boys."

Maury produced the almond, feeling a bit sheepish as he pulled it from his mouth. "Good work, Maury, what's your wish?" Grant was doing well at being friendly.

"He doesn't get a wish, it's just for good luck," LoBeth sounded like a wife.

Maury regarded the almond and held it away from Alex's reaching hand. "In either case, Abby and I have what we need. I pass this on to Renan, that she have good luck with her store."

As Maury talked my thought collided with feeling. We needed more good luck. We needed a house. I needed an interesting job. I wanted a new couch. A vacation. My wishes would always be second to Maury. Second to Renan. A cloud of welling feeling without a name ached. Last with a father. Second with a husband. Jon and Alex would leave me. I would lose them to women, wives, daughters. And I understood all of it. Pine Creek and the great hollow it had carved and left empty in Maury and his whole family made me feel puny and childish. I moved my arm, almost feeling Renan's bruises as my own and aching for Brad. My Sir Brad. I loved Sir Brad. Had I betrayed him? I had everything. Did people wish their good luck to brothers and sisters?

Is this what a larger family meant? I didn't know if LoBeth would wish Glen, Marjorie, Lee or Owen a stale almond in a famine. All this thinking was before Maury gave the almond to Alex and told him to chew it well while LoBeth applauded his altruism and handed Jon a clean almond from the cellophane bag.

167

9

Feeling fills me. Watching a buck breathe evenly.
Seeing my words hit home in the eye of a customer.
The light in my children's eyes when I walk in the door.
Renan's body. The peace of knowing I've done it right.

- Bradley Conrad Evans

The doors closed on an almond for good luck in 1994 and 1995 opened its doors with reason to believe it. Tomas was back in the states, and happy to stay in the army as an electrician. He was sure what he knew was transferable from setting up base camps in the desert to wiring buildings in Salt Lake. Meanwhile other people were caring for him as Chepita had by cooking his food, washing his clothes and paying the utility bills while he made friends from all over the country. His new hobby was to learn the Southern, Texan, Eastern, Californian and Midwest English languages so he could confuse Utahns. A new friend, an immigrant from Haiti, taught him proper Jamaican British English. Juan almost hung up on him on that call.

Retablos were hanging in every family home near and distant. Recently, Marcus' mother had worked several evenings with Renan piecing satin baby slippers next to a corsage ribbon and a row of men's shirt cuffs she pleated. I started a collection to see if I could be at all inventive.

"Maury, what if I used a hundred dollar bill as the centerpiece from which everything radiates to represent the joy my birth meant?" He shook his head.

"You need to work on forgiveness. I want you to learn what it is in case I ever need it."

For the retablo I started putting away baby shirts, ribbons and a wildly colored scarf from the 70's LoBeth had given me. I equated it with the best of Missy Mommy's hand to an awkward daughter she was shoving to adulthood.

Kelly and Jerry were still together and though no progress was made toward a ring or wedding date, they nuzzled like lovesick bears about to hibernate whenever we saw them. After they left our place on a Saturday night I was closing a bag of potato chips when Maury ran his hands all over my body like he was looking for candy. "Let me give you a Jerry hug." He finished with kissing my neck like Jerry had done to Kelly. "I'd like more of these. It would be okay." He laughed and walked away. "Meet you in the bedroom."

As I put the chip dip in the fridge, I remembered LoBeth's news of the day. Two men had killed their wives during December and one woman had killed her boyfriend when he announced he was leaving her for her girlfriend. I'd been married long enough to wonder about the energy to kill. With a job, two young boys, an apartment to clean and a husband to mentally dance around for enough affection and assurance, I didn't have time or enough information on how to kill him. But if Maury announced he was returning to Erica I'd give it some thought. I turned off the kitchen light, checked on the boys and went to the bedroom.

Marlon Evans, Brad's sixty-one year old dad died of a heart attack the last week of January. He timed it for a Saturday funeral which made it easier for Maury to be the family representative but he flatly refused. The bank vault door slammed shut and there was no negotiation. His eyes went so dead I stepped back. Instead I maneuvered my schedule while he watched the boys. When I stopped to pick up Chepita for the funeral, Felipa was ready and sitting on the couch like a regal queen mother waiting for her carriage. She was dressed in a heavy wool black dress with a thin matching belt and Peter Pan collar. A red silk rose was pinned on her heart side. She held a white handkerchief.

"Grandma Felipa wants to go," Chepita said, "Thank you for taking us, Abby."

The three of us were the Arias representatives. We waited in line for the awkward hello and I'm sorry funerals require. Brad was first in line, then Renan, Crystal, Sandy and Bonnie. Since Marlon's death was a surprise, everyone had a vacant stare like they were trying to breathe after a bully's full force belly slug.

"He shouldn't have left me. It wasn't the right time," Bonnie said to the woman in front of me. Her right hand clutched the corner of her husband's copper coffin and I had the uneasy sensation he could hear her complaint just as he had for the last forty years. She offered the same hand to me and thanked me for coming. Chepita was given a polite hug and Grandma Felipa was offered a handshake.

Courtesy and attention to detail in caring for the Arias family brought Bishop Erickson to the funeral. Chepita led us over to say hello after going through the line.

"The Evans family was a good match for Renan, Chepita. They are related to the Whitneys in my ward." Family connection through never ending cousins was a constant pastime and form of introduction in Utah. In a surprise move he turned to me. "When are you going to visit the church, Abby? We'd be honored to have you."

"Thank you Bishop Erickson but I'm not good for churches." We had both been polite with his veiled, 'Quit being a godforsaken heathen and amount to something or at least think of your family, Woman.' And I had answered with, 'Get way from me, you overbearing, self-righteous jerk.'

"Life doesn't have to be hard or alone, Abby. You will always be welcome." His voice was feather soft, his hair turning to thin white rabbit fur. Okay. Maybe Bishop Erickson was truly a good man and I was the overbearing, self-righteous jerk.

In the chapel we took seats toward the back for a view of the audience and program and no view of the casket. Carrie slipped in as the service started and sat by me. "I just came to sign the guestbook so Renan would know I was here, but I've got to get back to work. Tell her hello." She left after ten minutes.

I was fringe in Marlon Francis Evans' life, a doodad hanging at the edge without serious importance. It took the funeral to hear enough about him to feel introduced and hear new clues about Brad. I'd been to two LDS funerals. A high school friend's mother died and I'd gone out of a sense of duty. LoBeth made me go with her to an old Open Heart Anguisher's funeral who died of a life too filled with drugs. The family's last effort to save his soul was a funeral the deceased would have found mortifying, according to LoBeth.

I found their folksy style surprisingly entertaining and sweetly sincere as friends or family reviewed lives and stories. The first speaker was a childhood friend of Marlon's who looked ruddier and was a man still of the farm. Marlon was born in 1934 on a farm in Richfield, a community in the center of Utah. "They didn't know it was the depression because being a Utah farmer had always been a depression," he joked. It was a good LDS farm family childhood and as the youngest in a family of achieving older brothers, he made his niche as the most devoted reader and marksman. His favorite childhood book was Huckleberry Finn and he had trophies from shooting and hunting clubs every year from the time he was eight. In '49 when Utah experienced one of the most severe winters in history, fifteen year old Marlon supplied anyone in town who asked with deer to eat. Six years earlier his father had given him an 1890 Winchester .22 slide action rifle for target practice and small game. He became so good and smooth with his handling of the rifle his father began calling Marlon Six Fingers. By the time he was twelve he had saved for a bigger hunting rifle and with the help of an uncle bought an 1894 Winchester .30-.30 with a leaping deer engraved on the side.

Marlon's LDS mission was in Florida which made his mother proud and then he attended the University of Utah which was her lifetime embarrassment. Two older brothers graduated from Brigham Young University. Then he met the 'lovely and pure LDS flower' as Bonnie was described. The speaker paused and looked appreciatively at Bonnie and her womanhood before continuing. Marlon was a year from graduation and Bonnie was in her second year when she stole him away from Richfield to stay in Salt Lake. The speaker ended his first-hand childhood information with, "Together they worked to finish his college education and begin his business career."

Brad was the next speaker to continue his father's story. He stepped up to the podium surrounded by gladiolas and roses with resolve holding his chin tight. It quivered just before he spoke. He took a breath and began to read his words.

"My dad was my hero. When I was a kid he was a strong, good father. He was very strict about making beds, combing hair, taking care of my bike. All that stuff. I was a little afraid of him but it was a respectful afraid and I did as I was told. Mom was always behind him, believing in him, supporting him. They were always together."

Brad cleared his throat, glanced around and returned to his written words. "He could do anything from hunt and fish to make dinner. He taught both Sandy and me how to handle a gun and use it right. It was his idea to start a gun safety class for everyone who wanted to come. It was at our church and he held special classes in our basement where everyone got to see his collection and I was so proud. My best childhood memories are shooting and hunting with my Dad. Remember, Brad, he'd say, we're part of God's plan when we hunt with respect for life that gives us life." Brad stopped again to gain air. "I learned a person can change from him. That there are many sides to a person.

"When I was twelve he went to UCLA for a business course and he needed to be gone from September to June to graduate. Mom supported him in his career but it meant he would be away and she had to work. People didn't travel as much then and he only came home at Christmas." He looked at Renan whose dark hair twirled up in gentle curls. She nodded encouragement. "I learned from my dad that men can be strict and leaders and then gentle and still be a leader. There are different parts. My mom had to take up the lead while he was gone. She was a secretary at work every day. When my dad came home in June with a certificate the first thing he said was how much he missed us and he would never leave again. He was a different man after California. He only checked my bedroom once a week.

"He still took me deer hunting but he let his gun club membership lapse. October is beautiful in the high mountains, but it can be cold and mean as spit. As we sat hidden by rocks and trees and waited in grey dawn for the first light of day, he made me repeat after him, I kill with reason and humility for life; not revenge, not greed, not sorrow. When we saw the kill and I was ready to aim he made me say, In God. For food.

"Sometimes on school nights he sat at the dining room table with Sandy and me as we did homework. He liked to cook." Brad looked around with a true smile, "His favorite was what he called goulash and Mother always made a face when he made it but I loved it. Noodles, hamburger, sour cream and secret stuff he'd put in and never let us see. I think it was ketchup. Two weeks ago he made it for my children, Crystal, Rose and Daniel. We'll all miss it."

Before anyone realized he was finished talking he began walking back to Renan. I felt nosy peeking in the window of Brad's parents' marriage. Marlon had always seemed the gentle parent while Bonnie handled order and discipline. But maybe I didn't know what I was looking at. What did Los Angeles mean?

During the LDS prayer Grandma Felipa rocked back and forth, her lips silently repeating a Catholic prayer. When the presiding LDS bishop said, 'in the name of Jesus Christ, Amen,' she closed in traditional Catholic manner.

"Did Grandma Felipa have her funeral dress on?" Maury asked after I told him about the funeral.

"It was a black dress with a peter pan collar and belt at the waist."

"That's it."

"What do you mean funeral dress?"

"She'd missed the funeral in Pine Creek, but that dress was the first thing she bought in the United States and she wore it for a year for Emilio. Now she only wears it for a funeral."

"She was your official family mourner?"

"Every day we saw our sadness when we looked at her. But it was good because we were the only ones who knew it had happened and we had to have something to know our hurt was real and not imagination."

We were within a thousand dollars of the goal for a down payment of a house. Maury promised he would look at houses I thought were worth a second round saying, "You know what you want Abby Sabby, don't drag me to every store. I'll wear out. Just remember I want enough space for a new sound system and a desk for my computer." I dragged LoBeth, Kelly or Renan around to look.

It was the Sunday in April after the Oklahoma City bombing that Renan went with me to wander through houses. When she was with me I heard about how each house could be improved with paint, draperies, flowers and countertops. With Kelly I heard about closet space, bath size and number of electrical outlets if a beauty parlor was ever installed. LoBeth analyzed the kitchen and number of steps to the laundry room.

Renan had just finished telling me how properly hung drapes would frame the huge tree in the front yard as though it were a photo in the living room when I asked her how Brad was taking his dad's death.

"Not very well, Abby. It was a big shock and he's having to be the strong one for his mother, Sandy and Crystal, too."

"What do they expect him to do?"

"Everything. Sandy wants to cry and remember the good old days which Brad does not want to think about because it makes him sad. Crystal comes to our house and picks on Rose and Daniel if they're not quiet and respectful of their grandfather's death. She'll come around. She's thirteen and just started her periods. When I told Brad that he sat on the bed and it looked like he was going to put his thumbs through his eyes he was trying so hard not to cry. But the one that made him hit the ceiling was his mother. She called and said the toilet wasn't working and he needed to come fix it. It was 9:00 o'clock at night and Brad had been at her house at 6:00 that morning to help go through papers and he'd worked until 7:00 that night and lost a sale he thought was sure."

"So what happened?"

"He told her to call a plumber, he didn't really know that stuff and she said, I can't Brad. I can't have a strange man in my house. So off he went at 9:00 and didn't get home until almost midnight.

"But the worst part is she gave him Marlon's gun collection. She said she was keeping one handgun in the nightstand by the bed but otherwise he was to take them all."

"Oh." I didn't know how many that was.

"Marlon sold a couple a few years ago. He used some of the money for Sandy's master degree. He got $10,000 for one handgun. A Colt I think. They're in a gun cabinet and he borrowed a truck from work the next day and brought them home. I hate them."

"How many are there?"

"Only about six but I hate them. They make me squirmy."

"Sorry. But if they're locked and away they shouldn't be any trouble."

"Shouldn't. But I don't like them and Brad likes them too much. He touches them and he looks like a boy of ten and says, 'My Dad taught me how to use these.'"

"They're just mementos of his dad."

Another weekend LoBeth came with me to walk through a pre-planned series of realtor open houses in the Murray area, which is midvalley and midincome. It's less than half an hour to LoBeth's Sugarhouse house so she spent extra time championing the virtues of every one. Finally, she changed the subject.

"So how was the funeral and is everyone recovering?"

I told her about Chepita's old dress that was just for funerals, how

Bonnie had declared the death bad timing and Brad's words about his father. "He really made it sound like his father changed in Los Angeles. Bonnie had been a quiet good woman housewife and was forced to go to work and get stronger and he'd left as the family drill sergeant and come home a monk."

"Leaving home can change a person."

"What do you think happened?"

LoBeth held her cigarette out the window's top one inch and somewhat aimed her smoke the same way while I drove. "Who knows. Anything can happen when you leave home. You know my story."

"Well, yes, and it's a hard one."

"Not all of it. I had fun, too. But I met myself, Abby. I had to look at me. That's something you've never had to do." It had been a long time since I'd heard Golden Bitch.

"I think I know me."

"I'm sure you do. But going away gives a new side to things. Christ was gone for three years, Mohammad had a cave, Gandhi wandered somewhere and even Joseph Smith left Palmyra for a few years." She looked at me like she was flirting with Grant.

My life didn't need to sound inadequate next to four voices of God. "So do you think Bonnie knew what happened?"

"No, I don't."

"Why do you think no?"

"The biggest changes happen inside a person and they're not easy to talk about. It's my observation that marriage more often inhibits a person from growing and showing changes until they explode. Bonnie is a snappish woman but not a purposely cruel one and I think she felt left out."

Enough of the peanut gallery. Maury's odd interest in his study group and sudden withdrawal jumped to mind. "Is Grant in or out?"

"Definitely in. He makes love like a god."

"Makes love. That is so old, LoBeth. Screw or fuck or a new one is hook-up, even have sex is more precise. Especially for you."

"Your generation is wiping out romance."

Two months later when Renan went with me again she said Brad had been taking a handgun with a pearl handle to a gun store on Redwood Road four days a week. Sometimes he went during his lunch break but

175

when he went after work he came home smelling of metal and the heat of it was on his skin, hair, and through his clothes.

On an April evening when she was arranging snips of forsythia and grape hyacinth in a teacup she heard the banging of the gun cabinet door. She went to see what was happening and Brad had locked all the guns. He was shoving the cabinet to a storage closet beneath the stairs where he covered it with a blanket.

"Dad's dead and I don't need Mother," he said before he went to the shower. Water ran for twenty minutes before she knocked on the door and went in. Steam was so thick she could barely see. His clothes were neatly folded on the counter. He had taken the time to button his shirt and fold it as though it were for sale.

"Are you okay, Brad?"

"Yes. Say goodnight to the kids for me. I'll be in the bedroom."

Renan told me his hands were muscle in velvet that night. Her eyes dilated as she continued and shyly looked at me before finishing quickly, "It was a good night. I'll always remember that night."

"A good fuck, huh?"

"A very good one."

"But what was he upset about?"

"I found out later Bonnie went to Brad's work and they had a fight in front of everyone about Crystal."

The next morning Crystal was scheduled to stay for the weekend. Within moments thirteen year old girls can turn from giggling naive sex kittens to winsome little sisters to rapacious fairy tale monsters that need wide berth. Not that I was ever that way with LoBeth, but when Renan said Crystal had started her period neither she nor I had to say anymore to know what Crystal was capable of. Brad's efforts to keep back tears were understood.

Not much bigger than a golf cart, her mother's beat up four seater continued to run as Crystal got out and slammed the door behind her, Renan said. That wasn't unusual and it wasn't unusual when she came in the door surly and scowling. What was unusual was the dark straight leg pants she wore and the flowered long sleeve blouse buttoned to the neck. Crystal usually wore designer jeans and a white blouse with her hair as board straight as fashion required, but that day it was pulled from the ears to the back and gathered in a pioneer half ponytail while the rest fell in her semi natural curls for a look of a 1950's family photo.

"I'm here." The diva was on stage.

Brad nodded and Renan welcomed her as usual. Crystal settled with Rose and Daniel and the weekend started normally. The dinner table was the first time everyone sat together.

"That's a different style for you, Crystal," Renan ventured, "I haven't seen you in pants like that."

Crystal shrugged.

"It looks old for you. Kind of like Grandma." Brad was looking at his food. It was Bonnie's look of modesty and though not stylish, it was utilitarian and acceptable.

"It's what a woman of good morals and integrity wears."

"It was a terrible moment," Renan waved her arms while we were stopped at a red light on the way to the next house. "I had to move my feet to keep from holding my blouse closed." She put her left hand on her chest then, to still herself. Most blouses refused to completely hide the top of Renan's cleavage.

"What do you mean?" asked Brad.

"It means my mother dresses like a whore and Renan's not much better," her voice rose. "Women should be modest and virtuous and I hate living with my mother and seeing her life. I want to live with Grandma Bonnie where it's peaceful and good."

Brad glanced at Renan who felt a little sick. Rose and Daniel had never heard screaming at the dinner table from anyone except them so they were mesmerized. Brad clenched his fork like a sword but his voice was steady, "Don't ever talk about Renan that way again, Crystal, but you could live with us," his head bobbed, emphasizing the invitation.

"No! You don't understand." Renan said Crystal got up from the table. "I need a clean moral house where tithing is paid and scripture is read and people go to church. I want to live with Grandma Bonnie. Not with my mother who doesn't know one man from another and not with you who doesn't follow the church. You drink. You don't live the gospel." The quiet she left in her wake as she ran to her bedroom was only filled by her crying wails until the door slammed.

Renan tried to convince Brad it was a stage she was going through like sucking on a binky or carrying a blanket. Crystal was powerless to herself though powerful to everyone else. But Brad had been hit in the heart and the wound was deep.

It was a Saturday several weeks later when Renan finished the story. She and the kids came to have lunch with me at the mall while Brad helped Crystal move from her mom's to her grandma's. We were sitting in the food court with echoing cave noise of a thousand people. Rose and Daniel were happy holding French fries with ketchup like pencils, writing on the tray and dotting each other's hands.

"Maybe it will be good for Crystal. She'll learn being a good woman is boring." I tried to make light of it.

"I don't know. Plenty of women seem to make a life of it. Oh, Abby, don't you see? It's what keeps us separated from ourselves. Don't you see?" I must have looked blank and stupid because she went on. "We're all good women, but when we separate our sexiness and beauty and desires from our need to also be considered good and worthy we slowly kill our real selves, our whole selves."

I repeated her words back to her to make sure I'd heard them right. "Is that what you said?"

"Yes."

"Oh." I looked at her. "So you think we can have it all?"

"Well, don't you?"

"I don't know. You've given me something to think about. Since you've said it that way, I guess I have thought women are either one or the other. I didn't think slut or whore exactly, but maybe good vs. too sexy."

Her voice was curious. "Really? What are you and I?"

"In the middle." It was time for diplomacy.

Suddenly she leaned forward and looked deep in my eyes. "Abby, listen deep, listen deep." Her voice cracked a dream memory. The angel held Renan's voice in hieroglyphics.

Then she sat back, a returned person. "Not me, Abby. I want to be too sexy. Too beautiful. Too everything. I want Brad to feel hungry for me when we're apart. I want to live in beauty. I am a good person and I want to be the best mother ever and a business owner. I'm thinking of a name for the company. What do you think of using my middle name? Marolita's?"

"That's very pretty. It would work."

"Now if I can bring Brad around to be excited. He's been so down lately that I'm worried. Travis even asked him last week when he and Mistie and the kids visited and he didn't know I could hear. 'How is it, brother? You seem distracted.' But Brad didn't answer." She paused with a long breath. "I told him about the saved money two nights ago and we had a big fight about it." I looked for bruises but didn't see any.

Renan had a Mother's Day picnic and she generously invited LoBeth. Abuelita Felipa, Chepita, Tia Manuela and LoBeth each presided over one table while sitting in a decorated folding chair with a lavender satin skirt, matching polka dot bow draping down the back and hot air balloons standing at attention above their heads.

LoBeth looked like a queen whose identity was at last recognized. One daughter was not an adequate queendom. Carrie, Renan, Kelly and I were recognizable by our circle of spring flower hats with ribbons down the back worn by nymphs. We looked like over aged flower girls. If Renan had a flute, she would have taken the city. Pedro was the only person missing. The Mother's Day Buffet at the restaurant kept him all day.

Kelly was busy preparing the beginner assignment of salad. Over time I proved myself with rice and salsa, which was that day's contribution. It was unlikely I would ever be asked to bring chile verde, but on Saturday nights when he hadn't tasted his mother's recently, Maury insisted he liked my version. When I was sent out with napkins and salt and pepper shakers to put on tables, I saw Brad was giving his best smile to LoBeth. I took time to hear what they were talking about. She was asking about buying a new car which explained Brad's big smile.

"I didn't know you were looking for a new car, LoBeth."

"Just thinking about it, but Brad's making it sound like the best time this century to buy."

I smiled at Brad who smiled bigger and went back to follow Renan's directions. Kelly and all the mothers except Grandma Felipa and LoBeth were working in the kitchen. When Kelly saw me she put down the slicing knife and tomato and took my arm. "Can you come here for a minute? I want to ask you something." No one noticed we left for the quiet living room.

Her brown eyes were lasers. "Does Jerry always give Renan that expensive perfume, *Beautiful*?"

I answered yes. She looked away. An emotional ground she thought was hers alone, she now knew was shared.

"Why?"

"I don't know, Kelly, but he's done it forever. I don't think it means anything, really."

"They're not related."

"No. But they're kind of like brother and sister."

"He doesn't give anything to Maury." We stood quietly when Marcus walked behind us and out the front door to his car.

"He said it was a Mother's Day gift, a party thank-you."

"That's all it is, Kelly. All it's ever been."

When Daniel looked temporarily disinterested in knocking against his boy cousins until one of them fell down, I picked him up for an aunt hug. He smiled and kissed my cheek before I could kiss his and he stayed on my lap long enough to drink from my cup. He had a strong jawline. Jerry did, too. But Brad's wasn't slack. Daniel's eyebrows were long lazy rivers. So were Jerry's. Daniel's skin was tawny, the light year round tan people paid money to have and Renan called her own. Jerry's was camouflaged by year round sun. This child only looked like himself. Still young enough to hold an adult's heart for the hope and beauty babies bring. A blend of life impossible to dissect into orderly history.

Time was closing in on that Mother's Day. Events were circling closer than I realized. Now, I might recognize that but even if I had known something was going to happen, what would I have done? What was there to do? None of the events involved me. I was only a spectator.

Juan brought out the Mexican sombrero and as the May shadows lengthened he threw it on the patio. When Tia Manuela found the right music he asked his wife to dance.

As people were leaving I went to the backyard and pried off the polka dot bow where Chepita sat. "I hope its okay. I'd like to take this for a retablo." I said to Renan.

She lifted. "Take anything you want."

"Now you're getting the idea," Maury said when I showed it to him. I felt like a fake hoping to look real. I was gathering, saving, trying to participate in this family of a thousand players where memory was felt in color and feeling was danced in swirling circles around hats, but I felt as useless and extra as I had on the seventh grade girl's softball team.

LoBeth called the next day. I didn't want to take the time to chat. Monday was housework day and I wanted to take the boys to Liberty Park to ride the merry-go-round. But her voice was urgent and she talked quickly.

"I'm worried about Brad."

"What do you mean?"

"He had an intensity I've seen in some disturbed families around here when they come in."

"What?"

"I have a bad feeling about him. Something in the spaces between his words. They're not connected. When I asked him about Crystal and his mother I couldn't tell if he was going to cry or hit me. What's going on?"

"Crystal went to live with Bonnie and he's hurt she's not living with him and Renan."

"And…" she expected more.

"I don't know his whole life, LoBeth. Get out of those cookies Alex." I gave him a hand stop sign.

"He mentioned Renan was starting her business."

"She's trying to. You know about that. She's working on a lease with Mountain Plaza."

"Well, he's worried about it. Or angry. Or something."

"It is a big financial thing."

"He needs to see help. He's too wound up." I didn't answer. "I'm going to get names of two psychologists who are good with men and I'll be back to you. Gotta go now, Bye," and she was gone. What was I supposed to do? Call Pedro and give him LoBeth's vote? Call Brad and suggest he's crazy? Call Renan and say what? Call Maury and verify LoBeth could be nosy?

The doorbell rang five minutes later and Pedro was at the door with a lidded cardboard box big enough to hold a large pizza. I held the door open.

"I'm bringing Mother's Day presents. There were leftover pastries from the buffet yesterday and I'm bringing them to you and Renan. Take a few for LoBeth, too."

"Thanks, Pedro," the boys stretched to see what was inside the box. "You'll be glad you didn't have the cookie, Alex. These will be better." Eclairs, lemon teacakes and linzer tarts were inside.

"Take what you want, Abby, and I'll take the rest to Renan." I offered him coffee or a juice.

"Ah, La Flaquita, you wouldn't be flirting with me, would you?" His flashing look before turning to the door had the rumble of thunder. Was he teasing or was he testing? I needed time off from this family. It breathed heartbreak, sex and danger under its roof.

An hour later Maury called. He was leaving work to help Renan and he would call later. It was late afternoon before he called to tell me what happened. Pedro hadn't expected to see Renan's car at home on a Monday and he was planning to leave the pastries in the garage to be cool, but he rang the doorbell. Just as he was heading for the garage the door opened. Renan stood small and shrunken. Her dark hair hung without care and her hand held a robe closed at her neck. Pedro went from outside May sunshine to enforced darkness behind drapes where he forcefully took her arm and led her to kitchen light to see bruises and swollen lip.

Brad had started drinking at 2:00 in the afternoon on Mother's Day and continued past Rose and Daniel's bedtime. She didn't know what sparked his first hit because she had tried not to say very much as she watched him get drunker and drunker.

She weighed about 125 pounds; a steady but not impossible effort for an enraged drunk 190 pound man eight inches taller to lift and throw. Potatoes. It could have been apples in an autumn twilight twenty years earlier. Love makes us work. The little bit of love that comes our way we hurt, daring it to stand up for us and claim us again and again through our failings.

On the first throw she fell to the kitchen floor, quiet and non-resistant as she had to her father years before. She hoped the children would not hear. As silent as she, he picked her up by the arm, dragged her from the refrigerator, shook her and threw her like a shovel full of garden dirt to hit the refrigerator again. Perhaps she felt the silent watching shadows of her brothers and mother as her father hit her in his shocked rage of a lost son. Again he picked her up and threw her in a crazed dance. Her only noise was gasps for air as she hit the refrigerator and floor. His heavy breaths were measured, calculating and then quiet as air re-filled him for the work of throwing life away. He turned and walked to the bedroom to sleep.

Noiselessly and separately, Brad prepared for work Monday while Renan prepared Rose for school, gathered Daniel in her arms and returned to bed to cuddle him. Brad left at his usual time and Renan called in sick.

Maury later told me Brad was standing pale but smiling with a customer when he sighted Maury, Pedro, Juan, and Jerry walking toward him. The four of them stood in a line outside of hearing distance, but close enough to be obvious and present. When another sales man walked toward them, Pedro, who was the leader, shook his head no and they all looked at Brad. As the customer left the four of them walked to Brad who was rooted where he stood. Brad was told if he ever hurt Renan again these Arias men would beat the hell out of him. It was only because he was Rose and Daniel's father that he was being given one more chance.

The next day, on Tuesday, as morning light was stirring to bring sun, Renan called Chepita and said Brad had not come home.

10

*I told Abby she didn't need to be Catholic but it's
important to remember your life is a prayer to God.*

- Tia Manuela Arias Rodriguez

Monday was the men's day to gather and make rules clear among themselves. Tuesday was the women's day to comfort and assess the battlefield. Renan told me Chepita called Bishop Erickson announcing her sadness to God and then Tia Manuela who she wanted as company at Renan's. "Only two days earlier," Chepita said as Tia Manuela parked her car, "the house was a happy mask with windows as eyes and the porch was smiling and welcoming." Chepita finished when Renan opened the door. "Now the house is a deserted mask without happy eyes."

Renan held three year old Daniel. He was comforting her in the darkness of the heavy curtained room. His observant eyes darted from his mother to grandmother to aunt, assessing why he felt danger in their safety. Renan called the police at 3:00 in the morning but was told there was no report of a Brad Evans.

The three women and little boy began a day of waiting and drinking tea with sugar, eating cookies, weeping and saying Catholic prayer with Tia Manuela and an LDS prayer when Bishop Erickson stopped by. In the afternoon they finished clearing out the backyard of chairs with lavender satin skirts and polka dot bows.

Brad didn't come home. Tears streamed so steadily from Renan that her face became bloated and not her face at all. She didn't shower and her heavy hair hung without brushing or care. After returning home from work and showering, Juan gathered clothes and a toothbrush for his wife and brought them for her to spend the night with Renan when Tia Manuela needed to return to Grandma Felipa. When Juan entered Renan's living room, his daughter's ghost at age thirteen stood alone. His wife watched from the memory of Emilio's death, laying the failure of his manhood at his feet.

Chepita's eyes blazed when she later told me of this scene. The eyes of his women, more than his sons, surely surrounded his memories of the basement apartment in Salt Lake City on his return from Mexico. The now spiraling pattern of his wife standing back to watch him had haunted him since and now would haunt him twice. Maury later told me Juan said the weight of the protection of women was very heavy. His mother, sister, wife, daughter and now a granddaughter. All of them were his to oversee.

This time Juan walked to his daughter and lifted her to his arms where she cried tears welling in her heart since Pine Creek. Chepita, Daniel and Rose held each other as time fell away to Tia Manuela's soft praying and Renan's cries. When her hold lessened from exhaustion, he took her hands and pulled her away like she was broken pottery to mend.

He walked to the phone and called Pedro, Maury and Jerry to tell each one it was their responsibility to find Brad and bring him home.

Maury left the house at 8:00 to meet the others. He was not animated or happy when he recounted the night for me just before dawn when he got home. I was told only because it was necessary to let me know the situation. Otherwise, I could tell it felt like giving death entrance.

First they made calls. Jerry was told Brad hadn't shown up for work. Pedro assigned Maury to call Bonnie saying his voice was friendlier and sounded more gringo. The call had the expected response. Bonnie immediately called Renan, but it was Juan who answered and volleyed her fears and veiled accusations. Maury called Travis who said he would call old friends. When he called back there was alarm in his voice but no news. Pedro talked to Renan about any bars or hangouts where he might be found.

Jerry did the driving to Take One, a liquor club with restaurant service and Sail Away, a beer bar less than a mile from Brad and Renan's house. He was not at either one and their questioning was not welcome. While they discussed what to do next, Jerry retraced to a bar halfway between Take One and Sail Away featuring dancing women dressed in threads. "I would have stopped here from time to time," he reasoned.

Brad was not there. The gun club was closed. The next few hours were spent in an aimless search of parks, driving through cheap hotel parking lots and a careful cruise of the closest area of airport parking. By three a.m. they had revisited Take One and Sail Away twice. Neither Brad nor his silver SUV were to be found. There was nothing to do but wait.

Renan said the doorbell sounded like a trumpet through the quiet house on Wednesday. Travis was at the door and wanted the whole story. He'd called everywhere and Bonnie was near delirious. As she told him he saw the bruises.

"Brad did that?" When she answered he only stared.

Thursday Renan changed from sick days to vacation days to gain time for her face, arms and legs to heal. She also wanted to be home when Brad returned.

Friday morning she again called police. Daniel, her son to cuddle and be cuddled by, was in daycare but Chepita and Tia Manuela were at her side when a female police officer arrived. Renan told the story in humiliating sequence. The policewoman saw the fading bruises and noted them. She told them what the police could not do. They could not look for him. The officer was sorry, of course, but there didn't appear to be any reason to check on an adult who had cleanly disappeared after a fight with his wife and a confrontation with her family. They would release his license plate number and if it was spotted they would try to talk to him and say he was missed at home. Quietly, politely the officer suggested they hire a private detective and look into credit card transactions and be sure to check all bank accounts.

That evening when I returned home from Wanlass, Maury handed me cooling take-out pizza and directed me to the car where the boys were already strapped in the back. We were going to Renan's to make phone calls. For an hour Maury dialed and talked while Renan gave him statements of credit cards and bank accounts. In the end, a plastic pile of about ten cards lay like exposed worn underwear. Renan sniffled and patted Rose's head who was clinging to her like warm honey.

Credit card charges were recorded on two cards from San Diego. The checking account with an approximate balance of one hundred twenty-five dollars had not been touched and the savings account at a credit union had been reduced by half; leaving Renan four hundred fifty dollars. When the calling was finished, Maury and Renan faced each other over the dining table. The refrigerator, sink and cupboards framed Maury; a portrait of Brad, Renan, Crystal, Rose and Daniel on a red wall was behind Renan.

"We know where he is, Renan. What do you want to do?" Maury's voice was his softest last good-night whisper through bedroom darkness to the boys.

Her dark eyes blinked in childlike bewilderment. "Do?"

Maury sat up and rubbed his mouth. "We know where he is, Renan. San Diego. Probably at this hotel," he pointed to the words written on paper. "Do you want to call him? Do you want Pedro to call? Or me?"

For a full minute she looked unblinking through Maury. I sat at the side trying to see both but afraid of a breath's movement.

"I don't want to do anything. Not now. I want him left alone." She sat like a statue.

Maury and I put her children to bed while Renan sat at the kitchen table. Afraid to make protests under unusual circumstances, the children slipped quietly into sleep. We returned to the kitchen where Renan still sat and I put my arm around her shoulder and led her upstairs to prepare for bed. Maury gave Jon and Alex cookies and got a beer from the fridge before straightening the financial papers and sitting in front of tv.

Renan's bedroom overhead light would have been police interrogation so I sidestepped to a lamp on a night table while Renan leaned like a hungry orphan on the doorframe. The room was velvet, brocades, lace in dark green, a purple turning black with flits of lime and beige. The bed was not made. Renan did not move so I went to the closet and saw a nightgown and purple robe with lace on the floor. I handed them to her.

"I'll wait for you." Without looking at me she took the clothes and went to the bathroom. The toilet flushed, shower water ran, then it was quiet as she dried. Sink water ran, time passed and I hadn't done any thinking at all. Only listening. The bathroom was dark when she opened the door and walked toward the bed where I sat.

"Lay beside me, Abby. I need to hold someone." She turned out the lamp and we stretched over upturned sheet and bedspread and held each other, full as lovers. Her hair was wet and sweet. I pulled it away from my face to look for the light coming from behind the curtains.

"When I was a kid LoBeth and I would sometimes sleep like this."

What started as small tremors of cries Renan tried to keep back became a body moan and she held me tighter. "What am I going to do, Abby?"

I stroked her hair, "I don't know, Renan. I don't know." I patted her with my hand hoping to calm her. On her dresser I saw the moonlight reflecting sculpted Mexican silver from Jerry's mother's mirror.

"Stay with me, Abby. Don't go."

After thirty minutes she still wasn't soothed or asleep. I went to Maury with blankets and told him we needed to stay. The widened pupils of his eyes were tunneled to memory pouring through him from a time I didn't understand and a place Jon, Alex and I could not heal. I went back to the bedroom and held Renan as I had my boys. As I wanted Maury to want from me, from my womb to my heart.

In Crystal's room, Jon and Alex moved fitfully through the night. Maury slept with a blanket on the family room couch.

Monday Renan returned to work.

Households accustomed to revolving with the work of two parents are thrown into chaos when half the management team suddenly disappears. Everyone was on alert to help Renan juggle Daniel and Rose with day-care, school and dance classes. The week the house payment was due Pedro, Juan and Maury each gave her money for groceries. The whole family whirled around Renan and the children, hoping there would not be further fracture. Unannounced, Mistie came by with an envelope of money.

Work and raising children demanded Renan's attention and she returned to it with resolve. A workday was never missed, a sick day was not taken again. To crowd evenings with activity she took the children on picnics to the park and movies. Weekends were more difficult so she invited Chepita to spend one with her and the children. Another was spent with Chepita and Juan in the boys' old bedroom. A handwritten note was left on the kitchen table in case Brad came home.

On Memorial Day weekend Travis drove to San Diego. With the motel name Renan gave him, he found Brad. When he returned he was reluctant to give Renan details but he did give her a sealed envelope. Two hundred dollars in cash and a handwritten note were inside. "I need to think about things. I love you, Renan. Brad."

My Family, Mi Familia

We were all on a swaying temporary bridge over whitewater. As I watched tv evening news one night in June, trying to bore myself to sleep, I saw a pushing swirling sea of people surrounding the city government building like ants ready to carry it away. Earlier that day it was announced Salt Lake had won the 2002 Winter Olympics. We were on automatic pilot fed by shock, but life continued around us.

Life had a heaviness that made it an effort to get up in the morning and be cheerful with my boys. Stopped still in my tracks while doing housework, I suddenly came to with a rag in one hand and furniture polish in the other. Several people honked when I didn't move soon enough at stoplights. Customers had to repeat questions. My brain was stopping dead in its tracks to give itself time to heal because daily effort was crushing.

"It isn't us, Abby," Maury impatiently told me. "We're still in place. Why are you taking it like this?"

"I don't know."

"Maybe it's for the better Brad's gone. Who knows." I didn't understand his thinking or my reaction. Brad's absence didn't change the structure of my life but it felt like a bullet hole to a soft frill that protected my heart.

My future at Wanlass now spread before me as thirty years of repetitive days more grueling and brain numbing than high school. I stopped looking for a house. It was too much work. I was only capable of thinking of the simplest needs. Food, laundry, changed sheets. I didn't plan anything harder than taking the boys to the zoo.

Maury had his work. He was with a team of engineers and other brilliant people without any credentials at all. He was sure Virid was going to revolutionize music but it was going to take a concept few of them respected. Time.

Since he lost two jobs because of company money problems he wasn't sure the company should trust venture capitalists. But banks still believed internet dreams were a loser's sorry roll. They understood the business of trains, planes and automobiles but not computers, music and the internet. The career honeymoon was over and he realized work was work, occasionally but not commonly, interspersed with fun. Just like his marriage.

Renan did not attempt to call Brad but she saw his trail through two credit cards with food, gas, a few taverns and a clothing store. The end of

July she reluctantly closed the account. She could not afford his life as well as her own and the children's. She began making minimum payments on over credit balances. He did not call her.

Or Bonnie, Crystal or Travis. Bonnie called every day. "What happened that he left?" she finally asked. All she had been asking was if he was back.

"We had a fight." Renan didn't add anything and there was silence.

"What was it about?" she clipped.

Renan sat down by the kitchen table, glad the children were absorbed a room away with television. "I don't know why he got so angry, Bonnie. I don't understand it either. I wish he would come home."

"Crystal and I would like to take the children to church Sunday. Would you like to go, too?"

"No, I wouldn't, but I'll have them ready."

Carrie, Sofia, Marcus II and Roberto stayed with Renan during a weekend Marcus went fishing with his family. Carrie convinced Renan it was time to open her business and take her chances. The excitement of weekend talk soon wore away to practicality. The cash she had quietly saved would disappear the first month when she needed to pay a lease, phone, employees, vendors and advertising. She couldn't use equity in the house because Brad wasn't around to sign. Renan had never heard the term angel benefactor. But she had one.

On a Saturday early in August I went to Renan's to pick up the children to spend a weekend with us. "Oh thank you, thank you, Abby. I don't want Rose and Daniel away. They are my comfort," her voice choked as she let me in the front door. "But I have a lot to do if I'm going to open Marolita's and I certainly can't do it when I'm at work." This was the first time clear light had returned to Renan's eyes since Mother's Day.

Jerry was in the kitchen. Everyone knew he had been at Renan's several times. On a Saturday morning he taught her how to use the lawn-mower. On a Thursday afternoon he picked Rose and Daniel up from daycare when Renan worked overtime until 8:00. Another day he fixed a leg on Rose's bed that was loose enough to make her 'seasick when Mommy left the room.' Jerry brought a pillow with a unicorn on it to keep her nightmares away. Daniel received a teddy bear, 'to keep him safe at night.'

"Hi, Jerry." His hair, polished shoes, pressed shirt and pants were perfect. When he walked through half built buildings and talked to people scruffy from half a day's work, he must appear a precise military emissary from a demanding government. But with Renan, in a bright yellow and blue kitchen with red accents like passionate kisses, he looked like a man happy to fall to a woman.

"Hi, Abby. Kelly says hi."

"Say hi to her. What's she up to?"

"Work as usual. She just did her hair red. She looks like a movie star."

"Red?"

"Yes, Those Irish genes were a natural."

Renan came in holding two small suitcases and toys under her arms. "Guess what, Abby? You won't believe it."

"What?"

"Jerry's going to be my partner. He's got more money than a bank and we're going into business together."

I looked at Jerry for an explanation. "I haven't got so much money, but I make good money and I don't need so much either. I saved some and bought a little garage a few years ago that has equity. The same small repair shop has been in it since I bought it. I thought some day I could take up welding and make a statue. But Renan's ahead of me with plans, so I thought, good to see the brothers and sisters move ahead."

Happy voices full of planning ideas and partner plans were behind the door when it shut on the children and me. "I want Daddy," Rose said as I strapped her in Jon's seat. Daniel whimpered.

"I'm sorry, dear Rose and Daniel. I know it's hard to be without a daddy." It was all I could say, but at least I knew what I was talking about. Rose nodded in agreement before turning to look out the window as life's beautiful lost traveler.

I told Maury about Jerry helping Renan open the store. I was sure this was a good sign Renan was feeling better and life would return to normal. I was surprised when he looked down after I told him.

"He's giving her money?"

"No. They're partners. He'll own part of the store."

"He doesn't know anything about sewing."

"Maury, that's not the point. Renan can get going. She's always wanted to do this." He always wanted everything for his sister. What was the hold up now?

"I don't know." He was quiet and unwilling to talk.

On August 24, 1995 Windows 95 was released. Maury insisted we go out for dinner. He chose Sizzler. Big booths made children easier to handle in privacy, there was food for two generations, and we could afford it.

"Bill Gates is changing the world."

I continued peppering my salad, but I politely nodded.

"This is it, Abby. The computer is in!" and he clenched his whole arm.

"The computer has been in for a long time." Even I admitted it was here to stay.

"Not like now. Now it's going home. It's going to follow kids from school and mommy and daddy from the office. It's going home, baby." Again he clenched his arm. Jon imitated him with his arm and Alex popped his belly forward and laughed at his exposed navel.

"What do you mean?"

"Home computers are going to explode. They've been in offices, sure, but now the market will change. The software is going to go crazy. The banks will finally loan big on dreams; not just brick and mortar. We're in a whole new world, Abby. And I'm going to help lead it."

I loved Maury, Mauricio Antonio Arias. He was happiness, belief, optimism and breaking sunshine after rain. Brad's absence was losing its cutting glass edge.

On Labor Day I decided to start looking at houses again. Prices were moving up with the Olympics coming. Some people believed it would be best to wait until after the Olympics to buy anything more important than lip gloss. Life would return to normal and the Sultan of Brunai would leave with his skirts whisking in the wind of falling house prices. Maybe, but that was seven years off and I wanted to have a house now. I wanted earth. I wanted a basement, a rose garden, a garage I could make Maury clean. I called Kelly to go with me through a list of open houses with three bedrooms and two baths I had in perfect driving order of a section of the valley.

"Tell me what you know about Jerry's and Renan's relationship," she started as we headed south.

"First let me tell you, your hair looks great."

She ran her fingers through a burning auburn sunset. She really did look great. Red struck a fire I didn't know she had.

"Now tell me about Jerry and Renan."

"What do you mean?"

"I mean," she paused. Sideview substantiated her chest heaving, "I mean, I don't know if this is going to work at all. With Jerry. He and Renan are talking about business all the time. He's been at her house for every little thing. They're not related. It stinks."

"They've been family friends since they were kids."

"I think he wants to fuck her. If he hasn't already."

"I don't think so, Kelly." I felt obligated to say that but my loyalties to Kelly and Jerry started to pull to opposite sides of the ring.

"I do." Her voice was measured. She stopped talking as we pulled up in front of the first house.

We got back to their apartment at 5:30. I turned off the Toyota and looked at her. "Which house did you like the best?"

"Number three. It was in a good neighborhood, the rooms were semi-spacious and it had a basement area for LoBeth when she starts to kick off."

I hadn't thought of LoBeth ever kicking off. "What are you going to do about Jerry?"

"Love him as it is for now and leave him if he wants Renan," she almost tripped in the gutter pushing herself out of the car to run toward the building.

Private Tomas Arciniga Arias became Lieutenant Tomas Arciniga Arias. He signed up for one more go-round of military service and everyone believed he would sign up again until a distant twenty years passed. City pallor and aimless stooping shoulders with nowhere to go had changed to a ruddy well-fed frame standing tall and proud. When he stood for pictures with his brothers he moved from shortest and youngest to taller than Maury and brawnier than both of them.

At the Sunday welcome home dinner everyone took a shot at him. "My son, an Aztec warrior," Chepita had tears in her eye. "Hrumph," proudly grumbled Juan. "Your son, Pepito," said Pedro good-naturedly referring to Desi Arnez's bumbling stereotype side-kick in late night reruns. "Sell the bed, Pedro, before he comes back," added Maury. "Hey, Tomas, have any good hand to hand combat techniques you can show me?" asked Jerry.

On the way out the door for a backyard demonstration, Tia Manuela watched her nephew leave. "Tomas." She smiled and purposely flipped her hair to flirt. "The girls will think your pants are the Hotel Utah." We all looked at her.

"No ballroom."

Tia Manuela referred to the Salt Lake landmark Hotel Utah built in 1911. It was the city's premiere hotel but it never had an official ballroom as did the heathen Hotel Newhouse, that anchored the non-LDS end of the city.

Maury leaned and whispered, "Tia Manuela es mi familia's barometer."

Everyone went to the backyard to see the combat techniques. Pedro teased the puppy who had grown-up, "It's better to be a lover than a fighter."

"I get both." The Hotel Utah showed us that.

During his stay Tomas split time with Chepita and Juan in his childhood bed and at Renan's in Crystal's room. He was happy to be a playful indulgent visiting uncle but he was on a working vacation helping Renan. He prepared store shelving, a cutting table, and re-wired electricity for better lighting and six sewing machines. He was often at the thousand square foot space working alone all day. His evening progress reports included free lunches brought by girls in the neighboring sandwich shop on one side and offers from the female masseuse on the other side. After 4:00 Juan, Pedro or Jerry would stop by and help or take over. Tender computer fingered Maury even pledged two evenings a week to keep the store on schedule for a November 1 opening.

I was pulled in with Renan's sincere pleas for help to keep track of money. My training with Wanlass would make the difference of success or failure she said. It was all in my hands and she would be so grateful that she would pay me with money sure to pour in November 2. I was handed Renan's savings that had slowly grown to include four figures and Jerry's equity which was the substantial investment in Marolita's.

On an evening when Chepita and Renan were looking at fabric catalogues, and Juan was fixing a leak in the bathroom sink, Chepita whispered to Maury. His father would be giving him his underwear that night, so don't leave without it. Maury knew that meant they were giving cash from their savings which was kept in a not so secret box with Juan's clean underwear.

On the second Wednesday of October Renan walked in the door of

Marolita's with Rose holding one hand and Daniel the other. The children ran to Tomas who was fitting a board for the fabric displays. He stopped working to move dangerous equipment away and hug them. When he looked up he saw Renan had not moved and her face was an empty tank. Maybe Brad was home. "What's wrong, Renan?"

"I've been fired." The children ran to the back office where a tiny fridge kept juices.

"Then this dream is now reality for you."

She finished her re-telling to me that she, Nolan and half the department were let go in a surprise cleaning after a buy-out by a larger California company. There was no turning back.

On the last Saturday night before Tomas returned to the Army all five men worked at Marolita's. They were planning a tavern visit to give Tomas a beery good-bye. Kelly called me at home while the boys and I watched tv and ate ice cream.

"I'm leaving Jerry tonight."

"I'm sorry, Kelly. I wanted you and Jerry to last."

"Me too. But he wants Renan."

I was silent, unable to deny the truth. Kelly sniffled and blew her nose. "Jerry's willing to do anything for her. We've lived together three years but he never offered to start me in a hair salon and he knows I want one."

"I'm sorry, Kelly."

"I'm leaving a note, but since he's been gone all day and I know he'll be late, I've had time to move things out so he'll know. My dad's helping. I'm going home for now. I hate to live with my parents again but I don't have anywhere else to go." Gen had married a manager of a Colorado ski resort a year ago and Kelly's circle of unmarried friends had dwindled.

"I'm sorry, Kelly."

"I know. We'll talk later."

I pretended he was in private mourning because Jerry didn't say anything until Thursday night. He walked to me after changing the inner guts of a slow toilet we all hoped would be up to some public use. I was verifying a delivery of baby blanket flannel, as I would glass frames.

"You know Kelly left." A simple statement without loss or anger.

"Yes."

"I was sorry to see her go. I did love Kelly." Maybe he loved her like a replaceable bouquet of delicate fragrant flowers.

"She loved you." I bit my tongue. He nodded at the understood statement.

"Come see the gun I've hidden for Renan. I know you'll be here, too." It was deep under the cutting table on a shelf meant for scissors and yardsticks. He'd found Brad's collection and brought a Smith and Wesson .38 caliber revolver.

"This isn't a 7-11."

"And no one who is going to work here could put Maury down." Renan, Tia Manuela, Chepita, Carrie and I were dismissed as he gave his toothpaste ad smile and walked away to Renan for further work directions.

"I think Carrie could," I said to his back. A wave of plain tired sunk from my head to the floor so I sat to count bolts of flannel. After ten minutes the work was automatic and I didn't know what I had counted. I was thinking about Kelly.

That night when I pulled up to the apartment our windows were dark. I listened for the boys' breathing and tiptoed to Maury to lean down and kiss his cheek. Jointly startled and assured I was home, he was asleep again before I was out of the room.

During my Wanlass Manager Training there was a Problem Solving Seminar to 'improve practical problem solving' when dealing with irate customers, testy employees and 'general business management decisions.' The intense man who talked too loud for ten students in a small room, repeated that problems must be clearly written down. Benefits, drawbacks, and probable outcomes of every possible solution listed in their own column and considered.

The night's problem was: Is there a difference between love cautiously stepped into and freely given without stated obligation vs love wildly fallen into and then steadily given with expectation of return? It was a Kelly vs me man approach question. Jerry hadn't been the first she said she loved but he was the one she left the single life for to try her chances. She declared love without promises returned. I quietly, safely maneuvered around Maury like he was a butterfly to be bagged instead of a man to love. But after 11:00 at night, when dark moonless sky and a gentle fall breeze whisks dead leaves along the street and your insides are hot melting glass ready to flood with emotion you don't understand, and the aching need for love and touch you need and suspect others need is something you are equally afraid of, and gin with an ice cube feels like passionate surrounding arms that you haven't felt as often as you would like because perhaps you don't ask for it and a list written with black ink on white paper would only have tears muddying the stark lonely words written one by one from a blank heart it no longer matters. Besides, it wasn't a practical problem.

Marolita's skeleton was in place. Shelves were up, display racks lined in four rows, six sewing machines were installed in a cozy teaching circle, the toilet and sink worked, walls were painted a surprisingly neutral baby blue and the lights were brighter.

As the men gathered their tool boxes the women scheduled when they could help. Chepita, Tia Manuela, Carrie and I were all expected to work with hours tracked but no pay until the store had an income.

Renan's radiating presence would have been enough to invisibly invite all seamstresses driving by Marolita's, but the simple painted sign went up a week before opening. A few potential customers stopped in curiosity and said they would be back.

To celebrate the night before opening everyone was invited. Families poured in the store bringing food and drinks. A homemade paper banner was taped to a wall saying, Dios, bless this store. Cooking pots and slow cookers were placed on the cutting table as they arrived until barely an inch surrounded all sides. Four women brought beans and their four styles of cooking blended with the pots of rice, meat, piles of tortillas and shredded lettuce. Beer and soda were in ice coolers on the floor.

Children ran down the aisles bordered in silks while their parents either stood or sat on folding chairs they brought and told them loudly not to touch. Bishop Erickson scooted past the beer pretending it was not there. Tia Manuela dressed in her best church black stepped up beside him.

Both offered their respective blessings. With all arms folded Brother Erickson wished prosperity and good service to others. With all arms held high with a shot of tequila or soda pop, Tia Manuela called God to notice and bring good cheer. A flurry of head nods and signs of the cross finished the double blessings. Music played from a boom box and people jockeyed in line for dinner.

I took a second swallow of beer, looked around the twice blessed store and walked down the aisles. Later I would hear the term niche marketing, but that night I looked at Renan's choice of fabrics and ideas to seamstresses and I wasn't sure it could succeed. If her brain were reproduced in fabric I was standing in it. Velvets, satins, boucle, taffetas, silks, linen, crepe, georgette, ramie, lawn ringed the store in a well-dressed historical love story. Romance dripped from a length of laces, bows, ribbons. Only one partial row nestled simple flowered, plain and plaid cotton baby flannels. They were the store's lone tribute to the result of history's love stories.

On one side, above the bolts and down the whole length of the store were hanging Renan's retablos as inspiration. She had borrowed LoBeth's, Chepita's, Yasmina's and Tia Manuela's to hang for a few months to fill the wall. Rose and Daniel's were displayed on a far wall. Baby blue background invited the dimensional, emotional retablos to hang in splendor without competition. Renan hoped to introduce her personal art of love, pride and inner psychological work through fabric. It was a store of enjoyed excess, unselfconscious joy, and unrepentant beauty. It was a total reversal of my understanding of Salt Lake life.

People were in every area of the store so I hadn't noticed Tia Manuela and Jerry who were in a front corner. Jerry's right arm thumped his heart and his voice was intent, vivid. "Mi corazón, Tia Manuela. Renan is my heart. Brad sees her only as his, but she is me. Before God, she is me." I stepped back and they turned, seeing me.

As I left, I heard Tia Manuela say softly, "I know, Geraldo, yo se."

"If I'd known it was open range on religion tonight, I would have brought an Open Heart Anguisher," LoBeth who had been invited was beside me.

"I should have told you. Your retablo looks good up there."

"Yes. I've enjoyed it as much as I thought I would. Have they heard anything about Brad?"

"No. Not a word. We don't know if he's still in San Diego for that matter since the credit card was closed." Several seconds passed before I asked, "Do you think Renan should have gone to San Diego and demanded he return? Or get the hell out?"

"I don't know, dear," Ruby Reverie was truly thoughtful. "Remember our conversation about Jesus, Mohammad and Joseph Smith? Why hold Brad to a higher standard?"

I rolled my eyes. "I doubt even he considers himself in the same angst league and this seems so…so wimpy or uncaring. Cruel. Something. I don't know."

"Men and women together. The more I watch, the less I know. When I left the office tonight word was coming in of a domestic death in the south part of the valley. Police were calling our office for someone to come."

LoBeth walked away and I turned to watch the party. Color, music, voices in two languages, cowboy hats, full skirts, tight jeans, brown and white skin, smells of food, work, oils, satins, taffeta. All of it moved in and out of me in resonance I at once knew and didn't know at all. Sensation was of me and not of me. A deluge, a sweeping flood of history was at that moment meeting on land not settled.

Maury was down an aisle with Juan and Chepita. They had histories without me. They were stirred, trampled and beaten. Then they came, came here to me. To me as we stood on the concrete made by my ancestors to protect us from earth. Here I stood alone, the child of their conqueror left to fend without the father who changed them.

I looked at Maury and his family. They, too had been left. As hungry wanderers to this land no longer held by the stewards who were their northern cousins, they had lost the god of their childhood, the power of their language, the ways of their parents. I had expected them to be like me. What would be the lives of my boys, the keepers of the secrets and blood of both? The keepers of the strengths and the weaknesses.

Now, years after this story when I think back, I imagine this time as a small gold button that is far heavier than the size would indicate. Real gold buttons raise and slip into place to secure. They are strong and large enough to hold opposite sides behind, ahead and above as they bring two sides together to protect.

As I watched the celebration I felt part of who forced them away from Pine Creek without what measured justice could have given. When Maury's family came to Utah it was during a very short time of unquestioned white skinned rule. LoBeth believes beauty outlives. I have come to hope the heavy gold buttons of justice, love and forgiveness will secure and hold well against the cold in all of us.

Marolita's opened on time and was publicly announced with a Now Open banner and an ad in the free community newspaper. People trickled in and out and sometimes bought a few yards of beauty or a pair of scissors to cut it into form. The Now Open banner was replaced with a Holiday Fabrics banner and sales unsteadily improved.

On a Monday afternoon while Jon was in school Alex and I were at the store. Alex joined Daniel to run up and down the aisles with clear instructions not to yell when customers were in the store. I was working on balancing the books and Renan was cleaning the front window. When I finished I walked out of the small back office. The boys were happy and no one was in the store.

"It really is nice to be here, Renan. There's a feeling of peace and happiness that's a lot different than at Wanlass."

"Perhaps the feeling is in you, Abby. Not the store." She wiped the window.

"Maybe. It must be nice to own your own place."

"You're welcome to join me anytime. Quit Wanlass and be my manager. I only want to work with the fabrics and people."

"I'd love to but Maury and I have to get a house first. I need the job for that." She quietly agreed. The boys were running toy trucks up and down the aisle. "Isn't Jerry an owner with you?" I felt nosy.

"No. He loaned me the money, but that's all. His name's not on anything."

"He took a big gamble."

"Yes. He is a good man."

"He is. And I think he likes you a lot."

"We've known each other forever."

"Well, I guess it's time to go now. The bookwork is finished for today," I walked away for coats. Renan was looking through the pattern drawer when I came back.

"Abby," she began slowly, "Jerry has always been good to me and I've always loved him but I have Brad." Her head moved up and down to believe her words.

"You've been alone six months now. Kelly left Jerry because of how he feels about you." Words I hadn't intended spilled out.

She looked down and ran her fingers along the cabinet drawer. "Jerry and I have made love." There was nothing to say so I watched her slowly take a breath to gain time. "It's very good. Jerry makes me calm. Calm to keep Marolita's going. Calm to not cry too much in front of the kids.

Calm to talk to Crystal and listen to Bonnie yell. Calm to hear my mother's tears and my father's silence."

I put my purse down and hugged her. The hug was full arm, slow and body to body. Her bones and skin were of softly weaved cotton that met melted glass. She wept the quiet tears of children who don't want parents to hear. "I'm sorry, Renan."

She spoke into my chest like Alex did when Jon told him in a big brotherly snit he couldn't play with his friends. "I'm so lonely, Abby and I miss Brad so much. And I love Jerry. I love Brad."

"Renan, Brad's gone. Can you still love him?" Her full softness was disturbing. Holding her was far different than holding my three guys or LoBeth and I wanted to move. It felt like an embrace of love to myself and I didn't know how to accept it. The hidden streams of love in this family were far deeper, quieter and mysteriously hidden than the rocky western creeks I'd grown up around. I felt about to drown.

"I love, Abby, I love." She said as though she was telling me her eyes were brown when I should have known that. "I love because I want to love. When it is given I don't ever take it back. It burns from the inside out and warms me, warms Jerry, warms Brad. Brad will be back."

She pulled away to pick up Daniel who had come to join his mother and cry. Daniel's brows were heavy with his father's absence and his mother's cries. Comforting Daniel evened her voice and stopped the tears. "Brad loves me. It hurt him he could not always love tenderly. He did not learn how to love properly. But he loves."

"Mommy, hot," Alex joined us complaining of his coat.

"I'm sorry, Renan," I repeated as though I could make a difference. The tear session was over and we began straightening hair and wiping eyes, suddenly conscious we were in a store and anyone could walk in.

On cue, Bishop Erickson held the door open for Alex and me as we left. "Hello, Abby, hope you're doing well. Say hello to Maury and tell him we miss seeing him at church." I agreed to tell Maury hello, feeling like a second rate Jezebel, luring my man away from God.

Bishop Erickson came for Renan's house key so he and another church member who was waiting in the idling truck, could replace a garbage disposal. If Maury wasn't around, my female luring skills would mean I better have enough money in the checkbook to pay a plumber. I could call Bonnie for references. Maybe Bishop Erickson's work was a simple act of pure love.

February brought a raise for Maury. His team finished the musical background software for a series of computer games aimed at teen-age boys. Hands on tests had been spectacular. Everyone was sure the company would be selling internationally within eighteen months and on the stock exchange in thirty-six.

Euphoria of new frontiers in a cyberspace of imagination was picking up speed. It was soon expected all shopping in stores would cease and all commerce would be done from the comfort of a home computer.

"You'll see your customer on a screen," Maury imagined, "and you'll get a photo of his face you can fit glasses to and send them back for approval. You'll never have to be in anyone's sneeze space again, Abby. Except mine." I was telling myself the slamming and twisting lock of the bank vault was my imagination. Maury was brightly transparent and all mine.

"What about Marolita's? What about your sister?" He told me she would need to open a virtual reality store and do business worldwide instead of only Salt Lake City, because the new world was coming at her and stopping for no one. I suspected his otherwise knowledgeable reasoning didn't understand the female need to get away from home and dusting to touch, smell and see something other than a computer screen. Besides, I knew he'd noticed every female on the planet had a different body and none of us were about to trust a twenty-two year old techie's computer version of how jeans looked in the butt.

It was time to buy a house. We had the savings, the income and the need. Asking prices had walked up a ladder in speculation and excitement over the Winter Olympics and there was now a sense of urgency. Maury invited himself to go with me on a Sunday to look at open houses.

"Why didn't you like that one?" The boys were running in front of us to the car after looking at a four bedroom, two bath, twenty year old house with a study and a chain link fence.

"It was boring. It looked like every third house in Salt Lake. No imagination."

"So put imagination into it. The house was fine."

"The rooms were small. The whole thing needed painting."

After the next house he asked the same question.

"The kitchen was puny."

"LoBeth's is puny. My mother's is puny. Ours is punier. If we knocked out the wall and made it bigger to the backyard, what else is wrong with the house?"

"The bedrooms are smaller than a trailer. The closets couldn't hold your clothes."

Maury didn't offer to go with me again so I called Kelly. We'd hadn't had a good talk since she left Jerry so I convinced her to go to lunch with me on Sunday before we drove around.

"I don't really blame Jerry or Renan," she was angrily puncturing a salad.

"Why not?"

"They've known each since they were teenagers. I was the one who came late in the story. I didn't know."

"I'm sorry, Kelly," She thought I was saying I was sorry she had been the late actor on stage. What I was apologizing for was enforced blindness of the relationship and that I hadn't warned her.

"He always took her birthday and Christmas gifts and I tried to pretend they were sisterly things until I found out about the *Beautiful*. I asked him about their relationship once when he'd had too much to drink."

"What did he say?"

"Can I have more salad dressing?" she looked up and asked a passing waitress. "He said he'd always thought she was beautiful and kind. He started giving her gifts in high school like a lovesick kid and she'd give him a hug and kiss, just like a sister." We were quiet as she took a bite and seemed to need time to sort her words like she was also sorting tomatoes from cucumbers.

"They ended up going for a ride one night when he was seventeen and she was twenty. He parked and they started something. I don't know how far it went but he did say Renan stopped it and said, 'No, Jerry, we can't do this. You need someone more innocent and I need someone less.'"

"Huh," I avoided saying anything.

"Maybe Gen said the best thing. Want to hear?" I nodded. "When I told her we broke up she said, good. Kelly Sandoval sounds like a drunk Irish slut." We looked at our food. I understood and I didn't understand at all.

After years spent with one person and the only measurable result a broken heart, Kelly decided to be more scientific. A Santa Claus list for a husband was taped to her bathroom mirror. The jumbled order was: taller by at least two inches, good steady work in an office where clothes never met grease or mud, clean teeth, likes to camp for one vacation and go to New York for the next, easily adjusts to changing hairstyles, has sense of humor, occasionally buys fresh flowers, will be friendly with parents, loves her and she would love him. It didn't sound like an impossible list.

"And what's your house list? What are we looking for in a house, Abby?"

"I'm not as organized. I'll see the perfect house and it will speak to me."

"You can do better than that."

"That's how I found Maury."

"Really?"

I rushed to tell her details in the story she hadn't heard while I tried to bury Gen's statement.

On the last Friday in February snow weightlessly piled like bath bubbles. Dry snowflakes flew in whirls from a broom sweeping driveways, and promised spring. I stopped by Marolita's on my way home from Wanlass. I had promised to fill out a Personal Property Tax Form from the county that was due in March. Latin music thumping its beat greeted me before I opened the door. Closing time had passed but the door was open to anyone who cared to be lost in rich soft fabrics and hear the staccato laughter of women. I stamped my boots to remove snow. Chepita, Tia Manuela and Carrie had brought dinner and spread it out on the cutting table. Yasmina, Marta and Bernice were putting out drinks.

"Join us, Abby," Tia Manuela offered. "Renan called Chepita today and said sales were up fifty percent this month so I threw dinner together and here we are."

"Thanks, I will." No reason to turn down free good food. I'd stop for hamburgers for the neglected men at home. Everyone glowed in happiness for Renan and the store that was succeeding. Everything was going to be fine. Why had we worried at all?

After the paper plates were thrown away and the table wiped, Chepita started dancing to an old favorite by Lola Beltrán. When the mother of the family dances, children join so round the table we went, down the aisles, swaying our skirts or feeling free in our long pants to kick high. Smells of my snow wet hair, fresh oiled thread, silks from China, dinner of beans, meat, fresh lettuce and tortillas were all part of our dance. At first we were a friendly conga line but at the end of lining and taffeta we parted ways to dance our own free-formed twirls. Chepita led one group with her Mexican heoyyy cries and Tia Manuela led another answering her as longingly and fully. Arms swayed like willows in a wind, female hips followed the deep call of drum, horns, and guitar behind Lola's seductive yearning wishes. We were in the middle of *Huapango Torero*, laughing as much as we were dancing when the store door opened. I didn't hear or see but the laughing hooting calls of the women stopped and when my twirl led me around to face the front I also stopped. Music canopied the wordless stares of stilled dancers.

Brad faced us. Soft snowflakes lined his shoulders, making him appear a slightly out of focus, weary and soul saddened Jesus. "My Sir Brad," I said through the music.

11

I surrender in love to burn and then
I rise through ashes to love deeper.

- Renan Marolita Arias Evans

When I told LoBeth about the scene she believed she would have said, "Well (and her hands would have been on her hips, with an eyebrow lifted), Stud returns to face Bitch Revenge." I don't think Golden Bitch would have thought of it soon enough. We all stared at Brad while he stared at the stopped dancers. We were each other's last morning dream, already evaporating. Renan's slightest whisper was heard beneath the trumpets. Love and hope were wrapped in her soft sweet, "Brad." The barest lift of her hands brought him to her in an embrace made for the movies.

Under three minutes Chepita, Tia Manuela, Carrie, Yasmina, Marta, Bernice and I left with our coats half on and carrying awkward armfuls of bowls and pots. I was so overwhelmed I hope I didn't run red lights as I drove straight home. Buying hamburgers was forgotten and Maury forgot he wanted food while he wondered what should be done.

"Like what?"

"A man's gone for what, nine months? We should do something."

"Like what?"

"Did he seem okay? He didn't look deranged or anything?" I'd never seen deranged, but I did remember the heavy sadness of his shoulders and eyes.

"No, he didn't look deranged. Maybe lost and sad."

"Was Renan happy or afraid?"

"Neither, Maury. They were holding each other when we left. She wasn't afraid."

That seemed to be evidence and he was quiet for a minute while he thought it through. "Okay, then," he slowly gained speed, "We'll wait and see what happens. Let's order pizza." He was calmed enough to eat.

All we knew that weekend was that since the children were water coloring with Juan that evening, they stayed the weekend. Tia Manuela and Carrie were in charge of the store for the weekend. Word flew around the Arias family network like dust in a tornado, but the eye of the storm, Brad and Renan, were left alone. Pedro called Jerry so he wouldn't show up at the house. Jerry wasn't happy.

It was my usual Monday when I saw Renan again. Alex and I saw two customers walking about the aisles while a third was talking to Renan about signing up for her Wednesday class on designing retablos. Alex rushed to hug her leg and she turned her attention to him with a smile and slow sweeping of his hair. He let go, followed me back to the office and Renan returned to her customers.

It was almost half an hour before she walked back and opened the door, allowing Alex's escape. She stood watching him and the front door. Her pink long sleeved crushed velvet blouse was a Simplicity pattern shown on its cover on a schoolgirl in navy knit. Her chest rose and fell like deep trombone notes on a late and smoky Saturday night.

"Everything okay with Brad?" I sat at the desk, holding a pen.

"Yes, everything's fine." She looked to a back corner of the store that would be deep in shadows away from the parking lot light at night. "We made love right there. Good love. We made love all weekend."

She talked of underground caves and flowing rivers of human feeling that weren't mine and couldn't be mine. Since Brad left I once more stood facing the edge of my childhood's black abyss. When I met Maury I turned away from it, avoiding the swirl, believing it didn't matter and he could make it disappear. Hearing Renan talk I felt the crumbling shore under my toes. Brad's desertion, my father's ransom for freedom, LoBeth's boyfriends who left me before her, three uncles with distant lives. My grandfather's death. All were a disregard to my existence. All men left me broken, unable to allow the bravery it takes to sink, sink, die, die, be born, be born into another's fire; a fire throbbing and birthing for

207

some but I'm outside, feeling the cold too well. "So everything's okay?"

"Yes. He's home today, resting and sleeping. Tomorrow he's going to start looking for work."

"How did he find the store? Had you been talking with him?" I felt weak. Unable to hold the pen, I put it down. Something was draining from my body, out my chest, hands, bottoms of my feet.

"No. He called Crystal before he came home. He told her he was sorry for leaving and he would call her this week. Bonnie got on the phone and told him about the store."

A million questions had popped in Maury's and my conversations all weekend, but now all I saw was a woman lost in a mist of sex and the peace of believing her life was mending. I couldn't remember the practical and mean spirited questions like, what the hell was Brad thinking? She stepped back into the store when a customer came in. "I'll tell Maury everything's okay with Brad and not to worry about you. He's been worried." I turned away to wipe tears from my eyes that were for me.

"Yes, tell Maury that. It's true." She bent and kissed the top of my head, once again my gracious, loving woman teacher.

When I told Maury what Renan said, leaving out doing it in the corner of the store, he called Pedro. "Keep it casual. Renan's okay with it," was all I heard.

"What was that all about?"

"It was us who made him go. If Renan's all right with him coming back, we need to let him know we can live with it." Pedro was the delegation of one to extend the male hand of letting history fade. Was all this courtly or controlling? Protective or nosy? Having involved males in a girl's life looked to be a lot different than I had imagined. Maybe it was only Pine Creek working its sorrow, guilt and fear.

"Jerry was angry he came home." Maury's voice was informational.

"Why do you think so?"

"He'd take Renan and the kids in a second. He's never trusted Brad."

"Why not?"

"He thinks, and I'm sorry to say this Abby, but it's a lot true from the brown man view. White boys are taught they're on the top of the heap and they deserve better, better, better. When something goes wrong they don't know what to do. Brown men learn from their mamá's and papá's knees life is work."

I didn't have any white man in the world to protect except Brad. "That's not true. He was under a lot of pressure."

"Like?"

"Like you guys coming to him. Sales work is hard every day. Crystal accused him of being immoral. His dad died. His mother doesn't think he's succeeded. Not enough money. Renan wanted to start the store," I didn't like adding the last one because I thought Renan should have started the store, but it was a pressure for Brad.

Maury touched my shoulder, to calm me. "I know Abby and as I move into this white world of business and having plenty I understand even more, but half of what you said is white man expecting life to be easier and better for him. Everyone faces problems like that without fucking up the rest of their life. Even our women are white man's bounty. Brown women are just supposed to be handed over."

"But they're real problems. Real problems." I avoided the statement about brown women. I'd been handed over, deserted and overlooked, too. Something Renan hadn't experienced.

"They are Abby. I know they are. Life is a real problem. That's what I mean. You have to accept the problem and deal with it. Not let it deal with you." He sounded like an irritating book jacket. We were quiet, each of us lost in the emotional weight of our words. Maury turned it into a sociological discussion while I simmered in female powerlessness and Brad's right to his misery. "Latinos won't be more powerful because of our numbers. Not enough of us are organized or educated yet."

"What do you mean?"

"White boys are giving up the throne. They're too inbred and self-righteous. When they discover life has made them a burro, too many of them don't know how to make an honest living at it. They're trained to intimidate, fight and demand. Not live."

Life slowly resumed when Brad reappeared, just as it had when he left. My life certainly continued with a schedule of caring for males, Wanlass and a few hours at Marolita's. The difference was recognizing the heavy load I was carrying around in my head, making periodic drops to my heart, where I had to shove them back up where they belonged. A brain can turn things into cold results and data. A heart feels and aches. Subjects would pop into my mind without proper phrasing, such as beauty or desire. My mind would be jumbled with Renan's fabrics, lace, drapes in her living room, her jewelry, sunsets, the color of LoBeth's bright costumes and glowing smile when she was with the Open Heart Anguishers vs my twill pants, cheap wedding dress, plastic placemats, nylon nightgowns. The same thing happened with education, brothers and sisters, buying a house. When my heart ached, I worked like hell to kick them back up to my head where they could be isolated in sarcasm and defense before I cried.

I think another version of that was going on in Jerry's head. Probably he was thinking about Renan's hair, the curves of her body, Beautiful cologne, the quiet of his apartment now that he was alone eating from a can over the kitchen sink. He was not often seen and for the time being, he stayed completely away from Arias gatherings.

I believe from the bottom of her mother's heart Bonnie thought she was offering to improve her son's life when she called Brad a month after he was home. Renan said she told Brad she would pay for college if he would go. She said it was time to prepare for life. Brad insisted he was. He found a sales job at Kelson Industrial Heating and Air Conditioning and he expected to be top salesman in a four state region before long. "Education is the only way up," his disappointed mother said.

"But Brad, I'm not disappointed. I think you're doing great," Renan spoke from the heart of a woman who knew terror, the feel of rough blankets and work in a sugar beet field as a child. He buried his head in her shoulder and hugged so hard she squirmed. "He let me go, Abby, and I saw the sadness of the world in his eyes. I know the grief that doesn't end."

"What did he do while he was gone, Renan?" It was again a Monday afternoon between customers.

"He sold cars from a used car lot. Lived in a motel by the week. Watched tv and drank beer." She paused, "He did a lot of thinking, too. He's softer now. He smells like torn nasturtium leaves, peppery yet frail. I don't know all that he did, but he's changed. Last night he looked at the kids and me like he wanted to swallow us whole and keep us with him every moment of his life."

"Aren't you mad at him, too, Renan? Don't you just want to scream at him for leaving?"

She picked up a lace bolt and started wrapping it tighter but smiled,

"Yes, so I did. After he'd been home a week and the kids were asleep, I told him I was so angry I wanted to scream and yell and hit him. He said okay and sat on the couch in the family room. I punched him twice on the arm as hard as I could. Almost made myself fall down. Then I tried to scream but my voice cracked and it was like a nightmare that wouldn't come out. I cried instead. I hit him one more time and when he could tell that was all I was going to do, he put his arms around me and we made love."

"You could make a retablo from the last year of your life, Renan."

Her laugh was enjoyment of self-recognition as she moved hair behind her shoulder. "Yes, it has been different."

"He doesn't hit you. It's important he doesn't hit you." I realized the absurdity that it seemed okay, perhaps the right thing to do, for Renan to hit Brad.

"No, Abby. He hasn't hit me. Hitting seems to be out of him."

I reported to Maury who reported to Pedro. Everyone relaxed and let time and air heal the wound into visible scar tissue. Caution lay over the Arias family like a heavy coat in spring's too early warmth.

There was relief Renan's caressing deep beauty and feminine spirit ruptured into bloody fragments as a girl had mended to womanhood able to survive and be strong enough to build a life after Brad left. There was caution the man she still loved was as capable of surrounding her in safety, family and home as purposely hurting her beauty, abandoning her love and deserting her to find her way alone.

The alone I imagined for myself was not Renan's alone. Renan's feminine softness, LoBeth's calculated armor were frightening and sad. One looked vulnerable and weak. One looked hard and uncompromising. Neither was as they appeared. I had spent my life teetering in the middle, afraid to fall either way and drown in emotion or callousness. Renan and LoBeth were my examples of excess. Where would I be without Maury to walk around my protected female ideas, substantiating the structure I was safe in believing?

Renan's months without Brad brought life that had circled her for a very long time, waiting for an opportunity to reach her. When Jerry's desire and the dream of her store could materialize through Brad's absence, her life wrapped comfortably, warmly, creatively, lovingly around her. It was as though the fist of passion, the swirling in dangerous, overwhelming love had imprisoned her and his absence made her free.

An unexpected swelling of something close to but not exactly compassion for Brad rocked me enough that I called him at work and asked to meet for lunch. I needed to hear his words and look in his face without anyone else around. Maury didn't understand and wasn't happy but he had no reason to understand with two brothers and a sister to call his very own.

"How's Sandy?" I started as we sat in the booth of a steakhouse.

He closed his eyes as though remembering who she was. After a slow breath he answered, "She's fine. She's finally got a boyfriend. She'd do better if she'd just relax. I wish she wouldn't try to make Mom happy."

I thought of Kelly's Santa Claus list for a man, LoBeth's need to prove she wasn't from Utah's middleclass and my need from Maury to belong. Aims of white woman love. I needed to ask Chepita and Tia Manuela what they had needed. Deep from the colors and hunger of Mexico had they ever hoped for any more than the warmth of a kind man to hold children and bring food?

I answered when I saw him waiting. "Most of us would do better if we relaxed." His near twitching excitement and sparkling eyes of years ago were gone. He felt like sitting next to a tired, beautiful teacher who had drained away his knowledge to others and needed to sleep.

"Perfection doesn't exist as she wants it. I hope this man's going to be good enough. I'm afraid she's going to be alone and comfort Mother like a lap puppy."

"And Bonnie?"

"Mom's doing fine. She found a plumber and an electrician while I was gone. She has all the men she needs now."

I didn't remember his voice ever sounding like a soft breeze in June while he spoke LoBeth's spiked language. "How are you doing, Brad?" I jumped into my question. There wasn't going to be a better way.

"You want to know the truth, Abby?" He looked me in the eye for the first time and I nodded, curious what was coming. The waitress put a steak sandwich and fries in front of him and a baked potato and salad in front of me.

"I'm tired." He put ketchup on his plate and salted the fries. He seemed to need time to continue. The sounds of other people floated in back of us. "I'm tired and there's nothing to be done about it. I worked so hard before. Every day I looked in the mirror when I shaved and told myself it was going to be a great car sale day. Money was going to burst my pockets and Renan would always love me.

"But the harder I worked, the further I got behind. Sometimes I sold better than Oreos, but sometimes I couldn't talk a wino into free wine. Renan said it was the economy or a slow time of year. She'd cover for me. But I knew I was disappointing her. She wanted to start that store and I just couldn't see doing it. Not then. It was a honeymoon. Taking the kids to Disneyland."

"You've always been a great salesman, Brad. Look at you now."

"I like sales. It fits me. I need to learn this industry but I will and there's more money to be made than in cars. And better hours, even if some of them are out of town."

"Sounds like things are improving. Better than they were."

"Mother thinks I'm a slug cleaning toilets," he talked as if I hadn't said anything. "Renan's family treats me different but I know why. Crystal at least speaks to me. Said she's too old for sleepovers now but she'd come tend the kids. And she wanted money for designer jeans," he smiled a clear browed, easy dad smile. All that she did to hurt him and she got a dad smile. Now I knew what they looked like.

"Good. Teenagers are weird just because they're teenagers."

"I wish I hadn't run, Abby, but I did."

"We're glad to have you back, Brad. I missed you. I missed you very much."

Gratitude looked back. "Not everyone did. But I'm glad if you did."

"We're glad to have you back, Brad."

"Jerry's not. Jerry would like me to eat shit and die. He should have stayed with Kelly. It was shitty what he did to her."

"She's getting back in the dating scene. No one special yet."

"The only good thing he did was put the Smith and Wesson in the store in case Renan needs it. I'm teaching her how to use it but she doesn't like it."

"Yes, I saw the gun."

"I did a lot of thinking. I missed Renan and the kids so much. I thought of you, too." He lowered his head.

"Oh?"

"I almost told you when you asked me about Erica, but it's been another damn family secret. Just like Pine Creek." For the first time we looked at each other through Pine Creek's blood running over us. "Maury was in to women too fast for him. Erica was one. They were eating him alive and he didn't care. Pedro knows what's going on but Maury was only being used. Erica only wanted a tourist pass. Juan called you the Border Patrol because you eventually stopped all the traffic. Renan and all the women think you're the one who turned him into a man. But they'll never tell you. He's theirs."

He looked up to see me staring and hurried on, "And another thing. It's not for me, but it is for you. You should go back to school."

"Maybe I will someday when I have a house with room for a reading lamp." I couldn't comment on anything else.

He opened the door for me when we left and gave me a big shoulder squeeze before we headed for our cars. The first brotherly hug I ever had was from Jerry when he held my head like a jelly jar and called it a sandia. I felt special and cute in a little sister way with Jerry. When Brad held me it was as a brother of blood and tears. "Thanks for calling, Abby. Everyone seems to need to hear I'm back. I'm home."

"I'm glad, Sir Brad."

Later I marked this conversation as when my glass insides began to permanently melt. The internal shards of sharp cold glass that gave distance and protection to deal with Wanlass, Maury, his family, our boys, LoBeth and myself began a last meltdown. I would never again be able to have a moonlit private session of universal questions and heart breakdowns oiled with the comfort of liquor and wake up in the morning with all questions replaced on their organized brain shelf where they didn't interrupt daily life.

I had asked questions of Maury's love, his family's ache, LoBeth's motherstyle, whether I was a good mother, what sex was really meant to accomplish, the meaning of education, what a man might do if he discovered I hadn't been aborted and the routine of the working world. The next morning I would be comforted unanswerable issues dissolved with the sunshine of the day.

After seeing Brad's suffocating need for Renan, feeling her close weeping body and its rays of love and desire, after hearing Maury's cool assessment and LoBeth's self-protective jabs, and seeing that Jerry would never have his real love, while Kelly carried an ache by innocently giving true love, my internal shards of glass refused to protect me again. I did not understand anything.

Perhaps because I didn't understand anything I began to see differently. The structure of relationships and people no longer had to fit my judgments. Nothing had to change its shape to please me. Everything was frightening.

I didn't care if I found a house and I stopped looking. The beige apartment on Fifth East by the freeway overpass where Maury and I started trying to be adults with wedding rings and where we brought our boys home, well, we were just fine.

The boys were outside playing when the fourth Sunday passed and I didn't go to open houses. Maury asked why. I said it was too much work. I didn't want the burden of looking for a house. It felt like looking at myself as outdated red brick, overgrown dying trees and shrubs that would need love I didn't have, closets that weren't big enough to hold my sadness, small kitchens that didn't let women cook with love, and cold small dark bedrooms waiting to strangle all four of us. At the end I was sobbing and my audience was silent.

"I didn't know you thought you were a house, Abby Sabby," he drew me to him. "I'll go looking with you and show you how I see you."

I knew my outburst would be treated kindly, but it felt like purposeful kindness, not love. It was comfortable, affectionate and as reliable as animal crackers. Being scorched by Renan's passions defined the cold outside a roaring fire's heat. I hadn't an answer to what I wanted anymore or if kindness and passion only existed in different marriages.

Jerry didn't like being removed from the center of Renan's life. After a polite few weeks he stopped by Marolita's at odd times to see if she needed help. Regularly, he began stopping in on Wednesday at closing time when a retablo class started. He knew Brad's schedule and worked around it. Through the family grapevine he heard Brad was attending a sales convention in Phoenix and would be gone for two nights.

Jerry waited in his car when Renan turned the lights off after class at 7:00 p.m. and locked the store door. Fifteen minutes went by as she counted the cash and put it in a drawer for me. She checked the backdoor, went to the bathroom and put a new roll of toilet paper out before leaving the store. She was planning to drive to Chepita and Juan's for Rose and Daniel.

"Please let me take you to dinner," Renan reported he said. She admitted hesitating only a second. She missed Jerry. Instead of a restaurant he took her to his apartment where he had a takeout Italian dinner ready to be warmed.

"I know it's wrong, Abby, but he touches me so well and he made me feel so loved. So loved," she looked glassy. Renan's story was a movie and I couldn't stop watching, couldn't say anything. I just wanted to feel alive through the heroine I knew to be good, to have suffered and was not afraid to feel in ways I could not.

"Oh, Renan," my only words to her anguish.

"He said he loves me. Wants me and will never leave me like Brad did and will love my children as his."

I couldn't answer. "I told him, in the end, when it was all over and we had loved, that I could not leave Brad. He is my husband and I need to be with him."

I went home to Maury without a report. Maury was right to remind me it wasn't us when Brad disappeared. This family's passions knotted around my heart so tightly I felt suffocated. While working in silence between customers Mexican love ballads of Fernandez and Beltrán would swirl in my head in red, green and white. Family china six generations old, migrant farmlands of work and desperation, smell of oranges within breezes of ocean air, apples on a crisp sunny October morning, the aches of arms and backs leaning over sugar beets and a dark angel bringing me a letter began to feel as my own memories. I began to breathe and know a pain that was unspoken and held secretly instead of allowed to breathe air and heal.

The inside gut feel of white pioneers in heavy black clothes who knew land only as theirs and eyed passionate emotions with distrust was slipping. The sureness of living in only one heritage was frayed. When LoBeth said she was going to meet the Open Heart Anguishers the next week for a pot luck dinner I asked if Kelly and I could come.

She paused unbelieving. "Yes, Abby, I'll let them know. Bring anything but don't top my brownies." I told Kelly she was joining me.

"See a bunch of old women? Why not Slickers or we could try a new place?"

"I need a rest."

"Yes, I do, too." Kelly brought bakery rolls and I took a beginners salad.

The group had grown since I last attended over seven years ago. About thirty people filled their plates with overlapping piles of pasta, vegetables, cheeses and fruits. A deboned and decorated salmon was at the end. A buffet without tortillas looked incomplete.

"I didn't know the group was so large." Kelly and I sat by LoBeth, Judy and Susan.

Susan answered, "Foreigners are moving in from New York, Colorado, Ohio. You name it."

"So are you considered old timers now? Founding fathers?" I asked.

Judy and Susan laughed but not LoBeth. "You'd be considered an old timer, too, Miss. Not many of them grew up in New Age. Most of them came from Mormondom, being Catholics and a smattering of all those old Luther break-offs."

"Did I grow up an Open Heart Anguisher?"

"Got yourself thigh high in the doo-doo. And blessed you are, my child," LoBeth made the sign of the cross in front of me.

"Don't proselytize, LoBeth. This is a social," laughed Judy.

"What do you think, Kelly? Am I thigh high?"

"My parents would call you neck high." The conversation changed to Judy's new boyfriend and LoBeth needed to report Grant's stir fry technique.

On the way back to Kelly's I asked her what she thought of the group. "They're a good group of people, Abby. They're who you grew up around. They're your family." I'd gone home for comfort food whether I understood it or not. I did feel better.

Maury's patience and gentle persistence while showing me houses that needed originality to make them unique, resulted in our move to a new home we had 'toured.' He said it had large windows that let in enough light to match mine, a kitchen that demanded creativity in cooking, just like I had, a bedroom where I would have room to dance for him, closets that had never heard secrets and demanded colorful clothes, a family room begging for a family and last, an unplanted bare yard that would respond as Jon and Alex had to female love.

I didn't understand men's love at all. Maybe I hadn't been wanted at all by my father or deeply wanted by Maury when we met or married, but I had made a space in life with that man and two boys. I had tried to love and be good more than hurt and hate and be alone. And so had Renan. I didn't understand anything.

The house was in the southwest part of the valley where housing development lots are drawn like English labyrinth gardens. A mile of farmland was beyond the contractor's fence holding all houses in a surveyor's line and next year or in ten years the view would be the back of another house. It had everything I wanted and a few items I hadn't dreamed would ever be mine. A curving staircase to a second floor, a private bathroom off the bedroom, and a walk-in pantry started the list.

The first weekend we lived there I got both boys up on a counter big enough for them to sit on to make oatmeal cookies. Half the dough disappeared before baking.

"Is this a simple act of pure love?" Maury asked as Jon and Alex threw in raisins.

"No. It's teaching my boys to bake like their Uncle Pedro and convincing them I will always be the most important female in their lives."

"Cookie, Daddy?" Alex held out a ball of goo on fingers he had licked.

"That's a simple act of pure love, Maury." But he didn't take it.

Renan, Jerry and I had neglected to decide his loan check should be mailed. Since April's first payment, Jerry stopped by on the first Saturday of each month to check the plumbing, do any maintenance and pick up his check. He didn't ask for it and the first time he came by she only remembered after he walked out the door. She ran after him.

On the first Saturday in June, Jerry was adjusting the lock on the back door when Brad walked in a few minutes after noon with Rose and Daniel. Renan was ringing up a sale of yellow dotted swiss when Jerry walked from the back. Renan said they looked at each other like street dogs over a bone. "Brad," Jerry said.

"What are you doing here?" Brad's hoarseness made Renan look up but the customer writing her check didn't notice.

"Adjusted a lock," he gathered his tools to head out the door.

"Bye, Jerry," Rose said before sitting on the floor to read. She had already hugged his waist in greeting and now she waved. Four year old Daniel also wanted a hug before running a truck noisily along the sides of material bolts of imagined roadway. Brad held ground, watching his children treat Jerry with new familiarity.

The customer walked out ahead of Jerry and he leaned to open the door for her when Renan's voice stopped him. She was telling me the scene at our usual Monday visit, but this time she was distracted. "I got the check you wrote, Abby, and ran it to him. Brad just stood there and for the next hour I explained between people coming in and out that Jerry had loaned me the money to start the store.

"Then it got worse. Bishop Erickson came by. He said hi to Brad. He's known he was back since the beginning, but he was there to offer any help at the store or at home and wondered what needed doing. It's as though Brad is here in thought but no one expects anything of him."

Renan lifted hair off her forehead and held a pair of scissors by the cutting end while she tapped them in her other hand. Her body moved with her thinking. "Brad stood like a statue. When Bishop Erickson left I had another hour explaining things had broken while he was gone, I needed help, the children needed help and people helped."

"He must have known that."

"I guess not or he hadn't thought about it. He didn't stay. He left and didn't get home until ten. Eight hours of drinking and I don't know where he went."

"What happened?"

"He didn't talk to me and I didn't want to talk to him. He fell into bed and slept till noon."

I knew why I was Renan's new confidante, even usurping Carrie's position. I was close enough to care, I wouldn't hate Brad no matter what she said about him and I wasn't going to tell the family, which would break the cover of quiet she needed to deal with her marriage. I felt honored and since he wasn't hitting her I felt absolved of any need to tell anyone. It was a private matter just like Maury and I had from time to time.

The next Thursday the phone rang minutes after Maury and I fell asleep. He got up and took the phone out of the room. I watched his little butt that looked too small to sit on walk away without one tiny muscle falling to fat.

An angry, near screaming male voice was garbling something to be heard through the bedroom, down the hall and on the stairway where Maury stopped. The voice did all the talking. The conversation was only a minute and when Maury didn't come back to bed I followed. He was sitting in the kitchen with a glass of water held between his fingers, staring at the refrigerator for answers. Stark overhead light drained his beautiful color.

"Who was that?"

"Jerry. He said Brad and Travis just left his place. Brad was drunk and mean, kicked the door and demanded to know what was going on with Renan. When he said nothing, Brad said if he ever caught him by her again he'd kill him."

I poured a glass of wine. "What did Travis do?"

"Jerry said he stood there glaring like a pitbull. I guess Brad's on his way home. Drunk and mean." He dialed Renan who immediately answered and told her what happened. She was to call if she needed anything and if everything was okay. After he hung up he got a beer and we sat at the kitchen table with beer and wine in front of us for fortification. We wondered if our silence was the wrong thing to do. He'd kicked a door and yelled but he hadn't hit.

"I know all of this has to do with Emilio."

"What?" I heard the clock ticking and I looked at his smooth chest skin that I knew smelled of chestnuts and pine trees.

"Renan has been trying to fix her hurts with love ever since. For years she woke crying from dreams and Mamá would run to her. She said Emilio spoke to her as he lay there dead in the apple orchard. He told her to love because hate would kill all her brothers." He drank beer and I drank wine. "She felt so much. She always felt so much."

Silence and stark kitchen light beat around us.

"I'm sorry, Abby."

"Sorry?"

He rubbed his eyes, trying to erase thoughts. "Because she felt so much. Needed to love so much. To keep Pine Creek away. Turn hate and grief to love. I turned away. I closed inside, afraid to watch. Afraid to feel my own life."

Again we were quiet. "And you have suffered because I have not always loved you as you should be loved."

Silence is peace, deeply inward as a moonlit pool of water, and silence is rejection, left alone to feel its way without help. Maury gave me a sliver of his soul. I was not the love who received his deepest emotion. That was Renan. I was the one who helped him pretend he didn't live gripping the sides of an endless memory he couldn't forget. I was to hold open the gate and lead him from the heritage of his parents through the treacherous workings of the elusive fickle norteamericano. I was used in a blind masquerade so he could believe his path in life was easy when it was not.

I felt air coming in the window over the sink. Summer in Utah is the hot dry of a sauna burning the nose and causing lungs to clutch and suffer small breaths of hot air. Perfumed full baskets of bougainvilleas do not wildly bloom in mist and lust like I've imagined in the histories of Chepita, Juan, Tia Manuela and Abuelita Felipa. Summer in Utah is pruned trees and patterned flowerbeds self-righteously expecting a desert to pretend English propriety in a temporary show so we can believe our body desires and heart angers are hidden and in control. Utah believes justice is owned, beauty can be tamed and governable, love is orderly, desire a decision.

Half an hour later the phone rang. Brad had come home, not looked at or spoken to Renan and gone directly to bed.

Now that we had a house it was time to have Maury's family over for a Sunday dinner. When LoBeth first saw it she called me Queen Arias. Chepita looked overwhelmed at excessive luxury. She glanced at Maury hoping he hadn't gone mad spending money that would turn her grandchildren into beggars.

Juan shook his head, "Todos los norteamericanos son reyes pero no lo saben." Maury leaned and translated for me. Everyone else knew it was a generous but not over the top house for a young two income family in Salt Lake City, Utah, USA to feel entitled to.

The backyard hadn't received the female love Maury wished it yet, so only the children ran in the dust of farmland turned to housing while Maria Elena, Issac, Tiffany and Morrison were in the front yard by the mailbox where they could be seen. The adults moved around the house.

"Didn't I tell you, you'd get everything, Abby?" Renan said while she admired the kitchen. I watched for jealousy, knew it well enough to spot it, but it wasn't there.

"Yes, you did Renan. You were right."

"Waiting is always worthwhile."

"Now I know where to come for a night when Estrella kicks me out again," Pedro leaned against a wall, resting his thin randy self. The story of Estrella was a repeating pattern of wild claiming passion followed by anger in equal measure, dramatic kicking out of Pedro at 2:00 a.m., and her remorseful running to his parents' house to tearfully reclaim him at 5:00 a.m.

"Don't leave that woman to me," answered Juan, "I'll call the police."

"Then I'll come here when I no longer want her to find me."

Brad was in the family room with Marcus quietly watching basketball playoffs. When he brought his empty plate to the kitchen he leaned over. "I see you have a reading lamp. You must have plans."

After dishes were cleared, the women sat in my kitchen. It was pleasing they were complimentary of a house still wearing contractor white, cream and beige.

Now color floods walls in the new fashion of designers. LoBeth and her friends can barely leave a wall untouched. Paints named Caribbean Blue, Mexican Basket Red and Argentine Pampas are on walls from Maine to Alaska. Brown life is sinking in. Then, white people's walls were white. Then, my Tamayo print of the flying brown angel was the only thing on any wall. It was the first thing seen when someone walked in the door. It was a forewarning to any unknowing person they were in a border land.

Plain decorating or not, the women accepted my bare anglo skeleton that didn't have the grace of what they would do to frilly up everything. While we talked I saw Carrie reach to her purse and lift a wrapped gift to Renan who leaned down to put it in her purse. It was the size and shape of *Beautiful* cologne.

After everyone left I wiped the kitchen counter while Maury swept the floor. The boys were making noise in the playroom. With a house so big I was losing information of every little move they made, but they were very aware of what each other did. They didn't like being apart very long. The night we moved in Maury and I proudly gave them each a room. Maury was thrilled to give such a gift to his boys but the first night they were frightened to sleep alone and ended up in our bed. The second night they suffered withdrawal from each other and whined through the walls. So on the third day we put both beds in one room and declared a separate playroom for all toys.

I picked up a last fork for the dishwasher. I had a dishwasher! "Do you know anyone who would be good for Jerry? He's probably lonely."

"I'm not a matchmaker and Jerry's never needed one."

"I know but he needs someone." Maury only shrugged.

On the third Wednesday in July, Rose and Daniel were at Chepita and Juan's and Brad was at Kelson's. Jerry walked in Marolita's at 5:45 p.m. He hoped only to talk to her, delay her return to Brad, perhaps feel her against him, perhaps reach her body and the part of her heart he knew was his.

Marolita's Wednesday night retablo class was full. Students started arriving a few minutes before the store closed at 6:00 and it was often very busy in the last minutes of the retail day. Late customers needed help, the day's receipts were counted, students needed a friendly hello and phones still rang.

"Jerry, perhaps you should not be here," Renan left the side of a student showing her antique lace she had found in her grandmother's basement.

"Perhaps I need to be here," Jerry said he told her. He did not look at her as he began straightening bolts of fabric and pulling their ends out to look like dancing skirts. He had learned to cut the fabric for customers, service the sewing machines, read the numbers for patterns in the cabinet, and straighten the supply closet as he listened to Renan talk to her students.

By 5:56 he had answered the phone twice and put the day's receipts in the small inadequate safe. The phone again rang as Renan greeted a student at the door. It was quiet so he said hello again and then heard a disconnecting click.

The six students, four women, one teenage girl and a man, had brought boxes and plastic sacks of fabric memories. Renan's introduction was the various ways they could be arranged. Importance of each person, when or how they were important, or as she said, the feel of their personality and heart, all needed to be considered with color, form, available materials, and imagination. They were creating a tribute and work of art to be enjoyed for a very long time. They listened to her ideas and played with several layouts and designs before deciding. All the while they traded stories of who and why a person was represented with green tattered ribbon, a worn embroidered dishcloth, thick plaid winter wool, thirty year old buttons or strings of beads. Renan helped them choose complimentary backing or needed accessories from her store, ever gentle as she suggested alternatives and ideas for their life story or moment of remembrance.

Brad called Renan at one minute to 6:00, knowing she would soon be teaching. He wanted to settle what time she would be home and if he should bring dinner since she was getting the kids. It took the time from the disconnected call until 6:40 to drive home and unlock the hidden gun case.

His father's Ruger .22 was on the bottom green felt, behind the hunting rifles. He picked it up, feeling the grip of target practice, his childhood and his father. When his father said, good shot, son, he was so proud. He placed it on the glass coffee table in front of the tv. He sat down, ground his elbows into his knees with his hands, rubbing his chin and stared at the Ruger and a vase of wilting flowers. The hot blood metal smell of newly dead rabbits and deer was so strong in memory it overcame the warm petals drooping in heat. Fragrance leaked as they slowly died in water unable to sustain them. "I kill with reason and humility for life; not revenge, not greed, not sorrow." He heard his fourteen year old cracking voice repeating a promise to his father. The house was empty without her.

When the door closed on the last student Renan had only to pick up her purse, check the lock on the back door and leave. The long twilight of July made it difficult to see in the prismed window of the store as Brad sat in his SUV. He barely saw Renan bend for her purse under the cutting table and then turn to head to the back. Jerry followed. Brad got out of his SUV and walked to Marolita's. His hands were empty claws drawing up for battle. The Ruger was locked and returned to under the stairs. He refused to have a thought in his head. All messages were limbic survival to muscle. He pushed open the door, walked up the aisle of velvet and chiffon and stood by the cutting table, listening to the back door being locked.

Jerry followed Renan back inside the store. They saw Brad at the same time. He stood straight, his legs slightly apart, balancing his body that was ready to move any direction. Jerry moved from Renan and took a step toward the cutting table. Brad turned to keep him in straight sight. "Jerry, I'm just telling you what you and Renan's brothers told me." His voice was a slow thud. "Don't hurt Renan, Jerry."

"Move away, Renan," Jerry's was sharp as a cleaver. He couldn't measure the danger of staying or going, but he knew he was five years younger and in better shape.

Renan yelled, "No, Brad," and Jerry jumped to turn the store lights off. Renan moved toward Brad. Fading sun lengthened store shadows of red, pink, and yellow through the clean store window. Jerry pushed along the floor to the cutting table, rushing to act. Brad shoved Renan away, aware of the danger she was in with her closeness to him. He fell toward Jerry as the gun slipped into Jerry's grasping fingers. Brad hit Jerry on the chin, not realizing the gun was between them. When he moved back in his fall Jerry brought his arm up and Brad saw the Smith and Wesson waver in Jerry's hand. Brad's awareness became a hunter's full picture of Renan, Jerry, the room's map and total focus on the gun in the hands of a man who did not respect it.

"Don't use that, Jerry," Brad hissed through sweat and saliva, heaving from effort. Jerry did not give up the gun and he did not stop. They lunged together, kicking and falling over bolts of fabric. They turned on the floor as embracing brothers, rolling, kicking, pushing arms together in equal strength and anger and years of keeping away, years of hope, years of need. Both men struggled for control with left hand to right hand for the gun in the middle until its recoil broke their hold.

Racing air pushing from lungs and heart opened throat cries. Three times Renan's voice trembled as a swan's falling gasp from the sky. She twisted to the dark corner from the parking lot light as she might have the night Brad returned when they finished sex. On her back with legs and arms spread, her face turned, hidden by hair curling to hide her face. Her surrender to love that night. Her final payment for Emilio this night.

Brad leapt to her still crouching. He cradled her chest, arms and head with full heavy pressure to keep her together, warm, control the shaking. Shrieking, he told Jerry to call for help, she still breathed. When the call was made Jerry lifted a roll of pink satin, brought it to Renan and together, Brad and Jerry wrapped her tight, working to stop the red spreading from her back, around her body from the chest to her head, to her hips.

Renan breathed without words or sight, lost in the dreams of the dying. At the hospital her family's separate hearts, each with a different love and need from her were silent. Only the two men who held their separate secrets of her woman's heart and body were missing. A breath past the blackest night darkness when the touch of the next day's light promised dawn, Renan slipped from our lives.

The night dreams of heartache, fear and guilt within the Arias family had at last broken its festering blister to air. Its flowing oozing ache now flooded beyond Maury's family to cover Brad, Rose, Daniel, Jerry, my sons, and me. Its poison and tragedy could no longer hide.

Before the casket closed Tia Manuela held the opal necklace and walked with Juan to bury history. Juan weaved it carefully through Renan's stiff fingers. Her great-great-grandmother's legacy returned to earth where she held its hurt away from her brothers.

The cover of the funeral program had a picture of Renan and her children with a fragment of a poem by Jose Carlos Becerra. Pedro found it on the floor of Renan's bedroom after her wedding. He kept it in his wallet.

I have disappeared from my own creation
And will reemerge the day I break my death glass,
But then the accident can never be, the innocence of gesture;
No, it won't be possible to break that glass unintentionally,
Like a child with a ball
But head-on with a fist.

"With young people. Rose and Daniel need young people," Juan's tears filled dry deep creek beds down his weathered cheek. We were sitting in Chepita's kitchen. "Mauricio, Abby, you will raise los niños." Rose and Daniel heard their grandfather. Both fell deeper in Chepita's arms.

Over the next week I was at Renan's house gathering clothes and toys. Rose asked me to bring her mother's witch dress. I finally found it in a box hidden behind the empty gun cabinet. I held it up. The dress had strength of standing up to death and looking it in the eye. It brushed against my chest. As I tucked it back under its tissue my own chest hurt with what I would need to tell Rose about her mother. Beside it was a brown grocery sack of scraps. I found green velvet from the Thanksgiving dress, gold lame, pink velveteen and there was purple lace from the robe both Brad and I had dressed her in. With her sewing, with her heart, Renan always tried to mend.

Brad and Jerry told the same story. Both of them wore her blood and the smell of gunfire. Both of them left fingerprints. After four months of investigation, interviews, and whatever else police and prosecutors consider, they were charged with negligent homicide. Caught for murder that killed the woman they loved, they also paid for the murder that was never caught with Emilio.

No alcohol. No drugs. No pre-meditated intent. A legal gun. No prior records. No one with the will to fight. Good lawyers. Overflowing prison system. One year in the county jail to think.

It is Chepita and Juan who feel the passing years with the aging bones that make death welcome. Quietly, almost as one being with two moving parts they work and do. With the quietness of a closed church and the sturdiness of a bridge with each pillar deep in the ground, they do the work of daily living with a simplicity and devotion that is humbling. I have thought of LoBeth's story of the old people dying with their stories we never ask to hear.

The names I parceled my mother, Golden Bitch, Ruby Reverie, Missy Mommy and Drunk, have faded away. A large personality with many sides, barbs, opinions, loves and aches requires smaller personalities who love them to also split when they are loving, hating, arguing, laughing with the person. So I had split my mother into chunks, but now she is LoBeth, Mother or Sunshicloud. Her friends did know her better than I did. They accepted her careening swirling barbs and insights darting through black spaces to insist on enough room to be. Now I do, too.

When Brad was released from jail he returned to San Diego, a city where he knew he could be lost. He keeps in touch with his children but the pain is so great he is afraid his presence would hurt them more. He needs to heal where he can. The children need him. When he called last week I told him eight year old Daniel was up to my shoulder and ten year old Rose slept with his picture. He said he would be home before her next birthday.

Jerry is in San Jose. His belongings were in storage during his year in jail while he decided what to do with history's fragments. One brother was given the china cabinet and the other the sofa. He hand wrapped every thin china piece that belonged to his great grandmother in wraps of silk and tissue before giving it to me in four sealed boxes.

I watched him bring each box in and place it in a far corner of the unfinished basement. The gold hairs in his thick hair still glistened in the black but they were now joined with a small growth of grey by his temples. His love had been the most open to Renan I thought, as I watched him moving and stooping. When he finished he stood by his car door and looked at me. The sight in his eyes had changed. Now he recognized the self protective fear darkness has of light.

227

"Give my mother's hand mirror to Rose and tell her I will always love her mother. Save these dishes for Daniel. Tell him they hold his special history." I nodded. "Let me hug you, Abby. I need to say good-bye." We stepped together, into this last hug by my first brother. "Take care of yourself, Abby."

I did not know where I fit when I was Abby Baker. It is a simple name from my mother and now I accept it as her first gift to me. Abby Baker Arias. Here is a name of two histories, not fully claimed by either. It is the life's texture I want. To be seen by both and gripped by neither.

The first print in our house was the Tamayo angel forewarning dreams and visitors. The second was an apple orchard. Maury needs to see it to settle with peace as he can. Both of us need to understand the bravery and necessity of looking with full sight at life's blinding moments.

Rose needs to hold her little brother's hand and listen deep for their mother's voice. They will learn to lie side by side in an apple orchard, watch the night sky and hear her talk of love and life. Rose Graciela Madrugada Evans. Rose, grace in the small dark hours before dawn.

Discussion Questions

1. While on a date with Craig Spencer, Abby was surprised he thought happy went with love. What led her to this belief and do you agree? How does this belief influence her approach to life?

2. When Abby is at the front door of Tia Manuela's house before helping sew Carrie's wedding dress she is stopped with a new awareness of confidence or security in women who were brought up with fathers, brothers and uncles in their lives. What do you think of her conclusion?

3. Abby thought lack of knowledge of the father she had never met made it easier to accept his absence. Do you like to know everything or are some things better left unsaid?

4. What does Abby mean when she is talking with Kelly and she thinks married with child and unmarried with hope looked straight at each other?

5. Abby is suddenly overwhelmed with envy and remorse of her envy when she hear's Renan's sultry voice as she invites Jon to spend the weekend at her house. Do you think she perceives it is a cultural difference or simply a difference between females?

6. Abby compares her physical appearance with Renan's several times. How does their self-image affect a woman's behavior?

7. Abby comes to the conclusion it is better to send victims of tragedies caring thoughts instead of attempting to feel their pain. She reasons personal happiness is too fragile to have disrupted by a stranger's problems. What do you think?

8. LoBeth thinks people only face themselves or truly mature when they leave their area of birth. Do you agree, disagree and why?

9. LoBeth's belief is that the deepest changes in a person happen silently inside them and that marriage is more likely to inhibit freedom to change than encourage it. What do you think?

10. Why do you think Renan accepted Brad's physical violence to her?

Discussion Questions

11. Renan and Abby talk about being sexy vs good. Renan believes that having to choose one or the other disrupts a woman's sense of self. Do you think women are expected to choose one at the expense of another? If so, what does that do to their sense of self?

12. Abby compares her expectations of returned love from Maury vs Kelly living with Jerry without promises. Do you think genuine love has a right to expect return? If it is not returned does it alter the nature of the love?

13. In the story there are issues of family loyalty and relationships. What differences do you see as unique to a family, culture or are universal?

14. What differences and similarities between LoBeth, Chepita and Tia Manuela are a result of cultural heritage or simply being female? What about the differences between Brad, Maury and their families?

Abuelita ~ Grandma

Amigo ~ Friend

Anglo ~ Shortened version of anglosajón, indicating anglo saxon heritage

Apasionada mujar ~ Passionate woman

Bahía ~ Bay

Bebé ~ Baby

Braceros ~ A farmhand commonly referred to as a contract worker who came to the U.S. to work under the Bracero Program supported by the U.S. government to obtain workers during World War II.

Casa ~ House

Chiquita ~ Little one

!Cuídese mi hijo. Vuélve vivo! ~ Take care my son. Come back alive.

Cuñada ~ Sister-in-law

Dios ~ God

El servicio a Dios es mas grande que el pecado. ~ The service to God is greater than the sin.

Ella entra al matrimonio. Mi hija, al fin es bendecida. ~ She goes into marriage. My daughter is at last blessed.

Flan ~ Custard dessert with caramel topping

Garcia ~ A Spanish surname

Gracias ~ Thank you

Graciela en la madrugada ~ Grace in the small dark hours before dawn

Gringos ~ Foreigner, usually from North America

Hay, pobre de México. Tan lejos de Dios y tan cercas a los Estados Unidos. ~ Poor Mexico. So far from God, so close to the U.S.

Hermana ~ Sister

Hola ~ Hello

La flaquita ~ Little skinny girl

Lo que mas quiera es tener muchos nietos. ~ I want grandchildren all around.

Los niños ~ the children

Manuela, es una colcha. ~ Manuela, it is a quilt.

Mas vale vivo con cacahuates que muerto con rosas. ~ Better alive with peanuts than dead with roses.

Mi familia ~ My family

Mi hija al fin sera cuidada. ~ My daughter is at last taken care of.

Molé ~ A traditional Mexican sauce with, among other things, sesame seeds, chocolate and chilis.

Mi Corazón, embriego con su bondad. ~ My love (heart) I am intoxicated with your kindness.

Mi hijo ~ My son

Mi hija ~ My daughter

Nada ~ Nothing

Ojos muy bonitos ~ Very pretty eyes

Por favor, su madre ~ Please, your mother

Pobrecita ~ Pitiful little one

Poco tiempo ~ Little time

Pozole ~ A thick soup of pork and hominy, often topped with onion and cilantro.

Pues ella viene de tus huevos, pendejo! Estamos parados en un México muerto y abadonado, separado del corazón donde la bandera gringa vuela. Protéjela. ~ She is from your balls, bastard. We stand in dead, deserted Mexico, separated from its heart where the white man's flag now flies. Project her.

Puta ~ Whore

¡Que te chingues! ~ Fuck you

Que sea la que Dios quiera. ~ What God requires to live this life.

Retablo ~ Altar often arranged in homes for private worship.

Sandia ~ Watermelon

Senorita ~ Miss, or young unmarried woman

Si ~ Yes

Tia ~ Aunt

Todos los norteamericanos son reyes pero no lo saben. ~ North Americans are all kings but don't know it.

Torero huapango ~ Singing (or musical) bullfighter

Una colcha con corazón e historia desde el principio ~ A quilt with heart and history from the beginning.

Y mi familia ~ and my family

Yerba Buena ~ Good herb

Yo se ~ I know

Church of Jesus Christ of Latter Day Saints (LDS) Terms

Bishop ~ Designation given to a man giving rights and responsibilities to oversee a ward, including duties such as counseling, marriage, blessings, burials, etc.

Brother ~ Designation given to a man implying accepted membership and respect.

Fast Sunday ~ On the first Sunday of each month breakfast is skipped and what it would have cost is donated to church for charity use.

Gentile ~ By LDS definition anyone who is not LDS.

Hotel Utah ~ Built in 1911 the Hotel Utah was the city's premier hotel with restaurants, gift shops and meeting rooms, but not a designated ball room. It has since been renovated for church business.

Missionaries ~ At age nineteen members can elect to spend eighteen months in services to the church to proselytize.

Sister ~ Designation given to a woman implying accepted membership and respect.

Sunday school ~ Classes held on Sunday for children.

Ward ~ Geographic designation that comprises a congregation for an administrative division.